To JR
My gr...
God Bless you.
Allan Preston Brooks

KARMAKAZE

Copyright © 2011 by Allan Preston Brooks
Published by Lulu Press

All rights reserved. No part of this book may be reproduced, stored in media, transmitted or copied, in any form, or by any means, without prior written approval of the author.

Cover concept by Brian Darnell
Cover design by Dave Thomas
Set in 12 point Tahoma

Brooks, Allan P., 1951-
 Karmakaze
 / Allan Preston Brooks.

ISBN 978-1-257-87022-6

DEDICATION

This book is dedicated to Rebecca Suzanne Brown.
My soul mate.
At times the bane of my existence.
Always the love of my life.

Special Thanks

To my great friend Mickey Brooks for suggesting that I write <u>Karmakaze</u> and for being a friend that any friend would be grateful to have;

To Dr. Craig Nunn for being the friend of a lifetime to me, for teaching me so much and showing me the love of a brother;

To my parents Shel and Doris Fowler for their love, caring and support for such a wayward son;

To my sister Genie Rasmussen for being there absolutely every single time I needed her and for meaning so much to me;

To my sister Shirley Lamers and her family for their love, understanding and support;

To my son Michael Amos Connard who I failed miserably as a father, but who became a cherished friend nonetheless;

To Jean and David Bell for becoming like family to me and treating me like a beloved brother;

To Michael Barone for staying in touch with me for over two decades and going far beyond what is expected of a close friend;

To Penni Walker for doing me an incredible undeserved act of kindness that enabled a relationship with my son;

To David Boman, David Elam and Kirk Sarago for their patience, understanding and without whose assistance this project may have never been started, let alone finished;

To Peter Pressman and the Nashville Striders for their support and encouragement of literally hundreds of inmates as well as their kindness and generosity;

To Dr. Dan Haskins for his understanding and assistance which allowed for the rewriting this book so badly needed;

To all the people I have met behind this curtain of razor wire who have proved that wisdom can be acquired in the face of utter ignorance;

To all those I am forgetting who deserve my gratitude
Thank you all for helping me to overcome many issues, as I work on others, and for all the kindnesses shown to me. Your help was essential during my walk toward becoming a better human being.

KARMAKAZE
TABLE OF CONTENTS

INTRODUCTION

Part I   **FOUNDATION FOR FAILURE**
CHAPTER 1   MADDIE MAE
CHAPTER 2   WHAT A GOOD LITTLE BOY
CHAPTER 3   JACK vs. WILL
CHAPTER 4   GRANDFATHER
CHAPTER 5   ANOTHER FATHER FIGURE
CHAPTER 6   FIRST ENCOUNTER WITH DEATH

Part II   **A 60's & 70's REALITY SHOW**
CHAPTER 7   AH, YOUTH
CHAPTER 8   EDUCATIONAL TRAIN WRECK
CHAPTER 9   JULIE, JEFF & UNCLE SAM
CHAPTER 10   AN AFFINITY FOR VIOLENCE
CHAPTER 11   HIGH(ER) LEARNING

PART III   **SEX, DRUGS & ROLLING THROUGH THE 80's**
CHAPTER 12   NO JULIE = MARY ANNE
CHAPTER 13   COCAINE
CHAPTER 14   HANNAH
CHAPTER 15   JAMI
CHAPTER 16   NO HANNAH = JAMI, BRITTANY, CAROL, CANDY, ETC.
CHAPTER 17   HELLO ADAM!
CHAPTER 18   ANOTHER WAKEUP CALL IGNORED

PART IV   **NIGHTMARE TIME**
CHAPTER 19   AUGUST 13, 1989
CHAPTER 20   IN THE NEWS
CHAPTER 21   THIRTEEN AND A HALF
CHAPTER 22   GOOD MORNING DESPAIR
CHAPTER 23   BEING THE CAUSE OF GRIEF

PART V   **INTROSPECTIVELY**
CHAPTER 24   RELIGION...A SWING AND A MISS
CHAPTER 25   UNDESERVED LOVE
CHAPTER 26   THAT ABORTED CHILD
CHAPTER 27   THE UNKNOWN
EPILOGUE   ANOTHER TRIAL, ANOTHER JUDGMENT

PROLOGUE

* * * *

As I walked to my car, I realized that I had the gun in one hand and my briefcase in the other. I had no memory of picking up the briefcase. I also noticed that the entire front of my pants and shirt were saturated with a mixture of our blood, hers and mine. I reflected for an instant on how sticky it felt, and then in a near state of shock, I got into my car and drove away. I had no wallet or ID, but with three hundred and forty-four dollars I found stuffed in the glove box, along with an ounce of cocaine and three ounces of pot in the compartment behind the seat, I drove onto the entrance ramp of the interstate and headed…south.

I drove and drove…and then kept driving, oblivious to the fact that the blood all over me, my face, my hands and clothing, had dried. When I partially emerged from my mental fog, I pulled into a self-service carwash bay somewhere in Georgia. I got out of my car and used the carwash wand to clean myself, five minutes of soap, followed by five minutes of rinse, clothes, shoes, everything. I didn't give a damn.

My perspective at that time was that everything that had just happened was her fault and that now my life was over. I took off my T-tops, got back into the car, still soaking wet and lowered both windows. When I looked in the rearview mirror to examine my injuries, I was surprised to discover that I had one hell of a black and swollen left eye, so I put on a pair of very dark sunglasses to conceal it.

Back on the interstate, I sped up just a little and allowed the inrushing wind to dry me and my clothes. I stopped for some gas, and then drove all the way to Orlando. Once there, I got another full tank of gas and considered getting something to eat. Instead I used a drinking straw to snort some cocaine from a loose pile at the bottom of the console. Then I drove on, and I didn't stop until I reached Miami. I had been driving for nearly twenty-four hours. I was going to get a motel room, but it occurred to me that I should conserve as much money as possible for gas and food. At that moment I just wanted to think.

* * * *

If you've ever taken a standardized test, you're familiar with those little oval-shaped bubbles that must be filled in carefully with a number two pencil. You're supposed to match the question with the related bubble on the answer sheet. But if you accidentally skip a bubble and proceed to fill in subsequent answers, a situation might arise in which you correctly respond to each question, yet miss every answer. It's something of a phase shift error; one that begins innocuously and propagates silently.

The test taker might be shocked to see his failing score, unaware that a subtle alteration undermined the entirety of his preparation, knowledge and aptitude. A similar error can occur during human DNA replication with predictably disastrous results.

My life has been something of a phase-shift error with disastrous results. First there was a slight shift in the substance of my existence. As my life cascaded toward devastation, I was too intimately involved in the particulars to notice - that's the way these things work. By the time I realized that my answers were in the wrong bubbles, I was lying on a steel bunk deep within the confines of concrete and razor wire. Where was that first mistake? Which was that missed opportunity - that skipped bubble?

As I lay on the top bunk of my prison cell, I forced myself to delve deeply into my childhood and to consider the totality of my life. It was an unfavorable assessment. In fact, it bordered on iniquitous. My mind raced back as far as my memory allowed - to the time I stole five bucks from my mother's purse to buy a baseball glove from a neighborhood pal, all the times I was mean to my little sister and the time I was caught swiping candy from the local grocery store.

I had overrated myself and my abilities in every aspect; school, sports, my appeal to women, and even my ability to overcome obstacles like addiction and a propensity toward violence. Now, during this initial, crude attempt at self-evaluation through a distasteful regurgitation of prior bad acts, I concluded that I wasn't the person I considered myself to be. The life I led was far from exemplary. My lifetime of misdeeds pointed to an obvious conclusion - I had been a woefully inadequate human. While there were many people who thought of me as a good, dependable, intelligent and honest guy, the truth was that under the façade, I was a narcissistic, violent, lying, manipulative, misogynistic, drug-abusing miscreant.

With one exception, I had never been faithful in romantic relationships. Glimmers of loyalty appeared in platonic friendships, but I had never been the kind of a friend that a friend would be grateful to have.

I recall an aphorism about how we are not judged by our mistakes but by what we do afterward. Would 100 years of saintly behavior undo the deeds of the world's worst such as serial killers, child abusers, or monsters like Adolph Hitler or Ted Bundy? How about 1000 or 10,000 years? Can anyone ever atone for an act as heinous as molesting a child or for murder? Can atonement be reached through "becoming a better person" or by following the dictates of some worn-out, idealized, religious formula?

Regardless of what occurs after the fact, the abused child still becomes an adult saddled with an undeserved burden, the raped are still victimized by traumatic memories and an understandable mistrust, and the murdered remain dead. These crimes cannot be balanced by some set amount of subsequent goodness on the part of the perpetrator, no matter how sincere the effort.

People in prison are separate and distinct individuals. Like people in the free world they are a mix of good and evil. I knew, despite my "membership" in the prison community, that the vast majority of inmates are disturbingly similar. Samuel Langhorne Clemmons (Mark Twain) said, "If you want to see the scum of the earth, go to any prison at shift change." He must have spent very little time inside a prison; otherwise he would have known that the inhabitants of those prisons, not the guards, are a true source of earthly malevolence. There are exceptions. There are innocent victims of an imperfect judicial system, but they are a skeletal minority. There are those who have made a mistake toward the lesser end of the felony spectrum and those who make sincere resolutions to change. Some actually succeed.

Living on the inside, I realized that most prisoners belong in prison. They were little more than willing passengers on an inevitable trip toward their destinies with all their sad, ridiculous, worthless and pathetic lives. Countless times I saw some inmate pick up a Bible, Qur'an, or whatever holy book struck his fancy. He would brandish it or thump it at convenient and well-calculated times. Good-hearted volunteers were often duped, but few inside the system are fooled by such transparent duplicity.

Like me, most inmates knew the routine. Upon making parole, the convict drops his source of miraculous conversion, picks up a crack pipe or some other vice, gets strapped (armed) and reenters the familiar arena of drugs, robberies and other criminal activity. And when he appears at the institutional gates for a return engagement, he spouts the usual litany of excuses, blaming everyone but himself, and then renews the process of jockeying for another shot at freedom.

PART I   A FOUNDATION FOR FAILURE

"It was the best of times, it was the worst of times."
(Charles Dickens...A tale Of Two Cities)

CHAPTER ONE
MADDIE MAE

"Everybody needs somebody sometime."
(Dean Martin)

As far back as she could remember she hated her name. She loathed the way it sounded when her mother called, "Maddie Mae, oh Maddie Mae, come in for supper child." She hated the way it stared up at her from the paper on her homework. "As soon as possible," she thought, "I'll get it changed...something like Rita or Lana...now *those* are names." They're the names of movie stars, and that's what Maddie Mae wanted to be.

Why not? There had already been major changes in her young life. Born out of wedlock in Oklahoma to a banker's mistress, she was abandoned, adopted and whisked away to Nashville, Tennessee to live with her new parents, Howard and Birdie Springs. They were nice, God-fearing, upper middle class people who were unable to conceive. They were delighted to welcome Maddie to their family, and they offered tons of love to the beautiful baby girl. They nearly burst with pride the first time they attended church with their tiny angel, held securely in Birdie's embrace.

Maddie was a pretty brunette, intelligent and energetic. When she turned 13 she became acutely aware of the way men turned their heads in her direction. Maddie's mother Birdie noticed it too. She didn't like it, but Maddie took secret pleasure in the way grown men stared at her developing curves.

Maddie was also talented. And that talent was cultivated through the many lessons Birdie arranged. Maddie danced with refined elegance and was an exceptional singer. Her ballet, gymnastic and acrobatic classes paid off, too. Family friends told Birdie to take her talented daughter to auditions in New York or Hollywood. Birdie wouldn't hear of it. Maddie was to attend a local girl's prep school; a very prestigious one. Then she would matriculate at Vanderbilt University. But the good intentions and considered plans of doting mothers are easily derailed.

Maddie was barely 15 when 24-year-old Jack Collins entered her life. Although forbidden to date, her friend Irene convinced Maddie to meet Jack who was her boyfriend's buddy. Jack had just been honorably discharged from the army. He was 5' 8", and handsome, his head endowed with striking jet-black hair. Anyone talking with him for a few minutes would notice his extraordinary charisma and ambition.

The moment they met was magical. He was the most attractive man she had ever seen. She captured his heart so quickly, his head spun, nature took its course and a clandestine love affair followed, predictably ending with morning sickness and, to

Maddie's horror, a progressive swelling of her abdomen. Fortunately for Jack, things were a lot different then. Today he would be indicted and convicted on multiple counts of statutory rape and sexual molestation of a minor.

When Howard first found out, he wanted to kill them both, but his anger quickly settled on Jack. When common sense finally prevailed, everyone agreed that a hasty wedding was the best option. The nervous couple married in a small ceremony in a town just south of Nashville.

Little Joan Collins was born on January 20, 1945. This new, ultra-realistic, human doll enchanted her 16-year-old mother. But the novelty wore off as feedings and diaper changes turned to drudgery for the new mother. What had her life become? She wanted to be out with other girls her age, having fun, going to the movies and flirting with boys. As the days dragged on, Maddie's resentment and bitterness grew. The targets of Maddie's anger were usually Jack and little Joan.

Joan developed from an infant to a toddler and on into a precocious preschooler, but Maddie's animosity grew unabated. She hated being a wife and a mother. She was now 20 and her life felt empty and purposeless. She could have been an actress or a singer if only her mother hadn't been so stubborn. She began leaving Joan at Howard and Birdie's house and she stayed home less often. This greatly displeased Jack.

Then one morning about a year later, just after she sent Joan off to school, the familiar, distressing rhythm of morning sickness returned. She was horrified.

"Oh my God, oh no, please God please, please, please, please…I beg you please don't let me be pregnant again, please!"

For the next eight months Maddie agonized about how another baby would only worsen her miserable existence. After praying every night and day for it not to happen, I was christened Jeffery Holden Collins on September 7, 1951, kicking and red-faced.

A week later my mother was still crying into her pillow.

"I'm only 23 years old and my life is totally ruined. How in the world am I going to take care of two children? I feel like killing myself," she sobbed.

But the reality was that she *didn't* take care of the children. My grandmother Birdie babysat Joan more often while my mother went "shopping." She left me with Jack, who became more aggravated with each passing day.

It wasn't that Mom had no love for Joan and me. She loved us very much. But she had missed so much, practically all the good things about being a teenager. She wanted to be a good mother. She wanted to put our happiness and well-being ahead of her own desires, but she couldn't. She realized she was no longer in love with her husband and she wanted a change; a major change, and it had better happen quickly or she would go insane. She desperately needed something good to happen in her life. She was ready to act to make it occur.

A few days later she stopped by her parents' house. As they sat in the den, Mom came right to the point.

"Momma, I want...no...I need for Joan to stay with you for a while."

"Why on earth would you want that, Maddie?"

"Because I am about to lose my mind, Momma. Two kids are too much for me right now. Jack and I are constantly arguing, and Jeff is more than a handful. He's always getting into something that I have to clean up. I need a break, Momma. And if you don't let her live with you for at least a while, I swear that..."

"Maddie Mae Springs! You should be ashamed of yourself for asking such a thing."

Birdie adored Joan. She was the apple of her grandmother's eye and no child ever felt more love than Birdie showed that little girl. However, her feelings toward her own daughter were different. Mom ruined all the grandiose plans Birdie had made through her unplanned pregnancies. All the gossip of a forced marriage of her adopted daughter with a poor, uneducated soldier home from the war had been the social undoing of Birdie in her close circle of friends - at least in her eyes.

"Scandalous!" She had thought to herself at the time of the wedding. "What a shame, Lord Jesus me, what a crying shame."

"Momma, please, I need this!"

"Maddie, I raised you and I am getting old. That little angel is a wonderful blessing sent to you and Jack by the good Lord. You have two beautiful and healthy children and a husband who loves you. Do you know how many people would trade places with you?
Have you lost your mind, girl?"

Mom turned her tear-streaked face toward her father.

"Daddy, please help me. I can't take it any more. I need some help, please!"

"Don't say a word Howard, I mean it. Maddie, your father wouldn't be the one taking care of her. It would be me, and my health...well my health isn't what it used to be. I feel weak and I have dizzy spells all the time. I love Joan to death, I really do, but you're her mother and you're going to raise her. And that's final!"

My mother stood up and began walking briskly toward the door.
"The hell it is, you old bitch," she muttered to herself.

Within a month Joan was in a home for unwanted children, and more than a week passed before my grandparents found out about it. After Birdie was told what happened, she spent a week crying in bed. When she finally made it downstairs for the first time in days, Birdie was a defeated woman. Her health began a downward spiral as she became weak and sickly. She never recovered.

Now that Mom was free from my sister, all that was left to contend with was me. She continued to leave me alone with Dad several nights a week. One Monday evening, when Dad had finally had enough and gave her the ultimatum of being a wife and mother or else, she chose the latter option.

Dad immediately hurried into the bedroom to grab some belongings. Being a man of honor and character, he knew that he needed to leave before he did something that he would regret. But Mom wasn't finished.

"And you can take Jeff with you."

"That's fine Maddie, I will. Look, I'll take enough clothes to get us through the next few days and then I'll come back for the rest of it by the end of the week."

"You'd better because the locks are going to be changed as soon as I can get it done."

Dad barely looked up at her as he walked through the door with a bag of clothes in one arm and me in the other.

"Have a nice life, Maddie."

"Thanks, I plan on it."

Six months later they were divorced, with Mom willfully yielding custody of me to my dad. During this time she began dating a man named Will Pickett. He was about 6' tall and rather plain looking. He had dark brown hair with a face that revealed his friendly nature. The two married exactly 33 days after Maddie's divorce was final. They moved into a house that my grandfather owned and they lived there rent-free. Mom seemed happy with Will for the next 3 years, until the moment she became pregnant. They named their daughter Jeanne Pickett. Once again, Maddie found herself in that familiar, untenable situation.

My mother loved her children and she wished to be a good mother. But she never developed the maturity needed to prioritize maternal instincts over selfish desires. The dilemma was simple. She felt incomplete without a man, but with both a man and children, she felt suffocated. Her failure as a mother affected all three children, but I believe that it was hugely influential in shaping my personality and changing my moral fiber in a profoundly negative manner. My distrust of people grew as additional character flaws of my mother came to light.

I suffered a fear of abandonment by those close to me, especially the women in my life. These cumulative conditions were instrumental in my future date with selfdestruction. A pathological jealousy pervaded my most serious love affairs and must be partially attributable to a complicated relationship with my mother.

My mom fought serious psychological issues. She expected much more from life and she probably could have been successful in several different venues. However, reality frequently throws curveballs. The psychological legacy that she left me was my reality. It would be more than four decades later before I embarked on the difficult journey to understand and overcome these impediments to normalcy.

CHAPTER 2
WHAT A GOOD LITTLE BOY

"Cleverness is no substitute for true character."
(The Urantia Book)

My dad and I moved into my grandfather Howard's house. Dad began working for Howard's plumbing company and became a trusted and valued employee. My grandfather grew close to my father and soon thought of him as a son. In fact, the plan was for Dad to take over Springs' Plumbing Company in the foreseeable future.

My father cared for me with a powerful love; the kind that can only be understood by a father who has held his newborn child in his arms, felt the warmth, smelled that indescribable new baby smell and seen that first little smile. We were as close as a father and son could be. We did everything together. We were inseparable, except when he was working or the few times a month he would go on a date. We played baseball, basketball, went swimming and took long drives through the countryside. We often visited a farm owned by two of Dad's closest friends. We went to church every Sunday morning and again in the evening. Even well into adulthood, I still fondly recall those evening services with my dad. The pastor was a good artist and he created pictures with pastel chalks while delivering his message to the congregation. As a youngster, I would sit spellbound as the plain white paper transformed into a tranquil scene, like a cascading waterfall or a pair of praying hands.

I was an energetic youngster, athletic and bright. I was a good-looking kid with blonde hair, blue eyes and an engaging smile. Yet there was something about me. Something hard to put a finger on, but something not quite right. It manifested itself early on through a peculiar, hardened look in my eyes. A look that surfaced when anything negative was directed at me, or as a result of just about anything I didn't like.

There is an old black and white episode of "The Twilight Zone" starring Billy Mumy as this little demon-boy with super power. He causes anyone he doesn't like to vanish into some netherworld just by thinking about it. Then there's the episode of the animated series, "The Simpsons" in which young Bart Simpson, following a post-prank reprimand from the Reverend Lovejoy, sells his soul to his pal Millhouse for five dollars. While Mumy's character is totally unapologetic and even smugly satisfied with his deeds, Bart shows genuine remorse subsequent to his actions. I fell somewhere in between the two, and it depended on the perspective of the observer to decide on which end of that smugnessremorsefulness spectrum I belonged.

While I basked in the affection of a father who loved me, Joan continued growing up in the cold, austere environment of the children's home where Mom had abandoned her. About once a month, Dad and I would pay her a visit. Every time we went there I experienced unease, especially as we left. Much later in life I wondered why my parents had put her there and why Dad hadn't jerked her out of that dump. Neither Joan nor I ever had the opportunity to receive answers to those questions. I think I developed a sense of superiority at being a wanted child, as opposed to my less fortunate sister. This probably led to a sense of entitlement, another trait destined to cause me difficulty.

I hit the first grade running. I was very clever if not highly intelligent, and I was a step faster, both mentally and physically, than most of my peers. I liked school and excelled academically. That excellence was reflected in report cards with the exception of one area, behavior. When report card time rolled around, I received the highest marks, but always accompanied by a little note in the comments section such as, "Jeff is a very good student, but he does not always pay attention," or "Jeff has had to be disciplined for talking in class, disruptive behavior, etc."

My father talked to me about my conduct, but to no avail. The comments continued, along with exemplary grades, and because he was so proud of my academic achievements, he discounted the importance of those warnings. Jack Collins was convinced that I would outgrow the bad behavior. After all, I always behaved when he was around, and people always complimented him on how well-behaved and polite his "little man" was.

I loved my dad. My weekly allowance was a dollar. If I behaved that week, I received a bonus, a small Matchbox metal die cast toy car from the local toy store. I had been collecting them for a couple years and had close to a hundred of them. When my dad washed his car, I would wash some of my favorite matchbox cars too, especially the newest additions to my fleet.

Swimming with my father was my favorite activity. He took me to a municipal pool that had several diving boards, including a high dive platform. Under his patient guidance, I quickly learned how to swim, but it took a great deal of coaching and coaxing before I finally jumped off one of the lower diving boards. Then at the end of the summer, just before I started first grade, I jumped off the high dive platform…30 feet! I was proud, but not nearly as proud as my father, who was waiting for me down below. And that felt wonderful to me, because in my young eyes, he was Superman and I wanted to be just like him when I grew up.

He rarely left me with a babysitter except for the few times a month when he went on a date. Even then he usually bribed me to stay with the sitter or he would wait until I fell asleep. If those ploys didn't work he occasionally resorted to trickery. We would drop in on a friend under the guise of visiting, and then my father would slip out while I was distracted. This method almost always resulted in a crying jag, but eventually I would calm down and settle in with my hosts. One time we dropped by his girlfriend Sue's apartment for a real visit. She had a son about one year younger than me and we were upstairs playing. Dad had just stepped into the restroom when I came tearing down the steps.

"Daddy, Daddy, don't leave me."

"It's okay honey, he's just in the restroom...he'll be right out," Sue said in a reassuring voice.

"No he's not; I heard his car leave...Daddy!"

"Honey I promise you sweetie, he's..."

"I know my Daddy's car," I cried through a face full of tears.

"There he is Jeff...see, I told you honey."

When I looked up to see my dad standing in the doorway, I immediately ran and attached myself to Dad's leg.

"Your car is gone, Daddy."

"No it isn't Jeff. I'm right here."

"I don't care...I heard it and it's gone."

Then he walked me over to the front door to show me that I was wrong. He opened the door and pointed at...an empty parking spot. His car had been stolen.

"See, I told you I know the sound of your car, Daddy," I said as I looked up into my father's stunned face.

Like most little boys, I went through a phase when I really despised the fairer sex. After all, they all had cooties, didn't they? There was one little curly blonde headed cutie named Cassandra in my first grade class who had a major crush on me, and during nearly every recess she would try to kiss me. No way, Jose! I resisted her by shoving her aside and running for cover. Then one day after school I was ambushed on my way home. Cassandra and her big brother jumped from behind some bushes and grabbed me. There was no escaping those "cootified" lips this time. Her brother was in the fourth grade and about twice my size. He pinned me to the sidewalk as Cassandra pounced on top of me and gave me a big sloppy kiss right on the mouth!

"Yuck! Cooties!"

As soon as I could, I jumped up and ran the entire way home, all the while trying to decide which was worse, being manhandled by another kid or the kiss itself. If only I knew then just how much energy and attention I would be devoting years later to chasing after those "cooties."

I had a lot of friends. I was almost always picked first when my classmates chose sides to play games. More than a few times, I was the kid brave enough to stand up to the class bully or the one who defended some pal who was being picked on. Except for acting up in class, I was considered an excellent student, and the other children's parents all liked me because of my well-mannered behavior (at least in their presence.) In essence, I was deemed a youngster with great potential.

However, an indication of what was to come took place during a play date with my neighborhood pal, who was nicknamed Peanut. We were playing with our toy cars in Peanut's sandbox. Peanut decided that he wanted to play with the red roadster that I was driving down one of the sandy lanes in the box. The problem was that roadster was my newest and current favorite. When Peanut received my firm denial, he responded with a shove that sent me backwards, loosening my grip on the prized toy. Peanut scooped it up with what turned out to be fleeting glee, because my actions were both immediate and decisive. With one hand I flung sand in Peanut's eyes while using the other to rain down blows all over his body. Long after Peanut surrendered, I continued the assault and concluded it by pouring bucketfuls of sand on his head. I snatched my car from Peanut's grip and marched toward my house, leaving my fallen comrade sobbing into the sand.

As I rounded the corner of my house I felt a sense of power. But this sense of being the conquering hero was short-lived. Electricity moves quickly and the telephone call from Peanut's mother overtook me on my way home. As I opened the back door to my house, my sense of triumph transformed into alarm, when I saw the look on my father's face and his belt sliding through the last of his belt loops. Pain delivered and message received.

Another hint of things to come occurred at Vacation Bible School during a spring break from elementary school. My mother volunteered to teach children's Bible stories and when I saw that she was going to be the teacher, I figured that I had it made in the proverbial shade. In short order I proceeded to uncover unpleasant facets of my personality, still assuming I had complete immunity from punishment. I was wrong. Mom gave me a "time out" and directed me to a corner for thirty minutes. Within two minutes I launched my plea for clemency.

"MOM, I have to go to the restroom."

"You can…in thirty minutes. Now sit."

"Mom, I really have to go bad…and not just to pee."

"Well now, that's just too bad isn't it? You should have thought of that before you started showing your little butt."

"Come on Mom, I really need to go!"

"Jeffery Holden Collins, you are going to sit right there until your thirty minutes are up."

"Momma, please!"

"You heard me, Jeff. Now turn around, face the wall and be quiet...or I'll make it an hour. If you have to go that badly, go in your pants."

Accepting only momentary defeat, I whirled around in a huff.

"I'll show her," I told myself.

Since I didn't really feel an impending intestinal requirement, I wondered if I could actually conjure one up in my pants like she had dared. Summoning an inner strength, I silently and surreptitiously completed what turned out to be quite a bowel movement, the volume and bouquet of which surprised even the perpetrator.

The smell rapidly wafted through the small classroom as I sat quietly facing the wall, confident that my scatological accomplishment would convince my mother that I was a formidable foe. The other children got the first whiffs and as it floated gently down the rows of desks, the stench seemed to grow in potency. When it reached my mother she knew instantly what had happened and who the culprit was.

"Jeffery! You're in big trouble now little mister. Let's go!"

"What are you talking about Mom....?"

But it was too late to play innocent. She snatched me up by the arm so hard that my feet left the floor. She then marched me right out the door, down the hallway and out of the building.

"Jeff, I am so mad at you right now, I swear to God I could just..." her voice trailing off.

"Just wait until I tell Jack what you did...and in the church of all places!"

And of course she did tell my dad and once again Mr. Belt had an intimate meeting with Mr. Butt.

Another incident took place in the kitchen on a Saturday. Dad was outside waxing his car, and I was playing with my toy cars inside on a large area rug in the den. I suddenly had an inspiring idea which envisioned a catastrophic wreck involving a couple of my less cherished wheels...

"I'm gonna make it a big, *fiery* wreck. Man this is gonna be so cool," I said aloud.

I decided on a couple of my least favorites and then considered how I might actually get them to burn. I went to the kitchen cupboard and retrieved a can of lighter fluid. I took a look at the thick rug and decided that I needed a better place to stage what I hoped would be a dazzling performance. I scooped up the cars and lighter fluid and ran to the kitchen.

"The linoleum won't burn," I said out loud.

I cleared an area for the big scene, placed the cars in strategic positions, and doused them with generous splashes of lighter fluid. I realized that I didn't have a way to ignite the fluid so I went in search of a match. It took a few minutes to locate a box of matches. When I returned to the staging area, I saw that the lighter fluid had formed tiny rivulets gracefully tracing paths in various directions. I struck a match and held it close to each car, watching with delight as each one burst into spectacular flames. I slammed one into another, instantly burning my hand.

"Ow!" I yelled.

Then I noticed all the flames running towards the kitchen walls.

"Uh oh. Daddy!" I shouted.

But he was already in the doorway, having heard my initial cry of pain.

"Shit Jeff, you're really going to get it this time..." his voice filled with panic.

He grabbed the nearby fire extinguisher and saved the kitchen, the house, and maybe my life. And as soon as the fire was out, my rear-end received multiple licks from his belt. It was the worst whipping my dad ever gave me, and it turned out to be the last one I would ever get from my father.

So that's how it went. When I misbehaved, my father would become stern. When the misconduct continued, his belt came off and discipline was dispensed in the form of pain to my little rear end. That was the way his father had dealt with unacceptable conduct from him and his siblings, and that's the way he reacted when discipline was required. Children don't come with manuals, and most parents learn parenting through the models in their own lives, for better or worse.

Today most child rearing experts agree that spanking a child causes more harm than good, and psychologists hypothesize that children may suffer a lifetime of neuroses from a few swats on the behind. Experts argue that it's much more effective to take away a few privileges, such as a video game, and to calmly reason with misbehaving children. It would be easy to become self-righteous and, consistent with today's "blame someone else" mentality, to accuse my father and his belt of unbalancing me. I could claim that parental physical abuse was the spark that eventually grew to the conflagration of horrors I had yet to perpetrate. Some people might buy that. Not me. It's a load of crap and a lousy excuse for what really amounts to a lack of self-control.

People become successes and failures from all sorts of bizarre environments. Common sense and moderation appear to be better methods, but my dad did his best. I'm convinced that every whack he delivered to my young rump was delivered with a father's love. Regardless of the plethora of troubles I would face throughout my life, I will not attribute even a small portion of them to my father's disciplinary methods.

CHAPTER 3
JACK vs. WILL

There's something happening here, what it is ain't exactly clear.
(Buffalo Springfield – For What it's Worth)

After my parents divorced, years passed before I spent any significant time with my mother. When my dad was at work, I usually stayed with his girlfriend Sue. But when Sue accepted a new job, other arrangements had to be made. Since I was starting grade school that fall, I needed to have a place to stay until dad got off work. After a little anguish and gnashing of teeth, Dad struck a deal with my mother. She would keep me from the time I got out of school until around 5:00 PM, when Dad picked me up.

It was around this time that Mom and Will decided to get Joan out of the children's home. She had been there for five years. During those years her only regular visitors were my dad and me. We went there at least once a month to see her. I hated that place and it puzzled me as to why my sister had to stay. I loved my sister and I was sad every time we drove away without her.

When I began staying with my mom in the afternoons, Joan and little Jeanne were there too, so it felt comfortable at my "other home" just as it felt comfortable at home with my dad.

It was during the third week of this new routine that I nearly burned down the house while playing with my toy cars in my dad's kitchen. My butt and upper legs were still marked from the imprints of my dad's belt. I always changed from my school clothes to play clothes as soon as I arrived at Mom's house. My bruises were clearly visible for anyone to see. As I pulled down my pants, my mom walked into the room.

"My God Jeff, what is that on your leg?"

"I dunno."

"Come here honey and let me see."

I went over to her with my eyes averted, looking down at the floor. As she ran her palm over the welts on the back of my thighs, she pulled my underwear away enough to see other similar marks on my bottom.

"Jeff, did Jack do this?"

"Oh yeah…on Saturday."

"Why, what did you do?"

"I caught the kitchen on fire…I guess."

"How often does your daddy whip you like this?"
"I dunno Momma, whenever I'm bad I guess."

I looked up into her face, then down at the floor, shuffling my feet and feeling nervous about the interrogation and hoping more punishment wasn't in store. I looked back up again and saw tears coming out of my mom's eyes. Then my feeling changed from anxiety to confusion.

"Jeff, would you like to stay here with me all the time?"

"Can Dad stay here too?"

"No honey. I mean do you want to stay here with me…and with Will and Joan and Jeanne…would you like that?"

"But where would Daddy stay?"

"Daddy would stay at his own house. Jeff, your daddy has been mistreating you. I love you more than anything, and I can't let this type of thing go on. I want you to come and live here with us."

"Momma, I wanna stay with my daddy," I said as my eyes began welling up with tears.

Mom pulled me close and hugged me tightly.

"It's gonna be alright honey, I promise you. You're not gonna be mistreated anymore."

"But Momma…"

"Momma is gonna take care of it baby. Now run along and play."

So I went outside and sat in the backyard swing, as I wondered about what had just happened and worried about what it all meant. Thirty minutes later I heard the familiar sound of Dad's new Plymouth coming up the alley, and I was at the gate waiting for my dad before the engine stopped.

"Ready to go little man?"

"Yeah Da…"

"He's not going anywhere, you son of a bitch!"

Mom was stomping angrily toward us. She took me by the hand and pointed me in the direction of the house.

"Jeff, go inside and see what Jeanne is doing for me okay?"

I was slowly complying but when I got inside the kitchen where my stepfather Will was standing, I turned and looked back at my parents in the backyard. As I did, Will brushed by me, stepped into the laundry room and looked outside at the developing scene.

"Maddie, what's going on…what's wrong with you?"

"You've been beating him, Jack!" she screamed. "He's got welts all over his little back and legs, you bastard. He's not leaving with you. He's staying right here with me."

"The hell you say. Yes, I whipped him... I whipped him for nearly burning the house down this past Saturday. He's my son and he needs to be whipped when he pulls stuff like..."

"No he doesn't. No child needs to be whipped like that, and that one ain't gonna be whipped like that any more. He's staying here."

Dad took off running toward the house. He swung open the back door and saw Will blocking the inside door to the kitchen.

"Jeff, come on, let's go."

My mother stopped just outside the back door and said, "Will, do not let Jeff come past you."

Will looked at my father solemnly, "He's not going with you Jack."

"The hell he isn't, come on Jeff."

Dad looked defiantly into the taller man's eyes. He had been in plenty of scrapes in his life and had boxed for his unit while in the Army. There was no fear in his body, and his son was leaving with him. I began to come through the door when Will reached down and stopped me. I took a few steps back into the kitchen, my eyes wide with anticipation about what was about to occur.

"Get your hands off of him and let him come out. This is none of your business, Will."

"He's not going with you Jack."

"Oh yes he is."

Dad reached for me, but Will grabbed his left arm. And when he did, Dad shoved him. As I backed away from the scuffle in panic, it escalated quickly. Will swung with a right. Dad easily sidestepped it and landed a solid left and right combination to Will's jaw and nose. Blood appeared. Mom started screaming. She flung open the door and wrapped her body around Dad's back and dug her nails into his face, his shoulders and any other place she could reach. The blows had dazed Will, but my mom's attack from behind gave him a chance to recover. Dad turned his back to Will in order to ward off Maddie. Will grabbed him from behind in a chokehold. I immediately ran to my daddy's aid, attaching my body to Will's leg, punching and biting the man who was trying to hurt my father. But Mom quickly stifled my efforts, pulling me away from the fracas and back into the safety of the kitchen.

"Let me go!" I cried.

"No Jeff, you're staying here."

"No I'm not...Daddy...you let my daddy alone!"

By then my father was nearly unconscious. He had enough awareness to make one final attempt to escape Will's chokehold. He brought back his right elbow with as much force as possible and caught Will in the eye. Will released him and stumbled backward momentarily, but then he used his last remaining bit of energy to grab my dad in a bear hug and lift him off his feet. Dad was helpless because he was still trying to regain his breath. Will had him up in the air and then suddenly threw him forcefully onto the washing machine.

Mom had a tight grip on me as I screamed in horror at the unfolding scene. Dad hit the metal of the washer hard and I knew that he was hurt. He somehow rose to his feet and nearly tripped over the threshold as he stumbled outside.

He was so out of breath and in so much pain he could barely talk.

"This isn't over, believe that. I have legal custody and I will get him back. You're not going to take him away from me, Maddie."

As he staggered to his car, I cried for him, "Daddy!"

"It'll be okay little man. I'll see you real soon."

As the blue Plymouth started up and disappeared down the alley, I wondered how long *real soon* would take. It would take a while. I felt deserted again. And adding to that feeling was the unease of having just experienced my first encounter with adult violence.

There would be a custody hearing in family court four months later. During that time Will and my mother manipulated me to say what they wanted me to say. At the hearing, a lot of grownup men asked me a bunch of questions about all kind of things, questions I had already been told how to answer. But the most important answer was my reply to the most central question.

"Who do you want to live with son?"

At that time I had not seen my father for four months. My new home was a nice place and I liked living there with my mom and my sisters, and even with Will. I was a mere child and I had been under the influence of my mother, a master manipulator, for all that time.

"My momma, I guess."

And so it was. My mother now had custody and Dad got visitation rights with me every other weekend. From that day forward Dad picked me up at the end of the block every other Saturday morning and dropped me off late Sunday afternoon. Regardless of whatever else that was happening in his life, I remained the single most important thing for my father. He never missed a single weekend visit with me.

When my mother disciplined us she used a fresh switch. It left bigger welts than my dad's belt. Whether her thrashings represented irony or hypocrisy depends on the perspective of the observer. That's true a lot in life, I suppose. Obviously in retrospect, it was both ironic and hypocritical. My stepfather Will applied punishment with a paddle (from one of those "paddleball toys" that once had a small rubber ball attached by a long elastic band). Both systems of punishment were used on all three children, my 13-year-old adolescent sister Joan, two-year-old Jeanne and six-year-old me. All three disciplinarians in my young life dispensed liberal amounts of pain. I never understood why Dad's way was wrong while Will and Mom's methods were okay. When I finally realized the extent of my mother's hypocrisy, and how much of an emotional burden it put on my father, my resentment was nearly unlimited.

Two years later, Will left Mom. We asked her why he left, but she never answered. We never learned the reason for his departure. Although Jeanne did periodically visit with Will, who was her biological father, I never saw him again.

CHAPTER 4
GRANDFATHER

"Old man take a look at my life, I'm a lot like you were."
(Neil Young – Old Man)

Howard Springs was a moderately wealthy man. While he only completed the tenth grade in high school, he possessed excellent judgment when dealing with money and in business. He owned 25 rental houses in Nashville and the Springs' Plumbing Company, which he inherited from his father. I could always count on him for big gifts on birthdays and Christmas; like a shiny new bike or an expensive toy. He was the richest man that I knew, so to me my grandfather seemed like a millionaire. I was his obvious favorite of the three grandchildren, with Birdie showing a preference for the firstborn Joan and little Jeanne standing in the fallout of her grandparents' affection for her siblings.

Every time Pop visited his daughter and grandkids, I followed him out to his car as he left, because I knew that a dollar would eventually be slipped into my hand. I loved my grandfather, but I grew to depend on him as my own personal ATM machine; another impediment to my development into a responsible member of society.

During the summer months when school was out, Pop would stop by early in the morning and pick me up to ride along with him at least once a week, as he checked on the progress of the various jobs his company had going on throughout the city. I always enjoyed walking into a building with my "Pop," the boss of all the men working for Springs' Plumbing Company. I also loved to hang around the office and ask questions about what that thing was or how much this cost, etc. I knew a lot about the company by the age of seven, even how much money the employees earned. My dad worked there too, so I got to see him the first thing in the morning or when he came back in for supplies. Yep, I really liked hanging around the shop and all the workers seemed to like having a curious little fellow there as well.

Pop took me everywhere he went during the day, like the corner drugstore where Pop always called the pharmacist a "money grubbing Jew" right to the guy's face, but smiling as he said it. I couldn't understand why he called Doc that name, but since it was my grandfather I just assumed it was okay. I didn't care much for the profanity that Pop used either, especially in front of people I didn't know, but again, it was Pop, so it was okay.

Then one hot day in mid-July, we drove to check on a project that involved installing a long water pipe to a new building. When we pulled up, four workers were there with shovels in their hands, but only one of them was working, a black man named Charlie Holliman who must have been around 90 years old.

"Get your asses to work. I'm not paying you to stand around with your thumbs up your butts!"

They mumbled something under their collective breath, but nonetheless they all went grudgingly back to shoveling along with Charlie, who never once looked up from digging.

I noticed that Charlie never stopped working. The old guy was steady and thorough in his tasks, no matter how hard the job was or how high the temperature climbed. What I couldn't figure out was why old Charlie made nearly a dollar an hour less than the white guys who obviously did less work. I decided to ask my grandfather. When we returned to the car and were about to drive off, I said, "Pop, can I ask you a question?"

"Is there any way to stop you?" Pop laughed and then said, "Go ahead."

"How come Charlie works longer and harder than anybody else, but makes less money than all of them? It don't seem fair to me, does it to you?"

He was about to turn the key in the ignition, but paused for a moment, gripped the steering wheel and turned to face his young grandson with a broad smile.

"Well honey, that's because Charlie's a nigger."

"Well that don't seem right to me. He does more work than two of those other guys."

"Jeff my boy, there's a whole lot of things in this old world that ain't fair. You'll find that out when you get older, son."

I never forgot that conversation and the injustice of the situation. Charlie should have been paid the most of those four workers. But it taught me a very valuable lesson. I learned at an early age not to judge people by the color of their skin. I didn't like it when my grandfather cussed, but I liked it even less when he used racial names such as Jew, nigger or wetback. So I made a decision then and there never to use those words. And though I developed a plethora of other vices throughout my life, racism was never one of them.

I know my grandfather was a good person despite his racist views. He was an ignorant man who was like most of white America at that time. It was how he was raised and all that he knew of such things. The white man had been in charge for so long that anything different seemed backward or even uncivilized. Howard Springs possessed many good qualities, such as helping the needy and showing kindness and consideration to others. He doted on his wife Birdie, whose health had been on a constant decline since her precious granddaughter had been placed in that wretched home. Even after Joan had reunited with the family, Birdie remained sickly. Mom often displayed resentment toward her mother by calling her "that old faking hypochondriac" behind her back.

I spent a lot of time at my grandparents' home, especially on the weekends that alternated with the ones I spent with my dad. I loved to go there, to watch color television, eat big bowls of ice cream and best of all, cut the lawn using the riding mower! If Birdie felt up to it, we went out to dinner at one of the three or four restaurants we frequented, places where we were greeted by name upon entering the establishment.

I must say that Birdie had quite a flatulence problem. In fact she had what could be termed epic flatulence. Birdie and Pop claimed that her doctor (one of many) advised her to never suppress the need to "let one rip." Consequently, she did indeed let them "rip" - anyplace and anytime. She would let one go in a restaurant, in a store and even in church, when she felt well enough to attend. My grandfather's unabashed response to her ripping one was always the same.

"Atta girl, Bird!"

This always terribly embarrassed the rest of the family, particularly when there were strangers in the vicinity, but little Jeanne and I always got a good laugh when she let one rip (or at least a snicker or two until Mom gave us a sideways glance). Once while I was spending the weekend with them, I was upstairs in one of the guest rooms. Pop called me downstairs to meet the pastor of their church. I was nearly an adult at the time and for me the charm of Birdie's gaseous volleys had long ago worn thin.

"Reverend, this is my grandson Jeff."

"It's a pleasure to meet you young man. I hear that you plan to attend college when you graduate from…"

Birdie turned in her recliner and slightly lifted her left leg.

"BAARRRRRACKKK!"

"Atta girl, Bird!" my grandfather sang out.

I wanted to find a hole and crawl inside. Neither of my grandparents ever said anything like "excuse me," or offered the smallest, perfunctory explanation for polluting the air. Red-faced and holding my breath, I turned to leave the room.

"It was very nice to meet you Reverend."

"And you as well Jeff. Maybe I'll see you in church…."

"BAARRRRRACKKK!"

"Atta girl, Bird!"

In spite of all the attention that my grandfather lavished on her, Birdie didn't return much gratitude. In spite of waiting on her hand and foot, giving her total body massages, delivering breakfast in bed, etc., she was constantly complaining. One minute the house was too hot. The next it was too cold. He burned her toast, the toast wasn't done…blah, blah, blah. And the tirades were almost always followed by a healthy, "BAARRRRRACKKK!"

To which he would issue his standard refrain, "Atta girl, Bird!"

I wondered why she was so ungrateful for all my grandfather did. Then one day when he returned a few minutes later than expected from the grocery store and they didn't realize that I was nearby, I got the answer, albeit rather cryptically.

"Hey, baby doll, how're you doing sweetheart?"

"Don't you sweetheart me!"

"Ah honey, come 'on…give me a little

sugar." I shuddered at the thought.

"Get away from me. You've probably been fooling around with some cheap whore somewhere again."

"Birdie, please, that was so long ago…"

"Howard Springs, you made your bed…you used yourself up. You haven't been any good to me for years. Now leave me the hell alone!"

Good God, did she catch him screwing somebody or what?

I shuddered again at the thought of my grandfather and some old road whore naked in bed together and Birdie walking in on them.

"Wow!" I said to myself as I quietly eased outside.

Not long after that incident, I was alone in their house when Pop took her for one of her many doctor's appointments. I was in the basement snooping through some drawers, looking at some old pictures, when I spotted a huge mahogany chest in the corner that I had never noticed before. I walked over to it and pulled on the door…locked. I felt around the bottom and then the top until I found a key. It worked! I opened it and looked inside.

"Damn!" I said aloud.

The entire bottom of the inside, which was about two and a half feet wide and nearly six feet long, was literally filled with money. It was mostly rolls of silver dollars, apparently thousands of them, but there were also wads and wads of bills and thousands of half dollars, quarters, dimes and nickels, some in rolls, but mostly loose in the bottom.

"There must be a hundred grand here!" I nearly yelled.

I was beside myself over what to do. There was so much money and it was obviously just being thrown in there from time to time. No one could possibly be keeping up with how much was in there. I really didn't want to steal money from my grandfather, but man there was so much money. If I took a few dollars, it was a near certainty that no one would ever know. So I did take a few dollars; from time to time I took *much more* than a few dollars, somehow always justifying it in my head.

It really isn't stealing is it? I mean, he wouldn't care and when he dies, I'll get it anyway. Heck, if I asked him, he'd probably tell me to go ahead.

But I did not ask and the money did not belong to me. It was my grandparents' and it certainly was stealing, no matter how hard I tried to mitigate the seriousness of it in my mind. It wasn't like I had never stolen anything before. I got caught swiping a Hershey's Candy Bar from the little corner grocery store that my mom used to send me to for milk and bread. And I took five bucks out of her purse once in order to buy a baseball glove from a classmate. But I was busted both of those times. With this caper, the guilt had a good long time to ferment. It bothered me so much that after years of pilfering, I stopped my regular withdrawals altogether, but not until I had taken several thousand dollars from the chest. I had grown accustomed to having a lot of cash in my pockets. When I was younger I blew the money on toys, model car kits, junk food, and the like. As I grew older, the purchases changed to things like accessories for my car, gas, clothes and of course, I began spending some of it on girls.

It was several years before he confronted me about it, and when it finally happened, I acted like I didn't even know the chest was there. My grandfather loved me so much that he appeared to accept my lies, even though it was painfully obvious to the old man that his beloved grandson had been stealing from him.

Things were never quite the same after that deceptively minor confrontation. I sensed that although my grandfather never said so, he knew that I had been dipping into the chest of cash. At times his disappointment in me was almost palpable. It caused me enough shame in my own psyche that I vowed never to steal again, but I did nonetheless.

There are various forms of theft and anyone with average intelligence knows when you obtain something by some underhanded means, it is a form of stealing. I may have been clever enough to justify my actions in my mind, but I knew in my heart when I did something wrong, which turned out to be far too often.

CHAPTER 5
ANOTHER FATHER FIGURE

"OM MANI PADME HUM"
(Mantra of Bodhisattva Chenrazee)

In early springtime, about a year later, a new guy started hanging around the house. Mel Snow was a friendly and talented man. He was from somewhere in Pennsylvania, the first northerner I had ever met. He worked for a local tree surgeon, trimming trees and treating them for disease. Mel wore western clothes, including expensive cowboy boots and he fancied himself a budding country music songwriter. He talked funny, too...he said "yews guys" instead of "you all" and "leave it go" rather than "let it go." At least it sounded funny to me.

When he first showed up, it was like having a new neighborhood kid to play with. Mel did lots of things really well. He was only about an inch taller than my mother at 5' 7" and in great physical shape. He climbed trees like a cat, played baseball about as well as anyone I had ever known, and he could play the guitar too. He entertained local kids with his singing and strumming, or by playing games like "hide the flag" with them. He was a big kid and everyone liked being around him.

Then one day he sort of just moved in. I remember the morning I walked into the kitchen to eat breakfast and there he was, cooking scrambled eggs and bacon. A couple of months later little Jeanne started calling the guy "Daddy." Not me. No sir. I had a dad. Besides, in my opinion this guy wasn't *so* great. And country music? Please...I hated country music. So some resentment was there in the beginning for the new man in my mother's life, and it was intensified by the fact that Joan and Jeanne thought he was so swell.

The next time Pop came to pick me up, I told him about the man who was living in his house with us. He tried to downplay it, but I could tell he didn't like the idea. I also complained about the situation to my dad, who asked if I wanted to come live with him again. My father figured that since Mom was now "living in sin" with a man and his children were in the house, it might be grounds for him to regain custody. But it wasn't to be. Pop and Birdie invited all of us to their house the following Saturday morning. Ushering us outside to play, Pop shared his feeling about the living arrangements.

"Maddie, you and Mel have my grandkids in my house and you're not married. Now I know you're gonna say it ain't none of my business, but you're gonna get my two cents anyhow."

"Daddy, I know what you're about to say...we know it's your house and we know it's...I mean, they're your grandkids..."

31

"You're damn straight and it's about to stop, especially if you plan to keep staying in my house rent free. Hell, Jack's already talking to a lawyer about taking Joan and Jeff away from you. And believe me gal, he can do it if you two keep shacking up together without getting married."

"Daddy, we love each other…"

"Damn love Maddie! If you two want to keep those kids, you've got two choices, one being Mel changes his address and two…well I guess get married and I mean real soon."

"Mr. Springs, I love your daughter and all three of those kids like they were my own. I want to marry Maddie and with your blessings, and as long as she says yes…heck, we could elope today!"

No one said a word for a minute or so, and then Birdie lifted her leg…

"BAARRRRRACKKK!"

"Atta girl, Bird!"

My mom turned to her mother, "Momma, would that be okay with you?"

"Why certainly Maddie…those kids need a father."

So they got married the following weekend. It was the first marriage for Mel and the third time around for my mom. For the next few years we lived together in relative peace and tranquility, although I continued to brood about my new stepfather. I already had a dad and I didn't need or want an extra one.

When Mom talked with Mel about changing her first name, he jumped on board, urging her to get it changed to her favorite name, Lana, so she did. Joan, Jeanne and I all thought that it was a very strange thing to do. It took quite a few years before we adjusted to our mother being called Lana rather than Maddie.

Mel was a man with a great deal of ambition. He was convinced that one day he would make his fortune writing country music songs, inventing a new gadget, opening a chain of restaurants or something along those lines. And he worked at his dreams. He took the money he saved and bought a coin-operated laundromat. After trimming trees all day, he emptied out the machines and would often repair a washer or dryer that was malfunctioning until late that night. There seemed to be very little that the guy couldn't do. Then he would make himself available to the neighborhood children for fun and games. On the weekends he and Mom would sneak off for a drive, leaving Joan to babysit if Jeanne and I weren't on a visit with our respective fathers.

It wasn't that I hated Mel. I actually liked the guy. The underlying causes of my negative feelings were related to the fact that the majority of my mother's attention now went to Mel, and my natural loyalty to my real father. My grandfather also seemed suspicious of his newest son-in-law. There was something about the man Pop just didn't like. However, I appreciated the fact that Mel was very athletic. I didn't mind even that the guy was better at sports than I was, even if he was *much* better. Heck, the guy's tips had actually improved my baseball skills and my jump shot. I considered him a pal, but not much of a parent.

Another thing I disliked about Mel was that he never went to church, not that I loved going myself. I just objected when my mother forced me to get out of a warm bed on a nice Sunday morning, get all dressed up, and sit on those hard pews, listening to some fat man telling everyone in the congregation how terrible we all were. The threat of eternal damnation, as daunting a concept as it was, sure didn't appear to be curtailing all the evil being perpetrated in the world, at least from my angle. And no matter how much I whined, hemmed and hawed, I went to church. My mom made sure of it every week, and I got plenty of doses of Bible verses from her during our daily family prayer times too, although Mel rarely made an appearance for those either. The real kicker for me was looking back at the front of my house on those sleepy Sunday mornings and seeing Mel sitting there on the porch with a cup of coffee and the Sunday paper.

"Mom, can't I stay here with Mel?"

"No you cannot. You're coming with us."

"Why?"

"Because I said so, that's why."

"Well, why doesn't he have to go?"

"Because his mother isn't here making him and he's an adult…and you're not, that's why. Now come on."

"Man, this sucks!"

"Not another word Jeffery Collins, I mean it."

Then came the weekend of the "conversation." It was a beautiful June Saturday morning. My mother, now known as Lana, was at the beauty parlor. Jeanne was visiting with Will, and Joan was spending the weekend at Pop and Birdie's. My visit with my father was the next weekend; therefore I was alone with Mel.

"Come on Jeff, let's walk down to the park and play some catch and maybe get a little game going."

"Okay, just let me run in and get my glove."

So we went to the park and played baseball for a couple of hours with a bunch of my friends and then walked to the store for a couple of cokes. On the way home, we were just shooting the breeze about things…cars, sports, etc.

"So you'll see Jack next weekend, huh?"

"Yeah, we're going to the lake and he's gonna teach me how to ski," I said excitedly.

"Has he got a boat?"

"Yeah, he just bought it. It's only been in the water once."

"You know, have you ever noticed how much Joan looks like Jack?"

"Duh...he is her father too you know."

"But you don't look a thing like him."

"Whaddayamean?"

"Well you're probably gonna be much taller than him, you're blonde-headed and don't look anything like him in the face."

"So what Mel...what are you trying to say?"

"Nothing, it just makes you wonder."

I never forgot that discussion and what I took as Mel's deviously intended implication. I knew at that time exactly what the guy was trying to say. But I also knew who my dad was. It was Jack Bernard Collins and nobody was going to tell me anything different, especially some guy who thought he was Marty Robbins and Gene Autry all rolled into one!

Mel was always coming up with new ideas about how to make money, and some of them were pretty good. One day he revealed his latest inspiration to me. It involved him and "Lana" going into the entertainment business. They would call themselves "Roy and Lana Starr" and he would demonstrate his skills with guns, rifles, knives, whips, etc. on stage all over the country.

"What a dreamer," I said to myself. "It'll never happen, not in a million, zillion years."

But I was wrong. I underestimated Mel's determination and skill. The next week Mel began bringing home all kinds of things like lumber, western clothes, metal poles, drills, power saws and a welding kit. He spent every night after working at the laundromat in
the garage making gun boxes and some type of wooden thing that looked like an oversized coffee table. Mel fastened it on a metal stand he had welded together and gave it a spin. Then he put two braces near the top and a piece of heavy metal near the bottom. He gave it another spin and stepped back to survey his craftsmanship.

"Not bad, not bad at all, huh Jeffy boy."

"What the heck's that thing for Mel?" I asked, scratching my head in wonder.

"Well, your mom's going to stand on it...then it'll get a good spin, and while she's spinning around, I'm gonna throw knives at her."

"Right...sure you are Mel," said I sardonically.

"Oh, it's going to happen, you can take my word on it," he maintained.

And it did. He practiced for hours with cardboard cutouts at first and when he was certain that he could do it without any danger to my mom, he put her on it. He never missed, not once. In fact he never so much as nicked her or even slightly touched her with even one of the knife handles! And that wasn't all. There were whip tricks where he would light a match or take the fire from a cigarette in her mouth. He fired a rifle at the gun box with a knife in the middle and a burning candle on both sides of the knife from about fifty feet away, and he split the bullet and put out both candles! And these tricks, along with a myriad of others, were actual feats of skill, not illusions like many other performers used. This guy was good, very good.

They never made the big time. They covered the local circuits, appearing on programs such as the Three Stooges and Popeye kiddy shows in the Nashville area and a few other cities. But Mel's sights were on places like Las Vegas and Hollywood. Unfortunately however, it just never happened.

All of my buddies were very impressed with it all though and when Mel began teaching me how to do some of the tricks, I actually really enjoyed learning them. But all those things like the clothes, whips, rifles, ammo and supplies cost money, not to mention the traveling expenses. It just didn't pay enough to warrant continuing with the Roy & Lana Starr's Wild West Show, so it quietly met a slow and inevitable demise.

Later on during the first weekend of August I was outside goofing around in the back yard, tossing a football over the fence with Sam, one of my next door neighbors. All of a sudden something hit me right in the side of the head and I became instantly drenched.

"What the hell?"

When I looked up, there stood Sam's older brother Ned and his stupid cousin Jerry grinning ear to ear.

"Bull's eye...or should I say...Jeff's eye!"

They both had their arms full of water balloons.

"Splash!" ..."Splash!" Two hit near my feet as I dodged two more on the run for cover.

"Splash"

"OW!" I cried out as another one hit me squarely in the back.

"I'll show you clowns...just wait," I yelled as I sprinted into the house.

I needed some balloons. I'd show those goofballs. But there were no balloons...except those ones in the nightstand beside my mother's bed, the ones individually wrapped. I knew this because I had opened one up once out of curiosity, and decided that it was probably used in some medical application or procedure and of no use to me. I quietly snuck in their bedroom, walked over to the nightstand and opened the drawer.

"Bingo."

There were three or four boxes in the drawer.

"Man there sure are a lot of those things...I'll just take a few of 'em and they'll never be missed," I muttered as I scooped up about two dozen of the prophylactics packs.

Then I ran to the bathroom where I opened all of them up to remove the "balloons." I tossed all the wrappers into the commode and flushed them all at once, and then immediately darted outside to the water hose in order to fill them up with water. I filled the first one until it reached what I estimated to be an ideal size and weight for the purpose I had in mind. I ran to the garage and found an old cardboard box and brought it back to my filling station and then prepared the rest of them. After walking over to the area where the edge of the roof was the closest to the ground, I flipped the box over the eave causing it to land upright at the edge of the roof. After going back to get the ammo, I brought an armload back to the area directly under the box. I lobbed the first of them underhanded over the edge and gently into the box.

"Two points," I said quietly.

I repeated the process until all of them were loaded into the cardboard arsenal. Then I shinnied up the drainpipe and onto the roof, grabbed the end of the box and pulled it to the apex of the house just behind the chimney, where I could stay out of view of my next door foes.

"Now we'll see who's the best shot around these parts, you morons," I said to myself, as I sat down, leaned against the brick chimney and waited for my adversaries to provide me with targets.

It didn't take long. About ten minutes later the pair came out of the garage door laughing and joking about something, apparently not in the least concerned about my quest for vengeance. I grabbed a couple of balloons, got positioned behind the cover of the chimney and lofted the first one into a high arch.

"Splash!"

"Dang it, missed 'em by a foot," I grumbled as I began tossing one right after another.

"Splash... splash... splash... splash... splash!"

Two, maybe three, hit the pair right in the head.

"Goofball's eye! What a shot!" I yelled out with glee.

I was laughing out loud by now as I launched four more.

"Splash… splash… splash"

Ned and Jerry finally spotted me just as a water bomb hit Jerry right on his shoulder.

"Wham!"

"There he is…we're gonna kill you Jeff, you little bastard," one of them hollered as they ran for cover.

I was laughing so hard now, I could hardly breathe and when I bent down to grab another bomb, my foot kicked the box, which sent it skidding down the incline of the roof.

"Oh no…there goes my ammo!"

I reached down to grab it but it was too late. I watched helplessly as the box and remaining water bombs disappeared over the edge with a series of splats on the ground. I scurried over to the edge of the roof, scrambled back down the drainpipe and tumbled onto the ground. When I stood up the first thing I spotted was Mel looking at the box and the burst water bombs. He did not look pleased to put it mildly.

"Damn it Jeff, you're going to get it now boy. Not only did you clog up the damn toilet, you've been snooping in my drawer," he said as he began pulling off his belt.

"Stay away from me Mel, you're not my dad…you can't whip me," I said as I started zigzagging to elude Mel.

But Mel was too fast and he quickly caught me by the arm, just as he delivered the first of several lashes to my back and rear.

"OW! Stop it Mel you son of a bitch! OW!"

After about four more lashes from his belt, Mel let go of me and said in an eerily calm tone, "Now stay out of my stuff Jeff."

"You…you…son of a bitch! Just wait until I tell Mom…and Pop…and my dad. You're not gonna beat me with a belt…you…you son of a bitch!"

"Tell whoever you want…but like I said, stay out of my stuff."

When I told my mom what had happened, she got angry…at me!

Unbelievable! Just wait until I tell Dad Saturday morning. Then we'll see what he has to say about it…mister cowboy wannabe.

On Saturday, I woke up early, anxious to tell Dad about what Mel had done to me, which I did the instant I got in his car. My father was livid. His initial reaction was to go up to the house and kick the crap out of Mel. Then he decided that it would be better to take pictures of my butt and back, and talk to his lawyer Monday about regaining custody of me and maybe even Joan.

"Don't say anything about this to Mel or your mom, okay?"

"I won't Dad, I promise."

"If things go our way, you won't be living there much longer."

"That'll be fine with me Dad…I can't stand that jerk."

We had a great time that weekend at the lake, skiing and riding around in Dad's boat. He even let me drive it for a little while. I couldn't wait to be away from Mel and living with my father again. That Sunday went by much too quickly, and it seemed like no time at all had passed when Dad dropped me off at the corner late Sunday afternoon.

"Remember, not a word to anyone…not even your sisters for right now, okay buddy?"

"I won't Dad. I promise."

"Okay Jeff…see you soon…and I love you son."

"I love you too, Dad."

But it was August and the month of August would turn out to be the worst of those twelve somewhat arbitrary divisions we use to keep track of our time in this earthly realm, at least during the vast majority of my life.

CHAPTER 6
FIRST ENCOUNTER WITH DEATH

"I am no more afraid of what waits for me after death than I am of what was before my birth."
(David Hume)

It was Wednesday and a typical August day, stifling hot and not a breeze was to be found. I had been daydreaming most of the day about living with my Dad again. It would be so much better and I wouldn't have to see Mel's stupid face anymore either. Heck, the reason that I was with my mother now was because Dad had given me a few licks with a belt, and he was my father. But Mel beating me...well, that was a different story altogether. I hoped that my dad had already looked into it and that it would happen sooner rather than later.

After I moved to my dad's house again I hoped that he would look into getting custody of Joan, too. Mel and my mother were so strict with her, she could barely breathe. Why, they wouldn't even allow her to go to the movies on the weekend with a girlfriend or go to a sleepover at her best friend's house. Yeah, she needed to get away from there too. And as for Jeanne, well there was nothing I could do for her right now, but maybe later on...

I was in the back yard shooting a basketball at a crummy rim with no net that hung at a tilt over the garage door, when my sister Joan threw open the screen door and ran screaming toward me with a face full of tears.

"Jeff...Jeff, oh Jeff," she sobbed.

"What's wrong Joanie? What is it?"

"Our daddy's dead Jeff," she cried.

"Which one?"

"Huh?"

"Which one, which daddy?'

"Our daddy! Our real daddy...whaddamean which one?"

"What happened to him?" I asked.

"All Poppa said...was that a truck...ran over him...Oh Jeff," she sobbed.

I just stood there motionless, unable to speak.

"Oh," I said softly as I looked down at the ground, gently nudging the basketball with my foot. Having absolutely no experience with death, I was waiting on some type of weird internal autopilot to alert my emotional network as to the proper response. My sister stood there staring at me for a moment or two longer and when no further reaction seemed to be imminent, she whirled around and began running back toward the house.

"What's wrong with you, don't you even care? It's our daddy, Jeff, our real daddy," she yelled at me over her shoulder as she disappeared into the house.

It was as though I had been hypnotized. I stood there motionless, staring down at the basketball. Then all of a sudden I stepped back and kicked the ball with all my might. It slammed into the garage door and ricocheted right back into my face.

"Ugh," the sound came out of my mouth about the same time as the blood started pouring out of my nose.

Then I fell to the ground, crawled over to the garage and braced myself against the wall. The tears were flowing together with the blood, but I didn't care. My dad…my real dad…no, my **only** dad was…dead…my dad was…gone.

Mel came out the back door and walked slowly over to where I was rolled up into a ball as I sobbed into my hands, which covered my bloody tearstained face. I looked up for a moment to see who was approaching and immediately put my face back into my hands.

"Leave me alone Mel."

"Jeff, I just want you to know how sorry I am…and that I'm here for you if you need someone to talk to…that's all son," he said as he touched my hair.

"Don't touch me Mel…don't worry about me and I'm not your son. I don't need nobody…especially you," I said as I looked up straight into his concerned face.

"My God Jeff, what happened to your face?"

"Nothing…now leave me alone Mel!"

"At least come inside and let me wash that blood off your face buddy."

I stood up, threw my shoulders back defiantly and looked directly into his eyes.

"Mel, you can take your knives, guns and all your western crap and go straight to hell. I hate your damn guts and I wish that it was you that Joan told me was dead," I said as insolently as possible.

The next day Pop picked Joan and me up around 6:00 PM to take us to the funeral home. It had taken the morticians that long to prepare Dad's body for viewing due to the fact that his head had been crushed beyond recognition. He had been lying prone on a sidewalk looking down into a water main when a large truck backed up and over his head. He was killed instantly. At my grandfather's insistence, they prepared a fake head so that his grandchildren could see their father one last time. In hindsight it was a terrible decision, but I'm certain he had good intentions when the decision was made.

It was a dreadful experience for Joan and me. We were met at the door by countless relatives and friends of the family, and other people who I had never seen or heard of; strange women, their makeup all smeared with tears, hugging me and kissing my cheeks, and then attempting to wipe off the red lipstick...and men I had never seen shaking my hand and patting me on the head, almost all of them telling me what a good man Dad was, and saying how much I had grown since they last saw me. I vividly recall some lady coming up and giving me a big bear hug.

"Hello Jeff, I'm your Aunt Mildred from Texas. Do you remember me? Jack brought you down to my house when you were just a little fellow." "Yes ma'am I do," I lied in an attempt to be polite.

"How are you Aunt Mildred?"

"Oh honey, this is so terrible for all of us. Jack was such a wonderful brother. And he loved you and Joanie more than anything in this world," she said as she began to sob.

About that time I saw the casket out of the corner of my eye. I had never seen one before. It was maroon and shiny like the ten-speed bike my dad bought me to ride when I went to his house for weekend visits. The top was open and the inside looked like some white lacy curtains that were in my grandmother's bedroom. I turned and took a few steps in the direction of the casket, when Aunt Mildred reached down and took my hand into hers.

"Now darling, I need to tell you that your daddy is going to look different to you sweetie. They had to..."

But I pulled away and walked quickly to the edge of the casket. I looked down and saw my father's suit but the face, it wasn't my dad's. It looked like, like a...head...like a head off of a mannequin in some clothing store.

"Is that my dad? Aunt Mildred, that's not my dad!" I yelled as I began backpedaling away from the casket.

"Yes darling, that's Jack," she said as she finally caught up with me.

"It was God's will, Jeff. It's beyond our understanding, but I know that he's in a better place, and he'll be looking down on you and Joanie until we're all together with him in heaven."

"How do you know that Aunt Mildred...have you died and come back? Nobody knows what happens when you die. We may never see each other again," I said through a face full of tears.

"Now Jeff, you mustn't say things like that honey...you have to be strong Jeff..."

But I had heard enough. I turned and walked away, over to a section of empty chairs and collapsed into one of them. Anger, confusion, sorrow...I was experiencing so many different emotions that I couldn't process them all. Was this a dream, some type of weird nightmare? If it was, I needed to wake up in a hurry. But I was wide awake and the sight of that strange face and head attached to my father's body, all dressed up in his blue suit would haunt me for the rest of my life.

As most of the people there prepared to leave, all the friends and relatives once again assailed Joan and me with pats, hugs and of course, the red lipstick smearing kisses. They all said that they would see us at the funeral, which was scheduled for Saturday morning, and they made plans to eat at a local restaurant afterwards.

Joan and I returned home to an eerie silence. Mel and Mom were sitting outside on the patio and hardly moved for the next hour. I wanted to go outside behind the garage, but I didn't want to be around Mel, so I just stayed in my room. I was exhausted and shortly collapsed on my bed into a deep sleep.

I dreamed that Joan and I were on the lake with Dad riding around in his boat, water skiing and having a great time. Dad let me drive the boat while he took a turn on the skis, with Joan sitting in the back of the boat to keep an eye on our dad. When my father finally grew tired, he gave Joan the signal to stop the boat and then he let go of the rope. I drove over towards him and shut off the motor. Dad swam the rest of the way to the rear of the boat where the ladder was and handed the skis up to Joan. Then he grabbed the top of the ladder and pulled himself up so that his face crested on the gunwale of the boat.

"Jeff, Joanie, I love you both with all my heart, but I have to go away now, but don't worry because we'll all be together again one day soon."

With that pronouncement, Dad let go of the ladder, fell back into the water and disappeared. The dream continued with me waking up to see my father's fake head lying on the pillow right next to my face. Then I woke up for real, screaming so loudly that I probably woke up half the neighborhood. It took an hour for my mother to calm me down.

"It's okay baby, you just had a bad dream. Everything's okay," she said as she embraced me and tenderly stroked my face.

"But I saw dad's head when I woke up Mom. It was real."

"No honey, it was only a dream, a bad dream. You're okay now. I'm right here baby."

I felt exhausted as though I hadn't slept for days. My mom left the room and I sat up on the bed, thoughts cascading through my mind, each being shoved aside by the next.

I wondered why God had let my father die like that. Was this the will of the loving and merciful God that I had learned about in Sunday school? Was it the will of the "Father in Heaven" for my father's head to be crushed so horribly that a fake head had to be fabricated for the viewing? I thought about never being able to be with him again, never playing another game of catch with a football, never tossing a baseball in the front yard, never driving his boat around the lake with him skiing behind it and all the other fun we had together. All these thoughts continued to swirl around in my head. And as they did, I experienced yet another deep and foreboding sense of abandonment.

"Oh Dad, why did you have to leave me? God, why him, why not Mel or somebody else, anybody else…why God?" I cried.

The next day was Friday and that morning Joan and I were sitting out on the patio quietly. We were both thinking about going back to the funeral home and walking up to the maroon casket and seeing that awful fake head on our father's body. Mom and little Jeanne walked over to us. My mom sat in the chair between us and Jeanne walked over to me and put her hands on my knees.

"It's okay Jeffy, Momma said that your daddy's not dead. She said that we're all making too much out of this," she said innocently.

"What're you talking about Jeanne?"

Mom interrupted, "Jeanne, be quiet, you don't know what you're talking about. Now run along and play."

"Uh huh Momma, I heard you and Mel talking…" she said.

"Jeanne, I'm not going tell you again. Now go play, like I told you."

"What'd she mean Mom… when she said that my daddy's not dead?" I asked.

"Jeff, she's just a baby…she doesn't know what she's saying half the time. You know that. Now do you two need any clothes ironed for tonight? Do you know what you're going to wear?"

I knew that she was trying to change the subject, but I didn't care because I didn't feel up to continuing the discussion right now anyway.

"I don't want to go back to that place tonight," I said in nearly a whisper.

"Jeff, you have to go," said Joan adamantly. "That's our father!"

"Joanie, I can't…that head, that face, that's not Dad. I don't want to. I'll go to the funeral tomorrow, okay?"

"Jeff please, you have to, doesn't he have to go Momma?"

I glanced in my mother's direction and then quickly down at the ground.

"I don't have to if I don't want to, do I Mom?" I asked anxiously.

"No, you don't have to go honey."

Joan jumped up immediately and ran into the house crying.

I turned to my mother and said, "Mom, Dad is...uh...was my father, right?"

"Of course he was baby."

"Well then, what was Jeanne talking about?"

"Oh, she must have overheard us talking last night about how people are always making too big a fuss over such things and how I don't want everybody crying over me when I die...that's all."

"Mom, do you think that I should go tomorrow? I mean, do you think that it would be okay if I..."

"Honey, you paid your respects to him last night and you had a horrible nightmare because of it. Mel and I will completely understand if you want to stay here with us. As a matter of fact, why don't we all go to the park or do something fun instead? It'll be good for you to get your mind off of it and think about something else for a while."

I didn't go back to the funeral home that night. I stayed home with Mel, Mom and Jeanne. We grilled hamburgers and hotdogs, made homemade ice cream and played Monopoly. Afterwards, they asked me if I was okay and if I wanted to talk about Dad or anything else.

"I just don't want to see that ugly head again...you know?"

"Jeff I understand. I hated going to my dad's funeral in Pennsylvania last summer and I'm a grown man."

The conversation went on and on and somehow, by the time it ended, I had decided, or had been persuaded, that the best thing to do was to not go to the funeral. So I didn't.

Joan was livid with me for my decision. She refused to speak to me for nearly two weeks. Pop was fuming too, but not at me. He smelled a rat - two of them in fact. He knew that Mel and his daughter, who he insisted on continuing to call Maddie Mae, had manipulated me into skipping Dad's funeral.

I wasn't quite the same energetic kid for the next couple of months. I moped around the house a lot and didn't talk much to anyone. I continued the attempts to rationalize missing my father's funeral for years. I tried to convince myself that it wasn't that big of a deal, that I had done enough by going to the funeral home and by praying for my father.

The last thing I said to him was that I loved him. He knows that I miss him and hate that he died.

I initially blamed not going to the funeral on that awful fake head and the nightmare I had of it appearing on my pillow. Later on I would come to blame Mel and my mother for their apparent manipulation of the situation and for telling me that it was okay not to go. I even made an effort to persuade myself that Jack Bernard Collins may not have even been my real father, and if that were true, it would make not going okay. Nevertheless, in the end I knew that it was my responsibility alone to go. I was certainly old enough to make my own decision in this matter and no one had forced me not to go, and the older I became, the more it gnawed away at me.

Months later, I believe my resentment of my mother and Mel manifested itself in my first and only occurrence of sleepwalking. Psychiatry offers a myriad of theories on the causes of somnambulism, yet they all remain merely theories. No one knows the cause for sure. This episode happened in the middle of the night, just a few months after Dad died. Apparently I sleepwalked into my parents' bedroom, walked right over to my mother's side of the bed, pulled out my penis and began showering their entire bed with the forceful stream of urine that only the youthful can generate. Since some of it fell on their faces, Mel and Mom woke up immediately and turned on the light.

"What in the hell?" Mel yelled out.

"Jeff, what are you doing?" cried my mother.

I remained in the same position and continued watering their bed.

"Jeff!"

"I think he's walking in his sleep, Mel."

"I'm about to walk him okay..."

"No Mel, I've read where it's dangerous to wake someone who's walking in their sleep."

"Lana, he peed all over the bed and us! Whaddaya want me to do?"

"Sssh. Let's just try to get him back to bed. Then we can change our sheets and things."

I remained standing there for a moment or two after completely draining my bladder. Then I made a casual turn and strolled slowly out of their bedroom with Mel and my mom trailing behind me.

"Where's he going now?"

"Sssh. I think he's going back to bed."

But I walked right past the door to my room and out into the back yard. Then I just stopped and appeared to be surveying the darkness of the night.

"Mel, what's he doing?"

"How should I know? He's your son...you tell me."

"Let's see if we can sort of guide him back to bed."

So they gently steered me back to my room and somehow got me to lie down. Just as soon as I touched the sheets of my bed I rolled over onto my side and began snoring lightly, and that was that.

"Okay, come on and let's go change the sheets and pillow cases on our bed."

"What a night," whistled Mel.

The next morning they told me all about the previous night's activities, but I doubted the story, at least initially. It took taking me out to the laundry room and showing me the pee-stained bed linen to convince me that it had truly taken place.

I never walked in my sleep again, but I always remembered learning of the night I soaked Mel and my mother with urine. Years later I wondered if it actually had been triggered by some subconscious desire to retaliate against them for the things I judged them to be guilty of. Much later on in my life I realized that my judgment of my mother and stepfather was, at best, inexact.

Joan and I might have benefited from seeing a counselor to help us as we dealt with the untimely loss of our father. Apparently however, no one had the presence of mind to seek any form of therapy for us. We were left on our own to cope with the situation, and time would show that Joan was much better equipped psychologically to handle the burden than her brother.

PART II   A 60'S & 70'S REALITY SHOW

"I shouted out, 'Who killed the Kennedys?' Well after all, it was you and me."
(The Rolling Stones – Sympathy for the Devil)

CHAPTER 7
AH, YOUTH

"Life is tough, it's tougher when you're stupid."
(John Wayne)

It was a different era when I was growing up. I was around eight years old when I got my first taste of pizza and I loved it (even though a very hot piece of cheese worked its way loose and painfully attached itself to my chin.) There was no pizza delivery in my neighborhood then, but milk and the newspaper were brought right up to our front door every morning. The milkman brought the milk in glass bottles. He arrived about the same time as the paperboy with the morning newspaper. I, along with practically every boy my age that I knew, seemed to have the same job, delivering papers. The papers cost 15 cents apiece and I earned three cents from each one. There were approximately 150 houses on my route and I delivered the papers between 4:30 and 6:00 AM six days a week. Saturday was collection day and I visited each house to collect from my customers. My favorite customers were the ones who cheerfully handed over a dollar bill and said to keep the change. The least favorites never seemed to be home on Saturdays, even though I often saw a curtain move or a silhouette duck quickly out of sight as I left without getting paid.

Television was a very big deal back then. Everybody I knew had one, but they were all black and white sets with only three or four channels available. The first time I saw a color set was at my grandparents' house and I thought it was absolutely fantastic. Some people tried to make the picture bigger by putting a huge magnifying glass on the screen. Others who wanted a color set but couldn't afford one, bought these tricolor lenses and attached them to the screen of their black and white sets. The top of the lens was blue, the middle was red and the bottom was green, and the only way it could come close to working effectively was if the picture consisted of a big red fire engine that was parked on a nice grassy field under a brilliant blue sky.

Telephones were different, too. Most of my neighbors had a single phone in their house. All of them came in basic black, had rotary dials and were invariably located in the living room. Of course there were no cordless phones then, but you could order an extra long cord. Many people belonged to a "party line" which meant that three or more households had the same number, with each family having a slightly different sounding ring. You can just imagine all the fun the kids had as we eavesdropped on another family's conversation, and there was always the exasperation of people when they had to wait on an important phone call while some windbag yakked on and on.

Automobiles were power symbols then just like they are today. Huge metal monsters with fins, lots of chrome and loud, gas guzzling engines were the norm. In 1969, a new Chevrolet Corvette could be yours for about six thousand dollars. My grandfather bought me my first new car that year. That was when gas was only about 24 cents for a gallon of high-test fuel and at that time it was considered outrageously high.

The good old days had their problems too. Emotional wounds were still healing from the Korean War (or Police Action) when the casualties from Viet Nam began piling up, which caused so much sorrow for so many families all over our nation. During that war approximately 60,000 American lives were lost. At the same time abuse of drugs like marijuana, cocaine and LSD was becoming a national epidemic.

Americans felt immense pride as the United States sped past Russia and zoomed into the lead in the space race. Much of the world witnessed the Apollo 11 astronauts park their Lunar Lander at Tranquility Base on the moon. And as the Eagle touched alien ground and Neil Armstrong's "…one giant leap for mankind" message was proclaimed, it was apparent that this was an event that would forever be a highly significant milestone in the history of the progress of the residents of planet earth.

John Fitzgerald Kennedy and Martin Luther King, Jr. were two of our brightest leaders in that era. They were men who possessed the capability to make the world a better and safer place and possibly even to be catalysts for insuring that justice be much more evenly applied to all people. But it was not to be. Those brilliant beacons were snuffed out by bullets fired by cowardly assassins.

As the sixties began, Mel, Mom, Joan, Jeanne and I eased into the routine that most families find themselves in, and things seemed rather normal for a while. Mel kept on working hard at becoming rich, and eventually I grudgingly relinquished a bit of my sullenness and somewhat accepted Mel's role as my stepfather. We even began playing a little baseball and basketball together again.

Mom was strict with us, although she was much stricter with my sisters than she was with me. I was allowed to have a paper route, even though I was more than six years younger than Joan. Joan received the shortest leash and she bolted at her first opportunity to escape from under our mother's tyrannical rule.

Although Joan had recently turned eighteen, she was still rarely allowed to go anywhere without Mom. But she had been skipping class to see a guy named Robert Branch, a boy she had met through a friend at school. One day Robert proposed and off they went, straight to a justice of the peace. And just like that she was married. Mom was livid, but Joan was legally an adult, so there was absolutely nothing that she could do about it. Joan's elopement proved to be significant to my development, because it caused Mom to give me much more freedom. I suppose that in her mind, it would keep me from running away from home at my first opportunity as well.

During a downward trend in Mel's search for fame and fortune, he went to work for my grandfather's plumbing company. Initially, Pop was glad to hire him. Mel was bright, he caught on quickly and he was a good worker. Things went smoothly at work for nearly a year. Then an audit of the company books revealed that the sum of approximately twenty-five thousand dollars was missing. Well, Pop blamed Mel and Mel accused Pop of setting him up. Allegations and denials went on for some time with no resolution in the matter, other than Mel quitting. Of course Mom sided with Mel and I believed my grandfather. Mel tried to talk with me about it one day.

"Jeff, I swear to you, I never stole a cent from your grandfather, and it's important to me that you believe me."

"Pop wouldn't lie to me Mel and there's nothing you can say to make me think differently."

"Jeff, things aren't always as they seem, you know."

"And then sometimes they're exactly as they seem. Aren't they Mel"?

"One day the truth will come out about this and some other things you think you understand right now."

"What are you trying to say, Mel…are you making another insinuation that my father wasn't really my dad?"

"I'm just trying to…"

"Get bent Mel!" I yelled as I tore out through the back yard and disappeared down the alley in a flash.

I never talked with Mel about the missing funds again, although conversations and questions about Dad's paternity would grate at me for the rest of my life.

Mel returned to his ambitious, unfulfilled, pursuit of riches. Pop went on accusing his son-in-law of being a thief. He swore that the only reason he didn't have Mel arrested was because of his daughter and grandkids. Mel, on the other hand, simply quit talking about it.

With the relaxed rules that now applied to me, I was living the good life. My paper route, together with my mahogany ATM chest and the cash Pop frequently slipped in my pocket, gave me a lot of spending money. I frequently stayed out after dark, usually at the pool hall, where I learned how to play eight ball. I also wasted more than a few coins playing pinball. Even with the flipper machines eating a couple of dollars a week from my earnings, I still managed to save nearly three hundred bucks.

I had a plan…I wanted a motorcycle and as soon as I had enough for the sleek black 50cc Honda I had my eye on, I announced my intentions to my mom.

"Oh no you're not! I'm not going to pick up the phone and hear about you getting killed on one of those things. No sir!"

"Mom I could get killed just as easy on my bicycle, maybe even easier!"

"Jeff, you heard me. The answer is no…and that's final."

"It's my money. I earned it and I should be allowed to spend it…I'll bet Dad would have let me buy one."

"Well, he's not here is he? I'm your mother and I said no. Besides, you're not old enough."

"Billy Bowers is my age and he has a Harley 75cc and…"

"I don't care if little four year old Timmy next door has one. You're not getting one…at least not until you're older," she said, leaving the door open for possible future negotiations.

Nevertheless I did get the bike and I didn't even have to use my money to buy it. When Pop heard about Mom's refusal, he picked me up the next Saturday morning, drove me down to the local Honda dealership and paid cash for the bike along with a nice, shiny black helmet. Then I rode it home with my grandfather following behind in his car. Pop parked in the alley right behind the house, as I continued right on up to the patio where Mel, Mom and Jeanne were sitting.

Pop strolled up to them and said, "If you won't let him keep it here, he can keep it at my house."

In the end my mother relented and the little black Honda stayed. I suspected that it had more than a little to do with the fact that they were still living in one of my grandfather's houses rent-free.

From that day forward, I was motorized and zooming around the neighborhood. The paper route that used to take close to two hours to complete now took only an hour.
And little girls that I recently starting feeling attracted to seemed to be flirting with me more. What's more, I was now being pursued by some of the local coaches to play on local youth teams.

Thanks in no small part to Mel's coaching and tips, my jump shot was coming along nicely and my baseball skills were improving as well. I played baseball in the local Little League and was considered one of the better players. It hurt my feelings that no one in my family ever seemed to care enough to come and watch me play, but I refused to whine about it. I recall one night, the first time I turned on a high fast ball and got all of it. As I was rounding first base, I watched the ball disappear over the centerfield fence and wished that my dad was in the stands to see it. Besides the two or three little girls in my class that always seemed to be there when I played, the only familiar face I ever spotted in the stands was my brother-in-law Robert.

A few months later, trouble visited our house. Mel and Mom had been arguing for a couple of weeks when Mel suddenly moved out. I had mixed emotions about his leaving. While I had no great love for him, I knew that little sister Jeanne was crazy about the guy, and I could see how upset Mom was over the separation. Mom became pale and sickly, so much so that I began to worry about her. My worries metamorphosed themselves into a new hostility I exhibited in school.

On two different occasions inside of one month, I had to go to the principal's office for fighting. The only thing that kept me from being suspended was because the fight was initiated by older and bigger boys, and witnessed by a handful of classmates. When the potential trouble popped up, I reacted by punching them in their respective noses. Unfortunately, it was only a hint of the violence that would soon permeate my life.

I never did find out why Mel left. I only knew that it was deeply affecting my mother. She rarely ate, she stayed in bed most of the time and when I went into her bedroom to check on her, I frequently found her sobbing into her pillow. I knew that she had been going to see a doctor about once a week and I noticed more and more pill bottles on her dresser and nightstand. They had been separated for several months. Mel had come by a couple of times but, after talking for an hour or so, he left again as Mom cried and begged for him to stay.

One Friday night after one of Mel's visits, I went into her bedroom to see how she was doing. All the lights were out and the only illumination was supplied by the diffused light from the street lamps, coming through the slats of the Venetian blinds. She was sitting on the side of the bed, kind of hunched over toward a large dresser that was in the corner of the room. Even in the dimly lit room, I could see a metal object in her hand...a gun!

"MOM! What are you doing?" I said, my voice cracking and filled with panic.

"Mom, please...answer me, what are doing with that gun? MOM!"

She didn't even look up at me and said, "Go away honey, it'll be okay."

"What'll be okay? You don't look okay. Please Mom, talk to me...please."

"I just...just can't take it anymore Jeff. I...just want it all to stop."

She was slurring her words so badly that I knew at once that she had taken a bunch of pills.

"Momma, you're really starting to scare me. Why don't you give me that gun, okay?"

She mumbled something unintelligible and raised the hand that held the revolver.

"BAM!"

I nearly jumped out of my skin. She dropped the pistol onto the floor and collapsed back onto the bed. I flicked on the light and rushed to her side to see if she was shot.

Whew! No blood, she's okay. I thought.

Then I looked up to see my little sister standing in the doorway.

"What was that noise Jeff? What's wrong with momma?"

"Nothing Jeanne, it's okay. Momma is just tired and went to sleep. Be a good girl and go play, okay?"

"What was that noise?"

"I dropped something, that's all. Now please Jeanne, go play."

As soon as she left, I kicked the gun toward the wall and away from the bed. Then I picked up the phone and dialed the number of the place where Mel was staying. I couldn't help but notice that my hands were literally shaking as the phone began to ring. I glanced at the dresser and saw where the bullet had cut a shallow groove on its trajectory into the wall.

"My God Momma!" I said aloud.

"Hello."

"Mel, thank God...listen...Mom just fired a gun in her bedroom. I think she tried to kill herself. Please come over as soon as you can. Do you think I should call the cops...or...something? What should I do?"

"Calm down and take a deep breath. I'll be right there...and don't call anybody...just hide that 22 and be careful with it."

"Hide what?"

"The 22...the pistol Jeff, the pistol. Hide it and be careful. Just get it out of there. I'm on my way."

I cautiously picked up the gun, took it outside and looked for a place to hide it. Still shaken by what had transpired, I had difficulty finding a good place to hide it. Finally I just put it at the bottom of some hedges.

"That'll do till he gets here," I said aloud.

Then I ran back in to check on my mom.

"Asleep...good."

I looked in on Jeanne, who was playing in her room with her dolls. Then I went outside and sat on the front porch steps to wait on Mel. Five minutes later Mel's car screeched to a halt, his door swung open and he vaulted up the steps.

"Where's your mom?"

"Inside. She's asleep I think."

Okay, good...what'd you do with the gun?"

I walked with him over to the hedges and showed him where it was. Mel bent down and picked it up.

"Okay, good job buddy. Now relax. Everything's going to be okay."

After that night Mel moved back in and things got better at home. But my mother's health never completely recovered, and she suffered with fainting spells for the remainder of her life. She went to several specialists with no definitive cause ever pronounced. One physician recommended relocating to a climate more favorable for her condition. And since no other proposed cure was forthcoming, they began discussing such a move.

Months later I was called into the living room where Mel, Mom, Jeanne and my grandfather were sitting.

"Jeff honey, we want to talk with you about moving out west."

"Out west? Where out west?" I asked.

Mel stood up, "To Tucson, Arizona and we'd like you to come with us little buddy."

Pop shifted in his chair, "But you don't have to go if you don't want to. You have a couple of other choices."

"Like what kind of choices?"

"Well darling," said my mom, "I really want you to come with us. But if you don't want to, you can stay here in Nashville, or..."

"Where, with Pop?"

"No son, your grandmother's health is too bad for you to stay with us full time, but you could live with your sister and Robert...they already agreed to..."

"So that's it...those are my only choices?"

"Or..." said Pop, "You could go to a private school, a good one, a college prep school and I'll pay for it."

"I guess I'll stay with Joan and Robert. I don't want to go to some snooty private school...and I sure don't want to go be a cowboy," I said, deliberately cutting my eyes at Mel.

So Mel, Mom and Jeanne left for the Wild West two weeks later and I stayed in Tennessee with Joan and Robert. I felt resentment toward Jeanne for going even though she was just a little girl, and I felt abandoned by my mom for leaving me, a feeling I was getting far too familiar with.

The experience of living with my sister was short lived. I started staying out later, and when Joan tried to lay down the law, I bucked. I loved my sister and Robert was okay, but they couldn't get me to behave. They tried to reason with me, but I simply refused to yield to their authority. The last thing that I was going to accept was a third father figure. The experiment quickly ended and private school was the only remaining alternative.

Pop enrolled me in a very prestigious and exclusive military academy. I quickly adjusted to life at the prep school. The place focused on academics and sports with a little military training thrown in. Already excelling in sports to some degree, I relished the chance to learn how to play sports like football and tennis. I studied martial arts, too. Classes there were much more demanding than in public school, but I was up for the challenge. My first year classes included Academy English, Latin I, Advanced Biology, Honors History, Algebra I and Military Science Training I.

At the end of my first term I made the honor roll and had established myself as a pretty decent athlete. The sports program was considered as one of the best in the south, if not the nation, and the teams were constantly vying for the league championships in practically every sport. I loved being a part of this winning machine, even if it meant that I was a smaller component than I had been in the past. I had always loved baseball and basketball, and now karate became an additional passion.

I had a lot of great times in high school, memories that stayed with me forever. For the rest of my life I would recall a play I made during a home basketball game against our biggest rival.

>The coach was yelling, "Alright guys, let's work it around and into the paint."

But for some inexplicable reason, I immediately took a jump shot from nearly 25 feet from the basket. And as the coach screamed an obscenity or two, the ball hit nothing but net to the delight of the roaring jam-packed gymnasium. The ball went through so cleanly that it caused the net to whip up and fasten itself around the rim, which forced the referee to call time while the net was pulled down into place again. During the stoppage in play, the coach was giving me hell about shooting that far out, and the stands were exploding with a cacophony of appreciation. I just stood there grinning from ear to ear.

There was always something going on around the campus. I liked living in the dormitory setting. Yeah, I liked it there a lot. In fact, I liked it so much that I hated to see June arrive and the summer vacation begin. It meant going back to Nashville to live with my grandparents.

There were a few glimpses of trouble during my years at the prep school. When threatened by a classmate, I usually responded with a violent response and when a prank was being planned, I was frequently the instigator. Of course such behavior was met with stern and regimented discipline, in the form of whacks on my behind with a sawed in half baseball bat and swung proficiently by the commandant.

Nevertheless, I thrived in athletics and in the classroom during this time. Several colleges offered financial aid in the form of athletic and academic scholarships my senior year. I was even offered an appointment to West Point, the United States Army Service Academy. The string attached to going there was that upon graduating, each cadet was required to serve six years of active duty in the army. But I didn't care about that and at the beginning of the second semester of my senior year, I had planned to attend West Point.

That year, Mom, Mel and Jeanne returned to Nashville from Arizona. Mel had been successful in establishing a couple of profitable enterprises in Tucson, but Mom was homesick, and she talked him into moving back. So he put a couple of trusted friends in charge of his concerns out west and came back with the intention of replicating similar business ventures in Tennessee. He bought a couple of ice cream places, two small restaurants in downtown Nashville, and then opened up Mel's Plumbing Company. He also purchased a roller skating center that had two rinks, one for regular skaters, and a smaller one for private parties that could be rented for entire evenings. He owned five buses that went around the city to provide transportation for kids who lived out of walking distance from the rink. He was doing very well financially.

When I left school during spring break, Mom asked me to stay with them and I agreed. At first things went relatively well, with the exception of some residual negative feelings I had toward Jeanne. Nothing negative ever came from Jeanne. She loved me and was very proud of me. However, my resentment of my little sister for leaving with my parents remained fresh in my mind, and it expressed itself in the curt manner in which I reacted to anything she said or did, no matter how nice she was to me.

I returned for my final semester of school, feeling sad that it would be my final one, but simultaneously looking forward to what awaited me after graduation. My college plans were set. I formally accepted the appointment to West Point and was looking forward to getting a new car, promised by my grandfather for doing so well in school. But as the year rolled on, the requirement to serve in the army for six long years weighed progressively more and more on my mind. Additionally, my thoughts had been including the fairer sex for some time now. Although there were several local girls who had flirted with me, I never responded. It wasn't that I wasn't attracted to them or interested. I was. But my priorities at that time were my education and sports and they remained my main concerns all during high school. But now that my high school experience was coming to an end and I had achieved my goals, girls were moving to the forefront of my thoughts.

And West Point...did they even have female cadets there?

Graduation day was great. I graduated near the top of my class and was called to the podium to receive several additional honors, to the delight of Mom, Jeanne and Mel who were in attendance. That summer began in grand style for me. I received the promised new sports car from Pop, moved in with my folks for the summer and began working for Mel in order to save as much cash as possible for spending money in college. Life was good.

But change was on the horizon. I continued my undue mistreatment of Jeanne, and I was growing more and more suspicious of Mel's kindhearted treatment towards me. He paid me top wages and treated me like a son. He acted like there had never been a moment of strife between us.

I wonder what he's up to.

By the second week of my summer vacation, I had convinced myself that going to West point was not my best option. However, all of the earlier offers for financial assistance had been accepted by other students, so my choices were now extremely limited. There was one offer that remained from a small local Baptist college, where the basketball coach had invited me to walk on, with the promise of at least a partial scholarship if it proved to be a successful match. I went to talk it over with my grandfather the next weekend.

"Listen Pop, I can get into the school, that's no problem, but the tuition is going to be pretty steep at least for the first year until I can earn a scholarship."

"Jeff, I've paid for your education up to this point and I don't mind paying for it as long as you continue to make good grades. I want you to make something of yourself and you have the brains to do it. So don't worry about the money."

"Thanks a lot Pop...you're the best."

Later that summer when I was at my sister's house, Joan would inadvertently let the proverbial feline out of a certain paper container. I was in for a shock.

"Jeff, have you done anything with the money you got from Daddy's estate yet?"

"What money, from what estate?"

"From his insurance silly, and the money he left us in the bank. In fact you should be getting Social Security checks from the government because he died when you were under age until you turn 21. Didn't Momma or Poppa tell you about this?"

"What? Joan, this is the first I've heard about anything like that. Have you gotten anything from Dad's estate?" I asked with a look of bewilderment.

"Of course silly. How else do you think that Robert and I could have afforded this house?"

I didn't know what to think. Had my grandfather been lying all these years about paying for my schooling, clothes and all the other things he took credit for? And what about the missing funds he had always accused Mel of taking? Could Mel have been actually telling the truth?

Man, if Pop was lying to me all this time, I'm glad I got into his basement stash. Hell, I should go back for some more...and what if he lied about Mel?

It was very typical of the way my mind worked and the manner in which I would attempt to justify my own misdeeds throughout my entire existence.

I felt utterly confused as I left Joan's house that day. Part of me wanted to confront my grandfather and part of me wanted to go and talk with Mel, maybe even apologize. But in the end I decided to simply keep my mouth shut and observe things for a while.

Toward the end of the summer, I was in my room with the door shut, quietly packing some things I planned to take to my dorm room later the next week when school was to begin. I heard Mel and my mother arguing about something, so I walked over and opened the door a little bit.

"Lana, you have got to tell him the truth before we leave. You owe him that much."

"I can't, he'll hate me if he finds out…" she sobbed

"He'll hate you worse if he hears it from somebody else. Besides, you know that it's the right thing to do honey."

"I can't Mel, I just can't."

I marched right into the den where they were seated.

"Tell me the truth about what Mel?"

"Hey Jeff…I didn't hear you come in…how's everything going with…"

"The truth about what Mel…the truth about what Mom?" I demanded.

"It's nothing honey…"

"The hell you say. Now I want you to tell me what the hell you two were talking…"

"Jeff, I want you to calm down and stop talking to your mother like that right now," Mel said rather sternly as he stood up.

"And I want you to go fuck yourself Mel!" I shouted.

"Jeffery Holden Collins, you are not to use that word ever again in this house!" my mother interjected at once.

"Fuck, fuck, fuck, fuck…In fact, fuck you both. I'm tired of all the implications, innuendos and insinuations everybody in this **fucking** family has made about my father all these years…"

Mel stepped close enough to grab hold of me.

"I warned you about talking like…"

That was all he managed to get out. I was now six feet tall and my martial arts training and fight experience would prove too much for the older and smaller man. I delivered a right forearm smash right to his jaw and stepped back in order to get my leg completely extended for a roundhouse kick into his side.

"Oooh," Mel moaned.

Although the kick to his side must have hurt him, he was nevertheless able to throw a right hook towards my chin. But I was too quick. I sidestepped the blow, grabbed Mel's wrist and used his momentum to send him flying over the sofa and onto the coffee table.

"Crash!"

Then I went back to my room, grabbed my bags and headed out the door to my car, right past my hysterical mother.

"Jeff, honey…please wait!"
"Get the hell out of my way Mom…or I swear to God…"

"Jeff baby, please wait, please don't go…don't leave, not like this. We're gonna move back to Arizona soon and if you leave like this, I may never see you again. Please Jeff… "

"I couldn't care less Mom. You two deserve each other…and I hope that I never have to see either of you ever again!"

"Jeff!"

"Go straight to hell…both of you!!"

"Slam!"

The debacle that was to be my life was now well underway.

CHAPTER 8
EDUCATIONAL TRAIN WRECK

*"If a little knowledge is dangerous, where is the man
who has so much as to be out of danger?"
(Thomas Huxley)*

I was now homeless, albeit only temporarily. When I went to my grandfather and related the day's events to him, I received a couple of "Attaboys," along with five hundred bucks for school supplies and an offer to live with him and Birdie until school started the following week. But I was still thinking about what Joan told me about all the money Dad had left for us.

Had Pop taken credit for footing the bill for my education, when it had been my dead father who had been providing for me all this time?

Just thinking about what the truth really was, well it was infuriating, so I really didn't care to stay at his house either. So I called the college admissions office and received permission to move in a few days early. As I was leaving, Birdie insisted that I take one of her best quilts with me to keep warm in my dorm room during the cold winter months. Thanking my grandparents and saying goodbye, I opened my car door and stuffed the quilt into the storage compartment in the back and drove off. I felt a sense of freedom and exhilaration as I wondered what college life would hold in store for me.

It was a bad choice, a very bad choice. It was the wrong place, wrong time, wrong guy, wrong city, wrong planet, wrong universe, wrong, wrong, wrong. How wrong? It was a "sex fiend loose in a nunnery" wrong. After attending a regimented military academy for the past five years, a coed college was like living in a different dimension. There were girls there. There were pretty girls everywhere. And there was no one to tell me what to wear, to make my bed or clean my room. There was no trumpet blaring reveille telling me to rise and shine in the morning, and no one playing taps at night signaling that it was time to turn out the lights and go to sleep. I had my own car right on the campus! And there were girls everywhere! Pretty girls! Beautiful girls!

I registered for class and went to freshman orientation. They told us all about the campus, where things were located and answered a bunch of questions from us wide-eyed freshmen. I was told that there was a chapel service each Wednesday morning that everyone was required to attend, and any student who missed more than three times in one semester could be suspended.

"Big whoop," I muttered to myself.

The first week flew by. The first chapel service included the introduction of the basketball team, so I was there with all my teammates. I made it to all of my classes, even the boring Bible class that was a core requirement for graduation. And after eating a quick meal, it was off to basketball practice to earn that scholarship.

And everywhere I went, there were girls, pretty, beautiful, desirable girls. That weekend I met five, six, seven or more cuties at a freshman mixer. They were all talking and flirting with me, one right after another.

Man oh man, is this place great or what?

I took a pretty brunette named Becky out that evening and a beautiful blonde named Sabrina the next night. I got two respective goodnight kisses, but didn't even come close to my desire of having sex for the first time. After all, this was a Christian college and the girls, at least the ones I had met, all seemed determined to abstain from sex until they walked down the aisle.

Man, I'll be eighteen years old this next week and I'm still a virgin. Heck I haven't even seen a lousy nipple yet!

The next week I began to cut a class or two and the next week a class or four. And as for chapel service, please! I was way too tired from hanging out with my pals and chasing skirts all over the city. All the female students had 11:00 PM curfews on weekdays and midnight curfews on the weekends, but strangely enough the men had none. And although the basketball players were expected to be in bed at a reasonable time, there was no actual enforcement of this quasi-rule. Therefore, I would leave campus and meet up with some of my friends from my neighborhood practically every night.

We would cruise the local drive-in restaurants, chase after girls and get a six-pack or two of beer. The first time I tasted beer, I thought it was awful. I hated it! But all my buddies loved it, so I faked it. I would nurse a bottle for an hour if I could, or even pour it out on the ground if the opportunity arose. Everyone with me usually got drunk and had a good time, and I enjoyed myself while staying sober.

"I don't need alcohol to enjoy life," I said to myself as I laughed at the funny things my drunken friends would do and say.

I stayed out nearly every night until one or two in the morning and then snuck back into the dorm to collapse into my bed. Naturally this lifestyle eliminated nearly any possibility of making early morning classes, or for that matter, late morning classes. And chapel service attendance? Out of the question. In fact the only time that I actually attended chapel was the first week of school when the basketball team was introduced. And the only obligation I met on a regular basis was attending basketball practice.

Everything else…well I figured that I could always make up a missed class or two by getting someone's notes.

Sex was foremost on my mind. My friends were constantly bragging about nailing some new girl. It was as though I was America's last remaining virgin. A lot of girls had appeared to be interested in me, and while I had been out with several of them and had even seen a nipple or two, paradise continued to elude me. I was content with everything else in my social life. I had a nice car and plenty of spending money, but I wanted to join the club of sexual veterans, if nothing else to find out what was so great about it.

It finally happened during Christmas break. Everyone had gone home for the holidays, but since my mother, Mel and Jeanne had returned to Arizona and because I didn't want to stay with my grandparents, I stayed in my dorm room. That was just fine with me. There were no Bible-thumpers pestering me about going to church and my Nashville buddies were coming up to my room and hanging out practically every night. One night my friends Ricky and Tony were there.

"Man, that Belinda, I'm telling you Jeff, that girl is crazy and hot," said Tony.

"Oh yeah?" I responded, very interested, but feigning a cool cosmic disconnect.

"Let me tell you buddy, there is absolutely nothing that chick won't do," said Tony.

"Or anybody," laughed Ricky.

"Are you guys talking about Belinda Pepitone, that sexy blonde I always see at the community center when we play basketball and always hanging out at Shoney's? Are you serious? Man, she is fine! Come on though, you've got to be yanking my chain," I blurted incredulously.

"Yeah dude, that's her and she's been talking about how cute you are and what a nice butt you've got," teased Tony.

"Aw, now ain't that sweet," joked Ricky.

"Get outta here you two. I don't even know her, well barely anyway."

"Well she knows you old buddy, and she's been scoping you out for a while now…and I'm telling you, you could get some of that anytime you want it."

So the very next time I pulled into Shoney's and saw her, I made it a point to be hanging around her, just to see if I could find out if Tony and Ricky had told me the truth.

"Hey Belinda," I said as I walked up to her.

"Hello Jeff. Why, I didn't even think that you even knew my name," she sang as soon as she saw me.

"Now how could I not know your name *Belinda*?"

"Well this is the first time that I can ever remember that you've actually spoken to me without me saying something to you first. I mean, I've seen you at the community center a million times playing basketball and I've flirted with you so many times…"

"What….when?"

"You know exactly what I'm talking about Mister Big Shot with a new car and all the girls after you, Mister College Man."

"Oh yeah?" I stammered as I sensed a warm blush spreading over my cheeks.

"Yeah," she said with a big smile.

"Well I guess that I was really into a ball game or something, because I don't remember you ever flirting with me, but I sure remember you in those tight little yellow shorts, and I think that I would definitely remember any flirting…"

"Well, why don't you take me out to the lake, and I'll give you something that I guarantee you will always remember for sure!" she said with a sexy look which screamed out the real possibility that I was finally going to get lucky.

"Let's go!" I said, trying my best to contain my excitement.

As soon as I pulled up at the lake, I found a secluded spot without another car in sight. I parked and as soon as I turned off the ignition key, she was all over me. I began unbuttoning her blouse and at the same time, she was stripping off my shirt and unzipping my jeans. It was only a matter of seconds until we were both completely naked and squirming like snakes in a warm vat of Vaseline. It was much too cramped a space for what she had planned, but she gave me my first experience of oral pleasure, and to say I loved it would be the epitome of an understatement. But I was far from satisfied. I reached into the rear storage compartment of car and grabbed Birdie's quilt, got out and laid it on the ground.

"Jeff, uh…if you're doing what I think you're doing, I believe it's too cold for that, lover."

"Nah, I just heard on the radio…it's a balmy 40 degrees. Come on. Besides, I promise to warm you up."

So she tiptoed around the car to the quilt. We were both shivering from the cold and from nervous anticipation of what was about to happen. I pulled her close and then gently guided her onto her back as I lowered myself on top of her. Even though it was my first experience, instinct seemed to take over and I actually sensed what to do. The act itself was a marvel to me. It was better than anything I had imagined and the chilly weather only added to the exhilaration.

The feel of her warm, soft skin was absolutely incredible. But the smell, now that was another matter. And after it was over and we got back into the car for the ride back to Shoney's…WOW! It was unbelievable. I was too polite to say anything, but needless to say, my driver's side window stayed down all the way, even though it was December and 40 degrees. As good as it felt, I wasn't sure that I wanted to do it again, especially if they all smelled like that!

When I pulled back into Shoney's parking lot, I parked next to her car. She leaned over and gave me a big wet kiss. Then she pulled a pen out of her purse and wrote her phone number on my palm.

"That's my number…call me," she said, sliding across the seat, stepping out of the car and pausing to give me another sexy smile before she shut the door." "You know I will," I answered.

But I never did. Every time I thought about calling her, the memory of that odor overpowered my desire for a repeat performance. I wondered how anyone could look so good and smell so awful.

The following week I was at a local department store shopping for clothes when a girl named Janie Parnell, who I knew from my neighborhood, approached me.

"Hey Jeff, how are you doing?"

"Janie! I haven't seen you in over a year. You look great. How are you?"

"I'm fine. I'm graduating this year…I mean next year…you know, the end of this school year."

"That's great. Have you decided where you're going to college?"

"Yes, I got into Vandy! I'm so excited!"

"Janie that's great! Congratulations!"

"Thank you. Listen, I'm having a party this coming weekend…just a bunch of kids from school. There are a couple of my girlfriends I'd like you to meet. I think that you might hit it off with one of them in particular. Can you make it this Friday night?" "Well, I think that I can work it into my busy schedule," I joked.

That Friday night I headed across town to her get-together, and no sooner had I entered the door when a small throw pillow hit me right in the side of the head. I looked in the direction of the culprit and saw a very pretty blonde laughing.

"Oh, I'm so sorry. I was aiming at Danny behind you."
"That's okay, you can hit me anytime you feel the need," I laughed.

"Hi, I'm Julie Ross. You go to Stratford High School don't you?"

"No, I'm in college in Nashville. Janie invited me….and uh, my name's Jeff, Jeff Collins."

She was about the prettiest thing I had ever seen and I hoped that she was one of the girls Janie wanted me to meet. It turned out that she was the main girl Janie hoped to fix me up with, and once I got her number, we would talk on the phone countless times for hours and hours over the ensuing weeks. I hoped she would figure prominently in my life one day. It was a genuine wish that would be granted in time.

My second semester in college was much worse than the first. My grades were horrendous. I received an "A" in a Phys. Ed. course and the others were all marked with an "I", which stands for incomplete and turns into an "F" when not made up by the end of the next semester. But how could they have been any higher? I never went to class or to chapel service. As for the Phys. Ed. course, all the students who played varsity sports received an automatic "A" during the semester that their respective sport was in season. So my academic career was in the crapper and merely waiting to be flushed.

As for my social life, well that was going full blast. I was having sex with a couple of coeds, one of which being the brunette named Becky, who had initially claimed she was saving herself for marriage. I was still hanging out with my local buddies, wasting a lot of time riding around with them at night, cruising the local hangouts and checking out the ladies. I took Julie out a couple of times, but so far I hadn't even kissed her. I thought so highly of her that I was actually nervous about even trying.

As for basketball, I was doing okay, but seeing very little action, even though the coaches were always encouraging me and praising my hustle in practice. Then one day a teammate nicknamed "Horse" said something to me after practice in the shower that I took great exception to.

"Hey Jeff, where've you been keeping that little hot blonde high school honey?"

"None of your business, Horse."

"Seriously though, how old is she anyway...14...15?"

"Go to hell Horse!"

"Hey, no offense dude. But I was just thinking...do you think she could do anything with this thing?" he said as he grabbed his penis and shook it at me.

"Well, maybe so Horse, but not nearly as good as your mom did with mine...and half of the baseball team."

He hurled a bar of Dial soap as hard as he could, which struck me so hard in the butt that I could have sworn that someone could see the little hands on the clock. As soon as it hit me, I took two or three steps toward him and knocked him unconscious with one blow to his jaw. However, just as I swung, the coach was rounding the corner to the shower area.

"That's it Collins, you're out of here."

"But coach..." I protested.

"No buts...get dressed and get out."

"But you didn't see what happened before..."

"You heard what I said. Now hit the road and don't come back. You're through," he said as he turned and headed out of the locker room.

My playing days were over, at least for that school, and without the semblance of structure that the team afforded me, I had even more time to engage in my preferred activities - partying and hell-raising. I started hanging around with a few guys who were a year or two older, riding around with them a couple of nights each week, actually drinking a little beer and looking for girls.

One night in April I heard someone yell at me when I pulled into Shoney's. I parked and looked over to see my newest associates, Clark, Troy and Paul.

"Hey dude, come on with us."

"Where to?"

"Just to get some beer and scope out some tail."

I jumped into the back seat with Troy and settled back for a night of whatever. After getting some beer we drove to the other side of town to a park where homosexuals were known to get together.

"Hey Clark, where are we going man?"

"To get some money."

"What? What are you talking about?"

"You'll see."

Clark pulled up next to a Pontiac Bonneville with a guy who was looking at them with a weird smile on his face. As soon as Clark stopped, the guy made a kissing gesture at him.

Clark turned around and said, "Jeff jump up here and drive. Me and Paul will meet you guys back at Shoney's in about half an hour."

I got out and slid behind the steering wheel, while Troy flipped himself over to the front seat from the back.

"Hey Clark, what are you guys gonna do?" I asked nervously.

"I'll tell you later...hurry and take off before this guy gets nervous."

I assumed that Clark and Paul were about to engage in some type of activity with this strange guy that I didn't even want to think about.

Man, this is beyond creepy...this is the last time I'm ever hanging out with these guys.

Troy and I pulled back into Shoney's, parked and called in for an order of burgers, fries and shakes. After it came and we wolfed down the food, there was still no sign of Clark and Paul.

"Man, where are those guys?" asked Troy.

"I don't have a clue, but if they aren't back soon, we're outta here. I'm not sitting here all night," I said with conviction.

"How long has it been? Didn't he say thirty minutes?"

"Yeah and it's over an hour already...hey, isn't that the guy's car right there?" I asked rhetorically.

The same car that Clark and Paul had hopped into in the park had just pulled into the stall beside us. Clark was now behind its steering wheel, and he rolled down the window.

"Hey guys get out and come over here for a second. We've got something to show you."

"What happened to that guy?" asked Troy.

"Come here and we'll tell you...hurry."

We got out of Clark's car and stepped over to the stranger's big green Bonneville. I looked down into the car and saw Paul fanning out a bunch of cash. I also saw a roll of duct tape sitting on a pile of clothes between him and Clark. Both of them were grinning ear to ear.

"Hey man, what did you guys do to that queer?" asked Troy excitedly.

"Clark, you didn't...?" I couldn't even finish the sentence.

Clark and Paul just chuckled.

"Man, I don't want any part of..."

"Relax Jeff. We didn't hurt him. We just borrowed his car and his money for a little while," said Clark.

"Well, where is he then?"

"He's resting. Hey Paul, hit that auto trunk release in the glove box and show these guys what's in the trunk."

Paul opened the glove compartment, reached in and the trunk popped open. Troy and I walked back and peered into the trunk. There, bound with duct tape around his hands, feet and mouth lay the now completely naked homosexual from the park. He was squirming like crazy, trying to free himself and making a desperate sounding type of humming noise. Paul and Clark were laughing so hard that they could barely breathe.

I slammed down the trunk and backed up from them towards where my car was parked about four stalls away.

"Clark, this ain't cool. I don't want to be around anything like this," I said with sincerity.

About that time three girls who knew us came strolling up.

"Hey Jeff. Hey guys. What are you all up to?"

Clark leaned out the window a bit.

67

"Hey ladies, step to the rear of my fine Pontiac and see a most interesting display."

When they walked up to the trunk, Paul again released the latch and it opened as the three of them looked inside.

"Oooh. That's nasty…who is that?" they giggled and screamed.

"Ssssh. Quiet. Here comes Julie and Janie…hurry and close the trunk." "Hey guys, hey Jeff," Julie said as she and Janie walked toward them.

"Hey Janie, hey Julie…ah Julie, can I talk with you a sec…"

But Clark went into his "go see what's in the trunk" mode.

"Hey ladies, step to the rear of my fine Pontiac and see a most interesting display." They walked back to the rear and the trunk sprang open once again.

"Aaaiiieeeeeee!" Both of them screamed and ran frantically toward me.

They were terrified because by this time, the guy had freed himself and jumped out toward the two frightened teenagers. He took off down the street with only strands of tape covering a few places of his body, but the tape that remained attached was slowing him considerably. I stood beside the startled girls as Troy, Paul and Clark chased down the naked guy. They caught him in seconds and pushed him up next to a telephone pole. Clark ran back to the car, grabbed the duct tape and ran back to the pole, which had a fire alarm on it. They taped the guy with his back to the pole and when he was thoroughly secure…they pulled the alarm!

I was horrified.

"MAN…LET'S GET THE HELL OUTTA HERE!"

Every one of us bolted immediately. Car doors slammed, engines roared to life and tires screeched as the parking lot emptied. I gave the gas pedal quite a bit of my foot as I sped away in panic. The idea of returning to free that poor man flashed through my head for an instant, but unfortunately I lacked the intestinal fortitude and the integrity to do the right thing.

"Man those guys are completely nuts and I'll never get into another car with any of them. I swear to God. Man, those guys are going to end up in prison one day for sure!" I said out loud.

I made it back to the dorm, shaken but relieved to be far away from the mess.

Things continued as they had for the duration of my college experience. My partying then spilled over into the campus. I got caught with a coed in my bed, but she got into a lot more trouble than I did. And although I wasn't caught in the act, I was suspected to have masterminded a panty raid on one of the girls' dorms in the middle of the night. I was also the leading suspect in time-fusing cherry bombs in various places around the quad. Additionally, I had been cited by the university police for reckless driving. Actually, I had just finished a short drag race with another student when they pulled me over!

This sordid chapter in my life came to a sudden halt one morning in May during the final two weeks of the semester, when I was summoned to the Dean of Men's office.

"Come in and have a seat Mr. Collins...and close the door behind you," said the Dean.

"Good morning Dean."

"Mr. Collins, it has been brought to my attention that your academic effort at this school has been weighed and found to be...let's say extremely insufficient as to uphold the scholastic requirements of this institution."

"Yes sir, that's true, but I plan to knuckle down and..."

"Furthermore, Mr. Collins, I have received numerous reports concerning your behavior and your fondness for pulling juvenile pranks that most young men outgrow by the time they finish junior high school."

"Dean, if you're talking about the firecrackers, I knew nothing about that until I heard about it from..."

Dean Birdsong slammed his hand down on the desk and said firmly, "I am talking about it all Mr. Collins! The beer cans in your room, complaints about your driving habits on campus, pulling fire alarms..."

"But I never..."

"QUIET! I'm talking about not going to class, never attending our Wednesday chapel services, fighting in the locker room, getting kicked off the basketball team...and somehow luring young innocent coeds to your room. And this Mr. Collins...need I remind you...this is a Christian College!

I just sat there silently.

"Therefore Mr. Collins, I must advise you as to your options."

"My options sir?"

"Option number one, you may withdraw from this school voluntarily so that your transcript does not reflect that option number two was invoked. That way, if you ever decide that you want to actually earn a college degree, your record will not reflect an expulsion. Am I making myself clear sir?"

"Crystal, sir..." I said as I rose from my chair and started for the door.

"Jeff, I sincerely hope that you will use this incident as a learning experience and become the mature and responsible adult I am certain you can be in the near future. I will keep you in my prayers. Good-bye and good luck.

He then extended his arm, so I stepped back toward his desk and shook his hand.

"I'll be out by the end of the week sir...and thank you for at least offering me the options."

I went back to my dorm room and upon realizing how exhausted I felt from what had just transpired, I allowed myself to crumple back onto the bed. I just lay there and stared up at the ceiling for a long time.

"Man...I should have gone to West Point."

The golden staircase, which was leading to a successful future, was still there. But my actions were gnawing away at the handrails and weakening the foundation. I had been stirring up the cosmic force of karma, a concept dangerously misunderstood by most humans. The steps themselves were receding and the staircase was transforming into a slippery and a perilous ramp. I had begun an inevitable and dangerous slide toward tragedy.

CHAPTER 9
JULIE, JEFF & UNCLE SAM

*"Don't it always seem to go
that you don't know what you've got till it's gone."*
(Joni Mitchell – *Big Yellow Taxi*)

She might have made me into the man I was capable of becoming, the man I should have been. Julie. She was my only remaining sunny thought after I withdrew from school (one of my options) and I held on tight. We had been on about half a dozen dates and I realized early on that she was a very special girl.

Everything else that I considered important in my life had suddenly turned to shit. Thinking back on the events of the last 12 months, I managed to turn the responsibility away from myself. I blamed other people; my mother, my coach, Dean Birdsong, and many others. I had cultivated quite a flair for deflecting any culpability for my mistakes.

Since summer vacation had already begun, I moved into my grandparent's house without the need of explaining to Pop or Birdie about the meeting with the dean, and all the related implications. My plans were to find a summer job and enroll in another college by autumn. The job would be simple to obtain. Another attempt at a college education would be sidetracked for a while.

Julie. She was absolutely the best thing that ever happened in my life. She was extremely intelligent, pretty, athletic, personable, faithful and trustworthy. Years later as my life unfolded, I placed her upon a pedestal, and came to think of her as one of the finest humans to walk on this planet. I loved everything about her; the way she looked, walked, spoke, and kissed. I was infatuated with her almost the instant that pillow hit the side of my head and I turned to see that beautiful face. She was kind. She was gentle. She was talented.

Unfortunately for her, she fell in love with me. How or why she loved me were questions I often asked myself. The types of women I usually attracted were…well, loose women. When I ran across a virgin who wouldn't give it up, I quickly moved on to the next girl. If it was obvious that she was unyielding about waiting to have sex until after marriage, I saw no reason to wait around.

With Julie however, it was different. I knew that we weren't going to be having sex, at least for quite a while and that was okay with me. I was willing to wait for her…not that I didn't try mind you. But Julie Ross was a young lady with morals and goals, and nothing and no one could deter her from either one.

That summer we saw a lot of each other. I loved being with her regardless of what we were doing. We went everywhere together, to the movies, cruising Shoney's and to the park to make out. I took her all over the place, even to the community center while I played basketball. I found a job for the summer working as a lifeguard at a local pool and when she wasn't working, she was there, too. But when she wasn't there, the girls at the pool seemed to flirt unmercifully with me.

It's funny how some people will wait until they think that a person is in a committed relationship before they decide that such a person is desirable. But I only had eyes for Julie, at least at that time. To me she was the embodiment of female perfection and for a while, my relationship with her stifled my powerful desire for sex.

Someone once said that if you really are in love with someone, there is no way that you will cheat on them. The problem with me was that I probably lacked the capability to be truly *in love* with someone, even Julie. My disqualifying issues included a pathological need for sex, my egotism, an overpowering competitive drive and a narcissistic personality.

But I really did love Julie. That's a fact, but I was too selfish to give myself totally to anyone at that time. To really be in love with another person, the love for them must override your own self-interest, and not even Julie was capable of modifying that part of me.

I could easily envision being married to her. I just couldn't imagine never making love to another woman. And later that summer I started fooling around. First it was in the locker room at the pool with an attractive little redheaded lifeguard. She had been coming on to me for over a month when I finally gave in one evening as we were closing for the day. Then there was the neighborhood tart that lived two doors down from my grandparents. After I had finished mowing the grass one afternoon, she came into the garage as I was putting the mower away. I was dirty and sweaty, but she didn't mind a bit as she invited me onto the back seat of Pop's car in the garage.

From that point on I accepted sexual offers from any girl who tempted me, as long as her appearance met my external requirements. After all, I was nothing if not superficial.

This reckless conduct continued for most of the summer until the day I learned I was eligible for the draft by the Selective Service Board. It was the final time the draft would be used for Viet Nam and I was one of the first choices. When I inquired about status, I was told I would be inducted into the United States Army no later than December of that year. They also told me that I could volunteer for the draft in order to report early and get it out of the way. This appealed to me for a number of reasons. One was to simply get it over with. Another reason was to be eligible for the GI Bill, which would help to pay for a college education and to ensure that one day in the future, I would own my own home. Therefore, I signed a waiver to allow for an early entry and as luck would have it, I was told to report on August 25th. Once again the month of August was proving to be inauspicious in my life.

I told my grandfather, who was certain that the army would make a man out of me. He gave the plan his blessings. Julie cried about it for a while, but eventually came around to supporting my decision. I was a bit apprehensive about putting on a uniform again, but saw the advantages of being a veteran.

I had about a month before I had to report, so I took off for a week in Daytona, Florida along with two of my friends. This choice was noteworthy, because it showed that rather than spending every remaining moment with Julie, I chose to spend a week with my pals and chase wild women on the beach.

Weeks later I reported for basic training at Fort Campbell, Kentucky and because of my military training, I was immediately made the "Field First" or head trainee. Basic training was hard for most of the recruits, but I breezed through the eight week program and even made Trainee of the Cycle. My development as a soldier had a hiccup or two when I got into a few fights, but this seemed to be viewed as a positive characteristic by the majority of my superiors. After basic, I received orders to stay on the same post to play basketball for the post team. This happened because the post commander was a sports fanatic and he wanted to keep anyone who appeared athletic in order for them to play for his post in various sports.

I learned that I would probably stay there for my entire tour, and since it was close enough for me to see Julie a couple of times each week, I was very glad to get the news. However, when our post basketball team lost the regional championship game to Fort Hood in Texas by 44 points, my status quickly changed. Ten days after the debacle, I was called to headquarters to receive travel orders.

"Hey, Sergeant Williams, what the heck does RVN stand for on my travel orders?" I asked.

"Well, soldier...that would be the Republic of Viet Nam."

"Oh...okay...uh...thanks."

I saw my share of violence while in the army, although I rarely spoke about it. It was as if someone hit the pause button on the story of my life for that time and when the play button was pressed again, I found myself in Frankfurt, West Germany.

Germany was quite an experience. Upon landing there, I was totally drug free. I witnessed nearly a dozen fellow soldiers smoking hashish and shooting up heroin during my first week there. Other than the army, I had never been around drugs, with the exception of my mother's prescription medication. I was never tempted to try them until

I arrived in Europe. The vast majority of the soldiers there smoked hashish, a huge percentage dropped acid and a significant number used intravenous drugs such as heroin. Although somewhat curious, I continued to avoid drug use. Things changed when I began meeting the local girls. Practically every girl I met smoked hash. One night when I was out with a young and pretty fraulein named Monica, I succumbed to my curiosity. After we had sex, she talked me into inhaling a couple of hits from a bhang packed with some blonde Lebanese hashish which was laced with opium. After that night, I began smoking several times a week. Since I refused to stick a needle in my arm, I rationalized my drug use in my mind, convincing myself that only needle users were true drug addicts.

I also shunned popping pills until one night at a party in town, when another soldier slipped a hit of LSD into my drink. I thought that I was losing my mind. Somehow I navigated my way back to the barracks and took an hour-long shower…fully dressed! When I finally came down from the trip, I calmly walked to the culprit's room and knocked on his door. When the *drink-spiker* opened the door, I knocked him across the room.

"Put something in my drink again and it'll be a lot worse than that, you jackass," I said as I walked away.

Unfortunately, as I looked back on the experience of my first acid trip, I considered it somewhat enjoyable and tried LSD many more times in the future. The only misgivings I had about drug use was what Julie and my pals back in the states would think of me if they ever found out.

Although my official assignment was a clerical position, I actually played basketball and baseball for the regional U.S. Army team. We toured much of Europe and even once went all the way to Sydney, Australia for a basketball tournament. I sampled fish and chips in London, tasted a Wimpy's burger in a sidewalk café in Paris, devoured a deep dish pan pizza in Milan and bit into, but refused to finish, a nasty tasting foodstuff called vegemite by the people down under in Sydney. I was just cruising along the course of life, through the courtesy of a sinecure in the United States Army.

Julie wrote me faithfully all this time. I answered about every third letter from her. We talked on several occasions about her coming to Germany and the two of us touring parts of Europe for a couple of weeks, but I fretted about how this would cramp my style. I had met a lot of German girls and went to bed with a considerable number of them. I was constantly on the lookout for new conquests. Once when I went with some friends to a club in downtown Munich, we all decided to go to a brothel called Krazee Sexee. I entered with no intention of paying for sex, but when I saw an unbelievably beautiful and voluptuous whore, I gladly coughed up twenty-five American dollars for my first experience with a prostitute.

I had been in countless fights up to that point in my life and had never lost. That changed one night in a local pub in a small German town called Hanau. I was with three of my friends and four young frauleins. We were all stoned and becoming more intoxicated with each additional stein of potent German beer. When two guys at the bar asked us politely to hold down the noise a little, one of my pals took exception to the request.

"Fuck off comrade!" slurred one of my drunken companions.

"Care to step up here and say that again a little closer to my face?" asked one of the guys at the bar.

"Hey...ah...Jeff, how about taking care of my light work?"

With that said I stood up and walked nonchalantly up to where the two men were seated on bar stools. The one that had made the request seemed rather short and the other one was slightly bigger than me.

"Hey guys, we're just blowing off a little steam. We're really not looking for any trouble, so if..."

The larger man suddenly swung at me, but I sidestepped the punch and unleashed a series of blows that left the guy bloody and on his back at the base of his barstool. The smaller one took a sip of his cognac and coolly looked at me.

"Maybe you'd like to dance with me for a song or two...bitch."

I reacted the way I always had. I had learned to always try to get in the first blow, which I managed to do even on this occasion. In fact I landed several solid blows to my opponent's face. When the guy stood up off his stool, I stepped back and kicked him in the chest. This knocked the smaller man up against the bar and I leaned over, grabbed a half full bottle of beer and broke it over the guy's head. Then the guy looked at me seemingly unfazed!

"That all you got...sweetie?"

I swung as hard as I could, but I only caught air. The smaller guy ducked and caught a lot more than air. His first offensive action was a straight right that landed right in the middle of my face. I had never before, or since then for that matter, been hit that hard. That first blow alone nearly knocked me unconscious. Then the guy unleashed a succession of machine-like punches that found their marks. I was so out of it that by the third blow, I didn't feel the following punches or the kicks delivered to my ribs, chest and the side of my head. That is until I woke up in the ambulance on the way to the hospital. I found out that I had just stumbled upon an extremely tough little U.S. Navy Seal, and that in addition to the obvious black eyes, broken nose and fat lip, I had also received a couple of cracked ribs and a couple of loosened teeth. It was my first loss in a fight and by far the worse beating I ever experienced. It should have served as a valuable lesson for me concerning violence. Regrettably, it did not.

As bad as I was beaten in that fight, my injuries healed rapidly and I was as good as ever in a few weeks. I decided to take a few weeks leave in order to return to the states and see Julie. Feeling a little apprehensive about my illicit drug use being discovered by her and the rest of my friends back home, I nonetheless boarded a military aircraft and took off for Fort Campbell in Kentucky. From there I rode a bus to Music City, USA.

I hadn't told anyone that I was coming home. I planned it as a surprise for Julie, and besides, I wanted to show up unexpected just to see if I might catch her out on a date, or worse. After all, since I had been totally unfaithful to her while I was away, I imagined that she had been playing around, too. I was wrong. Julie loved me and she was true blue. She had been completely faithful. Her letters weren't merely words, and they spoke a truth that I could not find within myself. Her letters expressed her feelings and when she wrote about how much she loved me and missed me, it came straight from her heart. I was just too ignorant about the power of love and too narcissistic to treasure her feelings as much as they warranted treasuring.

She was sitting on her front porch when my taxi pulled into the driveway, and when I stepped out from the passenger side, she screamed and flew into my arms. If I only possessed the ability to feel the extent of love she held in her heart for me, that alone may have saved me.

Julie's parents liked and trusted me so much that they insisted that I stay in their guest bedroom. For the next few days Julie and I were inseparable and spent every waking moment together. Although I kept trying, Julie simply refused to have sex with me, and since I was happy just being close to her, I remained content with the celibacy. However after going to my grandparent's house and getting my car, I began scoping out my old stomping grounds.

The next day I dropped in on a couple of close friends. I had been anxious to know their reactions after they found out that I had been doing drugs. But as soon as I walked down into the basement bedroom and saw a pack of Zig Zag rolling papers, a water bhang and some loose marijuana in an overturned Frisbee, I realized that the soldiers and the good folks in Germany had no monopoly on getting high.

"Hey Bo, Howie…Gary. How's it going?"

"Hey dude! Man, we were just talking about you. Are you out?"

"No, I still have about another six months or so to go. I'm just here on a two or three week leave."

"How was Germany?"

"It's wild and crazy, Bo."

"What about those German girls? I heard they don't use deodorant or shave their legs or armpits. Is that really true?"

"Don't believe everything you hear Howie."

"Hey Jeff, I know that you've tried some of that good German hash…we heard that it's dynamite."

"Well I suppose that there are some things that you can believe Gary," I laughed. "Yeah, I managed to locate some."

"Maybe you could send us some in the mail…without a return address…I'll give you some cash before you leave," said Gary with a big wide grin.

"How much does hash go for here anyway?" I asked.

"Oh, anywhere from around five to ten bucks a gram, depending on the quality. How much is it there?"

"About a dollar a gram unless you buy in bulk…then it's cheaper…a lot cheaper."

"Man, let's do it…we could make a fucking fortune."

"Maybe Gary…but for right now, let's burn a few good old American joints."

And so we did, but I was already formulating plans in the back of my mind to make some serious money.

Later that day we went to the community center to shoot some hoops. I was now capable of dunking and I planned on impressing my friends as soon as the opportunity arose. The first time I found myself loose on a fast break I went up and slammed the ball hard…right off the back rim. While the ball was ricocheting high off the rim, I fell awkwardly and heard a loud pop. It was my ankle. I had to go to a doctor, where I learned that I had sustained a hairline fracture near my right ankle. I left the doctor's office with a huge cast on my right foot.

Great…now how the hell am I supposed to drive my car with this damn thing on my foot?

When I called Julie and explained what had happened, she got a ride from her brother over to Gary's and then drove me back to her house in my car. Now I was trapped! There was no way I could drive a stick with that gigantic cast on my foot. I had lost my mobility. Julie loved having me around and she loved catering to my every need. All that I had to do was rest and relax. I actually enjoyed the celibate and drug-free rest and relaxation I spent with her, at least temporarily. We played board games, ordered pizzas and talked about everything, especially about her coming to Germany in the near future. I felt very close to her during that time. I felt so close to her that I decided that I wanted to spend the rest of my life with her. At least that's how I felt at that instant in time.

It was a weekday morning and I was asleep in the spare bedroom at Julie's house. Mr. and Mrs. Ross were at work and her brother was at a baseball camp in Chattanooga. As I stirred and opened my eyes, I became acutely aware of someone crawling into bed with me…it was Julie…a very nude Julie!

"Good morning Mr. Collins," she whispered in my ear.

Then she pulled back the covers and gently worked my underwear down my legs and over my cast. Being a novice at such actions, it took a moment, but I didn't mind one iota. After getting me completely naked except for my cast, she mounted me, leaned forward and once again whispered into my ear.

"This is how much I love you Jeff Collins."

"Oh Julie, I love you too baby, more than anything else in this world and I always will."

Sex with her was different than with all the other girls I had been with. She was so innocent, so pure and our lovemaking was much more tender and heartfelt. She was wonderful and any man would have been lotto-winning lucky to have such a girlfriend. Even more, she was head over heels in love with me! But I was far too ignorant to realize how lucky I was.

I returned to Germany at the end of the next week. I really hated leaving, because we had been making love like minks for over a week by the time we said goodbye at the airport. We had worked out a plan whereby she would come to Germany around three months later, although I wasn't sure if I could wait that long to see her again. In fact, when I arrived in Germany, I avoided sex from even the most desirable of the German floozies. Before her plane landed in Frankfurt, I had worked out an agreement with the morning report clerk in my unit to allow me to take another two week leave so soon after my trip to the states, and I made a deal with a close friend to provide me with the use of his off-base apartment during her visit. I thoroughly cleaned the entire apartment and washed and waxed the old 1966 BMW I had bought for a song from a desperate soldier months before. Everything was perfect for her visit.

When I picked her up at the Frankfurt airport, she looked so beautiful, it nearly took my breath away. We drove to Hanau, entered the apartment, tore off one another's clothes and made love for the rest of the night. The next two weeks we toured Munich, Luxembourg, Paris and London. The first week was the happiest time of our entire relationship. By the middle of the next week, however, I began feeling…for the want of a better description, suffocated. I snapped and smarted off to her for no reason. I didn't even know where this sudden rudeness was coming from. Looking back on it later, it could have been a fear of commitment or apprehension of abandonment. In any event it was absolutely uncalled for and it left Julie feeling sad and confused.

At the end of her trip, I apologized for acting like a jackass and assured her that I loved her very much. She returned to the states thinking that I would return to her in under three months and that our relationship would bloom into a wonderful lifetime together.

As my tour was winding down, I began to prepare for my return to the states. I sold my car to a new lieutenant for seven hundred dollars more than I had paid. I also had a motorcycle to sell and the buyer was none other than my main source for hashish, a soldier named Vic, who had offered me two hundred bucks more than I had invested in the bike. I immediately agreed and said that I would deliver it to him that afternoon, which I did.

As soon as I walked into Vic's apartment, the potent smell of quality hashish hit me hard.

"Man Vic, I smelled that stuff when I was walking up to your door…you better be careful dude."

Vic stood there with a big stupid grin on his face and pointed to a big pile of hash bricks in the corner of the room.

"Holy shit Vic! How much is that"?

"A lot man, and I need to get rid of it fast. Need some"?

"How much for a kilo?" I asked as I thought back to my conversation with Gary in Nashville.

"Jeff, if you buy 10 of them I can let you have them for five hundred a piece…I need to move them out of here fast."

"TEN OF THEM…ARE YOU CRAZY MAN?"

"Well you tell me, how many can you afford"?

I thought for a moment or two.

"I'll tell you what…I'll give you thirty-two hundred bucks for eight of them."

"Man I need five per kilo."

"Vic, that's as high as I can go."

Vic thought it over for a minute and then reached into his pocket and pulled something out.

"Okay, here's what I'll do…since it's you and you're going home to your lady, I'll give you eight of them for thirty-five hundred and I'll even throw in this engagement ring.
It's a full carat and worth around three thousand bucks retail."

"Okay, it's a deal but you'll have to give me a ride back to the base in your truck."

So I got all of the hashish into my room in the barracks, locked the door and went out shopping. I had a plan. A friend that had finished his tour six months before had told me how to get dope back to the states, and I had paid close attention to all the details. I went to a local store and bought two rolls of masking tape, a couple of boxes of aluminum foil, a box of Saran wrap, and several household candles.

I brought all of the items back to my room and went to work. My roommate had been discharged a few weeks ago and had abandoned a big 200-watt Kenwood amplifier and a Pioneer reel-to-reel tape deck there...neither of which worked. After breaking the kilos into smaller portions so that they would be easier to work with, I began wrapping them in aluminum foil and then covering them with Saran wrap. I lit a candle and carefully covered the seams with candle wax. After I had done this to each of the packaged units, I repeated the entire process all over again, so that each of them now had two layers of aluminum foil, Saran wrap and were sealed twice with candle wax. I gutted both pieces of worthless stereo equipment, shoved as much of the hash as I could into them, stuffed some newspaper behind it and replaced the back cover. When I was finished I still had almost two kilos left, so I took a pair of German hiking boots I had purchased earlier and crammed them full. That was it...the task had taken me nearly three hours, but I was finished. Now all I had to do was put everything in the "home baggage" that I was sending back to the states. It would be shipped after I was discharged, and I could pick it up at Fort Campbell, Kentucky, the closest army base to Nashville.

I was supposed to be discharged a little more than two months after Julie had returned home, but the army let me go nearly two months early due to the phase down program, which was instituted in order to facilitate a significant reduction in the number of troops in Viet Nam at that time. When I heard that I would be home two months early, I could scarcely believe my good fortune.

I landed at the Nashville airport and Julie was there in the waiting area to pick me up. I was so happy to hold her, but I sensed that something was wrong.

"Is everything alright Julie?"

She said nothing but tears began forming in the corners of her eyes.

"Julie, what is it honey? What's wrong"?

She looked up at the ceiling and then right into my eyes as her tears began flowing down her beautiful cheeks.

"Oh Jeff...I...I'm...I'm pregnant!"

"Oh my God...are you sure?"

"Very," she sobbed into my shoulder as I held her tight.

I experienced a great number of emotions. They ranged from fear to anger. In between lay a thick layer of suspicion; suspicion about whether or not the baby was mine. My mind raced back to all the times I had wondered if Jack Collins was really my father. We walked out of the airport and got into her car. Before starting the engine she turned to face me.

"I've been to the doctor and I'm about 5 weeks along," she said softly through her tears.

"What do you want to do about it?" I asked rather matter-of-factly.

"What do I want…WHAT DO I WANT TO DO ABOUT IT? WHAT DO YOU WANT JEFF…WHAT DO YOU WANT TO DO ABOUT IT…" she cried.

"Calm down Julie, we're gonna work this thing out and everything's gonna be okay…I promise."

"So what are we gonna do?" she said as her crying jag subsided a bit.

"Well, we can get married and raise it I guess. I'll get a job and use my GI Bill to go back to school. I'll get my degree and…"

"Jeff, I want to go to college, too. I've been waiting on you to come home so that maybe we could go together. I don't want to have a baby right now. Someday, yes, of course, but not right now."

"Well tell me what you want…I mean what you want for *us* to do, because believe me, I'll do whatever you want. I'll be a daddy, I'll marry you. I'll support whatever you want, even an adoption or an abortion."

"Jeff, I…if I start to show, my daddy will be so mad and so disappointed and mother, well, I don't know what she'd do."

"So what are you saying, do you want to get an abortion"?

"At this point in our lives, yes. I just have to think that it would be the best decision we could make. I mean we could always have another child, several more in fact."

"Julie, you know that I love you and I've already told you that I'll support any decision you make…for us I mean. And after all, it is your body…your beautiful body." She smiled at me at last.

"Well, I found out that it'll cost about three hundred dollars."

"Don't worry about that, I have over thirty-seven hundred bucks on me right now."

"No, you're not paying for it all. I'm going to pay half of it myself."

And she did. We went to an abortion clinic the next week. On the 4th of April, the "problem" was solved, just like that. I felt extremely depressed, but I couldn't pinpoint exactly why.

Then summertime began for us two lovebirds. A local state university accepted us both and I was invited to walk onto the basketball team. I got a job earning good money servicing private swimming pools, while Julie worked as a cashier at a steak house. We spent a great deal of time together, but I still found time to smoke dope with my pothead friends and to fool around on her with my trollop of the week. During my job servicing pools, I was regularly offered opportunities to sample the wares of the bored, horny housewives on my route. And I did partake, at least with the ones that passed my superficial test...if they looked good enough.

I told Gary about the hash shipment and we drove up to Fort Campbell, where we picked up my property without a hitch. As we drove back to Nashville, we agreed on a deal whereby Gary would pay me about three dollars a gram or a thousand a kilo. I realized a small fortune as Gary began to rapidly unload nearly the entire batch for me. The hashish sold like hotcakes and by the end of the summer, I had profited nearly twenty thousand dollars in spite of smoking countless grams of the hash myself.

Gary made a lot of money, too. In fact, he made enough to buy a nice van with a custom paint job. One Saturday Gary met me at a local McDonald's to show off his new ride. After showing my approval for Gary's latest acquisition, we went inside for lunch. Once inside, I ran into a little redhead named Sheila, who everyone called "Red Hot." Sheila walked up to me licking her lips.

"Hey Jeff, let's go out and smoke a joint," she said as she gave me a prolonged hug.

"Okay little Sheila, let's go," I agreed, sensing her ulterior motive.

We went to the side of the restaurant where my car was parked and climbed in. We had no sooner finished with the doobie when Sheila reached over, unzipped my pants and went down on me right in the parking lot, in broad daylight.

"Wow, you *are* Red Hot, aren't you?"

"Yes I am and I wish that we could do more, but your car is just too little for what I had in mind," she said with a sexy pout as she resumed pleasuring me.

"Wait here...don't move," I said, zipping up and bolting back inside the restaurant.

I ran inside and got Gary's keys, ran back to get her and christened Gary's new van with Red Hot Sheila. When we finished and I was saying goodbye to Gary, he noticed the side of my neck.

"Dude, that little slut was hungry, look at your neck."

"Why…what is it?"

"It's a big old hickey…what'd ya think it was?" laughed Gary.

"Man I hate it when they do that."

The very same night while I was out at a bar with some friends, a very pretty, very slutty and very inebriated girl named Cheri suggested that I take her to the nearest motel and do whatever I wanted to do to her. And of course, I was more than willing to comply with her request. So we got a cheap room and went at each other like a couple of feral cats. She was a wildcat, a very horny wildcat. And before I could stop her, she had put another gigantic love bite on me, this time even higher up on the other side of my neck.

"Uh oh, that's not gonna be easy to explain to Julie. I need to avoid her for the next few days or so until these things go away," I muttered to myself as I examined the marks the next morning in my mirror.

She might have made me into the man I was capable of becoming, the man I should have been. Julie.

CHAPTER 10
AN AFFINITY FOR VIOLENCE

"Like a rock hurled into a hornet nest
Rage predictably results in regret
A malady with a cure often worse than the disease
Why surrender to the madness of wrath
Rather than summon inner strength to dispel the evil
Why allow it to live rent free inside the mind
Instead of enjoying the bliss of granting forgiveness
Perhaps perfection will be found when reaching angelhood
But was not Satan once called the perfect Son of the Morning?"
(A. P. Brooks - Anger)

So why did I cheat on such a wonderful girl, a lover who was so faithful and true to me, a girlfriend who would have never left my side if I had only treated her like she deserved? The answer could have been in my inherent character flaws, especially the ones that were most influenced by my environment.

Due to the unsightly set of suck marks on my neck, I had been avoiding Julie for nearly four days. But they were still fairly visible and anyone with half a brain would instantly know what they were. All my pals had been giving me the business about them for days. Around the middle of the week I went to the community center with Gary and Bo to play a little basketball. After playing two pickup games, I was so sweaty and hot that I pulled off my shirt and headed for the water fountain. A guy I knew fairly well named Butch was walking beside me when he noticed my neck.

"Hey Butchie boy, I thought you guys had us that last time...good game man."

"Damn dude, who's been chewing on your neck?" I was sick and tired of being needled about it.

"Well your little sister got me on this side but it was your girlfriend over here. Why do you ask?"

Taking great exception to my comments, Butch let loose with a vicious right aimed at the side of my head, and even though I was nearly quick enough to slip the punch completely, it caught me on the temple with a glancing blow. With my adrenalin now pumping, I retaliated with a series of left and right combinations and added a spinning right-legged kick to the right side of his head.

"Okay, okay man, I'm through...I'm..." gasped Butch as he held his hand to catch the flow of blood leaking out of his nose and mouth.

After seeing that he clearly had enough, I walked over to the water fountain and bent over to get a drink. As soon as the water touched my lips I saw her standing there staring at me with a disgusted look on her face.

"Julie, what are you doing here?"

"Well I came here to see you, since I haven't seen you since last Friday, and now I understand why."

"What are you talking about?" I said as it instantly occurred to me that the marks on my neck were prominently displayed for her to see.

"My God Jeff, you weren't even trying to cover it up. It's like you're proud of it." I walked toward her, unaware that she had only spotted one of them.

"Julie, hold on a second, it's not what you…"

Then, she saw the other side of my neck, with the larger of the two marks.

"Oh my God, there's another one! You…you son of a bitch! I'm not stupid…I know what hickeys are Jeff, and if you want to screw around on someone, you need to find someone foolish enough to put up with it. Don't call me, and don't come to my house…ever again!"

She took off running out the door of the center and onward toward her car. Dashing after her, I caught her just as she opened the door, and grabbed her hand.

"Julie, honey…please listen to me…"

She snatched her hand away determinedly and looked up at me, her beautiful cheeks streaming with tears.

"What is it Jeff? What possible explanation could you have for letting some tramp suck on your neck like that? Why don't you just go ahead and…TELL ME!"

"Julie you're way too upset right now. I'll come by tonight and tell you the whole story. Please give me a chance to explain it to you…"

"Don't bother, I think I'll go out tonight and get drunk at one of your hangouts. Maybe I can find somebody to suck on my neck…then you can see how it feels."

She jumped into her car, locked the door and sped away.

That afternoon I called her house, but she refused to come to the telephone. And later that night I drove by her house only to find her car gone from her driveway. Around 9 o'clock I went by Mickey Finn's, a local bar I frequented and there was her car, sitting right in front of the place. I parked, went inside and instantly spotted her at the bar with some guy trying to hit on her. I walked right up to them.

"Hello Julie…hey dude, take a hike," I said emphatically.

The guy was on the verge of objecting, but before he could, Julie jumped up and threw her arms around my neck and started kissing me all over my face.

"Jeffy, Jeffy, Jeffy! Hello Jeffy…I love you Jeffy!" she sang out.

"You're drunk, come on, I'm getting you out of here."

The guy was probably still considering a protest but when he saw the anger reflected by my facial expression, he thought better of it and merely wheeled around on his barstool and kept quiet. I led her out of the bar and got her into my car. As she sat silently looking out of the passenger window, I drove toward the lake, all the while, the rage in me bubbling and festering...my Julie flirting with some creep in a bar that way. I pulled into a parking spot that faced the water.

"What the hell were you doing back there Julie?"

"Just giving you a taste of your own medicine. How do you like it?"

"Whack!"

It happened so fast, I wasn't even aware that I had slapped her until it was too late.

"Oh my God! Julie I'm sorry...baby, I...I..."

She was crying softly, "How come it's okay for you to fool around on me, but I can't even go to a bar...and talk to someone?"

But by now I had an explanation for the hickeys and I had collaborated with a friend she didn't know, just in case she wanted proof of what I was about to tell her.

"Listen to me. I was over at Warren's house Saturday and there were these two crazy girls he knew...and they were real stoned and drunk...and Warren...he thought that it would be funny if they put hickeys on my neck...on each side of it. So Warren and another guy...they held me down and those girls did this. That's all it was though. They all had a big laugh, and I've been avoiding you because I knew you wouldn't believe me. But it's the truth. I swear."

"But you hit me Jeff...you hit me," she said softly.

"I know baby...I'm sorry...I'm so sorry. It will never happen again. It was just that when I saw you sitting there talking to that jerk, I nearly went crazy. Can you forgive me? Can we please put all this crap behind us? Please Julie, I love you and I'll never do it again. I promise...okay? Please"?

Julie bought my outrageous canard, which would become merely another entry in the collection of thousands of lies I was becoming so adept at telling her. We made up that night and for a while I treated her like a queen, like the way I should have treated her all along. I even temporarily quit fooling around on her, at least for several weeks when we began college.

Slapping Julie gnawed at me for a long time. I couldn't believe that it had happened. But it had. I had put my hands on her...on Julie. Julie! Many years in the future I would reflect back on this incident in my past. It was the first time, but regrettably, not the last time I would hit a woman. I wondered if something jammed deep within my psyche had been a contributing cause to such an action. But what? What could have made me do such a thing?

Up to that point I never considered my quick temper and my even quicker trigger to be a problem. I considered myself to be a guy who never looked for trouble, but on the other hand, I wasn't about to back down from anyone, even after my encounter with the Navy Seal in Germany. I took pride in my ability to defend myself and regarded it as an asset. I remembered from high school psychology class about how the primordial instinct of fight or flight was hardwired into the human race all the way back to caveman ancestors, and probably beyond. But hitting a woman, especially Julie, well that was a mouse of a different house. As a close friend of mine once said, it was as different as lightning and a lightning bug. And after that night at the lake with Julie, I vowed to myself that I would never put my hands on another woman in anger for as long as I lived.

The very next weekend, I was playing in a softball tournament for most of Saturday and Sunday. My team ended up winning the whole thing and afterwards, a lot of players on nearly half the teams agreed to meet at the nearest pub to throw back a few cold ones. The bar we chose turned out to be the favorite haunt of a local bikers' club and there were around twenty or so of them when nearly fifty players and fans from the tournament entered the establishment. Julie was there with me and everyone was having a pretty good time. There was a female biker chick sitting at the bar. She was about 5' 10" tall, weighed in the neighborhood of 220 pounds and her arms were covered with tattoos. She kept staring over at us, mostly at Julie, but she and I tried our best to ignore her. After the third pitcher of beer was ordered and delivered, I looked up and saw her signaling for me to come up to the bar. In spite of Julie's protests, I got up and walked up to the bar.

"Hey, what's up?" I asked.

"Nothing much, what is all this...you guys play for the Yankees or something?" she slurred.

"No we just got through playing in a local softball tournament, that's all."
"What's up with the little blonde bitch there?"

"That...LADY... is with me," I answered firmly.

"Well laaaa dee daaaa...ain't that special?"

"Okay ma'am or whatever you are..." I said as I started to step away.

"Hey punk, don't talk down to me like that...I'll kick the shit outta ya...ya piece of shit..."

"Okay, well you have a nice day...sir," I laughed.

"Wham!"

Suddenly she lurched forward and hit me right in the mouth. It was a good hard shot that rocked me backward for a second. Julie was wide-eyed as she watched the scene unfold, and she knew me well enough to know what I was about to do.

"Jeff, NO...DON'T!"

But it was too late. Before she could get the words out, I instinctively stepped forward and threw a straight right to her jaw.

"Crack!"

The woman crashed back into the bar and then kind of slithered down to the floor in an unconscious heap.

"Son of a bitch!" I said as I wiped the blood from my mouth and looked with wonder at the woman lying at my feet.

"Hey motherfucker...I'm gonna show you what we do to punks that beat on women around here," said a greasy looking biker.

The guy was huge and covered with facial hair. About ten or so of his buddies rose with him.

"That was a woman! You're kidding me! Man! I thought that it was some type of lab experiment gone astray, something like a cross between a wildebeest and a silver back gorilla. You know what I mean...something like...your mom probably looks like," I replied, now seriously hyped and primed for more trouble.

"Let's take it outside funny boy."

I backed up out of the place and into the parking lot as about a dozen or so bikers walked menacingly toward me. At the same time, my teammates and friends ran to their cars to retrieve a number of shiny aluminum bats, and then came close to my back to show their support.

And just as things were about to get very ugly, two cop cars came onto the property and three policemen and one policewoman got out.

"Okay, nobody move. Now what's going on? Jeff, is that you?"

I looked over at the cops and immediately recognized the female officer as the older sister of one of my friends.

"Hey Glenda...nothing, just a minor disagreement. But it's all okay...ain't that right fellas?" I said with a feigned attempt at peacemaking.

"Okay, you guys, let's break it up...everybody...either go back inside or get the hell out of here," said one of the male officers.

With that said everyone shuffled off towards their cars, motorcycles or back into the bar, except for Julie, me and the police.

"Hey thanks a lot guys. I thought that things were going to get hairy there for a minute."

"Okay buddy, you better get outta here, too. Now I know that you're not about to get behind the wheel are you?" asked the same male officer.

"Oh no way officer. My girl here hasn't had a drop. She's going to drive. Hey, thanks again. Bye Glenda."

"Okay, drive safe now."

It was the one time in my life that I was probably justified for putting my hands on a woman. Unfortunately, I would forsake my vow not to do so again far too many times. I was always able to rationalize my violence involving another man due to my early introduction to such behavior, when my father and Will fought right in front of me at my childhood home. And when I slapped, shoved, grabbed or otherwise put my hands on a woman in anger, I used my mother and my mistrust of women as an excuse. The problem was that deep down inside, I was aware that there is never any justification for the cowardly act of using force against someone smaller and weaker.

Maybe my mother's lack of parenting skills contributed to the anger I showed toward women, and maybe seeing violent behavior between my dad and another man at such a young age influenced my actions. Perhaps even the innuendos about my father's paternity played a part in the formation of my less admirable traits. In my innermost thoughts I often excused my actions because of my father's untimely death, along with things like the lies my grandfather told me concerning Dad's money. Unfortunately there were always enough excuses to justify my poor choices and bad behavior.

I wanted to be someone who did the right things, especially in difficult situations, just as I longed to become a successful and respected member of society; I just didn't want to put forth the required effort. Additionally, my upbringing probably added to the likelihood that I was well on the way to becoming a pathological misfit encumbered with delusions of grandeur.

Yet in the final analysis, each of us must accept the responsibility for our actions. If one believes in some type of a higher power, an intelligent cosmic force that dispenses justice along with mercy, if you will, then one believes in some form of karma. And karma, by definition, rewards and punishes for every deed and misdeed committed by each of us. My cosmic scale was unbalanced and leaning much too far in the wrong direction, and the future would reveal that retribution for my actions was looming and quite inevitable.

CHAPTER 11
HIGH(ER) LEARNING

*"The darkest time in a man's life is when he makes a
decision to obtain money without really earning it."
(Horace Greely)*

As Julie and I went off to college together, our relationship was the best it had ever been. She was delighted with the way I had been showing her love and affection and the amount of time we had been spending together. She still worried about my temper, and she certainly did not in any way approve of my use of marijuana. Yet, her enduring love for me caused her to turn a blind eye to my vices. She thought that in time I would grow out of those objectionable qualities.

I had it made. I was in an exclusive relationship with the girl of my dreams. Just the week before, Pop gave me ten thousand dollars for college and I had over seventyfive hundred in a savings account and another two grand in checking. And that was after I spent a big chunk of the cash generated through my hashish venture on a new black Chevrolet Camaro and a Yamaha 750cc motorcycle. Additionally, I was receiving significant amounts of money in the forms of government checks from both my GI Bill entitlement and my remaining eligibility from Dad's Social Security.

With Julie on my arm, a new car, my athleticism and an engaging personality, I quickly became a popular figure on campus. Julie talked me into running for vice president of the freshman class, which I did. I won easily. Ironically, the Student Government President appointed me Chairman of the Student Committee for the Prevention of Drug Abuse. Of course at that time, I was smoking the remainder of my hashish, along with copious amounts of marijuana.

Things went smoothly at first. I was going to basketball practice and even attending class every day and spending time with Julie several times a week. She joined a sorority, and I pledged a fraternity. I hit the books hard and by the end of first term, I made the Dean's List with a 4.0 GPA. My shot at an athletic scholarship was on the horizon too. It was the ideal college educational experience.

Then I began to slip. The first misstep was the weekend I was introduced to hallucinogenic psilocybin mushrooms. After downing six of the nasty things, I had sex with one of Julie's sorority sisters named Carol. The next weekend I took a couple of hits of LSD and bedded down with Carol's roommate Shannon, another one of Julie's sorority sisters. About a week later, I was in a bar one night when someone gave me two pills of a drug called Thorazine, which is often used as a powerful sedative or tranquilizer in treating mentally unstable patients. I woke up about 6:30 the ***next*** evening having missed basketball practice and all of my classes.

On top of these screw-ups, I began selling marijuana to my fellow students. But why? I had plenty of money and wanted for nothing materially. Maybe I did so in order to have a more abundant personal stash, or perhaps it gave me some sense of power by being the source of an important staple of college party life.

One night I went to a place near the river, called the cliffs, with an attractive member of the girls' volleyball team. Her name was Jana. We spread out Birdie's quilt that I had used in my first sexual experience and stripped down to our birthday suits. But one of Julie's sorority sisters had seen us together and rushed back to the campus to tell Julie.

Jana and I had just gotten busy when Julie stormed onto the scene.

"Hello Jeff...hello Jana. Having fun?"

"Julie, I..."

"Go to hell you jerk...and oh yeah, we are T-H-R-O-U-G-H!"

And we were, at least for a while. After about a month of pleading with her, she finally agreed to see me again, but only under the condition that we would both be dating other people. While I ostensibly agreed to this stipulation, I had no intention of allowing any other guy to see her. But it did happen. She went out on a double date with a tennis player named Adolph. I was in the frat house when Carol skipped through the door and plopped down next to me on the couch.

"Hey lover," she whispered mockingly while rubbing my inner thigh.

"Hey Carol, what's up"?

"Ask me where your girlfriend is."

"Okay, where's my girlfriend?"

"I just saw her and Liz at the steakhouse down the street...on a double date I assume, because they were with two guys."

"That's cool with me. We're seeing other people."

"Oh, really?"

"Yeah, really."

"So if I want to take you upstairs and screw your brains out, you wouldn't try to hide it from her?" she said with a wicked smile.

"Try me."

And she did. We went upstairs and had sex in a frat brother's bed but after I had satisfied my carnal impulses, I dressed and bolted out of the house. I sped over to Julie's dorm and waited until she returned.

I tried to act cool about it, but the truth is that I was livid when I found out that she actually went out with some other guy. And when the foursome pulled into the parking lot, I was primed for trouble. They weren't even all out of the car when I approached them.

"Hey Julie, what the hell do you think you're doing going out with this dweeb?"

"Listen asshole, I'm not someone that you need to be messing with...so run along and play," said Adolph.

I got right in his face and said, "Oh I don't know about that, you look exactly like someone I usually mess with."

"Jeff, please don't do this, please. Why don't you go back to your dorm and I'll call you in a little while...okay?" Julie pleaded as she tried to step between the two of us.

Adolph made a crucial mistake. He pushed her out of the way and turned to face me, as he said, "Stay out of this Julia, I'm going to teach your boyfriend here a little lesson."

"Pow!"

Adolph folded like an accordion when I hit him squarely in the nose.

"It's Julie ya jerk, not Julia...J-U-L-I-E. Now how about getting back up and teaching me that lesson."

"Hold up man, I think you broke my nose...no more," he cried.

"No more? Are you serious...that was it? That was my lesson?"

Right at that instant Adolph's friend Fred sucker punched me right in the eye. I never even saw it coming and the blow knocked me into some hedges. I recovered quickly, wiped my hand along my eyebrow and felt the warm flow of my own blood running down my face.

"Oh Jeff, you're hurt," screamed Julie.

"I'm okay baby...now then Freddie, let's see how you do when I'm looking."

I faked a left to Fred's stomach and slapped him with an open right hand. Then I faked a left to his head and punched him in the stomach with all my might. Fred doubled completely over as all of the air was forcibly expelled from his lungs. I then let loose with a right uppercut that straightened him all the way up and then dropped him back onto the pavement with a thud.

I walked triumphantly back toward my car, stopped and then turned to face Julie.

"You know, I really do love you and I'm sorry for all the things I've done to hurt you...I'll..." I stammered at a loss of what to say.

She offered a smile of understanding and compassion. She couldn't help loving me in spite of my actions, and although she was very astute in most areas of life, she was naive enough to believe her love could change me. And Julie's love might have been that powerful too. But without my commitment, that essential missing ingredient, the chance for the survival of our turbulent relationship was slim at best.

"What am I going to do with you? Come on, let's go up to my room and get you cleaned up," she said as she took my hand.

We were reunited again, a routine that would repeat itself many times throughout the next year. I kept fooling around on her, but I became more adept at concealing my infidelity.

The summer was good for us and our relationship. I once again appeared committed to her, which made her happy. But on the side, I was screwing around with several other girls. I was also becoming more heavily involved with dealing drugs. I had met a new friend named Jerry McCord who was a real wild child. Jerry was born with a silver spoon in his mouth and was connected to some serious players in the international trafficking of marijuana. He and I struck a deal whereby we, along with one of my closest friends, Howie Edwards, would take a rented Winnebago near the Texas border to pick up seven hundred and fifty pounds of weed.

Our trip south to the Mexican border was uneventful. When we arrived, we realized that we were about eight hours early, so we checked into a hotel. Then we visited a local whorehouse to kill some time. Next we went to a supermarket to buy twenty cases of Coors Beer to take back home, since it wasn't sold anywhere east of the Mississippi River at that time. Afterwards, we returned to our hotel room, counted out the cash for our drug deal, with the bulk of it being provided by Jerry, and headed for the planned rendezvous.

At the rendezvous the money was meticulously counted by the weed vendors, while we examined the quality of the product. After both parties agreed that everything was satisfactory, the packaged bricks were loaded into the back of the Winnebago and covered with a couple of heavy tarpaulins. We bullshitted with them for a few minutes, shook hands and got back into our respective vehicles and left.

The three of us were elated over how smoothly the deal had gone and we decided to break open one of the bricks and smoke some dope in celebration over our successful transaction. We were buzzed for the entire return trip and everything was fine until we passed the eastern city limits of Memphis. I was behind the wheel when a Shelby County Deputy Sheriff appeared on our rear bumper, flashed his lights and signaled for us to pull over.

"Be cool guys, it's probably just a routine stop. We weren't speeding or anything," I said as I tried to reassure both of them as well as myself.

I stepped out of the vehicle and smiled.

"Hello Officer, how are you? Anything wrong?"

"Let me see some identification young fella."

"Here you go sir."

"Now son, we've had a lot of reports about you young people smuggling that there Coors Beer back to Tennessee. Now son, you wouldn't have any of that there old watered down bear piss inside this thing, would you?"

Sir, I'm not gonna lie to ya...yes we do. We bought twenty cases down in Texas and they're right inside this rear door."

The Deputy stepped over to the door, opened it and then proceeded to count the cases of Coors as the covered mountain of reefer loomed ominously behind the beer.

"Yep, there's twenty of them *aw right*. Now son, here's the deal...I can either confiscate the whole kit and caboodle of 'em and arrest you boys for bringing untaxed alcohol across the state line...or...I can take half of 'em and go about my merry way."

"Officer, option number two sounds like a winner to me. Where would you like me to put them?" I offered with a friendly smile.

He strolled back to the rear of his patrol car and popped the trunk.

"Right in here will be just fine."

"Hey Jerry...Howie, come here and give me a hand."

We loaded the ten cases into his trunk as quickly as possible.

"Okay sir, thank you," I said as soon as we finished loading his alcoholic bribe.

"Okay boys...you boys drive safe now, ya hear?" he said as he smiled and got back into his cruiser.

"Yeah, thanks a lot...you asshole," Jerry muttered under his breath.

"Shut up man," I whispered as I good-naturedly elbowed him in the side.

"Let's get back to *Nashvegas* before they line us up before the local firing squad. I can't believe that he didn't smell anything when he opened that door with all that weed...man, his sense of smell must be shot to the curb or something," Howie said as he wiped his brow.

We finally made it back and by the skin of our teeth, as the three of us circumvented a lengthy stay in some federal penal institution. Nonetheless, the quality of the weed was superb and the local dealers and a multitude of eager potheads quickly snatched it up. Jerry made around forty-five thousand dollars, my return was about fifteen thousand and Howie made nearly two grand for himself.

Easy money...there's nothing like it.

Jerry and I would enter into quite a few other drug deals, although none quite as dramatic as that one. When school started we continued to hang out together even more. It was hard to decide who the bad influence on whom was. We were both wild and crazy.

Once we decided to open up a mini casino right in my dorm room. For marketing purposes, we went down to a pet store and bought a half dozen Siamese fighting fish of various colors, a large fishbowl and six smaller ones. We took them back to my dorm and put each fish into a separate bowl and then took bets on which one would win each battle. It was a huge hit. We kept ten percent of the bets, which more than paid for the fish, which only cost two bucks each.

We revisited the pet store each day until we had exhausted their supply of the fish and then simply began purchasing them from either of their two sister stores across town. The fish fight bets were getting bigger and bigger and all the while, Jerry was cleaning up with poker and blackjack games. Then one day I was told by the owner that we could no longer buy the fish at any of her stores, due to rumors she had heard about students using them to kill each other in "vicious fish fights." Sadly, my day as a fight promoter came to an end.

Jerry was always coming up with something crazy too. One day during the second semester, he came running into my room nearly out of breath.

"Hey man, we have to go to Churchill Downs man...tomorrow. My brother's a jockey there see...and they've been holding back this horse see...and he's racing tomorrow...probably coming off at about fifty to one. We gotta go. It's a lock man. I'm putting ten grand on it...gonna clean up dude."

So away we went. Along with a close friend of mine named David Beal, we ditched our classes, piled into David's Ford Galaxy and headed for the racetrack. On the way,
we smoked over half an ounce of reefer and drank nearly a case of beer, and every time we emptied a bottle we would throw it at a road sign. I hit a couple, Jerry never came close and David hit eleven in a row from the driver's side.

"You the man D Beal!" I said approvingly.

Somehow we made it to the racetrack intact, parked and ran to the betting windows to place our bets. The odds were 44 to 1. Jerry really did put ten thousand on the horse to win. I put down nine hundred and David bet seventy-five bucks. Then we walked to the end of the track where the horses enter the racing area.

"There he is...there's our moneymaker," yelled Jerry.

"Uh Jerry, I don't know a thing about horses, but why is there so much tape all over his legs," I asked.

"Relax, it ain't even gonna be close...you'll see," laughed Jerry.

He was right. It wasn't close. At the end of the race our horse was about twenty lengths away from the next horse...which was the next to last horse!

"Dead last, Jerry! You can really pick 'em man. Thanks a lot," grumbled David.

We all moaned in miserable unison as we returned to David's car for the return trip.

"Hey, at least we'll have a helluva story to tell, huh?" chuckled Jerry.

"Yeah, thanks a lot Jerry!" David and I said at the same time.

Jerry and I continued dealing weed along with the occasional batches of Quaaludes or LSD. Then one day during spring break, the inevitable happened. We were in Nashville, but the entire town appeared to be out of reefer, so we decided to drive back to the college and get half a pound of pot from the stash we had in Jerry's dorm room.

We pulled into the empty parking lot and I jumped out, ran up to the room and was back in a flash with a bundle under my arm. But when I put my car in reverse, the campus cops pulled behind me and blocked us in. They went back to the room and brought down the rest of our stash which totaled just less than three pounds. Then they arrested us and took us downtown to book us. Our bail was set at five thousand dollars apiece. I called the ever loyal and reliable Julie, who quickly rushed there with the necessary funds to set me free. Over a month later when we went to court, we were represented by a powerful Nashville attorney retained by Jerry's father who had "arranged" an agreement with the judge, whereby we would serve four consecutive weekends in the local jail. It was further stipulated that after our time was served, the charges would be expunged from our records.

Thus, I received my first taste of imprisonment. Julie would drop us both off at 6 PM on Friday night and faithfully pick us up at about the same time on Sunday for the duration of our term. Some punishment! Jerry smuggled hits of acid and numerous Quaaludes into the jail by sewing them into the lining of his jacket. We were put in an isolated cell together away from the *real criminals* where we had a 48-hour party each weekend. There was absolutely no lesson to be learned from this experience, which would later prove to be another cog in the machine I was building to assure my disastrous future.

Subsequent to this newsworthy event I was told by the basketball coach that I was no longer a part of the team, and of course I was no longer needed by the Student Government Council's Drug Abuse Committee, of which I had been a member for over a year.

Then one night a week later as one of the bimbos I was fooling around with snuck out of my dorm room, Julie was coming up the stairs to bring me some food left over from one of her sorority parties. She opened the door and found me lying naked on top of the bedcover.

"You're unbelievable!"

"What...what's wrong?" I said as I hastily pulled on a pair of sweat pants.

"I just saw that slut come out of here Jeff. What was she doing...cleaning up your room?"

"Julie I..."

"Go to hell...go straight to hell!"

She flung the food right at me, and as parts of a banana cream pie plastered itself to my face, my spontaneous reaction was a backhand to her cheek, which sent her tumbling down to the floor.

"Oh my God...Julie, I'm sorry," I stammered as I bent over to try to help her up.

"Don't you touch me ever again, you son of a bitch. EVER!"

"I'm sorry, but you..."

"Sorry won't cut it this time mister. You're not gonna...you can't hit me and then...just say you're all sorry about it and then expect for everything to be okay...uh uh...no way. That was the last straw Jeff. And I mean it this time."

But somehow, someway, later that night I talked her into meeting me and going for a walk around the campus quad. After over an hour of talking and handholding we stopped and sat down on an isolated bench. Next I pulled out the ring I had acquired in Germany during my big hash deal, got down on my knees and asked her to marry me as I pledged my eternal love to her. And for some inexplicable and unfathomable reason, she said yes.

At the end of the term we found an apartment and moved in together. We both found decent jobs and planned to work and take evening classes at another local college.

My grandmother Birdie died later that month on the second day of August. About a month and a half after her funeral, I went to see how Pop was holding up and to tell him that I was getting married. As soon as I pulled in the driveway, he came walking up to my car.

"Hey Pop, how're you doing?"

"Hey son...can't complain. Hey, guess what?"

"What?"

"I fucked Helen yesterday," he said rather matter of factly.

I wasn't sure what I had just heard.

"You did what...to who?"

"I fucked Helen, you know Helen...next door."

"Helen? Are you talking about Mr. McCluskey's wife...that woman who used to date
Dad when I was a little kid?"

"Yeah."

"Are you kidding me? When? Where? WHY?"

Pop just laughed as I shuddered as I tried very hard not to even think about the two of them rolling around naked.

"Well, I have some news of my own to tell you…Julie and I are getting married and the wedding is set for next month on October 19th. We both hope that you'll be there."

"That's great son…she's seems like a real fine gal. Congratulations. You both should be very happy together. Now Jeff, I want you to be good to her and treat her right, okay?"

"Sure I will Pop."

"Hold on a second…I've got a wedding present for you two."

Then he wrote out a check for twenty-five hundred dollars.

"Thanks Pop…thanks a lot!" I said as I gave him a hug.

I had gotten a job as a manager trainee at a local K-mart department store along with my buddy Howie. My bachelor party was planned for a Thursday night and as we left work, Howie laughed and said that we would probably both be calling in sick the next day.

That night nearly a dozen of my closest pals treated me to a mobile bachelor party for the ages.

We went to a couple of strip clubs, smoked about fifty joints and drank various kinds of liquor. Even though I was completely out of it already, someone thought it wise to give me several Valiums, which I immediately ate like they were M&Ms. Our portable party began breaking up around one in the morning, and by this time the only ones left *partially* standing were Howie, Gary Thomas and me. Gary was the only one who could even come close to driving, so he slid behind the wheel of my car. I flopped into the back seat and Howie got into the front passenger seat. It was decided that they would first drop me off at my place, the two of them would sleep at Howie's and then the next morning, Howie would drive my car over and pick me up for work. On the way home I suddenly experienced an intestinal requirement, the likes of which cannot be denied, at least for any significant length of time. Now at that time there weren't a great number of public restrooms available that late in Nashville. In fact there were none in the immediate area.

"Hey you guys, pull over, I gotta take a crap."

"Pull over where Jeff? There's nothing open this late man," replied Gary.

"Anywhere…hurry man, I gotta go bad!"

So Gary pulled over on the side of the road and I tumbled out of the car. I took an old newspaper that was in the rear floorboard and staggered over a little way from the road. I positioned myself on what turned out to be a slight incline, dropped my pants to my ankles and squatted down. But when I did, I fell backward down the hill about ten feet or so. Gathering myself, I stood up and repeated the same procedure, which was met with the same result. Finally after tumbling all the way to the bottom of the hill where it was relatively level, I was stable enough to do my business. The problem was that by now my pants had ridden up past my knees, and I was far too wasted to be conscious of it. So instead of dropping my business on the ground, I was depositing it directly into my pants. Unaware of what had just transpired, I thoroughly wiped the pertinent area with the newspaper, pulled up my pants and staggered back to the car, where I once again collapsed into the rear seat. As we continued on to my house, the odor began circulating throughout the car. We had just pulled into my driveway when the smell had become unbearable.

"Damn Howie, did you fart?"

"No…did you?"

"Uh uh, well Jeff must have shit in his pants. Come on, let's hurry up and get him inside."

So they got me inside my bedroom, threw me on the bed and began laughing as they told Julie what happened and advised her to sleep on the couch.

"Tell the Mad Shitter that I'll be by to pick him up about 7 o'clock," said Howie as they laughed all the way out the door.

The next morning, I woke up with my pants caked and plastered to my legs and butt. It was a difficult job, but after thirty minutes in the shower, I felt cleansed of my filth, but not my shame. Just as I finished dressing, Howie pulled into the driveway and honked the horn. I ran out and jumped into the car.

"Hey dude, I thought you said that we were gonna have to call in sick," I said proudly.

"Yeah, we're definitely heavyweight partiers for sure…and your pants man, they sure were heavyweights last night, too," he howled.

"Hey man, come on now, don't tell anybody at work about that man…please," I pleaded.

"I give you my word on our friendship, I will not tell a single soul at work today, okay?"

"Thanks man…I owe you one."

But as soon as we walked in the store, three girls that worked with us began smiling as they paraded past me carrying packs of Pampers and singing "*Good morning*

Mr. Mad Shitter."

Howie kept his word alright. He wouldn't tell a single soul at work. He had already called them and arranged for my further humiliation ***before*** he picked me up. My friends were unmerciful in regards to reminding me about that incident for years to come.

Julie and I married in October and it should have been the greatest blessing of my life. Her strength of character was much stronger than mine and she might have made up for what I lacked. But it was not to be.

I continued dealing pot and cheating on her, and I soon found another vice, gambling. I started with small bets on football games, but after I found that I was pretty good (or lucky) at picking winners, I bet more and more. Seasonal football bets overlapped into baseball in the spring and to playing poker machines and ultimately gambling junkets to Las Vegas. And of course the Vegas prostitutes were too much of a temptation for me, one of which gave me a venereal disease. The morning after I felt a burning sensation while urinating, I went to a health clinic where they told me that I had contracted gonorrhea. Realizing that I had likely passed it on to Julie, I asked the doctor for advice.

"Doc, I can't tell my wife. It would hurt her and then she might kill me…seriously!"

"Well, I'll tell you what. Just say that I said that it was N.S.U."

"What's that?"

"It stands for nonspecific urethritis, and you can contract it through nonsexual means. Then she can come in for treatment and you both can live in peace and harmony…IF you promise me that you'll clean up your act."

"Whew…thanks a lot Doc, and I will straighten up. I promise that I'll never fool around on her again."

But as soon as Julie and I had completed our prescribed course of penicillin, I was right back at it.

The next time I was unfaithful was shortly after that. Julie got an anonymous call telling her the details of the tryst, where and when. And when I came through the door, she went off on me. I was obviously caught and the guilt was too much for me to bear, so I reacted with the same type of response that I resorted to throughout my life…with violence. I shoved her up against the wall and told her to shut up and get out, which she did immediately.

She didn't tell me where she was going and it took nearly a month to track her down living in a tiny little town in Alabama and working at a pizza joint. Once again I begged for her forgiveness, promised to give up dope, gambling and my friends, who I unjustly blamed as the source of my inexcusable activities. Conning her yet again, I quit my job and moved down to the quiet countryside to live with her.

I found a job as the assistant manager of a convenience store and things were okay for several months. With no weed in my system and relatively very few skirts to chase, I rediscovered the many wonderful qualities of my wife. During those months spent in that hick town in Alabama, we were genuinely happy. In fact, I truly wish that we had never left that sleepy little village.

But eventually and predictably, I grew bored. I wanted to go back to school for my degree and so did Julie. We moved back to Nashville and planned to return to college that fall. We decided that since I still had most of my GI Bill entitlement left, I would attend classes and find a part time job, while she would work full time and take a few night classes.

Julie found a great job managing an apartment complex, which not only paid the bills, but also gave us a nice rent-free apartment. She hired me to clean and paint the apartments as they became vacant, which was a perfect part time job.

On the day of orientation and registration I had a meeting with my university counselor, Professor Milton, a pompous and pedantic Professor Emeritus from an Ivy League university.

"Come in and have a seat Mr. Collins."

"Good morning Doctor Milton."

"Young man, this meeting will serve as your required counseling session. Now then, do you have any questions for me"?

"No sir, I'm very eager to get down to work and graduate with a B.A., hopefully within the next two years."

"And then what…what do you plan to do with a Bachelor of Arts degree?"

"I plan on going to law school."

"Well Mr. Collins, I am what you could call a realist. And I must say that after objectively reviewing your transcript, I am of the opinion that you have had a…how can I say this tactfully? Thus far you have had a very checkered college career. Furthermore I feel an obligation as your assigned counselor to inform you that your chances of being accepted to any law school are very slim indeed."

"Well Professor Milton, I understand and appreciate what you're saying. I realize my current GPA is inadequate at this time to be accepted into law school. But I guarantee you that it will rise dramatically in the next two years and I plan on making a very high score on the LSAT. And your rough assessment just now, well sir, it will serve as further motivation for me…so thank you for your advice and for your time."

I was determined to get into law school and my efforts produced very good grades, grades that I had been capable of earning all along. Two years later at the end of my undergraduate studies, my GPA had soared from a dismal 2.55 all the way to a 3.39. And true to my word this time, I received one of the highest scores in the university on the Law School Admission Test or LSAT. And I accomplished all this while working part time in the apartment complex, playing intramural sports and smoking dope like Chief Wahoo with my latest collegiate acquaintances. And naturally I dealt pot on the side. To Julie's chagrin, I even grew a small crop of it in the woods behind our apartment.

I did somehow find the time to run football gambling tickets for students, with my major clients coming from the wealthy undergraduates along fraternity row. I was so busy that I didn't have time to chase after coeds during those two years. The only time I strayed was when I caught the eye of a stunning, raven-haired beauty named Tanya Chance. I believe Tanya met all the psychological requirements to be clinically classified as a true nymphomaniac.

During my first year back in school, I was sitting alone beneath a tree outside of a Geology classroom, when she walked up to me.

"Hey Jeff," she said as she flashed her dazzling smile.

"Hello...do I know you?"

"No, but I know you...my name is Tanya," she said and sat down on the ground beside me.

"You know me? From where?"

"Oh just around. I've seen you playing basketball and hanging around the campus, in the library...you know, around. You've got beautiful eyes and great legs. Has anyone ever told you that?" she cooed as she scooted her voluptuous body closer to me.

"Well Tanya, I appreciate that, but I have to tell you that I'm married."

"Ooh, I've never dated a married man before!"

I started to stand up, but realized immediately that I was quite aroused.

"Well I need to get on to class...we're supposed to be seeing some film on volcanoes or something. I'll see you later...I guess."

I then walked awkwardly into the amphitheater classroom and found an isolated seat near the top of the room. As soon as I sat down, the lights went out and the film began. Seconds later, someone walked down the same aisle and sat down next to me.

"Hello again," said Tanya in an extremely sensual voice.

She reached over and began caressing my genitals.

"Man this is like a letter out of Penthouse," I whispered.

"Oh it's going to be far better than any old letter, honey...I promise you that," she answered softly.

And with that said, she eased my shorts down to my ankles (with a little willing assistance from me), dropped to the floor in front of my chair and made good on her promise. It was one of the most erotic experiences of my life. And over the next decade, Tanya continued to pop into my life to offer me many additional similar trysts. Our relationship came with no strings attached, which suited me just fine, and it was quite a boost to my ego to have such a gorgeous creature at my beck and call.

I graduated with honors and was accepted by several law schools in the state. After discussing our options, Julie and I decided to move back to Nashville so that I could attend a night law school there. That way I could find a day job that would pay the tuition, since my GI Bill college entitlement was about to run out in less than six months.

Due to her experience and glowing references, Julie instantly found a job managing another apartment complex and I became the complex handyman. Both jobs provided adequate income for the two of us. I once again seriously hit the books and things were going smoothly during the first term of law school, when the situational ennui returned. And again I began smoking and dealing reefer and gambling on sporting events, although I wasn't nearly as successful this time around. My losses soon exceeded my dope dealing income and like most arrogant gamblers, I responded by making larger bets. This plan invariably turned into bigger paydays for my bookies, which in turn forced me to sell more dope. Julie protested vigorously, but to no avail, and each time she would complain, I in turn would simply tell her to stop her nagging.

Then one day the phone rang in our apartment. It was Tanya and she was asking me to come to her hotel room downtown and do lewd and lascivious acts to her body as soon as possible.

"I'm on the way!" I said as I bolted out the door.

Several hours later I walked back into my apartment where I found Julie, crying on the couch. As soon as I shut the door, she was in my face screaming and crying.

"You son of a bitch!"

"What? What did I do this time?"

"Jeff I was on the extension in the office when that little whore called you. I know where you've been. I can even smell her cheap perfume on you...you stupid jerk!"

She slapped me hard in the face and then swung at me again. I blocked her next swing and due to my instinctive tendency to defend myself, I slapped her face. My regret was instant, but too late.

With tears running down her face, she looked me directly in the face and said, "Go ahead and hit me all you want, because I promise you this Jeff Collins, you will never lay another hand on me again."

"Julie, hold on a second baby...I'm sorry, I..."

"Oh you're sorry alright...and you're about to be a lot sorrier. We are through...I've had it."

She quickly packed a few things and was gone within minutes.

In some twisted way I considered my relationship with Julie like some sort of competition. It was the way I would approach my serious relationships throughout my lifetime. I would do all kinds of incorrigible things that would cause the women in my life to leave, even to justifiably hate me. Then I would embrace the challenge of winning them back, and unfortunately for everyone concerned, I had quite a flair for it. But not with Julie, not any longer. My act had long since worn very thin for her. This time she was gone for good and there was absolutely nothing that I ever could do or say to get her back again.

PART III SEX, DRUGS & ROLLING THROUGH THE 80'S

There's an old story about good and evil. It's an analogy that compares them to two dogs inside everyone...one good and one bad. Which one we show to the world depends on which one we feed the most. I obviously fed the wrong dog.

CHAPTER 12
NO JULIE = MARY ANNE

Statistics tell us that one out of every four people in this country is mentally unbalanced. Think of three people that you know well. If they seem okay, then you may be the one.

Julie was gone. That cold sobering fact finally became clear after nearly two weeks of denial. She was kind enough to call from Jacksonville, Florida to let me know that she had initiated divorce proceedings. And as mind-boggling as it was in light of all the appalling things I had done during our five-year marriage, she said she would always care about me and wished me well. Reality gave me an additional smack in the face two days later on a cold rainy December morning, when the new manager of the complex knocked on the door and announced in no uncertain terms that I was to immediately vacate the premises. She also informed me that my services as the complex handyman were no longer needed. I was homeless and jobless, but as luck would have it, only for one afternoon.

Later that day I bumped into a college buddy named Roy Stewart. Roy was in desperate need of a roommate and of course I was willing to move in at once. Then later that night at my new hangout, a bar called The Gold Mine, I ran into a fellow named James Sullivan, the regional manager of a national chain of electronic stores. For whatever reason, the guy took an instant liking to me, and offered me a sales position in one of the Nashville stores. I told him that I was going to law school, but when he said I could earn well over a thousand dollars a week, especially during the Christmas holidays, I decided that it would be best if I made some serious money and put law school on the back burner.

So I dropped out of law school, but in good standing and with the hope that I would return in the near future. I went to work selling televisions and stereo equipment and the paychecks astounded me. It was the holiday season and the stuff was practically jumping off the shelves. I was making nearly two thousand a week! The problem was I wouldn't see a paycheck until I had been there a month, since they held the paychecks back a month as many employers do. And aside from five hundred bucks I had left after paying my part of the rent and security deposit, I was as broke as I had been in a while. I had always thought that dealing pot would provide plenty of cash, but it had been dry in town for several weeks. And even when the supplies were once again available through my connections, I lacked the necessary capital to invest in such an illicit business, thanks in no small part to my gambling debts. I had to come up with another plan, one that would yield quick returns.

So I contacted an old associate. The guy was known to make a vehicle or two disappear from someone's driveway or garage, never to be seen again. I wanted him to work some of his magic on my Oldsmobile Cutlass, which he did without delay.

While I was waiting for the check to be cut by my car insurance company, I decided that I would file a claim with the company providing my renter's insurance, too. Since I had access to my company's receipt book, it was a simple matter to forge half a dozen or so receipts for the televisions and stereo equipment that I claimed were stolen from my apartment. After calling the police, who filled out a burglary report, all I had to do was file another fraudulent claim and wait on the check.

In the meantime I was running dangerously low on cash. Although I was making pretty good money from selling electronics, it would be two more weeks before I was paid. And while my schemes to defraud the insurance companies had been successful, those checks would not be available for at least another week, either.

So in the meantime I did what came naturally...I partied and chased after women. I went to the Gold Mine nearly every night and more often than not left with a different woman. But now my singular criterion that she meet with my degree of superficial attractiveness was expanded to include a second requirement. She now had to have a car, because mine had *disappeared.*

Until the insurance company coughed up some funds I had to rely on friends for rides everywhere. Work was no problem. My job was less than a mile away and I had walked there several times. At night I would hitch a ride from someone who lived in the same apartment complex to the downtown area, and I usually managed to get a lift back home, if not from the floozy of the night, then from someone I knew from the Gold Mine.

I kept running into this eye-catching blonde Amazon at the Gold Mine, and every time I saw her, I came on to her. I usually said something highly suggestive whenever she walked by.

I often led with something like, "Whoa girl, I'm telling you that as long as I have a face, you have a place to sit down."

Such lewd comments usually garnered a smile from her and were followed by a standard brush off, like "You're cute but I'm here with somebody, but maybe one night you might get lucky...so don't give up."

I didn't. Every time I saw her, I'd flirt with her and toss out another provocative comment. She was in the Gold Mine almost as often as I was, so our paths crossed quite a bit. And then one Friday night I finally got substantially more than a smile.

"Hey Mary Anne, are you here with your boyfriend again tonight?"

"Actually, he's not my boyfriend anymore…we're just sort of hanging out together."

"Well then, can I buy you a drink, an automobile… a condo in Hawaii?"

She laughed and said, "Why don't you take me back to your place and then we can see what happens after that."

"There's a small problem. You see, I'm sort of in between vehicles right now and…"

"Are you telling me that you've been hitting on me for the past two weeks and you don't even have a car?"

"Well…yeah…but you have one, don't you?"

"Jeff…you know what…you're a real trip. Okay come on, let's go, but you're gonna have to drive because I may have had a little too much to drink."

It turned out that she had drunk too much indeed. As soon as we arrived at my apartment, she grabbed my hand and pulled me into my bedroom and kissed me passionately. Then she took a step backwards.

"Let's get naked!"

Thinking that to be an excellent suggestion, I immediately began shedding my clothes as she undressed and then stood completely nude before me.

"Wow Mary Anne, you're incredible," I said as I surveyed her awesome body.

But just as I was about to pull her close, she turned and ran to the bathroom, where she began hurling into the toilet.

"Damn, I guess she really did have too much to drink," I said aloud.

But she snapped back quickly. She gargled with mouthwash, came back into the bedroom and apologized, as she at last slivered her naked form alongside mine. We made love for over an hour and for whatever reason, she fell in love with me. In fact she began virtually moving in the very next day. Every time she came to my apartment, she would bring more and more of her belongings, starting with makeup and other feminine items, which preceded clothing and even a piece of furniture or two. Although I was a little surprised at how fast it happened, I didn't object to this sudden development. We were extremely attracted to one another and she seemed to love having sex.

Now Julie Ross and Mary Anne Petron were about as different as a bunny and a werewolf, and the only common denominator between the two was a shared love they had for a certain cad named Jeff Holden Collins. Julie was innocent and pure of heart. She wanted to have children and she didn't like drugs. She rarely drank alcohol and the only times she had used profanity around me was when I had committed some terrible breach of trust in our relationship. Furthermore, she was a genuine Christian who went to church regularly.

Mary Anne on the other hand was a perfect candidate for one of those "Girls Gone Wild" videos. She was a 5' 9" natural blonde bombshell. To call her statuesque would be no exaggeration, yet to say that she was striking would be more accurate than to say she was beautiful. Whenever she entered a room, heads turned. Her appearance was enhanced by the miracles of medical science. She had cosmetic surgery for breast augmentation and a nose job. Her hands were her nicest feature. They were the sculpted hands of a hand model. They could have been featured in television ads holding up a jar of mustard or demonstrating a lightweight vacuum cleaner. Instead they cut hair. She was a barber, a very good one. She made decent money and even seemed to enjoy the work.

Mary Anne had a few issues all right. She had a propensity to personify absolute bitchiness, and she was at least a borderline alcoholic and just as big of a pothead as me. She had been with many men, perhaps even surpassing my number of sexual partners. She also had a temper that rivaled my own.

Intellectually, I was beyond her reach, and throughout our relationship, I frequently used this advantage against her. I bested her in arguments, unfairly confusing her through Byzantine mazes of circular logic or by using words I knew exceeded her understanding. I rarely missed an opportunity to point out her intellectual inferiority. Several other areas of concern about her would manifest themselves in the months and years ahead, but for the time being, I was content with her. Superficially she was perfect for me.

Julie called me one day to discuss our divorce plans, and somehow I talked her into having what I termed, a rational face-to-face discussion before forsaking our marital vows. She agreed to talk with me, but demanded that it take place in Florida. She saw no reason to ever return to Tennessee.

Although I still had no transportation, I agreed to her terms, adding that I would be there within the week. I then turned my attention to Mary Anne and her car. When I went to work and picked up a paycheck for seventeen hundred and fifty dollars, I told them that I had to quit due to a "family emergency." And since my car insurance had yielded a check for forty-four hundred bucks and my renter's insurance coughed up a little over three thousand, I had enough capital to manipulate Mary Anne into a trip to Florida under false pretenses and still have plenty left to get back into the drug dealing business.

I told her how great it would be to lay around with her on the sunny beaches of Daytona and make love to the sounds of the ocean. Naturally I withheld my real objective for traveling to the Sunshine State, which was to reunite with Julie. Mary Anne agreed that it was a wonderful idea and we left that night for the sunny shores of the eastern Florida coast.

We drove to Daytona Beach in her car, as my grand plan to win my wife's heart yet again was set into motion. I used the travel time to conjure up an elaborate lie in order to take her car and drive the short distance from Daytona Beach to Julie's apartment in Jacksonville.

"Mary Anne, I have a surprise for you."

"What is it?"

"Well, you know that I'm married, right?"

"Yeah, but you told me that your wife lives in another state somewhere…right?"

"Yeah, she lives in Jacksonville, about an hour from where we'll be staying on the beach."

"Yeah…so…"

"Well you see Mary Anne, since I met you, I decided that it would be great to go ahead and get my divorce out of the way. That way if our relationship keeps developing as well as it has been so far, then we'd be free to…well, you know."

"Oh Jeff, that would be wonderful, but why are you telling me this?"

"Because I want to go to Julie's and pick up some paperwork in order to expedite this thing."

"Okay, do you want me to go with you?"

"No Mary Anne, I don't think that would be a good idea. Seeing me with someone else this soon would only anger her and I'm trying to end this thing peacefully. So what I'd like to do is use your car, run over there and get the paperwork. It won't take but an hour or two, three at the most. Would that be okay with you?"

"When do you want to do this?"

"Oh, anytime this week. Let's enjoy a few days of sun and fun before tackling the unpleasant task of dissolving a marriage. Let's say around Wednesday night…would that be okay with you?"

"And you'll only be gone for a couple hours?"
"Right, three at the most."

"Okay then honey…sure."

What a prolific and creative liar I was!

We spent the next two days lying on the beach, getting high and drunk during the daytime and making love at night, just as I promised. Then on Wednesday evening I left for Julie's around six in the afternoon. I arrived at her apartment determined to win her back, but after spending over four hours trying to convince her that I had actually changed, I realized she was going to use her good sense and say no to my pleas for another chance this time. I left there a defeated man. I had driven away the greatest thing that ever happened to me, and I had no one but my stupid pathetic self to blame.

As I approached the hotel in Daytona, I glanced at the dashboard clock.

"Damn, it's five after twelve!"

As soon as I opened the door, I knew that I was in for a wild ride. Mary Anne was drunk and angry.

"Hey you mother fucker, where have you been with my car? I was about to call the fucking cops on you."

"Okay calm down. It took a little longer than I thought..."

"Why didn't you call me and let me know where you were?"

"Mary Anne, I'm sorry. But everything is okay now and..."

"You've probably been screwing her, you bastard!"

"Okay, you're obviously drunk, so I'm just gonna..."

"Spppt!" she spit right in my face.

I couldn't stop myself. My hand seemed to have a mind of its own as it took off towards her cheek and completed a firm open-handed slap.

"Whack."

"Don't ever spit on me again Mary. I haven't been screwing anybody but you...you stupid bitch!" I yelled.

"Oh Jeff, you're right...I'm sorry honey...I love you. Let's not fight anymore...please," she sobbed.

So we made up and spent four more days in Daytona before going home. On the way back I faced the stark reality that I would have to find another job and a car as soon as possible, but since I still had about eighty-three hundred bucks left, I was certain that it would be enough to jumpstart my once thriving pot trade and at least put a down payment on another car.

Once again I hit the ground running and remained lucky. I scoured the classifieds, and picked up a cherry 1977 Chevrolet pickup from a desperate seller for only twelve hundred and seventy-five dollars. The truck would have been a bargain at twice the price. I secured a decent-paying job with a local beer distributor and then submitted my application for the upcoming term of law school. Finally, I made a five-pound purchase of some high-grade marijuana. I was set. Things were about to go my way, at least on the surface.

Cash began rolling in again. My decent pay from the beer distributor was chickenfeed compared to what I was making dealing weed, and I was hitting on my sports bets at a pretty good clip too. I decided that it was time to invest in something tangible, so I started hunting for a house. Mary Anne was excited about it and offered advice on the size and location, but I merely acted as though she was helping me to make the decision. I found a nice three-bedroom place near the lake. It had a dark room, a finished basement and a privacy fence, which I felt was necessary to conceal anything I deemed confidential enough to keep out of the eyesight of nosy neighbors.

Then one day a few months later while walking across the mall parking lot, I spotted a gentleman struggling to carry his purchases to his car. I offered my assistance, which was gladly accepted. We walked together until we came to a gleaming high end Mercedes Benz.

"Young man my name is L. P. Sprye and I really appreciate your help."

"Good to meet you sir. I'm Jeff Collins and you're very welcome," I replied with a firm handshake.

"May I ask what you do for a living Jeff?"

"Well, right now I work for a local beer distributor during the day and I go to Law School at night."

"I tell you Jeff, I'm a pretty good judge of character. And well, I own several businesses throughout the south and I need a bright young fellow like you for a very important position in one of my factories here in middle Tennessee. It would be a factory rep type job. It would pay well and the man who I hire will have a very good future, providing he's a self-starter who is willing to travel. Now tell me Jeff, how much are they paying you, if you don't mind me asking?"

"Oh, about twenty-seven thousand plus a bonus…just under thirty a year."

"Well, if you can come to my office this week, we'll go out to lunch and by the time we finish eating, I'll bet you agree to come and work for me."

"But I work every day sir. That would be very difficult."

"Jeff, if it works out, I'll start you off at thirty-five thousand a year and give you a five thousand dollar raise every other month until you're making…let's say…sixty thousand a year. Now that's more than double what you make selling beer."

"Mr. Sprye, I'll see you tomorrow at lunchtime," I said with conviction and another firm handshake.

"Let's make it around 11:30 in the morning…here's my card. Jeff, it was a pleasure to meet you. I'll see you tomorrow."

The next day I had lunch with Mr. Sprye and agreed to be his company's factory representative. I quit working for the beer company, which didn't trouble me in the least. But the new job required a great deal of travel and that was a problem. There was no way that I could stay in Law School and work for Mr. Sprye too, so I reluctantly dropped out of school again. At that time I had every intention of returning one day in the near future.

When I told Mary Anne about it, she sat there open-mouthed and questioned the truthfulness of my claim. As difficult as it was for Mary Anne and my friends to believe that a perfect stranger I met in a parking lot had given me such a fantastic job, it was typical of the exceptional opportunities that seemed to magically present themselves to me throughout my outwardly charmed life.

I loved the new job. My main responsibility was to make sure the company's vast array of customers all over the nation were happy with the products and the service they received. I was in California for two or three days one week and in New York the next. Then I would check on the clients around Tennessee and Kentucky and throughout the southeast. Mr. Sprye liked my attitude and work ethic a great deal, so much so that he paid me even more than he had promised by the end of the first year.

Mary Anne didn't like staying alone for days at a time all that much, but I was generous and decent to her. I left her with plenty of cash and weed and I let her use my new sports car whenever I had to fly - if my business destination was too far to drive. I frequently splurged on new things like cars, boats, big-screen TVs or practically anything she wanted for the house. Life had regained its previous luster.

Within around nine months of shacking up with her however, I detected an iciness that I hadn't picked up on before. How I had missed it was perplexing, because she was now giving frequent, convincing imitations of a very cold fish. The change in her demeanor appeared for no apparent reason and without provocation. I also discovered that she had Herpes Simplex II, which caused blisters to form on the most intimate area of her body. And when the blisters appeared, she told me that we wouldn't be able to have sex until it cleared up. Those episodes generally lasted for an entire week. I never considered the fact that by abstaining during her outbreaks, Mary Anne was actually protecting me from contracting the viral STD.

For me, those latest turns were totally unacceptable, because I wanted sex a couple of times each day. I also realized that Mary Anne had a severe prescription drug addiction. She was hooked on barbiturates and often ate as many as half a dozen Valiums when one of her blisters was present. The drugs just contributed to her recurrent, steely, bitchiness.

Her good points were still obvious to me though. Thanks to cosmetic surgery, her body was very appealing. She was an awesome cook and she kept the house clean and neat. She was a great barber and gave me top quality haircuts absolutely free. Sex with her wasn't that great any more but it wasn't that bad either. It just didn't occur close to the frequently which suited me. I began regarding her more like one of my male friends who I partied with rather than a lover. One thing about having her as a girlfriend that had startled me from the beginning of our relationship was that whenever we would visit her parents, the two of us would smoke pot with her father right outside in his tool shed. I always regarded it as a little weird but kind of cool just the same.

After we had been together nearly two years, the relationship had evolved into a strain and a pain. From my perspective her negative features completely overshadowed her assets, and she could be such a bitch! I realized that I was not in love with her. I still liked certain things about her, and maybe I even loved her a little at the start of our liaison, but certainly not any longer. That was about the end of my affection for Mary Anne Petron.

About this time I started seeing prostitutes on a regular basis. I planned on ending the relationship with Mary Anne sometime soon, but I was just too busy with my job, dealing large quantities of weed and partying every weekend like the world was about to end. So instead of scoping out my local stomping grounds for a new girlfriend, I satisfied my sexual urges with call girls.

Another change was on the way. One of the greatest love affairs of my life was on a collision course with me, and it would remain one of my top priorities for most of the eighties. However, this time it was not a woman.

CHAPTER 13
COCAINE

"Driving that train, high on cocaine,
Casey Jones you'd better watch your speed.
Trouble ahead, trouble behind,
And don't you know that notion just crossed my mind."
(Grateful Dead – Casey Jones)

The first time I had ever seen cocaine was when someone traded me an eighth of an ounce of it for some killer weed. I put it into the freezer and forgot about it for a while and when I finally remembered it, Julie had inadvertently thrown it away while defrosting the freezer. I wouldn't see much of it again for several years. When I did, it changed my life.

I was at a party one Saturday night with a bunch of wealthy acquaintances when my close friend, Warren Best, pulled me into the garage.

"Here Jeff, try a little of this."

"A little of what?"

"Peruvian Flake my friend, all the way from South America. Here, try a line or two. Let me put some on this mirror for you."

He took a Coors Beer mirror off the wall, wiped it with his shirt sleeve and dumped nearly a half an ounce of the powder on top. Then he pulled out a credit card and made several thick lines out of the fine particles, each one about a foot long. He pulled out a crisp one hundred dollar bill and rolled it into a tiny straw. Bending forward he hoovered an entire line up his left nostril, shook his head and repeated the procedure on the other side. Then he handed the bill to me.

"Here you go, do two of these."

"All of that?"

"Yeah, get you a good buzz!"

So I snorted as much of the stuff up my nose as I could, but when I ran out of breath, I looked down and saw that over half of my prescribed dosage remained.

"Come on, don't be such a wussy, get it all."

So I bent forward with determination, took a deep breath and snorted the rest of the lines.

"Whoa man…wow," I uttered as the rushing sensation permeated through my body. It was the closest feeling I had ever had to having sex and it was a case of "love at first snort."

Depending on who you are and where you were raised, you probably have some thoughts concerning the evil power much of the world knows as Lucifer, Satan, Beelzebub, the devil, etc. For people who believe that such an entity exists, it is submitted for your consideration that he must have enjoyed a major role in concocting the poison we call cocaine. The drug inflicts significant amounts of misery on humanity. If you've never tried it, take this sincere piece of advice and don't just say no, say "Never!"

While I unquestionably had other issues that led to my undoing, my decision to begin a love affair with cocaine was one of the key stepping-stones on my way to disaster. But just as I had done in the army, I rationalized that since I never stuck a needle in my arm, I wasn't a junkie or a dope addict. In fact I was an advanced pothead and had just taken my first giant step toward becoming a full blown coke addict.

Cocaine was expensive and I spent a lot of money in a hurry. In the next month I spent over a thousand bucks on the stuff and realized that the only way that I could keep a sufficient supply of blow was to deal it along with weed. Although I was a competent drug dealer, I had long since broken one of the most important tenets required of the most successful dope vendors...*do not use your own product*. I got away with smoking some of the profits in my marijuana business, but coke was a different animal, and I soon began snorting more and more of it. Furthermore, everyone I knew loved doing it. Mary Anne had often used it before she knew me and now that I was keeping a stash, well that was fine and dandy with her. She was voraciously vacuuming up the coke I left for her when I went away on business, and I soon discovered that she had also found my hiding places in the house and she was pinching off those supplies as well. She was what is known in the business as a "true coke whore." And for that matter, I was the male equivalent.

As for me, whenever I snorted a few lines of the stuff, I found that it would increase my already ample predilection for promiscuous fornication. And since Mary Anne had major limitations when it came to pleasuring me, I found even further motivation for locating other women to fulfill my physical desires. I learned that being a purveyor of fine blow endowed me with some interesting fringe benefits. It provided extra income (a large chunk of which usually went up my nose), a sense of power, and I instantly became the favorite customer of nearly every bartender I knew. There was also the pleasant surprise of turning into an object of affection for countless wild females. Girls began throwing themselves at me like I was some kind of rock star. I even had to turn down a few of them, ones I had lusted after for a while.

"So many coke whores, so little time," I mused to myself one night in the Gold Mine, when several of them were competing to lure me to their beds.

In addition to my genuine trips out of town, I frequently merely pretended to be away on business, all the while pulling an all-nighter with the skank of the moment. I'd spend the night in her bed or in some motel room in the city.

We all have certain natural limitations and I was no exception. My candle was burning at both ends and bending in the middle. I liked my job a lot, but the lure of easy money from dealing coke, along with all the perks made my decision simple. I couldn't do both, so predictably, I chose the path to chaos. I quit a dream job in order to focus on making some serious money, which meant moving larger quantities of illicit product. Realizing that some type of front was needed in order to justify all the cash that dealing coke generated, I decided to procure a real estate license.

In short order I took an accelerated real estate course, found a broker to sponsor me and passed the state exam. The astounding thing was that as soon as I was licensed, I began listing and selling properties. In my first three months I made over twenty-four thousand dollars without much effort at all. I could have been extremely successful in real estate had I actually applied myself. What a fool!

Cocaine is insidious for several reasons and one of them is the lure of easy money. At that time a kilogram cost between fifteen and twenty-five thousand dollars, depending on the quality, the dealer, and where you bought it. The normal process was to take the thousand grams in that kilo and *cut* it with various substances such as Vitamin B12 powder or a corn derivative called Isotol. Both of these *extenders* were easily and inexpensively purchased at any health food store.

Some dealers actually put a thousand grams of cut into the thousand grams of powder, thereby doubling the amount of their inventory. And if a dealer sells 50 of the resulting 70.5 ounces for two thousand apiece and partied with the rest...well, simple math shows the potential profit. This business was now my priority and everything else took a back seat. I moved more cocaine with each passing week and saw the cash start to pile up. Instead of investing in something sensible such as CDs, mutual funds or blue chip stocks, I chose to spend a great deal of it on grownup toys, junkets to Vegas and call girls.

Mary Anne assumed all the extra cash was the result of my drive and ambition, because she was under the impression that I was still working as a factory rep as well as selling real estate. This worked out well since it continued to provide me with a valid excuse for being away from home. Once I was gone for nine straight days. She believed that I was working my way through the major cities of Arizona, New Mexico and Texas.

In fact I had never left Nashville, except for two days when I traveled to Miami and back to pick up a large supply of powder.

I kept finding better sources until the day when my friend Warren introduced me to his main supplier, an El Salvadorian expatriate who had been educated in the United States. He went by the name Manny. Manny and I hit it off from the very beginning. I thought the guy was okay, but the fact he was always armed with a pistol or an Uzi, caused me serious concern.

Thus far my only experiences with guns had been in military school, in the army and the night my mom fired a pistol in her pseudo suicide attempt. My memories of my mother's action that night held a very powerful and negative association with guns for me. Nonetheless, I started hanging around with Manny and his friends, Ramon, Felipe and Jesus. Manny proposed that Warren and I fly to South America with them to pick up a load of blow.

"Man, I don't know Manny...all the way there and back...I mean, what if we get caught?"

"What if we don't...and besides, think of how much cheaper you'll be getting it, not to mention how much purer it will be than the weak shit you sell. Come on Jeff, life was meant to be lived my friend and remember, evil spelled backwards is live!"

Manny kept after me until I reluctantly agreed to fly to Peru with them. Manny offered his solemn word that the first time would be just a pleasure trip to show me how simple it was, and no cocaine would be smuggled back. Felipe piloted the plane which landed somewhere along the coastal region of Northern Peru. It was a four-day long nonstop party. After seeing how the cocaine was processed, the six of us had a grand time sampling the local cuisine and chasing the senoritas, as we snorted coke, drank tequila and smoked marijuana. Manny kept trying to talk me into helping him transport some cocaine back to the states, but to no avail.

However, I finally agreed to help him once the coke was actually back in the country. I listened carefully to Manny as the plan was laid out, but resisted hearing about the minutiae of the logistics. I just didn't want to know any more than I absolutely needed to. It was agreed that on a certain day, Warren, Howie and I would wait at Manny's house for a call. We would then quickly proceed in a large custom van to one of four areas, all of them very rural and isolated and within an hour's drive from Manny's home. Upon our arrival, a plane would fly extremely low over the designated area and ten heavy-duty duffle bags would be dropped out. Each duffle would contain fifty kilos or about one hundred and ten pounds of cocaine. Manny tried over and over to brag about some type of ingenious apparatus he has engineered to accomplish the drops, but I steadfastly refused to listen each time. We were to retrieve the bags and head to Manny's to wait on him and Felipe. During the first five trips everything ran as planned. I made tens of thousands of dollars from the deals; I wasn't even sure how much. I just knew that it was a lot. Manny paid fifteen hundred per kilo. He offered them for sale to me for four thousand, which was quite a deal.

Then there was our sixth mission. We followed the same routine, but this time Manny provided us with an old beat-up Volkswagen van, which was very uncomfortable for the guy in the back, who usually turned out to be Howie. On the way to the drop zone, we had a flat tire. It took thirty minutes to change and by the time we got there, the bags were already on the ground. We scurried to pick them up, but after nearly an hour of searching, we had located only nine of the ten. During the previous five runs, we always found all ten duffle bags right away. This was because other than a few trees and a couple of shallow ravines, there was nothing to obstruct our view at any of the four locations. This particular morning it was very cloudy and had started to drizzle. We located nine of the bags easily, but we just could not find the tenth one. After searching for more than an hour, we reluctantly gave up the search and returned to Manny's house.

When Manny arrived and heard the story, he immediately started to rant. He never called out any specific name, but each of us heard his threats to blow off the head of the one who stole from him.

"I swear on my momma, I'll shoot you and then I'll gut you if I find out one of you mother fuckers got it."

"Manny, man use your head…how could we have done it? We were all right there together. What probably happened is somebody came by and made off with one of them before we had time to get there because of the flat tire on that piece of crap you left for us to drive," I declared in our defense.

"Jeff, that's probably right, but if I find out that that *somebody* you speak of is actually one of you guys or someone you know and this was a planned rip off, then he better put his head between his legs and kiss his ass goodbye."

Manny was livid when we left and swore that he was going to get to the bottom of it, and by midnight he had called each of us up and threatened to shoot all of us just to get the thief. Then the next morning he called us all again saying that the bag better turn up sometime that day or else. I was pretty scared and I didn't know what to do. I knew that I hadn't done anything underhanded and I was just as sure that Warren and Howie hadn't either. However, I also knew that Manny was one crazy son of a bitch and capable of following through on his threats.

 It was late that afternoon when I rolled myself a big fat joint, turned on the five o'clock news and sat back on the couch to get high. No sooner had I finished smoking the joint, when the teaser for the next news segment suddenly grabbed my attention. There on the screen was some country looking bumpkin, smiling a big yellow toothed smile and holding a very familiar looking heavy duty duffle bag!

"You will not believe what was in this bag that fell out of a walnut tree on this gentleman's property and nearly hit him as he was out driving his tractor. Be sure to stay tuned…we'll tell you all about it…next," said the anchorwoman as they went to commercial.

I nearly jumped out of my skin. I snatched up a tape, popped it in the VCR and hit the record button. Then I watched the next segment, which included the part about the authorities opening up the bag and pouring out the neatly sealed plastic containers of beautiful pure Peruvian Flake right into the rear of a DEA van. Then I dialed Manny's number.

"What an idiot," I said aloud as I waited on him to answer.

"Hello."

"Hey man, it's Jeff. I'm on my way over to your place. Please don't call anybody and threaten to shoot them…just don't move until I get there, okay?"

"Okay man, come on over. What's up anyway? You got my bag, man?"

"I'll be there in ten minutes…you'll see."

When I walked into Manny's place, an Uzi was prominently displayed on the end table and a pistol grip was sticking out from under the sofa.

"Geez Manny, how about putting those damn things away."

Then I walked over to his VCR, popped in the tape and hit the play button.

"What's that Jeff?"

"Just watch."

We both watched and listened as the farmer told his story about how the bag fell out of a tree and about calling the sheriff.

At the end of the segment, I looked sideways at him and said, "Satisfied?"

"Man what a dumb ass that dude is. That stupid motherfucker just gave away a million bucks."

"And you were about ready to shoot us Manny…all of us."

"Man, you're okay Jeff, I knew that you were a smart dude and that I could count on you. I owe you big time. Here, take this with you as my gift of thanks." Manny then handed me two whole kilos to thank me for solving the mystery!

During the drive home, it all felt like a dream.

Yeah that's what it was…a dream. It was a dream, right? Or was it?

What it actually was was a perfect example of one of my many close calls in life. And once again something - luck, fate or whatever you want to call it - had helped me out of yet another jam. I was leading a charmed life, but my long string of good fortune made me oblivious to that fact. I suppose that I felt as though I was entitled to good luck, just as I felt entitled to my athletic and intellectual gifts.

It was in the middle of August when my sister Joan called to tell me that Pop had died after falling down some steps at the back of his house. A flood of memories flashed through my mind, including the death of my father. And again, I wondered about Mel's innuendos that Jack Collins was not my real dad. The funeral was extremely depressing. I couldn't wait to escape and get high. I loved my grandfather, despite the misgivings I had concerning money.

The phone rang as soon as I returned home. It was Jerry McCord's mom telling me that Jerry had been shot in a drug deal that had gone bad. She asked me to be a pallbearer. It was a rough couple of weeks. I had come close to being shot by a crazy coke smuggler and I had lost a grandfather and a friend and gone to their funerals.

I kept dealing weed and coke, gambling, running around with wild women and blowing big chunks of cash. And in spite of wasting huge amounts of money, I was still accumulating more than enough to make me nervous. Thousands of dollars were stashed in various hiding places throughout my house, and I had already opened up several savings accounts at local banks, but I was afraid to put more than twenty-five thousand dollars in any one account. I wanted to avoid attention. Then something happened that would be of significant help in dealing with my peculiar problem of having too much cash.

Arnie Abbott was a real estate agent who worked for the same broker as I did. I had partied with him countless times and had been selling him cocaine for a while. One day we had gone over to look at a forty-four acre piece of land I had listed for sale. Arnie had a client who was interested in purchasing it, so I met him there to give him a tour and a rundown on the property as far as the zoning and so forth. Afterwards, we rode over to my place to smoke a joint and have a drink.

"Hey, do you have any coke?" he asked.

"Arnie...are you serious man?" I replied with a smile from ear to ear.

"Well then go get some and let me turn you on to something my girlfriend showed me. It's called 'freebasing' and Jeff, let me tell you, it is awesome!"

I left the room and came back with several grams of powder.

"Arnie, you're not gonna waste this now, are you?"

"Just wait and see, you're gonna love it."

Now if there is anyone who doesn't know how to turn cocaine into its freebase form and wants to learn the technique, you won't be finding out from me. Cocaine is like a cancer and freebase, or crack as it is currently known, is its wicked stepmother.

Besides, if you're that desperate to discover how to do it, you can always ask someone fresh out of prison, because the vast majority of losers more often than not seem to possess this type of information.

After he cooked up a batch, I put it in a small glass pipe I used to smoke reefer, lit it up and instantly determined that this method was far better than merely snorting the powder up my nose. It gave me such a profound sense of euphoria that I could barely contain myself. I quickly memorized Arnie's recipe to the letter before taking him back to his vehicle. I then rushed back to my house, got an eight ball out of my stash and cooked up my first batch of freebased cocaine. I spent the rest of the afternoon in La-La Land as I sunk into the couch. Realizing that it was nearly time for Mary Anne to get home from work, I hurriedly threw some clothes, toiletries, a couple of ounces of blow and the pipe into a travel bag. I jumped into my car and took off for the Hyatt Hotel downtown. And after blowing off all my appointments scheduled for the next two days, it was just me and my newest flame, freebased cocaine.

Despite my distorted mindset at the time, I quickly found one negative aspect related to my latest obsession. After smoking a bowl of the stuff with an attractive hooker, I discovered to my horror that my *equipment* steadfastly refused to cooperate. This occurred whenever I was under the influence of freebase. Reefer, alcohol, cocaine powder and other drugs never presented such a problem, but this latest habit precluded any activity in the sexual realm. This charming Lady Freebase was a jealous lover! The situation provided me with quite a quandary.

Since I possessed an oversized sex drive, smoking the stuff definitely came at a price, but it made me feel so...different, so singular, so good. It offered an escape. It yielded a sudden, powerful, undeniable feeling of vigor that was itself a duplicitous distortion of reality. I knew that the stuff was really just a chemical reaction. It was simply an excess of neurotransmitters that overloaded my nervous system, but only those foolish enough to have partaken in this fetish of crack cocaine can relate to its potent hold. No woman had ever had the power to control my sex drive, but this drug did. I had to make a decision. Because of freebase cocaine's effect on my love life, I limited the amount I smoked. Even so, I still managed to make time to tangle with my freebase siren a few times each week.

When I told Howie about my chemical discovery a few weeks later, my friend was eager to try it.

"Let's go do some now," he suggested eagerly.

"Nah...we can't, the bitch is home. She doesn't even know I'm in town and I want to keep it that way."

"Then let's go to my apartment."

"Okay, but first let's stop by the head shop. I want to buy a new pipe and some more screens."

We completed our errand to the local drug paraphernalia store and drove to Howie's apartment.

"Uh oh, ain't that Sarah's car?" I asked as we pulled into the parking lot.

"It's okay, she wants to try it, too."

"How do you know that? I thought that you just heard about it from me today."

Howie shrugged his shoulders and said, "Nah man, there's a big article about it in this month's Playboy. Come on in and I'll show you."

As soon as we entered the apartment, I started the cooking process. I couldn't wait to demonstrate my expertise in preparing the concoction and for Howie and Sarah to sample the results of my talent. The entire time it took for me to get everything ready, Sarah was reading the article in Playboy about how addictive and dangerous freebasing was and how it was rapidly becoming an epidemic in America. The article did nothing but to further pique our interest and sense of adventure. We smoked all of the cocaine that I had brought and then sat around laughing at everything for over an hour, even at the blank TV screen. (The set wasn't on.) It then dawned on me that I wanted to be alone with some more dope, so I said goodbye to my vibrating pair of friends and headed home.

People were always stopping by my house at any time of the day or night. Usually they would park in the driveway and then go around the back of the house to see if my car was under the carport. If it wasn't there, they would look in the garage windows to see if I was home. Mary Anne generally left for work around 7:30 AM, so it was possible to wait until she left, go inside and do whatever I needed to do, like pick up more cocaine, and then leave without her ever knowing I had been there or even that I was back in Nashville.

If I could get away with it, I would use the time alone at home to freebase for several hours. The problem was the impromptu visitors that frequently dropped by. Therefore, I decided to conceal my presence from such annoyances. I went into the garage and painted all of the windows black on the inside, so that no one could look in from the outside to see if I was at home. After I had pulled my car inside and shut the garage door, I could suck in as much freebase as my lungs would hold in complete solitude. Problem solved.

My blackened windows and withdrawal from my friends were predictable steps on my downward path, an apt metaphor for a life darkened from within, a stepwise progression orchestrated by a willing protagonist. Anyone watching from outside could see my ruinous future, but I eliminated that possibility by closing myself off to everyone that cared. I had simply moved another step closer to the predictable misery awaiting me. Another step closer to inflicting more pain on others, another step closer to the decades of self-inflicted misery I would earn for myself.

CHAPTER 14
HANNAH

"They had one thing in common, they were good in bed. She'd say, "Faster, faster, the lights are turnin' red."
(The Eagles – Life in the Fast lane)

I had wished for her. I longed for a woman that made my heart skip a beat and not just at the beginning of a relationship when every girl is sexy and exciting. I wanted that same feeling after the hundredth, the thousandth and the ten thousandth time we made love. I loved her even before I knew her.

Howie, Warren and Manny and I had gone to a strip club called The Finest. Manny rented a stretch limo and picked us up to go partying. We had already visited two or three bars earlier and all four of us were drunk, stoned and coked up. As we were walking up to the door, I spotted her getting out of the car. She was absolutely the sexiest woman I had ever seen in my life. There was something about her that acted like a "Jeff magnet." I was drawn to her like a man dying of thirst would be drawn to a clear mountain stream.

I continued to stare as she walked toward O'Malley's, the restaurant across the street.

"Hey Jeff...Come on man," said Manny, breaking the spell, but only for a nanosecond.

"You guys go ahead. I'll be there in a minute," I replied, returning my gaze to the goddess walking into the building.

I waited for a few minutes and then crossed the street to the restaurant and went inside. There she was behind the bar, beginning her shift as the bartender. I was drunk, and not being the bashful type regardless of my mental state, I walked up to her, ordered a Crown and water and said the first thing that popped into my head.

"My name is Jeff Holden Collins. I saw you from across the street and I felt an irresistible urge to meet you..."

"Yeah I saw you staring at me when you and those guys got out of that limo."

"By the way, what's your name?"

"Hannah."

"You've got a beautiful voice Hannah."

"You're laying it on a little thick aren't you honey?"

"Look, I've seen and been with women from all over the world, and this is the first time that I've experienced an epiphany from merely looking at a beautiful girl."

"Well, aren't you the sweetest thing. Here's your drink. So what happened to your friends?"

"Over in the strip joint I suppose."

"Oh I see...and you're over here talking to me," she said as she flashed the sexiest smile I'd ever seen.

"Hannah, I'm certain that you have a boyfriend and probably another dozen men that want to be...but...how about meeting me for a drink later on tonight?"

"No."

"No?"

"Yes. No I don't have a boyfriend and yes, I think I will meet you for a drink. I'm only working a four hour shift tonight, so I'll be out of here by midnight. Where will you be?"

"Do you know where the Gold Mine is?"

"Yeah... I can probably make it there by around 12:30. Okay?"

"Great...I'll be there waiting for you, Hannah."

I sat there for the better part of an hour, nursing my drink while staring at her and talking with her as much as possible. The place was getting pretty busy so I downed my drink, said goodbye and walked back across the street. I went inside and saw Manny, Howie and Warren stuffing dollar bills in the thongs of assorted strippers and having a great time. After sitting there for over an hour, I realized that I was only thinking about Hannah and not even paying attention to any of the half naked women in front of me. Therefore, I somehow forced my drunken crew members to tear themselves away from the strippers. They weren't anywhere near ready to leave yet, but I demanded that they take me back to my car. Grumbling and cursing at me, they reluctantly left with me and took me back to my car. I then immediately sped off to the Gold Mine to wait on Hannah. She never showed. I waited until 1:45 AM and fended off several coke whores, hoping that my fantasy girl would walk through the door any second. I finally gave up in disgust and drove home, where I quietly and reluctantly crawled into bed with the refrigerator I called Mary Anne.

When I woke up the following morning, my first thought was of Hannah.

"Screw her...I'll bet that's not even her real name," I said to myself.

I just couldn't get her out of my head. But I decided that I could and would forget about her in no time, with a little help from some new friends. I grabbed a few things along with a big bag of coke and drove to the Opryland Hotel and got a room. For the next two days I called up escort services and partied with call girls. I had to keep hitting the local ATMs for cash, because I didn't want such charges appearing on my credit card statements. The second night I didn't sleep at all and when I went to the nearest ATM at 4:30 in the morning for another withdrawal, I was denied further funds. I had drained over three grand from my checking account in less than forty-eight hours!

"Damn it, the check for my mortgage is gonna bounce unless I get to the bank fast," I said aloud as the sun began to peek up over the horizon.

I checked out of the hotel and sped home. I took five thousand dollars from one of my more ingenious hiding places, one that Mary Anne hadn't found and pilfered from. It was only a few minutes past seven, so I grabbed a quick shower to kill some time before the bank opened. Next I rolled a couple of joints and drove to the bank. It was about fifteen minutes before the bank was supposed to open, so I decided to wait in the parking lot. Right at the exact second that I took the first hit off of a joint, one of the tellers pulled up next to me and honked her horn. It was Jami, the pretty redhead who worked the drive thru window. She got out of her car and walked over to my open passenger window. We had been sort of flirting back and forth for months and each time I pulled into her lane, her eyes and her comments became more enticing. Initially she came off as too prim and proper for my taste, so I just chalked it up to some innocent flirtation.

"Good morning Jeff, What are you doing…been on an all-nighter?" she sang as she smiled at me through the window.

"Yeah, but it feels like an all-weeker," I laughed.

"And it looks as though you're still going," she said, staring at the doobie in my hand.

"Yeah…well, hey Jami could you do me a big favor? Would you take this cash and put it in my checking account? I lost a lot of money…ah…playing poker last night and I had to really crank on the ATM, and I need to get it deposited fast to cover some checks that are already in the mail."

"Well, I'd be glad to do it for you Jeff…under one condition."

"And what's that?"

"That you come back about noon and take me to lunch," she cooed.

"Okay, that's a deal…but you'll have to call and wake me up about 11 o'clock. I need to go home and get some sleep. My number's…"

"It's on the deposit slip Jeff."

"Okay then. I suppose I'll talk to you later."

So I went home and fell asleep. It seemed like I had just dozed off when the phone woke me.

"Hello."

"Hey Jeff, are you awake?"

"Jami?"

"Yeah, it's me...are you coming?"

"Yeah... ah, I'll be there...noon, right?"

"Yes, noon. Okay then, I'll see you in an hour." I picked her up in front of the bank.

God, she's absolutely beautiful.

We went to a barbeque place near the bank. As soon as we had taken our seats, a lady approached our booth.

"Honey, I just had to come over to tell you that you have the prettiest head of hair I have ever seen in my life."

Jami looked up with a warm smile and said, "Why thank you!"

She shucked off the compliment like it was a little salt on the table in front of her.

She seemed so unassuming and down to earth.

"So listen mister big partier, I got your deposit done...and here is your receipt."

"Thanks, I really appreciate it."

"Oh that's okay, you can make it up to me when you take me out this weekend."

"Jami...you see the thing is...I'm kind of living with someone right now and...it's not working out very well lately, but she's still there so..."

"It doesn't sound like you're very happy, and if you want to get to know me...I don't care."

"Well, okay then. Let's do it."

She wrote down her number on a napkin and slid it over to me.

"Here's my home number...or you can reach me at the bank. Now I need to tell you that I have a little boy. I'm a single mom. His name is Johnny and he's four years old. Is that a problem for you?"

"Oh no, not at all. I love kids."

We ate and I took her back to work and agreed to take her out Friday night.

"Thanks for lunch. I guess I'll see you Friday," she said.

"Okay, I'll give you a call, Hey Jami, what's your last name?"

"Martin...Jami Martin...bye," she said as she turned and walked toward the bank. But she didn't even make it to the door before my mind turned to thoughts of Hannah.

The next day I lied to Mary Anne. I told her I had to go to Atlanta for a few days. I packed and drove to a local hotel. That night I went back to O'Malley's and there she was, pouring drinks and oozing sex appeal.

"Hey, what happened to you the other night?"

"I am so sorry...a friend of mine called with a minor emergency and I had to go help...sorry," she nearly sang as she cut her stunning eyes at me.

It was the same look that had been haunting me for the past three days.

"That's okay. Would you like to meet me tonight?"

"I can't tonight. I simply have to get some rest. But I'm off tomorrow and I'll meet you whenever you want tomorrow night...okay?"

"Okay, I'll be at the Gold Mine...about eight?"

"I'll be there, I promise."

I walked into the bar at 7:50 PM the following night, thinking that she would probably stand me up again.

A girl like that isn't going to be...

My thought was interrupted by the vision of her. She wore a blue blouse and a black skirt and looked incredible as she sat gracefully on a stool at the bar. As soon as she spotted me, she flashed a big smile and waved me over.

"Hey Hannah, you made it."

"I told you I would."

"Great, wanna go get crazy?"

"Sure."

We got into my car and rode all over the city smoking dope, snorting cocaine, laughing and talking. We hit many of the waterholes I frequented. She was amazing. I found out that her name really was Hannah, Hannah Jane Preston, and that she was twenty-three, which was eleven years younger than me, not that I cared.

"Well Hannah, it's midnight, what do you want to do?"

"I don't care, whatever you want."

"What I'd like to do is take you somewhere and make love to you until the sun comes up," I said with a smile.

"Talk is cheap boy, I'm from Missouri, show me."

I gunned the engine and steered my car in the most direct route to my hotel. When we got into the room and shut the door, I was more anxious for this sexual experience than ever before. I was literally quivering with anticipation of what was about to take place.

We stood by the bed kissing for several minutes and then she undid my belt, unzipped my pants and let them fall to my feet. I slipped off my shoes, stepped out of my pants and slowly undressed her. She was wearing neither a bra nor panties and in no time she stood before me with nothing on but black high heels. She was 5' 9" with shoulder length light brown hair and her blue eyes were deep enough to dive into. Every part of her beautiful and athletic body fit perfectly with each connecting part, and the cumulative effect rendered her ravishing. She was so dazzling that I stood awestruck for a moment with my mouth agape.

As I stood mere inches from her and looked into her eyes, the experience brought to my mind the somewhat peculiar impression of a flawless and succulent peach that had just ripened to perfection and was begging for me to take a bite.

"Well lover, are you going to finish getting undressed or are you just going to stand there and stare at me," she said with a sexy smirk of a smile.

I practically tore off my shirt, peeled off my socks and slid my shorts down to the floor and stepped even closer, pressing my body to hers as we embraced. We kissed for what seemed like a very long time, but paradoxically felt like an instant. We made love...it was tender, it was rough, it was slow and it was fast. It was beyond the descriptive power of a Shakespearean play. It was frenetic, wild and intense. It was passionate and sweet, and for me, it was addictive.

If we are fortunate enough, we humans occasionally come to a point during our brief stay on this physical plane, when we literally sense that we have encountered an extraordinary opportunity for something truly incredible. For me, meeting Hannah was an occasion that propelled me to another plane. It was one of the rare times in my life that I glimpsed the potential for a literal transformative experience. Many people who knew me felt that my best chance for such a treasure was my marriage to Julie. But it wasn't. For me, Hannah was much more than Julie could be, more than any woman before or after her. It was as if the actual essence of her had been hardwired into my soul before either of us had been born, and maybe, just maybe she was a woman who I could fall completely in love with, totally and completely.

We stayed in bed all night. We were both completely worn out as we relaxed in each other's arms until we drifted off to sleep. When the morning sun began streaming through the window, I awoke to being tenderly aroused by her soft and tender touch. The chemistry was electrifying, like soul mates who had searched for several lifetimes and had finally completed their quest at reunification. I felt as though I was in far over my head, but I was already too captivated by her to think about it. At that moment, I didn't want cocaine or reefer. I didn't want another woman. I just wanted her.

The noted novelist and playwright W. Somerset Maugham once wrote that no man wants to be with a woman for longer than five years, or words to that effect. For me, Hannah rendered that theory quite inane.

I hated for the experience to end, but Hannah needed to get back to her car and I had a couple of appointments I needed to keep, so we showered, dressed and left arm and arm. When we pulled along side her car, she leaned over and kissed me passionately until the morning traffic honked for us to move out of the way.

"Can I see you again tonight?" I asked.

"You better! Call me later today, okay?"

"Wait! I don't know your number."

"It's in the book under Don Preston, on Morning Glory Drive."

"Is he your husband?" I gulped.

""No silly, he's my father. Call me…bye."

I drove off in a daze. My head was spinning. For the rest of that day and for the rest of my life, I would never be able to get her out of my mind. Not that I wanted to. Well actually, there would be times when I tried to stop seeing her, even thinking of her, but my love and my physical desire for her would never permit it.

For the next two weeks we spent nearly every night together. I would stop by my house to get some clothes, make a few calls, do a couple of dope deals, even sell or list a property. Then I would tell Mary Anne another lie about having to travel to Knoxville, New Orleans or to Timbuktu…I didn't care. I didn't even care if the story sounded implausible, and I didn't care whether or not she believed it. Then it was back to the hotel where I would call Hannah. I took her everywhere, to lunch, to dinner and to meet my friends. We went for walks in the park, skiing, swimming and to see movies. She was far and away the greatest lover I had ever encountered, yet she was so much more. I loved the way she walked, I was entranced by her voice, and I loved the way she squeezed and held tightly onto my arm when we were together. Her laugh, her sense of humor, even her natural aroma, they were all intoxicating. She was pretty, athletic and bright. She was the song that I couldn't get out of my head, and never wanted to. I met her father, Don Preston, and her sister Corinne and felt instantly close to them. There was so much of Hannah in them that there was no way I could not like them.

Those glorious weeks zoomed by quickly as Mary Anne grew increasingly suspicious. One Thursday night when Hannah was working late and I was in desperate need of some sleep, I decided to go home to get some rest for a change. I hadn't had sex with Mary Anne since meeting Hannah and I didn't plan on it that night - or ever again. I came in, greeted my live-in human icicle and went upstairs to shower. After drying off, I walked back to the bedroom and opened the door to a surprising sight. Mary Anne had lit a couple of scented candles in the dimly lit bedroom and was lying on the bed in a very skimpy and very sheer teddy. She was propped up on several pillows and appeared to be under the influence of barbiturates and alcohol.

""Hey baby, come on over here and let me please my man," she slurred.

I have to admit that she looked pretty good, but compared to Hannah, she just wasn't very tempting. She had grown so bitchy, distant and sullen in the past year. And while a portion of her moodiness was certainly caused by my behavior, I believe she came by most of it naturally. We had been living together for over six years and sex with her had become emotionless and boring. I just didn't want to make love to her anymore. That ship had sailed.

"Mary Anne, I just want to go to sleep. I'm beat, maybe tomorrow night..." I said, ironically invoking one of her common refrains from long ago. She had used it often in the past when I had attempted to initiate lovemaking.

"What's wrong, your little sluts wearing you out?" she stuttered.

"Yeah, that's it Mary Anne. My little sluts...all my little sluts are wearing me out. Listen here you pill-popping popsicle of a coke whore. Remember all those hundreds of times I wanted to make love to you, but you almost always had an excuse...remember? 'I have a headache...my back hurts...I'm tired...I have a blister.' Do you remember all those lame-ass excuses Mary Anne? Well it's my turn tonight, but I don't have an excuse. I don't need an excuse. I have a reason, a good one. It's because I DON'T FUCKING WANT TO!"

And with that said I turned and slammed the door and stomped off into the guest bedroom, locked the door behind me and collapsed into the waterbed.

I woke up Friday morning and realized I needed to stop by the bank and make a deposit on the way to an appointment for a client's house closing. I was already in the drive through lane when the thought of the long forgotten date with Jami popped in my mind. Other cars had already pulled in behind me, so there was no escape.

"Oh crap," I said as I pulled in front of the tube delivery and she cut her eyes at me.

"May I help you?" she said rather frostily.

"Hey, I'm sorry about two weeks ago. I had to go out of town on kind of an emergency...and I lost your number. "I'm really sorry. Here's a make up present for you."

I took a big fat joint, stuck it in my deposit envelope and sent it through the tube to her window. She opened the envelope and gave me a big smile. Then she wrote down her number and stuck it back in the tube along with my deposit receipt.

"Thank you, but this doesn't make up for standing me up. So you better call me!" "I will, I promise," I said as I drove off with a sigh of relief.

That evening I left and didn't even bother to make up a lie about going out of town. I packed a bag and left Mary Anne sitting in the den with a Frisbee full of pot, a couple of grams of cocaine on a mirror and about seven Valiums on the coffee table. She also had access to a small refrigerator filled with beer and wine coolers.

"Have a good weekend Mary Anne. That should be enough booze and dope for you, at least for tonight."

"Fuck you, you bastard."

"Later...and don't wait up."

Then I drove over to Hannah's. I had told her that I was living with someone after our first night together. She responded with something like, "Well that bitch has got to go," to which I laughed and nodded in complete agreement.

We sat on her father's front steps and I told her what had happened with Mary Anne the night before.

She looked into my eyes and asked, "Jeff, are you screwing that psycho?"

"Hannah, I have not so much as touched her since long before I met you. I swear to God."

She didn't seem to believe me, but I was telling her the truth. Of all the women in my life, those before her and those after her, she was the only one I would even come close to remaining faithful to. As long as I had her as a choice, there were simply no other options I seriously considered.

We went to the downtown Hyatt and stayed Friday and Saturday night. During the day we went to movies, to a friend's house and to the park. We had more sex than I thought possible. We once made love twelve times in twenty four hours! When I told one of my friends about it, he laughed and said that it was outside the realm of possible human achievement. I merely smiled. And as for freebasing, it was out of the question. There was no way that I was willing to pass up a chance to make love to her. Weed, powder, and liquor did nothing to impede my libido, so they were acceptable. But freebasing? No way, at least not when she was around.

Sunday afternoon we checked out of the hotel and went to a restaurant for a late lunch. I went to the payphone to check my messages.

"If Mary Anne's still there, tell the bitch I said to pack her things," laughed Hannah.

I dialed my number and the phone rang a couple of times before Mary Anne picked up the receiver.

"Hello."

"Uh Mary Anne, it's me. I called to get my messages. Has anyone called for me?"

"Jeff, I'm leaving. I'm going to take some things today and move in with my sister. I'll come back for the rest of it later this week if that's okay."

"Sure...okay," I said, trying very hard not to sound too happy about it, even as I felt waves of elation ripple through my entire being.

"If you want to talk about this or need me for anything, I'm leaving my sister's number here on your desk by the phone."

"Okay."

"Jeff I want you to know that I still love you."

I didn't know what to say, so I didn't say anything.

"Goodbye Jeff."

I hung up and returned to the table.

"Well, I didn't get my messages, but Mary Anne's moving out," I said as coolly as possible.

"Great, let's go to your house. After we change the sheets, I'm going to screw your brains out mister."

"Promises, promises...show me. I'm from Missouri too," I said smiling as we walked out together.

We had already had sex in nearly every room in her father's house, plus a wild escapade on the stairs. We had sex one night in front of the Gold Mine in my small sports car and more than once in broad daylight in a public park. And during the next week we christened every room of my house. We did it at night in the hammock in the backyard, on the deck and one night even right in the grass! She was insatiable and I was ravenous. If the Olympics had a fornication category, we could have easily medaled. I was so happy and content with her as my girl. Never before had I been so consciously grateful for anything. A few days later things began to look less rosy.

She was supposed to come to my house the following Tuesday night, but she never showed. I called her father and her sister. They hadn't heard from her. I stopped by O'Malley's, and was told that she hadn't been to work for the past two days. I tried to find her for two more days and nights and just as I was about to give up, she showed up at my house. I asked her where she'd been, but she just said that she had been on a binge and not to worry about it. When I pressed her for details, she became defensive and said that it was none of my business.

"Hannah, don't you know that I love you, you silly girl and that I want everything about you to be my business? You haven't been fooling around on me have you?"

"No I haven't but, let me tell you right up front that I don't like it when a guy gets possessive and starts checking up on me. You just need to trust me"

"Okay, okay...I apologize. And I do trust you," I said, trying very hard to stifle my jealous nature.

We made up with a night of hot and passionate lovemaking. But the nagging suspicion that she had been with another guy never left my mind. I began suspecting her of infidelity more and more and I began accusing her of it more often as well.

Two weeks later, she disappeared again. I was irritated, but I didn't want to make too big a deal out of it. She showed up at my house around two-thirty in the morning after being MIA for nearly two days. After my usual accusations and her ensuing denials, we made love until we passed out.

I suspected that her job as a bartender at O'Malley's had something to do with her disappearances, so the very next morning I asked her to quit...for me. To my surprise, she willingly agreed.

"I've got another job offer anyway at a tanning salon. The hours are better for me and I want to go back to school anyway."

"That's great Hannah!"

Then I snatched her up, took her into the bedroom and made wild passionate love to her. I was sprung like a worn out pogo stick!

Unfortunately my jealousy and her disappearing acts didn't stop with her job change. The next time Hannah took off, it was for almost an entire week. I was fuming about it on a Friday afternoon around three o'clock when I still had not heard from her. Not surprisingly, I failed to recognize that my insane jealousy was more than likely the major cause.

"Man, the hell with this. I'm not going to sit around waiting on her to call," I said as I picked up the phone and dialed the number to the bank.

"First American Bank, this is Jami, may I help you?"

"Hello Jami, this is Jeff. I know that it's Friday and you're probably busy. Do you have time to talk?"

"I've got a few minutes. What's on your mind Jeff?"

"I know that it's short notice, but I was wondering if we could get together tonight."

"Ooh, I just made plans with a couple of girlfriends. We're going to Major Wallaby's to eat and then to Bennigan's for drinks. We should be there around ten o'clock. Why don't you meet us there?"

"Okay, I'll try my best to make it."

That'll show Hannah.

I took a long hot shower around eight o'clock, shaved, dressed and headed downstairs to the garage. I opened my car door, slid in behind the wheel and started the engine. I punched the garage door opener and when the door opened enough, I put the car in drive and started out of the garage. I almost hit Hannah as she suddenly appeared right in front of me. I slammed on the brakes, cut off the motor and got out. "Well, it's awfully nice of you to show up. And thanks a lot for calling, too." "Please don't be mean to me," she said in a little girl's voice.

"Hannah, I know that you've been fooling around on me. I'm really tired of all this shit."

""Jeff you're wrong. I'm sorry that I haven't called baby. But I'll make it up to you…let's go inside."

We did. I turned the answering machine on to catch any calls. Then we ordered a pizza, watched a movie on cable and then made love for hours.

Hannah suddenly departed from my life again just weeks later. I had grown weary of the game, but at the same time I was crazy about her. All she had to do to make me get over my frustration and jealousy was to show up at my door. I only wish that I had known at that time that Hannah's disappearances had more to do with the drug abuse, jealousy and instability in my life than anything going on in hers.

The next time she left, it was about two days into her absence when I experienced a vivid, erotic dream about the two of us together. This dream preceded countless other sexual dreams of her that recurred throughout my life, but this particular one was quickly etched into my memory and remained there. She came to me in a vision and half sang and half spoke in a melodious voice. We were making love when she suddenly stopped and told me to listen carefully to her. I awoke drenched in sweat, found a pencil and wrote down the words as best I could remember:

Let restlessness befall you

Be sleepless with thoughts of me, only me

Desiring me, only me

Possessed by me, only me

Obsessed by me, only me

Now I control you

Your thoughts

Your breath

Your body

Your heart

Your heart is mine

Your soul is mine

It was true. I belonged to her, body and soul. My love for her was deeper than words could possibly express.

Far too often passion doesn't feed on contentment, but rather on complications. I was becoming more distrustful each time Hannah withdrew from my realm. For me, this automatically led to jealousy, which further fueled my predilection for violence. These issues added to my ever-increasing passion for her. It was a love that was becoming pathologic, unhealthy and dangerous.

Now Hannah attracted men like bees to sugar. This was never more obvious to me than whenever we were in a club or restaurant. In my mind every guy in the vicinity coveted my woman and sometimes very openly. At first I merely smiled and laughed it off. But as time went on, I suspected that she often egged them on unmercifully. Hannah's beautiful blue eyes could instantly express whatever emotion she wanted to convey. In my opinion, she was too flirtatious and even more so when she was with me. One night at the local Bennigan's we were sitting at the bar. I noticed three guys next to us overtly ogling her. I had all I could take when the guy closest to us leaned over and whispered something to her.

"Hey dude, if you have something to say to my girlfriend, it might be wise to say it out loud and if I were you, I'd say it in a respectful tone."

"Oh yeah? Well I was just telling her how nice her ass was. That's all."

"Jeff, please don't start anything in here. He's obviously

drunk." I then stood up and stepped between Hannah and

the guy.

"I tell you what pal. Why don't you just say one more out of the way thing to her and see what happens."

"Is that so?" he said as he looked first at Hannah and then back at me.

I imagined that Hannah gave him another sexy look, then offered the same look to his two friends and finally she looked back at me.

"Try me," I said calmly.

"Well then, hey baby, how about going out to my car with me and seeing how much of this you can handle..."

"Wham!"

I unloaded a cocked right fist to his jaw, which dropped the smart-ass like a sack of flour. And as the jerk was falling, I hit him with another straight right to his nose. He was out cold. I turned to the other two.

"Either one of you got anything to say to her?"

"No, no...that was between you and Freddy. We're not involved man," one of them said as the other one quickly nodded in agreement.

"Well be sure to tell Freddy that he should learn how to hold his liquor better and how to speak to a lady, especially one with a date."

With that said I then pulled Hannah towards me, threw her up over my shoulder in a fireman's carry and carried her out of the place. I carried her all the way to my car before I gently set her back on her feet and opened her door.

"You are such a redneck...I don't know why I'm so crazy about you," she said as she wrapped her arms around my neck and kissed me.

"Me either…get in and let's go…you know, you're gonna get me in a lot of trouble one day."

We went back to my house and once again made love until we went to sleep in each other's arms.

The next morning I woke up to the sounds of Hannah yelling something from the bathroom. I immediately jumped out of bed and ran to the door.

"What is it baby? What's wrong?"

"Look at that crazy bitch!"

I stepped over to the bathroom window and looked out. Hannah's car was parked down in the driveway, and Mary Anne had her door open and appeared to be going through her car. I jerked open the window.

"Hey Mary Anne, what the hell do you think you're doing?"

Upon hearing her name, she stepped back from Hannah's car holding a pair of Hannah's pants up in one hand and a pair of her barber scissors in the other. Then she starting cutting them up!

Hannah pushed me aside and yelled, "Hey you crazy bitch! I'm gonna come down there and kick your ass, you stupid bitch!"

"Oh no you're not. She's got a pair of scissors. Let me handle this," I said as I stepped in her way to block her from leaving the bathroom.

Then I dashed downstairs but just as I got there, Mary Anne jumped into her car, locked the door and peeled out of the driveway. Hannah was right on my heels and was already examining the inside of her car when I turned around.

"Jeff, she cut up my clothes and ripped up my textbooks…this is all your fault."

"How the hell do you figure that, Hannah?"

"Because you stopped me from kicking that bitch's ass!"

"Hannah, she'd already done it and she was pulling off before I could get down here. Come on now, be reasonable honey."

"Fuck you. I'm leaving. I'm not taking this shit."

With that said, she got into her car and left me standing alone and extremely puzzled in my driveway.

About ten minutes later the phone rang. It was Hannah calling from a phone booth a mile away.

"Jeff, your psychotic girlfriend just tried to run me off the road," she cried into the phone.

"Is she still there?" I asked with a great deal of concern.

"No, she just took off."

"Stay right there, I'm on my way. We'll call the police and…"

"No, I'm not calling the police, Jeff. Just leave me alone and don't call me anymore."

"But Hannah, I…"

The phone went dead. She had hung up.

That afternoon I dialed her number and she answered on the first ring.

"Hello."

"Hannah, it's me, will you please talk to me about this?"

"Yeah, I'm sorry. I was just so upset. It's okay sweetheart."

"Okay then…great. Let's go somewhere to eat tonight and maybe to a movie. Okay?"

"I can't tonight Jeff. I have to go to Greenbrier for a job interview. Let's do it tomorrow."

"Well, okay. Are you telling me the truth?"

"Yes honey. Everything's fine. Call me in the morning at the tanning salon."

"Alright baby. I guess that I'll see you tomorrow then."

"I love you Jeff. Bye."

I didn't see her for three more days, when she rang my doorbell at 1:30 in the morning. I was livid at her latest absence, but relieved to see her. I opened the door and just held her in my arms for a while.

"You don't have anybody here with you do you baby?"

"No Hannah, there's no one here but you and me," I said softly.

We went back to my bed and undressed. I began making love to her with even more than the normal amount of zeal. I was on top of her and looking down at her with a worshipful look on my face. Then Hannah uttered one of the most enigmatic statements I had ever heard.

"You're gonna get me pregnant boy," she said with her sexy smile and gave me that look only she could give with those eyes - those wonderful, erotic, beautiful blue eyes.

"Hannah Jane, you are something else, and I love you more than anything," I said as I collapsed onto her.

A few nights later I was supposed to pick her up at the tanning salon. I pulled up in front and turned off the ignition. I saw her in the window and waved. She motioned for me to come inside.

"Are you ready?" I asked upon entering.

"Shh, there's no one here…I want you to see something…follow me."

"Well if there's no one here, why do I have to be quiet?"

"Because, I'm supposed to be locking up and leaving. So be quiet," she said with a sly smile.

She took me by the hand and led me into a large tanning room with a soft thick mat on the floor. She then began to undress. The room was dark except for the soft bluish glow of the light emanating from the tanning bed. She looked incredible.

"Let's go mister...I want you NOW!"

Who was I to disagree? She was awesome. And even though I was constantly suspecting her of fooling around on me, I was nuts about her. Except for disappearing for days at a time, she was the perfect soul mate for me. We made love right there on the floor and when we finished, she kissed me for a very long time.

"Jeff, I love you so much. I'll love you forever."

"You're unbelievable Hannah and I love you too."

We dressed and left in my car. She wanted to stop at her father's house for something so we headed that way. When we pulled in the driveway she turned to me with a very serious look.

"Jeff, there's something that I need to tell you."

"What is it baby?"

"You're gonna get mad at me."

"Why Hannah, what did you do?"

"Do you remember that night when I went to Greenbrier for a job interview?"

"Yeah...so?"

"Please don't be mad at me..."

"What did you do Hannah? Just tell me."

"Well that's not where I went," she said as she began to cry.

"Tell me," I said as my voice became louder.

"Don't be mean to me," she said in her little girl's voice.

"Tell me Hannah, please."

"I went to a motel with this guy I met. You're constantly accusing me of fooling around...and...I just couldn't stand it any more. And after that nut job Mary Anne cut up my clothes and tried to run me off the road that day, I just..."

"Are you telling me that you screwed some other guy Hannah?"

"Oh Jeff, I'm so sorry. I love you so much. And I promise that it'll never happen again, I promise baby," she cried.

I simply couldn't stop myself. My left hand bolted out and delivered an openhanded slap on her left cheek.

"You whore! Get out! And don't ever call me. I'm sick of your act. I mean it. Now get the fuck out!"

Bawling uncontrollably, she got out of the car.

"Jeff, please, can we just talk about it? Please, I love you. I'm sorry…"

"Go call that guy you went to the motel with and talk to him. We are through. Get fucked. I never want to see you again…EVER!

I reached over and slammed the passenger door, started my car and peeled off down the street, not even bothering to wipe away the tears streaming down my face. I was crushed. Despite my genuine emotions, the hypocrisy of my actions and judgments remained totally alien to me. The windows to my center of logic and reason were blackened from the inside, just like the ones in my garage.

CHAPTER 15
JAMI

Behold the maiden with the long, beautiful hair.

With Hannah, I experienced the highest of highs and the lowest of lows. She gave me my greatest joy and her disappearing acts and infidelity inflicted me with my worst heartache. It had been an entire week since I had hit her, cussed her out and drove off leaving her sobbing in her driveway. I had hoped that she would call me, or better still, ring my doorbell in the middle of the night, but I hadn't heard a thing. I desperately wanted to call her, but my pride wouldn't allow it.

In a pathetic attempt to get her out of my mind, I started partying like a college kid in Daytona Beach on spring break. While I was throwing back several cocktails at a nightclub called Chevy's, I ran into a very attractive blonde I had known for years. Her name was Bikina Vandelay. She was an aspiring part-time model/singer/songwriter from Brisbane, Australia. Bikina stood 5' 11" with light blonde hair and bright green eyes. She was a statuesque traffic stopper. We had gotten drunk and high together and had sex on numerous occasions. I liked her a lot and she was undeniably beautiful, but for some unknown reason, I wasn't that sexually attracted to her. There was no *wow factor* for me.

We remained friends and continued to be sporadic lovers, especially when we ran into each other when we were both alone and drunk. Today's generation would call it "friends with benefits." We both understood that our relationship was primarily a platonic one. Bikina was between relationships too, so our pseudo agreement worked out well.

One Friday night, Howie and I were drinking Crown Royal, doing lines of coke and smoking reefer in my den, when Bikina walked in through the sliding glass door that led to the patio at the rear of the house.

"Hey guys…whacha doing?"

"Hey B, come on in and have a drink."

"Okay, but just for a little while. I need to go somewhere and unwind…I want to boogie tonight baby!"

"Howie and I are going to hit Chevy's in about an hour…why don't you go with us? We can all fit into Howie's truck, if you sit on my lap," I said with a good-natured smile. "Okay boys. I guess I'm with you guys tonight, you lucky dogs."

"Wouldn't that be lucky dingoes?" laughed Howie.

After ingesting sufficient amounts of drugs and alcohol to render us quite merry, we drove down to the nightspot, where I paid the cover charge for the three of us. Bikina wanted to dance, so she and Howie went to the dance floor while I headed for the bar to order drinks. While I was attempting to get the bartender's attention, someone came up behind me and covered my eyes with their hands.

"Guess who," sang a familiar female voice.

"Man, I hope it's a naked Sharon Stone!" I laughed.

"Close, very close," she said.

I turned around and looked into Jami's beautiful face.

"Hey Jeff, want to make another date with me and then blow me off again and again?"

She had been drinking…a lot. She poked me in the chest only somewhat playfully.

"Hey Jami. Hey listen, I'm sorry and I apologize. I had…let's say an ongoing problem during that time, which has recently been resolved."

"Four times Jeff! You stood me up four times!"

"Four times?"

"Four…one – two – three – four…FOUR TIMES MISTER!"

"Again…I apologize for all four of them. What more can I say?"

"Hmmm…well…there is one way you can make it up to me," she said in a suggestive tone as she leaned closer to me.

I was quite buzzed, but still acutely aware of how extraordinarily pretty she was. I was thinking how her brilliant green eyes accented her beautiful hair, hair that was the color of red flames. Jami was about 5' 6", which was a bit short for my taste, my preference being 5' 9" - the ideal height for a woman in my opinion…the perfect height…Hannah's height.

Damn it…why can't I get her out of my head?

"Hello…planet earth to Jeff!"

"Oh sorry…I was awestruck by your incredible beauty, madam," I said as I bowed, took her hand and gave it a kiss.

"You're full of it Jeff," she said, pulling her hand away.

Then I added, "Okay then…seriously, what may I do to please you and atone for my multiple transgressions?"

She became very serious and looked directly into my eyes.

"If you're really serious, you can come to my little boy's birthday party at Chucky Cheese this Saturday afternoon at 2:30…the one a mile down the road from the bank on the way to the mall."

"Right, and that'll make up for all four times?"

"That's what I said. Just give up your Saturday afternoon for me. But...and I mean this with all my heart...THIS IS YOUR LAST CHANCE WITH ME BUDDY!"

"Okay, okay, I'll be there. I promise."

"I don't want your promise. I want you to be there, okay," she said in a soft voice as she looked up at me and smiled.

"I'll be there, come hell or high water"

Howie and Bikina suddenly appeared from the crowd of people all around us. They were sweating after having danced for four or five songs. I handed drinks to them and Bikina leaned in and kissed me on the cheek. Jami cut her eyes at Bikina and then back at me, apparently trying to figure out if there was something going on between us. I introduced everyone and then Howie asked Jami to dance with him. As they headed off to the dance floor, Bikina nestled up close to me.

"Is that my competition?" she teased.

"No, she's a teller at First National where I bank. We've been flirting with one another for months. We went out to lunch one day, but that's it. I mean with Hannah and everything...but she's so pretty. I can't figure out why a girl that hot would chase after any guy. Man she's hot, don't you think so Bikina?"

"What am I, chopped liver," she said as she gave me a punch in the side.

"You know what I mean Bikina. Anyway, I have a date with her this Saturday. A date with her and her four year old son Johnny," I laughed, all the while wondering about Hannah, where she was, who she was with and if she was thinking about me.

As the following Saturday rolled around, I had every intention of going to the birthday party at Chucky Cheese's. I hadn't heard from Hannah. I'd driven by her house a few times, saw her car there and kept going. I missed her terribly, but figured that it would be better, no matter how difficult, if I just stayed away from her. It was a little before one o'clock in the afternoon so I still had plenty of time to get ready.

It had already been an excellent Saturday. First I woke up and looked over at the gorgeous 26-year-old Bikina lying in bed next to me, which caused me to recall the activity we were engaged in only a few hours earlier. Later that morning, I listed a very nice house in an exclusive area of town and received an offer on another one of my listings.

I had stopped off at the supermarket and bought a ton of groceries, including a load of steaks, shrimp and beer for any potential party in the near future. On top of that I made three dope deals that netted a tidy profit of three grand, not bad for a half day's work. I was relaxing with a big fat doobie when Bikina came bouncing down the stairs.

"Good morning, I mean good afternoon beautiful. I was beginning to wonder if you were in a coma."

"Hey lover, I'm taking off. Hey give me a hit of that."

"Okay B. I guess I'll see you later," I said as I handed her the joint.

"Are you gonna tell your new little redhead what we did last night?" she teased.

"You know it. In fact that's probably all we'll talk about," I laughed.

"Jeff, are you really going to her little boy's birthday party?"

"I can't think of a reason why not, can you?"

"Yes I can. Any fool can plainly see that gal is already crazy about you, and she seems like such a nice person. And I'm sure you're going to break her heart, especially when Hannah pops back into the picture."

"Now, how can you say such a thing Bikina?"

"From my own personal experience with you lover," she said as she bent down, kissed me on the lips and walked out the door.

I watched her ass as her hips traveled out of sight. My attention to her backside was interrupted by the gloom of an extremely dark afternoon sky. A huge storm appeared imminent and it caused the sky to appear as though it was seven o'clock at night.

I took an extra-long shower, standing in the pulsating stream of water and letting it massage my shoulders, all the while hopelessly trying not to think of making love to Hannah in the same shower. Disgusted with my failure to keep her out of my thoughts, I turned off the water and looked at my watch. It read 2:17 PM.

"I need to step it up a little, don't want to be late for Chucky," I said out loud with a chuckle.

Suddenly, a clap of thunder sounded and a bolt of lightning struck very close by as the electricity went out and everything became dark. The sky had blackened to midnight tones. Permeating darkness appeared all around me.

"Oh, oh, this ain't good," I said as I stood naked in the bathroom and felt around for a towel and the hairdryer.

Realizing that the hairdryer was useless without electricity, I thought about all the food that I had just purchased and how it would spoil in a refrigerator with no power.

"Man, this really blows," I said as I finally found a towel and wondered if I had a flashlight somewhere in the house.

I stumbled around in the dark for a while, as the storm continued to rage. The only source of light was a sporadic flash of lightning, which lit up everything for a moment, only to plunge back into total darkness. I groped my way down the stairs to the den where I last remembered seeing a cigarette lighter. I found it, gave it a flick and decided not to waste the opportunity. I lit a joint and relaxed until everything outside died down a bit. It was a couple of minutes after I had finished smoking the doobie when the phone rang. I looked at the fluorescent numbers on my watch dial that read 2:44 PM. I felt for the receiver.

"Hello."

"Jeff?"

"Yeah."

"I cannot believe you. I should have known better."

"Oh Jami, I'm glad you called. A storm knocked all the power out. I'm sitting here in the dark."

"Stop lying Jeff, I'm only a couple of miles from your house and all the lights are on here."

"Hey I'm not lying. I am sitting here in my den in almost total darkness. I just looked out the window. The storm has eased up but my neighbor's house is dark too. If you don't believe me, drive over here and see for yourself."

"Forget it Jeff...and you can go straight to hell!" she yelled into the phone and slammed it into its cradle.

"Imagine that. They get madder when I tell them the truth," I laughed out loud.

About half an hour later I slid open the sliding glass door and stepped outside. The storm was over and radiant sunlight was streaming through the broken clouds. A beautiful rainbow appeared over the lake just a mile down the road from my house. All of a sudden Jami's car came to an abrupt halt in the driveway and she opened her door.

Uh oh, this could get ugly.

I stood there trying to organize some thoughts in my stoned mind, but then I looked up and saw that she was smiling.

"Maybe she's deranged," I said under my breath as I eyed her carefully for a bazooka or some type of weapon.

"Okay...I was wrong and I apologize," she said.

"About what?"

"Your lights silly. I didn't believe you and I was so mad at you that I got my ex-husband to stay with Johnny so I could drive over and catch you in a lie. But when I turned off Anderson Road and saw all the Nashville Electric Service trucks out on a Saturday afternoon and all the dark windows in the houses on your block, I realized you were telling me the truth. And...whew, I'm out of breath. So I'm very sorry I didn't believe you."

"Jami, it's okay. So do you need to get back to the party or what?"

"No, it's breaking up about now anyway and Johnny's gonna stay with his daddy tonight, so I'm free to do whatever I want."

"Well look, I'm starving. I was planning on some good old Chucky Cheese pizza, but then Mother Nature took control...soooo, you wanna ride with me somewhere to get something to eat real quick? Then we can come back here and make plans or just kick back for a while."

"Sure, I'll go with you," she said with a big smile.

As we drove down the street, I wished it was Hannah that was sitting beside me. I forced the notion out of my head and concentrated on Jami's beautiful face. As I glanced at her, I couldn't help but be puzzled by her relentless pursuit of me. She must have had countless men tripping over themselves just to talk to her. Maybe the multiple times I had stood her up caused her to view me as some sort of a challenge, because any woman who looked like that could have her pick of any man she wanted.

"Jeff! Jami to Jeff, are you stoned?" she giggled.

"Oh sorry, I was just...never mind. And yes I am. Would you like to be?"

"Why yes I would," she laughed.

"Well then, let me pull through this drive-thru to get some munchies and we'll head back to my house where I will do my best to comply with your wishes my fair lady," I replied.

As soon as we got back, we sat on the sofa in my den, where I rolled her a huge joint to smoke while I scarfed down an order of a Big Mac and fries. When we were both done, she immediately scooted over next to me, grabbed my face between her hands and gave me a first-class kiss. And after a few minutes of making out, she began unbuttoning my shirt and unzipping my pants.

"Ah Jami, if this is headed where I think...and hope it is, maybe we should head upstairs to my bedroom."

"I thought you'd never ask. Let's go."

We walked casually back to my bedroom where we finished undressing as she proceeded to kiss me all over my body. Once again Hannah began invading my thoughts as it dawned on me that Jami was about to become the only woman I had sex with other than Hannah since we had met. (I had conveniently and typically forgotten about Bikina.)

We fell onto the bed where she made slow and delicious love to me until the sun dipped under the horizon. She wasn't just beautiful; she was also a very good lover. As I lay there in the afterglow of ecstasy, I mentally compared sex with Jami to sex with Hannah. It was really no contest. As beautiful and stimulating as Jami was, compared to the pleasure I got from making love to Hannah, sex with Jami seemed almost pedestrian.

"Jeff, did you like that?" she asked as she snuggled closer to me.

"Did I like that? Are you serious? I feel like making a commercial, and telling everybody that I'm sure glad that I bank at First National Bank!" I laughed.

Then I held her in my arms until I recuperated sufficiently for an encore performance.

If it had been another time, she might have been just what I needed, but it wasn't the right time. It was a very wrong time. My feelings for Hannah were too powerful to be happy with another woman, no matter how beautiful.

Nevertheless, I began to experience a powerful attraction to her. Her looks aside, she was a very sweet, loving and personable woman, and I soon discovered her to be an exceptionally good mother to her little boy. We went out to dinner that evening and then back to my bed where we remained until sunrise. Jami had to leave in order to pick up Johnny from his dad, so she got up, showered and dressed. But before she left, she gave me another passionate kiss.

"Hey Jami, how old are you anyway? You're over eighteen aren't you?" I laughed.

"Well if I ain't, it's a little late to be finding out now, isn't it? Seriously though, I'm twenty-three. How old are you?"

I immediately realized that she was the same age as Hannah. Everything seemed to conspire to remind me of her.

"I'm an old man. I'm thirty four...old enough to be your..."

"My lover...and you sure didn't seem very old to me last night."

"Hey, I was just trying to keep up."

"Now tell me the truth? Is this going to be a one night stand for us?" she asked as she looked up at me with a solemn expression.

"Jami, I think you already know the answer. I'm planning on us repeating last night as soon and as often as possible."

We did. Our relationship took a little more effort on my part than I was accustomed to because of her son, but I didn't mind. Johnny and I got along great. And since little Johnny spent two weekends every month with his dad, Jami and I could spend every other weekend together. That is, until one night when my kryptonite resurfaced.

It was a couple of weeks later on a Friday night when Jami took Johnny to a friend's birthday party, so I went out alone. I was sitting at the bar in the Gold Mine and talking with my friend Larry, the bartender. We were talking about sports, women and the usual inanities when the telephone at the bar rang. Larry answered and stuck the receiver out towards me.

"It's some chick for you dude."

"Hello."

"Hey," said an extremely familiar voice.

"Hannah?"

"Yeah, what're you doing?"

"Nothing, just sitting here talking to Larry. What do you want?"

"Ask me where I am."

"I don't care where you are. Here Larry, hang this up."

Larry hung it up and seconds later it rang again.

"It's her again," he said as he handed the receiver back to me.

"Hannah, please stop calling here. This is a business phone and you're gonna get Larry in trouble."

"Well, ask me where I am and I'll stop."

"Okay Hannah, where are you?"

"Your house," she said calmly and hung up.

I handed the receiver back to Larry, ran to the payphone, stuck in a quarter and dialed my number.

"Hello," said the proprietor of my heartstrings.

"Hannah, what the hell do you think you're doing?"

"Waiting for you, lover," she said and abruptly hung up.

I handed Larry a twenty for my tab and ran to my car. As soon as I hit the interstate, I floored it and sped the twelve miles to my house in less than ten minutes. I was so mad at her...of all the nerve...breaking into my house. And I was determined not to allow myself to be seduced...not this time. This time it was going to end for good. As I took note of her car parked in front of my house, I pulled into the driveway and then all the way around back, got out, slammed the door and ran inside. Hannah was sitting on the sofa in a tight-fitting yellow jump suit and a pair of red high heels. She looked fantastic. But that didn't matter, not tonight.

Tonight I am strong.

"Get out Hannah," I said softly as I tried to remain composed.

She had helped herself to a glass of whiskey from the bar, which she sipped and then set onto the coffee table.

"Are you sure you want me to leave?" she asked as she unzipped the front of her jumpsuit all the way down to her waist.

"Yeah, I'm absolutely one hundred percent sure. Get out."

She stood, pulled the jumpsuit from her right shoulder and then from the left and allowed it to fall to her feet, revealing that she had nothing on beneath. Then she stepped gracefully away from the crumpled clothing and toward me.

"Are you real sure baby?"

I gulped back my raging desire for her with every fiber of my being and snatched a bottle of whiskey from the bar.

"Real sure Hannah," I said, somehow choking out the words as I began to pour whiskey all over her head and naked body.

I poured with one hand and guided her in the direction of the sliding glass door with the other. I tossed the nearly empty whiskey bottle onto the sofa, picked up her jumpsuit, slid open the door and nudged her through it. She then turned around and gave me the look I had missed for so long now.

"Please baby...I love you," she said through a face streaming with tears.

"Too late for all that," I said as I threw her jumpsuit in her face, slid the door shut and closed the curtains.

My hands were literally shaking as I walked over to the sofa and sat down. I lit a joint and inhaled as much of it as my lungs could hold and then held it as long as I could. I coughed out the smoke, picked up her glass and drained the remaining whiskey.

"Ah, that's better," I said, feeling fortified and powerful from the reinforcements of weed and alcohol. I felt a sense of pride from rebuffing the one woman I thought I could never reject. I took another long pull from the joint, stood up and walked to the door. I pulled open the curtains and then the door. She was still there, standing with her jumpsuit clutched to her breasts and crying softly with her head hanging.

"Why are you still here?" I asked in a stern tone.

"Don't be mean to me," she said in her little girl's voice and with THE look.

That was all it took. There was no way I could resist her any longer. Giving in to my immeasurable desire, I pulled her close and we stumbled back inside. She was still drenched with whiskey, but I didn't care. In seconds my clothes were off and we were squirming together on the floor of the den. Our white-hot passion caused any prior lovemaking session, even involving the two of us, to pale in comparison. When we finished, I noticed that the sliding glass door was wide open. Anyone could have dropped by and gotten an eye full, but my focus at the time didn't allow my peripheral vision to operate. Figuratively and literally, I only had eyes for her. I rose from the floor and hurried toward the door.

"Damn Hannah, let me close the door before someone walks in on us."

I started to slide it shut, but she stopped me, took me by the hand and led me into the backyard. We were both completely naked. She began kissing me and massaging my body with her own. In a very short time, we were making love again while standing upright and holding one another tightly. It was as if our two bodies had morphed into one.

Sex with her was so exhilarating and I was absolutely crazy about her.

When it was over we went back inside, dressed and sat down on the sofa.

"So Hannah, do you wanna tell me where you've been?"

"Do you wanna tell me who you've been screwing?" she countered.

"Me? You've been gone for over a month!"

"It's your own fault. You broke up with me. Remember?"

"Hannah, you're the one who teleports to some other dimension on a regular basis. And I don't want to get into a big argument with you about this, but you're driving me nuts. Things will be going okay between us and then …POOF! You're gone. And to where? Where the hell do you go and who are you with? Why won't you tell me? I mean it couldn't be any worse than telling me that you went to a motel with some guy and screwed him all night. Hell, you've already done that. So I'm asking you to tell me. I'm crazy about you. I love you. Does that mean anything to you?"

"I love you too…and I haven't been screwing anybody, I swear. I've just been doing a lot of dope and…"

"But you can do as much coke as you want right here, anytime you want it. Hell Hannah, why would you go somewhere else?"

"I…I've been shooting up and I knew you wouldn't like that. But I stopped and I won't do it anymore. And I won't disappear anymore. If you'll stop accusing me of fucking every guy you see, I promise it won't happen anymore. I love you baby…okay?"

So I was back with Hannah. I didn't want to hurt Jami, but Hannah was always going to be the love of my life. I avoided talking with Jami for the next few days, and toward the end of the week I called her and told her a big lie about having to go to Dallas, Texas during the weekend that we were supposed to spend together. I calculated that this deception would give me two extra weeks to cultivate a plausible reason to end our relationship.

On Thursday night, I was supposed to pick up Hannah from the tanning salon at 8:30, so I stopped at the Gold Mine at seven o'clock to have a drink and kill some time. I walked to the back of the bar and saw Bikina sitting on the last stool and leaning against the wall for support. She appeared to be very drunk.

"Hey you…you…Lothario!"

"Hi Bikina. What'd you call me?"

"LOTHARIO, he was a character in 'The Fair Penitent'...this play that..."

"I know who Lothario was Bikina. Why are you calling me that?"

"Isn't it obvious?" she slurred.

"You're drunk."

"Yeah and I'll tell you what. I was drunk last night too, when I ran into your little redheaded girlfriend at Chevy's...and we had a very loooong conversation."

"Bikina, what did you tell her?"

"I told her all about your little succubus named Hannah."

"BIKINA YOU DIDN'T!"

"And how she's got some type of spell on you and how you can never love anyone else as long as she's around...and how stupid you are and how...how much I love you and how much I hate her...and..."

"Thanks a lot Bikina. I was gonna tell her in a better way, but since you took it upon yourself to meddle in my business, THANKS A LOT!"

"But you are my business and I love..." she slurred, reaching desperately for me.

"Fuck that," I said as I stepped back, spun on my feet and stomped out the door.

My jealous nature continued in regards to Hannah, so in less than two weeks, she went MIA again. I went to her place to pick her up on a Wednesday night and found no car and no Hannah. Her father, Don, told me that he hadn't seen her in two days and had assumed that she was staying with me. I politely thanked him and left in disgust. I went down to Chevy's where I ran into Jami and her friend, Daphne Hershey. They both lit into me and began telling me what a slime ball I was.

"Come on let me have it. Get it out of your system and make yourself feel better," I said to Jami, refusing to even acknowledge her busybody friend.

"There isn't a guy in here that wouldn't lick the bottom of her shoes just for a chance to go out with her, you moron," said an obviously inebriated Daphne.

"Well then Jami, why don't you take them off and hold 'em up, because I'd really like to see that," I replied as I grabbed my drink and headed for the opposite end of the bar.

"Fuck you, jerk!" said Daphne.

"No, thank you Daphne. I think that I can do much better than you. And I'm certainly not into that shoe-licking fetish that you seem to be into."

An hour later, I was sitting at the bar and talking to an attractive oriental cutie named Kathy I had been intimate with once before. Jami walked over and put her arms around my neck.

"Jeff, Daphne's gonna be mad at me but I don't care. Will you please take me home with you?" she whispered in my ear.

I immediately excused myself from Kathy and guided Jami through the busy club. I took her home for several reasons. The first reason was to get even with Hannah for her latest caper. Another reason was to show Jami's loudmouthed friend Daphne that what she thought didn't mean spit, and finally because I really liked being with Jami.

The next morning, I woke up early in order to get Jami back to her house. Johnny was staying with his dad and all she needed to do was run in and change clothes, since she had already showered at my place. I pulled up to the curb and Jami started to open the door. Then she suddenly stopped, turned back and kissed me passionately.

"You know that I'm madly in love with you, don't you? And as for Hannah, you'll find out one day that she's no good for you," she said softly.

I offered no reply and drove away in a fog. For some baffling reason, one of the most beautiful women I had ever known had just told me that she loved me while the woman I was crazy about was growing ever more elusive. I was torn between my heart and my head, with my heart belonging to Hannah and my head split somewhere down the middle.

That night Howie, Bikina and I barhopped all over Nashville. We were four or five sheets to the wind, sitting in a booth in the Gold Mine around one o'clock in the morning.

"An undeniable fact in the face of it my good man," said a very intoxicated

Howie. I was equally smashed as I responded, "In the face of what Spiro baby,

the world?" "No man, *it*, you know, the cosmic *it*," said Howie.

"You guys are drunk and goofy," added Bikina.

"Yes we are," we sang together in extreme disharmony.

"So Jeff, let me ask you a question," said Howie, suddenly turning serious.

"Shoot my good man."

"Why is it that you've been acting so demented when it comes to Hannah, all kidding aside?"

"What're you talking about Howie?"

"Well let's examine the situation for a moment. You ran off what I consider a goddess, because of her and…"

"Whoa! Hold on a second. Are you calling Mary Anne a goddess? Are you insane? Although she is kind of cold and stiff like a statue, so I guess she could be a statue of a goddess, but…"

"Wait a second, hear me out. As I was saying, you ran off Mary Anne and you're blowing off one of the best looking women I've ever seen, not to mention snubbing this awesome looking gal sitting right here with us, who is obviously nuts about you, but who you continually take for granted and treat like one of the guys. All because of Hannah. So I guess what I'm trying to say is…WHAT THE HELL IS WRONG WITH YOU?"

"Come on Howie, you know that I love her."

"But why? I mean she's okay but I've seen you with so many other hotter women than her. Personally, she doesn't do that much for me."

"That's your opinion Howie," I said, now feeling a bit agitated.

Then I added,"Look, sex with her…is like…like nearly a spiritual thing for me. She's like my soul mate and making love to her is like…a religious experience." Suddenly Bikina jumped up and ran crying to the restroom.

"Dude, you sound just like some crazy chick…talking about me," roared Howie as he doubled over with laughter.

"You go to hell Howie! Go straight to hell!" I said firmly as I stood up, threw down a wad of bills for our tab and left.

Hannah called me the next day and said she was going to start attending Narcotics Anonymous meetings and asked me to go with her. I agreed to go with her to the first one, but afterwards said that I wanted no part of it. I promised to take her to and from the meetings but said that I didn't need to go to them. I said that I was strong enough to quit using drugs anytime I wanted. I just didn't want to quit at that time. So Hannah started going to the meetings and true to my word, I drove her to them and picked her up.

One night I pulled up and saw her hanging all over some huge guy who looked like an NFL offensive lineman. Even though she introduced the guy to me as Jerry Davidson and introduced me as her "honey," I went off on her on the drive home accusing her of screwing around again and threatening to whip the human tree trunk. This guy was about 6' 5" and had to weigh in the neighborhood of around 330 pounds. If the beast ever got a hold of me, he could have easily snapped my neck like a dry twig, but that prospect didn't faze me. I figured that as long as a guy had a jaw and I hit him hard enough, the law of gravity would take over and provide the desired result. That's concrete proof that love can cause a reasonably intelligent person to think like a lunatic.

When I went to pick Hannah up at her next meeting, a member of her group told me that she had already left with Jerry. I stopped at the nearest phone booth, looked in the phonebook and found his name. Then I dialed his number. Jerry answered.

"Hello?"

"Let me talk to Hannah."

"Sure, just a sec."

"Hello."

"Just what do you think you're doing?"

"Nothing, just watching a movie," she said calmly.

"What do you want me to do, come over there and whip that guy's ass just to show you I can?"

"Don't be such a redneck," she said and hung up the phone.

I stood in the phone booth and called back about a dozen times asking the guy to come outside and threatening to beat the hell out of him. The last time I called, Jerry told me that she had gotten tired of me calling and left.

"Look, nothing happened dude. All she did was talk about you."

I hung up, went home, closed all the curtains, took the phone off the hook and freebased until midnight. A few hours later I finally began coming down. I started to cook up another batch, but something extraordinary occurred. I sat back on the couch and began thinking about God and the cosmos and decided that it was time to pray. It was the first time I had prayed in many years. The prayer was rambling and discursive, but sincere. I asked for the wisdom to determine if God even existed and for the strength to straighten up. The path my life had taken was no longer the direction I wanted to travel.

God, if you really do exist, please help me. I feel so lost and confused right now. I'm making such a mess of my life and I want to be a good person. And as for Hannah...I...I can't help who I love, but I can't do this much longer. I'm afraid that I'll do something really stupid if things keep going the way they are. I'd really appreciate some answers, like just what I'm supposed to believe, so please, whatever you can do, I'd really appreciate it.

For the next few days I refused to talk with Hannah. She phoned me every day, but every time she called I'd accuse her of screwing Jerry or some other guy in her group and then slam the phone down. Then on Friday afternoon, Jami called.

"Hey what are doing tonight?"

"Nothing that I know of. Why?"

"Well, I talked with Daphne today and she wants to go down to the Gold Mine tonight and make nice with you. So will you meet us there tonight around eight for some drinks? Then we could head down to Chevy's for a while, and after that you and I can go back to your house and I'll show you how much I love you. Okay? Please say you'll come."

"Okay beautiful, I'll meet you guys down there."

I got there about five minutes early and found a parking place right in front of the place. My T-tops were off but since I could see my car from inside, I decided to leave them off. As soon as I walked in the door, I saw the two of them sitting in a booth. Two husky guys were standing next to them, trying to pick them up. But the guy who was hitting on Jami was wasting his time, because she was a one-man woman and the only man she wanted right then was yours truly.

I slid into the booth beside Jami and smiled at the two guys. I suddenly realized how good looking Daphne was. She had jet-black hair, brown eyes and a flawless, tanned complexion to go along with her terrific body. She was hot, but I still resented her for dipping her pretty nose into my business. And I was great at holding a grudge.

"Hello ladies, you're both looking exceptionally lovely tonight."

"Why thank you sir. Wanna be friends?" said Daphne as she beamed a radiant smile in my direction and stuck her hand across the table."

"Yes, that'd be great Daphne," I responded as I shook her hand to seal the deal, all the while imagining what it would be like to get naked and roll around with both of them at the same time, perhaps even later that very night.

Jami interrupted my lewd thoughts, "So why don't we have a few drinks and then head over to Chevy's for a while?"

"Yeah, that sounds good and we can take my car since all three of us can fit comfortably," added Daphne.

"Only if I can sit in the middle," I laughed.

We had a couple of rounds and got ready to leave for Chevy's. I paid the tab as the girls went to the restroom to snort some blow from a vial I handed to Jami. Minutes later they returned with grins on their pretty faces.

"Listen, why don't you guys go get your car and pick me up out front? I need to put my T-tops on and grab some weed and coke from the car."

"Okay, see you in a few minutes," said a beaming Jami.

I then went out to the car and put the top over the driver's side. Then I grabbed a handful of drugs from the console and shoved them into my pockets just as Daphne's car pulled up along side of me. I was about to get out and put the other top on when Hannah suddenly appeared, reached in to unlock the passenger door and jumped inside the car with me.

"Hello lover," said a delicious looking Hannah Jane.

"Hannah, what the…"

Jami immediately began screaming, "Is that Hannah. Is that that bitch? Jeff Collins, you better tell that slut to get out of your car right now. I mean it. It's time for you to be a man and make your choice. So who's it gonna be? Choose her or me!" I hesitated.

"You've got five seconds Jeff," said Jami as she grew more furious by the second.

I looked at Jami's beautiful, angry face, then at Hannah and next back at Jami.

"Jami, I'm sorry…"

"Fuck you Jeff, you two deserve each other. And don't you dare ever, and I mean EVER, call me again. Let's get out of here Daphne!" she said through a face full of tears. "SCREECH!"

"Well, I guess I win the prize, huh?" said my glowing dream girl.

As always, she looked incredible and as always, she was my choice, my only choice. When she was an option, there was simply no competition. We went back to my house, where she practically ripped my clothes off and seduced me like only she could. We made love inside and then I led her outside to the hammock on the deck. I positioned her on it and then straddled it. At that moment I loved her so deeply and at the same time I so passionately despised her itinerant tendencies that I made love to her with powerful and purposeful thrusts. I unleashed my unbridled passion upon her, like I was trying to ram her all the way through the cloth fabric of the hammock, subconsciously affixing her to one place, at least for a while.

Her response to such a furious and frenetic pace was to look up at me with a pure lustful delight and say, "Now you're fucking me 'Collins style' baby!"

She was perfect for me. Everything she did when I was with her was right. Our sexual chemistry was fantastic, beyond fantastic. It was pure ecstasy.

The next morning I drove her home.

"Hannah, we have to get all this crap straightened out. You know that I'm crazy about you, but we can't keep this up."

"It's gonna be okay sweetheart. I'll come over tonight and we'll talk about it as much as you want, okay?"

It never happened. I didn't hear from her all day and when she hadn't arrived at my place by eight o'clock, I called the tanning salon. They said that she no longer worked there. I called her house, but Don hadn't seen her either, so I just gave up and went out clubbing.

I came home at one in the morning to find her car parked in my carport. As I walked towards my back door, I saw her sitting in a lounge chair, sobbing uncontrollably.

"Hannah, what is it…what's wrong honey?" I asked as I tenderly touched her shoulder.

"Oh Jeff, I was just raped!" she cried as she grabbed my hand and pulled it to her face.

"When? Who? Tell me what happened!"

"I was on my way over here and I had a flat tire on the interstate. Some guy in a Johnson's Dairy truck stopped to help me. He said that my tire had a nail in it and it would have to be fixed at a gas station. He tried to put on my spare but it was flat too. Then he offered to take me to a gas station, so I got in the truck with him and we went to a gas station and they fixed it. I called you, but you weren't home. And then he said that he would take me back to my car if I didn't mind stopping at the dairy for him to log in or something. I looked at the nametag on his shirt and it said Louie, and he seemed like a nice guy. I didn't know how to get a hold of you or Daddy, so I got back in the truck. Then we went inside the place where he worked and things started feeling kinda weird to me. There wasn't anybody else there, at least that I could see, and then he drove the truck into some kind of big metal room. He called it a sterile room or something like that. Anyway, I started to get these weird vibes and told him I wanted out of there and then he grabbed me and held me down. Oh Jeff it was awful. I tried to push him away but he was too big. His breath was horrible. His teeth were all brown and his body odor, he stunk so bad. There was nothing I could do…and then he took me back to my car. I cried the whole way and when we got there, I just jumped out of the truck and let him put my tire back on. I thought about hitting him with the lug wrench, but I was so scared of him. And then he just got back into the truck and drove away without saying a word. Oh Jeff!"

She collapsed into my arms as I stood there with my mouth open. I was considering whether or not she might have made the whole thing up. But Hannah had told me so many details and appeared to be genuinely upset, so I believed her. She couldn't be lying, not about something this serious.

"I'm gonna kill him. I'm gonna go over there and kill the son of a bitch."

"No Jeff, I don't want you to get in trouble because of this."

"Well, what do you want to do? Call the police?"

"No, I don't want to go through all that stuff. I just want to forget it and…"

"Forget it? No way Hannah! I have a couple of friends, one that has worked at that place for over ten years and another that used to work there. I'm gonna get them to check this out and then I swear to God, I'm gonna go over there and beat the holy shit out him."

The very next day I contacted the two guys I knew, and they both confirmed her story about the returning delivery trucks needing to pull into a room they called the sterilization bay. The one who still worked there confirmed that a big fat guy named

Louie with bad teeth did work on a delivery route in the area and at the time Hannah said it happened. I had heard enough. He said Louie drove a green Dodge truck with a white camper on the back, and he generally got to work around twelve noon. I decided to meet the guy for "lunch" the following day.

I had been waiting in my car in the dairy's parking lot in front of the company vehicle entrance since a little before eleven o'clock when I saw the green truck pull into the lot. I got out and stood in the back of my car. The truck stopped and two men got out and began walking in my direction. The passenger was a small bald headed guy, so I looked past him at the driver, who met Hannah's description of her attacker. When they got within about ten feet, I stepped into their path.

"Hey Louie, how ya been old buddy?"

"Hi, how ya doing there? Do I know you?"

"Nah, you don't know me, but you know my girlfriend. It seems as though you stopped on the interstate and helped her with a flat tire the other night. Remember her?"

The guy looked nervously at his friend, who instinctively backed away. Then Louie looked back at me as he nervously shuffled his feet.

"Anyway, I just thought that I should stop by and give you something for what you did. Soooo..."

I kicked him right in the nuts. Louie bent over in agony and I straightened him back up with a knee to his face. I hit him as many times as I could. I blasted him in the jaw, nose, eye and anywhere else I could land a solid punch until the big guy fell down in the gravel blubbering like a baby. A group of men had come outside from the plant to see what was happening.

"Hey, what's going on?"

I gave the guy a well-placed kick to his stomach.

"Well, I'll tell you. This big ball of pus picked up my girlfriend the other night under the pretense of helping her with her car trouble, and then he brought her back here, and then this piece of shit raped her in your sterilization bay. Ain't that right Louie?" I said right as I kicked him in the chest.

Louie was bleeding badly and obviously wanted no more punishment, so I backed away a few steps.

"And I'll tell you all something else. If he wants you to call the cops on me, please do it. You can tell them my name is Jeff Collins, because I'd like for them to arrest him for rape even if I have to go to jail with him. And besides, if I do, I'll be able to beat the shit out of him the whole time I'm there."

I started to walk away, but stopped, turned around and stepped back in front of Louie.

"Oh yeah, one other thing, I got your home phone number and I'm gonna call your wife and explain to her how you got so beat up so you won't be able to explain it away with some big lie, you sorry pervert. And I'll leave my number with her in case you want to get a hold of me again for another little chat. Okay you piece of trash?"

Before leaving I delivered one final kick, but this time it was to Louie's buttocks. I then walked calmly to my car, got in and drove away.

That night I picked up Hannah and brought her back to my house. We ordered a pizza and watched a couple of movies. I sat next to her on the couch with my arm around her for the entire time. I was hesitant to do anything else. I didn't know how to act or what I should do. All I knew was that I loved her more than anything and wanted to protect her from harm. Later we went upstairs to bed and it was the first and only time that we didn't have sex when we were in bed together. I held her in my arms until I heard her snoring ever so lightly, and only then did I drift off to sleep.

I woke up the next morning to a noise which sounded a lot like my car pulling out of the driveway. I looked over at Hannah and discovered an empty place where her body had been several hours earlier. I got up and walked through the upstairs part of the house and when I didn't find her I went downstairs to the den. No Hannah. Then I opened the sliding glass door and looked out into the empty space under the carport where I had parked my car.

"What the hell!"

I went over to the couch and sat down to try and figure out what had happened. I thought that smoking a joint might help, so I reached under the couch to pull out the Frisbee that I kept my personal stash of weed and cocaine in....**empty!** Not only had she driven off in my car, she had either smoked a half-ounce of weed and snorted about four grams of cocaine or taken off with them. I went outside and thought about my next move. What if she got pulled over by the cops and they found the dope? What if she had a wreck? Should I call the police and report the car stolen? I went back upstairs and dialed the number of a friend named Danny Gains. Danny used to be a cop, but was now a fireman who sold a little weed and frequently bought coke from me. When I told Danny about what happened and asked him what I should do, he told me not to call anyone and that he would come over right away.

Danny was there in about ten minutes since he only lived about three miles from me. His plan was to get in touch with his brother who was still a cop and somehow try to get her pulled over discreetly, but before he could pick up the telephone to put the plan into action, it rang and I answered.

"Hello."

"Hey..." said a familiar sounding voice.

"Hannah, where the hell are you? Are you okay? Where's my car? And what the hell is wrong with you?" I yelled into the phone.

"Stop screaming at me."

"If you don't get my car back over here real fast, I'm gonna do a lot more than scream. Listen, I've called the cops and they're already here, so you better hurry up," I lied.

"You have not."

"Would you like to speak with the officer standing right next to me?"

"Yeah, let me talk with him. I'll bet that he sounds a lot like you." I handed the phone to Danny with a cryptic wink.

He went right into the act, "Young lady this is Officer Powell and I suggest that you return this gentleman's vehicle to him at once, because once a stolen vehicle report is issued, there is going to be a great deal of trouble for anyone involved."

"Okay, okay, I'll bring it back right now. Let me talk to my boyfriend again please." Danny handed it back to me.

"Hannah, you'd better hurry the hell up."

"Look, I know you're real mad at me right now, so I don't want to come over there. I'll leave your car in the parking lot on the corner, the one at the bank where your little redheaded girlfriend works. I'll be there within thirty minutes and I'll put the keys in the ashtray. And we can talk about this later...bye." Then she hung up.

How the hell did she know where Jami worked?

Danny was running late for his tee time at the golf course so I thanked him and said goodbye. Then I went to one of my hiding places, pulled out some reefer, rolled a fat joint and smoked it. I realized I had to get my car back from the bank somehow and before I gave serious thought to what I was doing, I had dialed the number to the bank where Jami worked.

"First National Bank, this is Jami, may I help you?"

"Ah...hello Jami, please don't hang up. It's Jeff..."

"I know who it is. What do you want?" she said coldly.

"Look, I know you're mad, probably still mad as hell at me, but I need a huge favor. You see...well, Hannah stole...ah...took off in my car earlier this morning and she's supposed to leave it in your parking lot."

"Yeah...and?"

"She said that she'd put the keys in the ashtray and I was wondering if you'd drive it to my house. If you will I'll take you to lunch or let you punch me in the face, whichever you'd prefer."

"OH MY GOD!"

"What?"

"Jeff, your car just pulled into the parking lot and a black limo stopped right behind it. Now Hannah's getting out of it. She just looked over here and flipped me a bird! That bitch, I hate her. She got into the limo and it's pulling away. Yep, there goes your slimy girlfriend."

"So Jami, are you gonna help me or not?"

"Okay, I'm gonna do this for you. Don't ask me why. And I'm not sure which one I want in return, the punch or the lunch."

Jami drove my car back at noon and we went to lunch. I apologized for what happened in front of the Gold Mine and asked for her forgiveness and if she could possibly see her way clear to maybe one day at least being friends. It took some convincing, but by the time I took her back to work, she was smiling and she even gave me a little kiss on the cheek.

That night I went out and really tied one on. I was so drunk that I had to take a taxi home. I walked into my house and stumbled back to the bedroom, where I found Hannah sound asleep in my bed! I walked over and snatched the covers away, revealing her beautiful nakedness.

"Hey baby, where you been?" she murmured as she opened her eyes.

"I hate you, or at least hate loving you," I said under my breath as I undressed and lay down beside her.

The sight of her naked body was irresistible, especially in my drunken state. But drunk, stoned or stone cold sober, the sheer essence of her had long ago pierced my heart, enveloped my soul and for the rest of my life I would be drawn to her like a moth to a flame. She had a hypnotic effect on me, or perhaps it was something more spiritual. Whatever it was, my passion for her transcended space and time. My desire and love for this woman existed metaphysically outside the farthest reaches of human intimacy, a singular bond, unique and unparalleled on the terrestrial plane.

During the following week, our time together was blissful, reminiscent of the moment when we first met. I loved her regardless of my suspicious and jealous nature and the admonitions from my friends. Hannah and I were both hopelessly blind to our problems. All I knew was that when I was with her, I was happy and content. However, as you might expect, one heaping dose of heartache was waiting on me right around the corner.

CHAPTER 16
NO HANNAH = JAMI, BRITTANY, CAROL, CANDY, ETC.

"The chains of habit are too weak to be felt
until they are too strong to be broken."
(Samuel Johnson)

It was a beautiful sunny Tuesday afternoon. I had just signed a listing agreement for a home a few streets over from Hannah's house, so I decided to drive by to see if she was home. Her car was in the driveway, so I pulled in behind it. I rang the doorbell and she opened the door. Her face was red and wet with tears.

"Baby, what is it...what's wrong?"

"Come on in...I was just about to call you..."

She led me into the den where we both sat down on the couch. She reached over and took my hand into hers and looked down towards the floor.

"Jeff, I have to go away."

"Why? Are you joining the army or something?" I asked nervously but with a slight grin.

"No Jeff, I'm serious. I have to go to a hospital."

"A hospital...why Hannah?"

"For several reasons. I have to stop using cocaine...and I...I mean, a psychiatrist Daddy took me to said that I have something called 'King Baby Syndrome'. And well...there are a couple of other things..."

"What's 'King Baby Syndrome'?"

"Oh Jeff I don't understand it. I just know that it supposedly causes me do some of the things I do, like abusing drugs and hiding from you and..."

"Is this a joke Hannah? Are you pulling a late April Fool's Day prank on me or something?"

"No Jeff, it's the truth."

"And you're leaving, just like that?"

"Yes."

"Today?"

"Yes, in a couple of hours when Daddy gets home."

"But what about us? When will I be able to see you again?"

"I don't know."

"But I love you."

"I love you too, but this is something I have to do, before things get so out of hand they can't be fixed."

"And where is this place?"

"It's a hospital in Columbia, South Carolina that specializes in the treatment that I need."

"South Carolina?"

"Yes, Columbia, South Carolina."

"Well, when can I come and see you?"

"I don't know. I'll call you and tell you as soon as I find out."

I felt helpless. I just sat there looking at her. Hannah leaned over and started kissing me. I stood up and pulled her close. We embraced for several minutes, just clinging to each other, while I wondered if it would be the last time I held her in my arms. I led her upstairs to her bedroom and undressed her. She reclined on her bed while I took off my clothes. Then I made love to her as tenderly as possible. It was one of the gentlest and most wonderful experiences I ever had, and when it ended we stayed united as I softly kissed her all over her face.

Then it was over. We dressed in total silence and went downstairs, just as her father's car pulled into the driveway.

"Well beautiful...I...I guess that I should leave."

"Okay...Jeff. I love you very much and I..." she said as the tears began to flow.

I knew that I needed to leave before I started crying as well, so I pulled her close for one final embrace.

"Hannah, I love you more than anything and there is nothing I wouldn't do for you, and girl, that's forever. You call me as soon as you can, okay?"

"I will, I promise."

She kissed me passionately one last time and then I left. On the way home I began to consider the reasons Hannah gave for leaving. If her cocaine habit was the major reason, then I had been a major contributor to the problem. After all, I was the main source of all the blow she wanted. On top of my pathological jealousy, my cocaine business was often a factor in our arguments. We both had been living very destructive lifestyles for a long time.

Did I cause all this? Oh God, did I? Is she leaving just to get away from me? Oh my God, no. I thought.

Life goes on; at least until death pays us a visit or until we choose to end it ourselves. And so it went with me. I kept on making loads of cash dealing weed and cocaine and even made some decent money from my side job as a real estate agent. I started seeing Jami more often, but our relationship was far from exclusive, at least from my perspective. I resumed my habitual one night stand routine and in spite of all the coke whores willing to spread their legs for me, I frequently phoned escort agencies for hookers.

Why I continued to pay for prostitutes was something of a mystery to me. Maybe it was the exciting thought of a sexual dalliance with a strange woman, who would be intimate but still remain a stranger. Maybe it was just because I was a sex addict. Whatever the reason, my practice of bedding call girls continued unabated.

Hannah called collect several times each week and we talked for hours. When my next phone bill arrived it was over fifteen hundred dollars, but I didn't care. I missed her and our only remaining connection was her sweet voice on the telephone. I needed to grasp on to some type of link to her.

She had been gone for almost two months, when my friends began noticing how wild I was getting. I pulled all-nighters several times a week and screwed anything attractive that would lie on her back for me. I stayed at the Gold Mine even after it closed. The bartenders and managers gladly obliged since I was generous with my cocaine. When the managers decided that it was time to go home, I often went to an after hours club until the sun came up. On the rare occasions when I hadn't found a willing coke whore by then, I would go home and call an escort service.

I was freebasing more and more. Being with Hannah had restricted my freebasing habit, since I knew its effects on my sexual activity. But now with her out of the picture, I freebased as often as the urge arose. And the urge increased with each passing day. Additionally, I was growing more violent. I found my way into a fight nearly once a month, usually while playing basketball or outside of some bar.

There was a panhandler that habitually hung out in front of the Gold Mine who went by the nickname of Lobo. Whenever he saw my car pull up, Lobo hurried over because I always gave him a dollar or two. One night Jami and I parked right in front of the place and true to form, Lobo lumbered over.

"Excuse me sir, do you think you could spare a couple of bucks for some...ah...so I can get me a sandwich?"

I pulled out a big wad of bills, found a ten-dollar bill and handed it to him.

"Now Lobo, I want you to take this ten and go down to the liquor store and buy the biggest bottle of wine you can get. And don't you let me see you eating any food. I want you to come back up here and show me just how big a bottle you got, okay?"

"Yes sir and thank you sir," said the grinning, wide-eyed Lobo as he snatched the bill from my hand and weaved his way down the street.

"Jeff, that was mean," said Jami as we walked inside.

"Jami, don't think for a minute that he was about to spend it on anything to eat. Just wait and you'll see what I mean."

Sure enough, Lobo was back within fifteen minutes. He looked in the front window, saw us and tapped on the glass. When we turned in his direction, he pulled out a huge bottle of Boone's Farm grape wine from a brown paper bag. I let out a big laugh and gave Lobo the thumbs up sign.

The next week Bikina and I parked in the same area and once again, here came Lobo. As he paused to ask for a handout, I reversed the field on him and said quickly, "Hey man, do you have any spare change on you?"

"Ah…nah…ah no man…sorry," he stammered.

"You know, sometimes you can be a real jackass," Bikina said elbowing me in the side.

"OW! Hey, I was just messing around with my buddy Lobo here. Ain't that right Lobo," I laughed as I pulled out a wad from my pocket and handed him five bucks.

About two weeks later as I was leaving the Gold Mine alone around midnight, I spotted Lobo and another guy walking up the sidewalk. When they were less than ten feet away, they stopped. I could tell that they were drunk and I expected to be asked for some cash for their next bottle. Instead, the fellow with Lobo pulled out a knife and waved it in my direction.

"Give me that roll of cash you got there in your pocket!"

We were now about seven or eight feet apart. I took a hard look at the guy. The unknown drunk was rocking back and forth unsteadily and his hand holding the knife was shaking. I waited as the bum rocked backward on his heels and then forward towards me…then backward again. The next time he came forward I stepped forward about three feet.

"Oh, you mean this roll?" I said as I put my hand in my pocket and simultaneously lifted my right leg. Using a downward kick, I sent the heel of my right foot crashing into the drunk's right kneecap.

The guy immediately dropped the knife and fell down on the sidewalk, screaming in agony as Lobo took off running down the street. I started to take any money the guy had on him, but thought better of it. Instead, I reached down, picked up the knife and tossed it onto the roof of the Gold Mine. Then I walked as calmly as possible to my car.

"Hey Lobo, don't be asking me for any more money either, you hear me? You dirt bag!" I yelled as I got into the car and drove away.

I never told anyone about the incident, because at the time it didn't seem like a big deal. I just went home, cooked up a big batch of freebase and smoked it until the sun came up.

A few days later I stopped at a convenience store to buy some rolling papers. I was sitting in the car rolling a joint when another car pulled up next to me. It was Mary

Anne and she appeared quite intoxicated. She got out and stood next to my car for a second as she looked down through the t-top.

"Hey Jeff, roll me one too," she said.

"Sure Mary Anne, jump in."

"Hi Jeff, how you been?" she asked as she opened the door and slid into the seat.

"Okay I guess, how about you?" I replied as I began rolling her a joint.

"So where's your little tramp of a girlfriend? Did you get tired of her and run her dumb ass off too?"

"Hannah? Dumb? Are you kidding? Didn't you hear?"

"Hear what?"

"She was just nominated for this huge literary award," I lied.

"What!" she stammered wide eyed as her jaw literally dropped.

"Yeah, she's like the youngest person ever to be nominated. It was for the Pulitzer Prize for excellence in the field of literature. She wrote this novel and it seems as though she's a lock to win it, which includes a check for one million dollars. So she's far from dumb. And no, I didn't run her off. She's in New York for the announcement ceremony at the end of the week."

A stupefied stare swept across Mary Anne's face.

"You got any coke on you?"

"No, actually, I've been trying to quit using cocaine and get away from that business. With Hannah's sudden literary success and all, I'm hoping that she'll support me while I pen my first novel, with her guidance of course," I continued to lie while struggling to avoid laughing in her drunken face.

"Well all I know is you lost the best thing you ever had when you lost me."

"Is that so?" I said as I handed her the joint.

"Let me tell you something Mary Anne, **Hannah** is the best thing I ever had or ever will have for that matter and no one, especially you, is even ballpark close when it comes to her."

Mary Anne opened the door and got out, but continued standing in the open door, staring at me.

"You make me nauseous. You know that?"

"Mary Anne, do you realize that what you just said is that you yourself are the cause of someone becoming sick to their stomach. That may be true, but what I think you *meant* to say is that I 'nauseate' you. Now that would be the proper word. And if Hannah were here, she'd tell you the same thing."

"Go to hell you bastard. You'll never get any more of this. I wouldn't screw you again if you were the last man on earth!"

"Mary Anne, if I was the last man on earth, I would be far too busy to service your frozen skanky pussy, now wouldn't I?" I howled with laughter." "I hate you!" she screamed as she slammed the door.

"Then I suppose a blow job would be totally out of the question." I roared, laughing at her as much as at my own use of the hackneyed retort.

"Go to hell you bastard!"

"Okay then, and you're welcome for the doobie," I snorted as she stomped off.

I hardly ever thought about Mary Anne, but since she had both insulted Hannah and presented me with the challenge of getting into her pants again, I quickly determined that I'd show her a thing or two. I was not a decent guy and my devious mind was already calculating new ways to humiliate this woman – a woman I cared nothing about.

A few days after my recent encounter with Mary Anne, I left a message on her answering machine apologizing for what I said to her. I followed up by sending her a dozen roses, delivered to her at work. The flowers included a card asking her to forgive me and to consider being friends. When I came home the very same day, I laughed out loud as I played a message she had left on my answering machine, inviting me over to her sister's house that night at 7 o'clock.

When I arrived at her door, she ushered me downstairs to her bedroom.

"We're all alone tonight so why don't you make your self comfortable and I'll be right back," she said in her most seductive tone.

I walked into the candlelit room and sat down cautiously on her bed.

"I hope she doesn't come running back in here with a meat cleaver," I said to myself only half jokingly.

When she returned, she was wearing a sheer black negligee that left little to the imagination. She bent over, switched on some mood music and then turned toward me.

"I think that you'll probably want to get undressed. Then I'm gonna do whatever you want me to," she purred.

And she did. It was probably the best sex the two of us ever had - with one another anyway. She was trying hard to please me and I was gladly going along with it. I ravaged her viciously because I continued to hold a grudge for her negative comments about Hannah. In fact, I enjoyed it more because I had closed my eyes and fantasized that the woman I was with was actually Hannah. When it was over, we were both sweaty and exhausted.

"Whew! Now wasn't that a lot better than screwing that awful tramp, baby?" she whispered in my ear.

I immediately got up and began dressing.

"Actually Mary Anne, I've got to tell you…no, it wasn't better at all. In fact it wasn't even remotely close to the *worst* sex I've ever had with Hannah. Wait a second…there was no worst time. There was no bad time. It was just incredible every time," I said as I finished putting on my clothes.

She was just lying there with an incredulous look on her face.

"Now if you'll excuse me, since I assumed that you'd offer yourself up like this, I took the precaution of making an appointment with the vet for a flea dip," I said as I began walking out of the room. I was not a nice guy at all.

"I'm gonna get you Jeff Collins. I swear to God, you're gonna be sorry," she screamed as I disappeared up the stairs.

As time went on I began to talk with Hannah less and I saw more of Jami. I really liked Jami, and for whatever reason she was totally in love with me and made no secret of it to her friends. My friends knew it too. The problem was that I was not going to be faithful to her. I knew I would never be faithful to anyone, with the possible exception of Hannah.

Jami had idealized notions of love and she considered our relationship to be exclusive. I had different ideas. Jami was somewhat restricted because of her son, which gave me the time and freedom to troll for strange and willing girls any time I desired. I desired a lot.

A week or so later I came home to find the sliding glass door to the back of my house wide open. Drama was a recurring theme in my life and one which reflected my inability to resolve the many social and ethical dilemmas roiling through my life. I went inside and discovered a number of things missing including two 17" television sets, a case full of audio cassettes, a brand new microwave oven, some cocaine and weed from two different hiding places and approximately four hundred dollars in cash. It occurred to me that the culprit was more than likely Mary Anne and when I found ripped up pictures of Hannah strewn across my unmade bed, I was certain she was the thief. That pushed me over the edge and into a raging fury. I picked up the phone and dialed her number. I only reached her answering machine, but began screaming into the phone just the same.

"Okay you dim-witted whore, you thieving piece of shit. Are you so stupid to think that I wouldn't know who broke in and stole all my stuff? I swear to God that if I ever catch you in my house again, I will literally kill you with my bare hands, you useless…frigid…coke whore of a skank. And if you don't believe me, just drop by for another visit and see. I'll show you how fucking deranged I can get. Then they'll find you in a ditch somewhere, you thieving piece of human shit! And if you think you're getting away with breaking in here and stealing from me, you're sadly mistaken. You're gonna pay for every fucking thing you stole, you nasty canker sore of a herpetic bitch!"

It was an impulsive and stupid move. Mary Anne edited the tape and took it downtown to play for the police, who immediately asked the night judge to issue a restraining order, which required me to stay at least five hundred feet away from her at all times. A violation meant ten days in jail. When it was served three days later, I laughed and actually thanked the sheriff's deputy who served the papers.

"As if I needed any motivation to stay away from that psycho bitch! I only wish it was for five hundred miles!" I laughed.

A couple of weeks later Jami went to visit her sister Pepper in Savannah, Georgia. She asked me to go with her, but I declined, thinking it would be a great chance to chase more wild women and do some freebasing.

On Friday night, I struck out alone. I didn't want anyone slowing down my hunt for a good time with a strange woman, or two. I stopped by Friday's to prime the pump, and was sipping on a glass of whiskey and water when Mary Anne appeared out of nowhere and sat down beside me. I stood up and threw both hands into the air.

"Whoa! I don't want any trouble. I'm leaving," I said in a voice loud enough for anyone in the general vicinity to hear.

I paid the tab and hightailed out of there with a sigh of relief to have dodged any possible drama. I walked to the Gold Mine and had several drinks at the bar as I scoped out the available talent. An exceptionally pretty girl named Brittany Webber, who was a part time hostess at Friday's, came and sat right next to me. I had flirted with her on several occasions, but considered her to be too straight-laced and perhaps even a bit too young for me.

"Hello Jeff, what are you doing tonight?" she said with a glowing smile.

"Looking for you. Hey, how about you and me going to hit half a dozen bars before I take you home with me?" I said half jokingly.

"Well, this might just be your lucky night," she replied.

At that moment Mary Anne walked up to us and sat on the empty stool on the other side of me, deliberately brushing against me in the process.

I turned to her and said, "Mary Anne just leave me alone. You know that I don't want any trouble."

"Hey, I'm gonna screw every cop in Nashville if it'll get you ten days in jail," she hissed.

"You'd just give them some type of VD," I laughed.

She picked up my drink and threw it right in my face and then slapped the hell out of me. I instantly and instinctively jumped up and away from her. Then from the other end of the bar came one of the bouncers. It was a bespectacled guy named Duncan Petty. Unbeknownst to me, Mary Anne had been dating the meathead for over a month. While running toward the scene, Duncan turned a heavy class ring around on his finger and then used it to smack me right in the back of the head. I wheeled around and threw a hard right, which shattered Duncan's nose and his glasses. It was a vicious blow that rendered him nearly unconscious, but I applied a few additional shots to his already bloody face for good measure. The other bouncers grabbed me and forced me outside. Figuring the cops were surely en route, I decided that it would be best to leave.

The next day, I learned that a warrant had been issued for my arrest for violating the restraining order. I called up an attorney friend of mine named Tom Macklin, who arranged for me to turn myself in with a minimal amount of hassle. My trial date would be in three weeks, so all I had to do was post five hundred dollars bail.

"What a conniving whore!" I said aloud as I drove away from the police station.

Since I had Brittany and a couple of other witnesses who agreed to testify as to what really happened, Tom assured me that the case would almost assuredly be dismissed, but that didn't happen. The judge turned out to be a man-hating shrew that took one look at me and decided that ten days in jail would be a fair punishment for the likes of me. As the bailiffs led me out of the courtroom, I glanced over at Mary Anne. She was grinning ear to ear while surreptitiously flipping me a bird. I was taken to a cell where I remained for the next six hours while Tom worked on my appeal bond. It was for ten thousand dollars. I called up Jami and told her where to get the money from my house.

Jami immediately left work and hurried down to the courthouse to make my bond. As I walked out the door of the police station with her, I realized how loyal and true this beautiful woman was, and at that instant I sincerely wished that I was capable of really falling in love with her. However, no sooner had the idea occurred to me, when thoughts of Hannah immediately flooded my mind. Any consideration of being in love with Jami popped like a balloon kissing an open flame.

That night I called Hannah and told her that I was flying to Columbia on Friday and wanted to see her. She agreed. The next day I went to a jeweler and bought an engagement ring. I was going to fly there and ask the love of my life to marry me. To hell with everything and everybody else. So without telling Jami or anyone else, I flew to Columbia, South Carolina. She was waiting for me as I deplaned into the terminal and she looked fantastic as always. We went straight to a local motel where we tore off each other's clothes and made love for nearly an hour. Then we showered, dressed and went out for dinner. I was planning on proposing to her after dinner, but during the meal she told me that she had been dating someone on a semi-regular basis. I tried to play it off like it wasn't that big of a deal, but inside, the thought of her caring about someone else was killing me. I kept the ring in my pocket as we finished and left the restaurant. We spent the rest of the weekend together, and I returned to Nashville on Sunday afternoon. When I left, she put her arms around me, kissed me passionately and told me how much she loved me and how she couldn't wait to see me again. I reciprocated with the same sentiments and walked away, but I was already determined to get over her.

I considered her leaving Nashville as abandoning me and dating another guy as a betrayal of our love. At the time, I was oblivious to my own serious problems, which included a predilection for violence, being a drug dealer, drug abuser, and my struggle with sexual addiction. If I had only recognized my own flaws, I might have successfully dealt with some of these issues. That in turn might have allowed Hannah and I to live a long, happy life together. But our lives fell woefully short of a fairy tale.

I returned to Nashville and dove into another coke-laden sex spree. When Jami was occupied, I screwed every decent looking woman who came within range of my manipulative, disingenuous charms. A rare exception was Hannah's sister Corinne, who I'd met on several occasions. We had met for drinks, smoked pot and just talked as friends. She was about the only attractive woman I never tried to conquer. I wanted to talk with her because she was so close to the situation, and I hoped that she would commiserate with me over my deteriorating relationship with her sister.

Two weeks after my trip to South Carolina, Jami was spending the weekend at my house. While I was in the shower, Jami rifled through my briefcase and found a copy of the plane ticket to Columbia. She immediately ran up the stairs, burst into the bathroom and ripped open the shower curtains.

"You bastard! You...you lying no good son of a bitch!" she yelled.

"What the hell? Am I on Candid Camera?" I joked as I stepped out of the shower and wrapped a towel around my waist.

"Go ahead and make jokes Jeff. Just go ahead, but I'm telling you right now that you're messing up a pretty good thing."

"Jami, what the hell are you talking about?"

"When's the last time you've seen Hannah, Jeff?" she asked, as her chin began to quiver.

I just stood there, dripping wet and silent.

"I'll tell you when, two weeks ago. That's when you snuck off to South Carolina to fuck her, didn't you?" she said, as she flung the copy of the airline ticket at me and began to sob.

I stood there and remained silent.

"Say something you son of a bitch!" she shouted at the same instant she slapped my face.

Straight away I grabbed her by the throat and shoved her into the door.

"Don't ever put your hands on me again, Jami...now get out!" I said through gritted teeth.

"Don't worry, I'm gone!" she said as she went flying out of the bathroom.

I knew that I was caught and had no reasonable lie cocked at the time to offer in my defense. I resorted to another common ploy of mine; righteous indignation with a splash of violence. I habitually used this diversion in a futile attempt to cover or distort the fact that I was guilty of whatever I was being accused.

"Screw her...the nosy bitch," I said aloud as I finished toweling off.

I had just finished getting dressed when the phone rang.

"Hello."

"Hey there good looking, what're ya doing?" asked an unfamiliar female voice on the other end.

"Well, I suppose that I'm about to go and see what kind of trouble I can get into. Who is this anyway?"

"Do you mean as many times as you've hit on me you don't know my voice? Why, I'm quite insulted. It's Brittany, Brittany Webber...you know the one whose pants you're always trying to get into," she giggled.

"Well in my defense we've never spoken over the phone, but let me state for the record that I'm very glad you called. What's up?"

"I figured that since our date was so rudely interrupted by your crazy ex-girlfriend a few weeks ago, it was about time to cash in on my rain check. I get off from work in thirty minutes. Would you like to come down and pick me up?"

"As a matter of fact, yes I would. I'll be there before you get off."

I sped down to Friday's and picked her up. She was pretty, very pretty. I asked her where she wanted to go and when she said my house, we made it there in record time. We smoked a few joints, did a few lines and had a few drinks, and before long we were rolling around naked in bed. After an hour of sensual pleasure, I got up to take another shower.

"Damn you're gorgeous," I said as I gazed down at her body.

"Why thank you sir."

"Brittany, how old are you anyway?"

"Ah…I'm twenty–two. Why, does it matter?"

"Not as long as you're over eighteen, it doesn't."

The following week she was taking a shower at my place after another wild lovemaking session. Stealing a move from Jami's playbook, I spotted her wallet lying on top of her purse. I picked it up and opened it to check out her driver's license. It revealed to my dismay that she was about three weeks shy of her eighteenth birthday! When she came back into the room, I went off.

"Damn it Brittany, you're not twenty-two, you're not even eighteen! Are you insane? Do you know that I could be arrested and go to prison for statutory rape? You need to leave girl, right this minute!"

"Jeff, relax baby…calm down. I'll be eighteen on the 24th of this month. It's okay."

"No it's not. Now I mean it. You have got to go and NOW! So call me in a month or something. You are beautiful, but not beautiful enough to go to prison over."

Ladies were always available and I was lucky enough to have a few exceptional women, women who I believe genuinely loved me. I supposed I possessed skill, experience and a little charm, but my ample supply of cocaine remained the true magic potion that seduced the vast majority of my sexual liaisons.

That night I stayed home and called an escort service. The girl calling herself Shannon was an attractive hooker whose real name was Candy Zahn. She was 5' 8" tall with long dark brown hair. She had a fantastic body with no need of help from medical science or the plastic industry. Candy was twenty-four and loved to party. She seemed instantly attracted to me, my inexhaustible supply of blow and my insatiable sexual appetite. At the end of our first session she asked me if she could come back to see me after she got through working, and I agreed. Our relationship quickly moved from one of prostitute and john to one where she chased me all over town. I enjoyed having sex with her, but she was far too clingy for my taste.

Therefore I limited our relationship to mere "booty calls" whenever it suited my desires. Candy reluctantly consented. She began to tell me she was in love with me, but I think that her love was focused more on my supply of cocaine than anything else. That fine white powder was the tantalizing bonus that blinded her to my promiscuity. I was pleased with the arrangement, but if I had known how prominent a role she would play in my imminent self-destruction, I would have run from her like she was a house on fire.

Then Carol Wilbrooke entered my life. I met her at a Kroger's supermarket in the produce aisle. She was twenty-seven years old and fine beyond description. She looked a little bit Polynesian with a flawless olive-green complexion, jet black hair and beautiful doe-like eyes. She wore an extremely tight pair of hot pants and a small halter top, which revealed an unbelievable body on her 5' 3" frame. I stopped in my tracks and was admiring the vision as she bent over a display of oranges. She glanced up at me with her erotic, exotic eyes. I was caught!

"See anything you'd like to take a picture of?" she said sardonically with a hint of seduction thrown in.

"Yes, as a matter of fact, I certainly do. I see something that looks nearly too good to eat...and the oranges don't look half-bad either." She turned to face me.

She is smoking hot!

"Do you ever have any luck with such a corny line?" she laughed, her smile growing wider.

"Well, since that's the first time I've ever used it, why don't you tell me?" I said, continuing to stare at her.

"What's your name?"

"I think it's Jeff...yeah that's it...Jeff. Would you care to come back to my house and get acquainted?" I asked, unable to take my eyes off her, but swinging for the fences nonetheless.

She stood there looking directly at me for a while, glancing back at the oranges for a moment, apparently considering something further for a few seconds and then turned back to me.

"Oh, I don't know Jeff. I never even talk to men who hit on me, especially in the produce aisle but I might be up for a little fun. Just what did you have in mind?" she said while looking me up and down.

"Well...ah, what's your name?"

"Carol."

"Well Carol, I live about two miles from here and I was thinking that we could go back to my house and do some blow and see what happens, if that's something you might be interested in. So how about it?"

"I know you won't believe this, but I have never done anything like this in my entire life, but what the hell, let's go. Just wait for me out front and I'll follow you."

When we got to my place, I threw an entire ounce of blow onto a mirror in an attempt to impress her. She bent over directly in front of me and vacuumed up most of a gram with one nostril and another half gram with the other side. I sat behind her enjoying the view of her cute little wiggling butt.

When she finished, Carol turned around and said rather nonchalantly, "Well, now I suppose you'll want to take me to your bedroom and screw me until I scream."

I certainly did. I couldn't believe how lucky I was to have met such a looker - in a grocery store of all places! After we were worn out from having sex, I learned that she was married and lived just three blocks away. I had never fooled around with a married woman before, but I couldn't help myself. She was so sexy. She even made me forget about Hannah, at least for a while. However I soon found out that Carol had a few issues of her own. She had a bit of a problem with alcohol, and she suffered from anxiety attacks about her husband finding out about our affair. And since her husband went out of town every week on his job as a traveling salesman, there were plenty of opportunities for us to fool around.

During this time I continued with my other vices too. I hadn't talked with Jami since our fight in the bathroom, so I was seeing whoever I wanted and whenever I wanted. I continued to smuggle cocaine with Manny from time to time and I was freebasing more frequently. In less than three months, I had emptied three separate bank accounts to the tune of over sixty-two thousand dollars! My obsession with freebasing when mixed with my gambling, dope dealing, screwing one coke whore after another and calling escort services, was helping me to spiral out of control. How I avoided contracting HIV from all the women I had sex with is anyone's guess, but the smart money would have to be on some type of divine protection. One thing was certain...I needed to check myself, and fast.

One Friday afternoon I pulled up to my driveway only to discover that it was full of cars. I parked in the front of the house and walked around back, where I saw more than a dozen of my closest friends waiting on me. Bikina, Howie, his latest girlfriend Sarah, Bo Cusack, Gary Thomas, Wes Morgan, his wife Tina, Tom Macklin, my attorney, and several others were sitting in lounge chairs on the deck and throughout the back yard. They all stood when I walked up. Even Jami was standing over by the sliding glass door! "What is this, an extremely early surprise birthday party?" Bikina took me by the hand.

"Let's go inside," she said too low for anyone but me to hear and with the lingering vestige of her Aussie accent.

"Okay, but you know I'm not into orgies," I laughed nervously.

They all packed into the den and had me sit in a chair in the center of the room. Bikina walked up to me, took my face in her hands and brought her face within inches of mine.

"I want you to promise to listen to us Jeff... okay?"

"Ah...okay...let 'er rip. What's up?" "Everyone in this room cares a great deal about you...some more than others," she said as she turned and looked in Jami's direction.

"Okay, well I care about you guys too…and?"

"We all want you to know that lately you've been behaving like a stupid, stupid moron."

"Well thank you Bikina, for such a warm and heartfelt compliment."

"Jeff, if you really put your mind to it there's very little that you're not capable of accomplishing. You could be practically anything you want in life, but it's painfully obvious to everyone here that you're totally out of control. You drink too much, you smoke too much pot and you're doing way too much coke…way, way too much. And every time we see you lately, you look like you haven't slept in days. You need to take a long serious look at yourself and maybe go check into a rehab center, or whatever you need. You've got a lot of people who'll stand behind you, but you really need to do something about it. We all love you and it hurts us to stand around and watch you turn into a real jerk and ruin your life," she said as her eyes began to swell with tears.

I sat still, looking around the room at the faces of all my friends etched with care and concern. I didn't know what to say. On one hand I wanted to feel irritated about them sticking their noses into my business, but their honesty and sincerity was obvious. The only emotions I felt were love, appreciation and humility.

"Wow…I really don't know what to say guys. I guess I should say thanks, thanks for being such good friends…and as for the partying, well yeah, I've been hitting it a little hard lately. But as for doing too much blow, don't worry, cause I've already decided that I'm toning that down…a lot," I lied.

Everyone there came up to me and gave me a hug and said a few more encouraging words. It reminded me of the Wednesday night prayer meetings that my dad and I used to go to when I was a little kid. Jami was the last to approach me. She put her arms around my neck, keeping a little space between us, but I pulled her close and gave her a big hug.

"Bikina called me at work and asked me to come here. At first I started not to come, but…I really do care about you, you big dope," she said as tears cascaded down her face.

"Thanks Jami and I'm sorry…for everything," I said softly.

"I really do love you, you know," she whispered in my ear.

I just wanted to be alone for a while and let it all sink in, so I lied and told them all that I had an appointment to show a house to a couple of newlyweds. After they filed out, I walked over to the couch and collapsed on it. Thoughts raced through my mind about so many things. I knew that I was out of control just like Bikina had said. I knew that I had made some terrible choices and taken some insane paths in my life.

As the Russian writer Aleksandr Solzhenitsyn poignantly said, "The line separating good from evil passes…right through every human heart." I had allowed this line to drift too far in the wrong direction. There was plenty of good in me, but it was obscured by the terrible and selfish decisions I routinely made. I began a rambling prayer.

"God I know that a lot of the things I've been doing are stupid and insane, like causing Julie to leave me, dropping out of law school, using drugs, selling them, SMUGGLING THEM AND FREEBASING. Man how stupid can I be? But I want to straighten up. I really want to. So I'm asking you for some help here because I've obviously made a huge mess of things and Hannah…well I guess that I'm asking for some help to get over her and go on with my life since I don't appear to be what she wants. Heck, I think I'm the main reason she left Nashville in the first place. I'm lost here and I really would like to have some answers, so please give me a little guidance, if you're really out there and if you're actually listening and care about me. I suppose that's about all for now. I'm gonna try to do better. I'm gonna try to be a better person…so thanks for listening, if you did."

I sat on the couch for a few more minutes and then got up and rounded up the three freebase pipes I had hidden in various places throughout the house. One by one I smashed the pipes to pieces by hurling them into the metal trash can outside in the driveway. And just like that, freebasing was a thing of the past. This decision and subsequent action demonstrated that I was capable of overcoming major obstacles, and freebasing was a pretty serious obstacle to overcome. I never freebased again. Unfortunately, freebasing was the only vice I overcame that day.

The next night I called up Bikina and asked her to meet me at the Gold Mine. When I got there she was waiting at the bar.

"Come on Bikina, I'm taking you to dinner,"

"Okay, but what's the occasion…are you feeling okay?" she said with a smile.

"I just want to thank you for putting that little reality check together for me yesterday. I really needed it. You're the best," I said as I gave her a kiss on her cheek.

We went to a restaurant called the Polaris, which sat atop one of Nashville's higher buildings. It was a romantic place and the entire restaurant rotated, enabling the diners to see spectacular views of the downtown area. We ate our meal, had a few drinks and talked for a long time. The two of us were actually rather close friends. I loved her, but not in that "take your breath away" type of love. She wasn't really like the proverbial *sister to me* since we had sex on countless occasions, but I cared deeply for her on a platonic level. It was difficult for me to explain to other people. In fact, I had a little trouble understanding it myself.

I ordered another round of drinks and while we were waiting, Bikina took both of my hands into her own. Her face took on a serious expression.

"Jeff, there's something that I've been meaning to talk with you about."

"Well, go ahead beautiful."

"Seriously now, listen...it's pretty obvious how I feel about you and...and I know you care about me. But you aren't in love with me. You'll never be in love with anyone as long as Hannah's stuck in your head. And I'm okay with that. You'll always be very special to me regardless of who you're with. Anyway, I've given it a lot of thought and I've decided that we should...well, that our relationship should...that we should stop sleeping together and just be friends.

"Bikina, you're wrong. I do love you, but in a way that's difficult to put into words. But as for us having sex, my feelings for you go beyond anything limited to a category - like the sexual genre. You've been such a great friend to me and whatever you decide is fine," I said as I squeezed her hands and smiled.

At that instant Daphne walked right by our table, but I was so preoccupied with our conversation, I didn't notice. Daphne gave us both a quick glance and scurried to the telephone to tell Jami what she assumed was happening.

Bikina and I finished our drinks and then left arm in arm. Though neither of us was certain that we could remain platonic, the plan was to be *just friends* from that point forward.

The next day, Jami drove to my house after work. I invited her inside, but noticed an air of belligerence about her that normally wasn't present.

"I tried calling you, but I only reached your machine, soooo...what did you do last night?" she asked.

"Oh not much...went to the Gold Mine, got something to eat, hung out, you know, the usual."

"Were you with anyone?"

"No, why do you ask?" I lied.

"Because, Jeff, I just wanted to see if you'd tell me the truth. And I should have known that you wouldn't. You're such a lying bastard," she said as her voice rose.

"What the hell are you talking about Jami?"

"I'm talking about you and your so called little *friend* going on a date."

"Okay, you're right, I should have been honest. Bikina went with me to eat. I wanted to thank her for getting all you guys together for my...ah...intervention. But it was nothing. In fact we talked about how we're just gonna be friends."

"Jeff, you don't take just a *friend* to a romantic place like the Polaris and besides, Daphne called and told me how you two were all over each other all lovey-dovey,"

"Well Jami, for your and that nosy whore's information, we *are* just friends and we weren't all over each other and if you don't like it, then leave me the hell alone."

"I don't believe a word you say you lying son of a bitch. Fuck you!" she screamed.

"Been there, done that," I wisecracked.

She tried to slap me, but I caught her arm and gave it a twist.

"Ow! You're hurting me...let go," she yelled.

"Well then stop trying to hit me!" I said as I continued to restrain her.

"Yeah, you're real brave aren't you, picking on a defenseless woman," she said as she began to cry.

I let go.

"Just go Jami and leave me alone."

"Don't worry, I plan to. Go to hell!" she said as she wiped her cheeks and ran out.

"Women, it seems like it's even worse when I tell them the truth, especially her," I sighed aloud, fondly remembering the day of the power outage, the first time we had sex.

A week passed. The phone rang.

"Hello."

"Hey Jeff, it's me, Brittany!"

"Uh...yeah...well..."

"It's the 24th today, my birthday. Now I'm legal! Can I come over?"

"Oh...well sure, why not? Come on over."

So we started going out. She still had to use a fake ID to get into bars and nightclubs, but since she was stunning and no longer jailbait, I really enjoyed being with her. We were dating for about two weeks when we ran into Jami at Chevy's. As she walked past us I said, "Hey Jami, still mad at me?" "Go to hell!" she snapped as she whizzed right by. "I probably will, and hey, maybe I'll see you there." "Who was that?" asked Brittany.

"Oh just a former friend of mine, I suppose."
The next day was the 3rd of July. I answered the phone.

"Hello?"

"Hey, you got a minute to talk with me?"

"Jami?"

"Yeah."

"Sure, what's up?"

"I guess that was your new girlfriend I saw you with last night, huh?"

"Yeah, I guess you could say that, why?"

"She's very pretty."

"Uh thanks. Ah…Jami, why are you calling me? I mean after…"

"I wanted to know if you'd sell me some pot. It's the 4th of July tomorrow and Johnny's spending it with his dad and I…"

"Well sure, come on over when you get off work. In fact, I wanted to apologize to you for the last time you were here, so come on by. As a matter of fact, why don't we do something tonight?"

"No, I don't think that would be a good idea Jeff. All we seem to do is argue. Look… I just want to drop by and get some weed from you if it's okay."

"Sure Jami. Okay then, I guess I'll see you about 4 o'clock then."

"Okay Jeff. Thanks…bye."

Ten minutes later the phone rang again.

"Hello."

"Jeff, it's me again. And I changed my mind…we can go out tonight, if you still want to."

"Alright then, but are you still coming over this afternoon?"

"Yeah, I'll be there around 4 o'clock…bye," she almost chirped into the phone.

"Man, what the hell did I just do?" I said out loud.

Jami came over and we made up. I was supposed to go out with Brittany, but I blew her off for another chance with Jami. We went out to eat and then back to her place where we spent the night together. The next morning I woke her up and said I needed to leave.

"I've got to run home real fast but I'll be right back. And we'll call Howie and Sarah and then we all can take the boat out to the lake if you want."

"How about if we just go by ourselves and take that inflatable yellow raft of yours out to that little cove you took me to that day, the one where we were the only boat around, remember?"

"Do you mean to tell me that you'd rather go float on that old rubber raft than ski and ride around in my boat?"

"Yes Jeff, I want us to spend the entire day alone together. No alcohol, no cocaine…just you and me…please?"

"Sure, okay, if that's what you want, that's what we'll do. But how about a joint or two…would that be okay?"

"Sure!" she laughed as she ran into my arms and began kissing me.

We stood there and held each other tightly for a moment.

I went home and took care of a couple of prearranged coke deals. Afterwards, I gathered up everything that we would need and stuffed it into a knapsack. I went into the garage and shook my head and laughed out loud as I admired my shiny new speedboat.

Well, if it's a smelly old rubber raft she wants, that's what the little lady will get.

I had bought the thing at an army-navy store years before. It was so big that half a dozen adults had once fit inside when we went sledding down the hill in front of my house that past winter. The sides were so high that you could lie down inside of it without being seen from the outside; a feature not lost on my libido, as I mulled over some salacious plans. The raft was far too bulky even in its deflated state to fit in the back of my twoseater, so I grabbed a foot pump, the raft, knapsack and the quilt Birdie had given me years ago and tossed it all into the bed of my pickup truck.

Jami had packed us a tasty lunch of submarine sandwiches, chips, cookies and apple pie, along with a cooler filled with ice and soft drinks. We drove to the place she had talked about. I inflated the yellow monster, which took nearly half an hour even with the foot pump, as Jami sat on the quilt rolling joints and smiling up at me.

It was a fantastic day, a beautiful, perfect day. The cove was small and isolated, so much so that only two boats came within view the entire afternoon. We spent the entire day together, just the two of us, just like she wanted. We smoked a few joints, stuffed ourselves silly and relaxed on Birdie's old quilt in the warm sun. We talked and laughed and had a wonderful time. Then we launched the raft, which Jami christened "Old Yeller." We drifted into the middle of the cove and my earlier thoughts of fornication began to solidify. We made slow and passionate love inside the comfort of the air-filled chambers until we realized that Old Yellar had run aground, and we had drifted all the way to the other side of the cove. We were both laughing as we got back into our swimsuits and I paddled back to the launch site.

After I finally managed to pull the raft out of the lake, Jami threw her arms around me, gave me a big kiss and whispered in my ear, "Thank you for doing this for us. I had a wonderful day. I love you."

As the day came to an end, we deflated Old Yeller and threw everything back into the pickup truck. I realized what a good time we had and how much I hated for the day to end. I couldn't recall a more enjoyable day in my entire life. Though there was one small thing that kept nagging at me…thoughts of Julie had been popping into my head for most of the afternoon and even after I had reflected on it for quite a while, I couldn't understand why for the life of me.

CHAPTER 17
HELLO ADAM!
"Let a hundred flowers bloom; let a hundred schools contend"
(Mao Tse-tung)

Jami and I had been spending a lot more time together since our pleasant and romantic 4th of July. She was so beautiful and I was actually beginning to love her. Yet there were several impediments that kept that special emotion from reaching fruition for me.

The top two obstacles were my love for Hannah and my own selfish nature, both of which continued to battle for supremacy in the hierarchy of my disturbed mind. Other problems included my love of drugs and money, and of course my weakness when it came to having sex with different women. After all, I could resist everything except temptation itself. But I really did sincerely care a great deal about Jami, and things had been going great for a couple of weeks.

I continued to fool around on Jami, even though I had cut my philandering back a little. I would pedal my bike the three blocks to Carol's house at least once each week when her husband was out of town. I'd stash it in her bushes and party with her for a while. Additionally, I frequently spent the night at Brittany's apartment, especially during the weekends that Jami had responsibility for little Johnny.

One Sunday morning in late July, I woke up in Brittany's bed with her naked body wrapped around me. I remembered only that I had been exceptionally drunk the night before. I got up, stumbled out of Brittany's bedroom, used the toilet and called my house to check my messages. Several friends wanted some coke or weed and then I heard a frantic message from Jami.

"Jeff, it's me...it's very important that I talk with you as soon as possible. Please call me as soon as you get this message...bye."

I tiptoed quietly back to Brittany's bedroom and peeked in. She was still asleep, so I shut her door and went back to the phone and dialed Jami's number.

"Hello."

"Jami, it's me. What's wrong?"

"Oh Jeff, please come over here right now. I need to talk with you." I could tell that she had been crying.

"What is it Jami, tell me."

"I don't want to talk about it over the phone. Please come over here right now. Please, I need to see you," she said and then began to sob over the phone.

"Okay, don't cry honey...I'm on my way."

I went back to the bedroom to get my car keys, woke up Brittany and told her that I had to leave. I made up a lie about a dope deal that I needed to take care of as soon as possible. She tried to entice me to crawl back under the covers again, but I somehow found the strength to resist her powerful lure, at least this time. Then I made it out to my car and started out for Jami's apartment, wondering just what the hell was going on.

As soon as I walked in the front door to her apartment, Jami threw herself into my arms and began weeping uncontrollably.

"Oh Jeff, I'm so sorry. I didn't mean to do this...I swear," she stammered in between sobs.

"Baby, what is it? Tell me...whatever it is..."

I guided her to her couch and sat down beside her with one hand rubbing her back and shoulders and the other holding her hand.

"Jeff, I think...I...I'm pregnant," she said through her tears.

"Are you sure?" I asked as my face turned a shade paler than normal.

"I've had morning sickness...nearly every day for the past week. I really think I am."

"Do you have one of those home pregnancy tests?"

"No."

"Well look, I'll run down to the drug store and get one. I'll be right back. It'll be okay honey."

I hurried to the drugstore and was back in a matter of minutes. She unwrapped the kit and went into the bathroom. While she was in there, Julie inexplicably popped into my thoughts again. Jami came out and handed me the testing kit.

"Here, take it. It takes a few minutes before the little negative or positive indicator shows up in the little window."

I sat down on the couch and held it in my hand for the better part of five minutes before looking down at it.

"What's it say?" she asked softly.

"Positive," I said in a whisper.

"I'll bet it happened on that day we spent at the lake on your raft."

"Jami...I...what do you want to do?"

"What do I want to do? What do you mean by that? If you're even suggesting that I get an abortion, NO WAY!" she said, her voice rising and cracking.

"No...no...of course not...that's not what I meant at all," I answered and at the same instant understood the apparently random onrush of thoughts about Julie.

I considered the possibility of some higher power causing such thoughts to permeate my mind. I thought about Julie and the baby we could have had, how old it would have been by now? 13? 14? 15? How great a mother she would have been, how having that baby may have stopped me from getting so involved with dope. Of course that would have been a lot of pressure on an infant!

"Jeff…HELLO JEFF!"

"Oh sorry…I was just…look Jami, the last thing in the world that I want is for you to have an abortion. It's just…it's just that I need a little time to clear my head and think about it, okay? This will all work out…I promise. So don't worry honey. I'll call you later this afternoon."

I went home in a state of confusion. I just wanted to be alone, so I pulled my car into the garage and closed all the curtains. Then I went down to the den and sat in silence, mulling everything over in my abnormally dope-free head. Suddenly the phone rang and broke my concentration.

"Hello."

"Hey," said an eerily familiar female voice on the other end.

"Hannah? Is that you?"

"Yeah it's me. I'm coming to Nashville on Tuesday and I'd like to see you if you have the time."

"Are you coming back for good?" my voice rising a few octaves and betraying my optimism.

"No, I'm just coming to see Daddy for the week, but I hope to spend some time with you too, okay?"

"There's nothing I'd like better," I said helplessly as the thought of her instantly pushed everything else out of my mind.

"Okay baby, then I'll see you on Tuesday. So tell all your other girlfriends that you'll be busy for at least a couple of days, okay?" she laughed.

"Okay Hannah, call me as soon as you get here."

I called Jami and told her to give me until next week to think about things, ensuring that I would be free to be with Hannah as much as possible. Then I called Brittany and told her that Jami was pregnant. She immediately hung up on me. My understanding with Candy was that I would call her whenever I wanted to get together, so that wasn't a problem. And then there was Carol, my married paramour. Since I only had Carol left to deal with, I called her and told her a lie about going to Florida for a few days and that I'd hopefully see her next week.

All day Tuesday I was preoccupied with thoughts of Hannah. I went to a real estate closing and barely heard a word they said. I came home, thoroughly cleaned my house and had just sat down to smoke a joint when she pulled into the driveway.

"I thought you were gonna call first," I said as I half walked, half ran to greet her.

"I couldn't wait to see you," she said as we met with an embrace and a passionate kiss.

We hurried back inside, practically tore off each other's clothes and made love until the sun went down. I was once again in seventh heaven with the girl of my dreams. I let the answering machines catch all my calls as we ordered a pizza and sexually explored one another until we were both exhausted and had passed out with our bodies intertwined.

When I woke up the next morning and looked over at Hannah, I realized that I was still crazy about her and that I always would be. However, my next thoughts included Julie, Jami and two babies, one of which I planned on raising and loving.

Hannah told me that she planned to go back to Columbia in a few days. I was a little sad, but I also felt a little relieved. I had a baby on the way and I was trying to focus on making sure this child would be okay. Nonetheless, I avoided everyone and everything as we spent the next two days together. Then Friday morning arrived.

"Okay, I guess I'm out of here. You seem kind of distant. What's the problem? Don't you love me anymore?" she asked as she kissed me goodbye.

"I love you Hannah. I'll always love you…and that's my problem," I said as I held onto her tightly for a moment before letting her go.

She left that morning, and although my love for her would never fade away, I felt that I had finally seen the last of the ultimate love of my life.

Afterwards Jami called me from the bank. She asked if I would go with her to the doctor for her first sonogram that afternoon. I agreed and picked her up. We drove to the appointment in relative silence. After we arrived and were called into the back for her examination, I sat and watched in awe as the doctor pointed out the penis of my baby boy. A son! I was going to have a son! I had so many thoughts going through my mind at the same time that it felt as though my head might literally explode. Fear collided with joy and confusion as a plethora of emotions permeated my being.

As we drove back to the bank, I kept looking over at Jami. She was so beautiful and radiant. And somehow, I'm not quite sure how, words began coming out of my mouth, words that seemed to flow on their own volition, with no need of thought or effort on my part.

"Jami," I said very seriously.

"Jeff," she said mockingly with a deep voice.

"Jami, ah...how would you feel about moving in with me, you and Johnny of course?"

"Are you serious?" she asked, disbelieving.

"Yeah, I'm serious. I want to take care of you and..."

There was an eerie moment of calm that caused me to glance over at her. Her face was aglow with the most dazzling smile I had ever seen.

"So, do you want to?"

"Oh Jeff...OH...YES, YES, YES!" she screamed and grabbed me around the neck.

"Oh Jeff...I love you. I love you. I..."

"LOOK OUT!" I said as I gave the steering wheel a twist and veered out of the way of oncoming traffic.

"Whew! Damn Jami, you almost killed the two...ah...the three of us," I said to her as she continued to smile at me.

"I love you Jeff Collins, I really do."

She looked so happy, and then it happened. I couldn't help myself as the words slipped over my tongue and out of my mouth.

"I love you too, Jami."

I knew that the only woman I actually loved was Hannah, but damn it, I was determined to love this beautiful redheaded mother of my unborn child, who for some incomprehensible reason was obviously crazy about me.

I dropped her off at the bank and went home. I put my car in the garage and closed all the curtains, because I wanted to be alone. Then I went down to the den and got down on my knees and began to pray.

"Okay God, if you're really out there and you care about me at all, I really could use some help about now. I feel as though you're probably the cause of me suddenly thinking about Julie and her abortion and everything, so if you're trying to tell me something, I'm listening. So please, help me deal with this. I want to be a better person. I want to be in love with Jami. I want to be a good, no a great father to our son...and a good stepfather to Johnny. I want to quit selling dope and I want to stop using dope. I want to stop screwing around on Jami. So please God, if you're out there and you're listening, and you care about me, how about a hand?"

Jami's lease was up in about six more weeks so we agreed that she and Johnny would move in with me around the first of October. In the interim I went through some near-miraculous changes. I stopped pulling all-nighters, I stopped seeing Candy and cut way back on my cocaine use. I began to actually apply myself as a real estate agent and I had soon listed and sold several very desirable properties. I went to a furniture store and bought a crib. I made a miniature basketball court under the carport for Johnny. I landscaped my lawn and planted a couple of fruit trees and some flowers...FLOWERS!

All my friends could barely believe all these transformations they were witnessing, and they were impressed. What they didn't see was the fact that I was still dealing and using cocaine and marijuana, and I was still drinking, albeit to a lesser extent. And although she was the only one, I continued to see Carol whenever her husband was away. I had improved somewhat, but still needed a massive amount of work before I could be considered a good person.

I made a considerable commission when I sold an enormous house in west Nashville to a wealthy elderly couple, Herman and Rosalyn Reeves, who appeared to instantly develop a fondness for me. Mr. Reeves, a top-level executive for a global conglomerate, offered me a position as a factory representative. The money he offered was surprising, but I politely declined. However, shortly thereafter I was practically forced to reconsider. I was assured that travel would be limited and told that I could continue to sell real estate. I just could not turn down such a deal. Once again, I was leading a charmed life.

Jami and Johnny moved in with me the following week. When Jami told me that she was quitting cigarettes, drugs and alcohol during her entire pregnancy, I questioned her resolve, but I shouldn't have. Jami gave up all of those harmful substances and never failed to demonstrate a tremendous love for our baby. And while I did not stop my involvement with drugs, I did feel an enormous sense of pride for the mother of my son.

Then I suddenly decided to finally end my infidelity. I bicycled to Carol's place three days before Jami moved in and one of our regular trysts ensued, but as I was leaving, I told Carol about Jami's pregnancy and how I thought it best if we didn't fool around anymore. She didn't believe for one second that I could resist her, but when I turned her down the next time she called, she understood I was serious. If I had also stopped using and selling my two drugs of choice, my life would probably have turned out very differently. Unfortunately for me and the other people in my life, my character was much too weak.

Jami was ecstatic with the perceptible changes in me. We spent a happy holiday season together as a family and looked forward to the first part of April when the baby was due. A Caesarean section was planned for the delivery and I wanted to be in the delivery room for the birth. As my friends sat around in the waiting area, Adam Holden Collins was delivered by C-section, gently cleaned and then handed to me. I looked down on my son with overpowering and overflowing love. The little guy weighed in at seven pounds and 14 ounces and was a perfect, beautiful baby boy.

"Hey little guy, I'm your daddy and I'm gonna love you and take really good care of you," I promised.

It was the 4th of April, exactly 16 years to the day from Julie's abortion, and when I thought about it, I experienced an uncomfortable feeling in the pit of my stomach. Ignoring the sensation, I handed Adam back to a nurse, leaned over and kissed Jami. Then I bolted down to the waiting room to tell my friends that everything was okay. Wes, Tina, Gary, Sarah, Bo, Gary and Bikina were among those waiting on the news. As soon as I entered the room and told them that both mother and son were doing great, Bikina jumped up and grabbed me around the neck and gave me a kiss on the cheek.

"Congratulations Daddy!" she sang out with a big enthusiastic smile.

"Thanks Bikina and everyone else too. Hey, they're taking him to the nursery in a little while so let's all go down there and you guys can see him for yourselves."

After standing around and talking for a while, we walked to the nursery to check out one of the newest members of the human race. And while standing there admiring young Adam, another new father walked up to see his own new baby.

"Jeff, do you know who that guy is?" Gary whispered.

"No...who is he?"

"Man, that's Steve Winwood!"

Steve Winwood's band was one of my favorite groups. Hannah had gotten me to listen to them one night when we were together and I instantly loved their music.

"Excuse me, are you Steve Winwood?" I asked as I extended my hand.

"Yes I am," he said as he shook my hand.
"I'm a big fan of yours. Are you a new dad, too?"

"Yep, that's my little girl right there in the front row."

"She's beautiful. Congratulations...that's my little boy right beside her. Man I wish that Hannah...uh...I mean...ah...Jami was here to meet you..." I stammered.

I felt everyone staring at me in disbelief at the words that had just come out of my mouth.

Soon everyone left the hospital except for me. I stayed in Jami's room until after dark. After making sure she was all right, I kissed her goodbye and told her I would return in the morning. On my way home, I stopped at a convenience store for gas and as I was exiting the place after paying for the gas, Mary Anne came walking right up to me. Tom Macklin had my violation of the restraining order dismissed several months before, but he had warned me to steer clear of her at all costs. This was no problem since I loathed her and considered her to be mentally unstable.

"Hey Jeff, I heard that you're going to have a baby. Is that true?"

I threw both arms up in the air, sidestepped her and began jogging to my car and laughing out loud.

"Wait a minute. Let me...can I talk to you for a second. Hey Jeff." I continued to laugh as I closed the car door and drove away.

We brought Adam home the next day and everything was great in our happy little home. I was working and making very good money and along with my dope dealing, I was beginning to save up a nice nest egg. Jami was a wonderful mother. She doted on Johnny and little Adam. I loved my little boy with a love more powerful than I imagined possible. And I loved the way Jami interacted with Adam and Johnny. I admired the way she tenderly went about such simple tasks as giving Adam a bath. Every motion she made demonstrated how much love this beautiful, effervescent, young woman held in her heart and how much joy motherhood provided for her.

When Adam would wake us up in the middle of the night for a diaper change or wanting to be fed, it never bothered me. We would take turns getting up to tend to him, but I preferred for Jami to get up. This wasn't because I wanted to stay in bed, but because I enjoyed witnessing all the love, tenderness and caring that radiated from her as she ran to take care of the baby...my baby...our baby. And each time she rose from our bed, there was this little thing she'd always say so very softly to Adam:

"Just a minute...just a minute...Momma's coming...just a minute."

It was the sweetest thing I'd ever heard, a simple little group of words that would stay with me for the rest of my life. "Just a minute...just a minute." I was beginning to love her.

One Friday afternoon we dropped Johnny off at his father's for the weekend and then headed to the grocery store. We filled the basket with our selections and I pushed it to the checkout line. I was bent over making goofy faces at five-month old Adam when I noticed a pair of black high heels walking toward us. The woman stopped right next to the cart and I looked up. It was Carol, who was looking particularly stunning that day.

"Oh, what an adorable little baby. Is it a little boy?" she asked as she smiled flirtatiously at me.

"Yep...he's a boy," I answered, wishing she would retreat from the obvious.

"What's his name and how old is he?"

"He's five and a half months old and his name is Adam," said Jami, adding a frosty edge to her tone and stepping closer to me.

"Well aren't you just a little cutie. Why I'll bet you'll grow up to be a real heartbreaker just like your Daddy. Isn't that right precious?" she said in baby talk as she bent over towards Adam and cut her eyes up at me.

During the ride home Jami fumed until she could no longer contain herself.

"Who was she, Jeff?"

"Who?" I asked with an aura of sainthood.

"You know exactly who I'm talking about. That little slut that was flirting with you back there."

"Me? Heck, I thought that she was flirting with you, little man," I said glancing at Adam.

"Go to hell Jeff."

"Damn Jami, I haven't done a thing. So go ahead and get mad if you want to, but you'll be angry over nothing," I said indignantly.

We pulled into the back of the house and I jumped out and began unloading the sacks of groceries. She picked up the baby and stepped close to me, kissing me on the cheek.

"Okay, I'm sorry. Okay? Can we just forget it?"

"Sure," I said as I carried the bags into the house.

Then just as we entered the den together, there was a female voice leaving a message on the answering machine. It was Tanya Chance, the nymphomaniac I had known since college.

"Hello Jeffy, it's Tanya. I'm gonna be in Music City next weekend and I was wondering if you'd like to get together. I'll be staying at our favorite hotel, The Hyatt and I'm sure you remember that I have virtually no gag reflex to speak of...soooo...I'll call you back later next week."

"You son of a bitch!" she said as she stomped up the stairs with the baby.

"Oh come on Jami, I haven't seen that girl since...hell, way before I met you," I said as I followed her up the stairs and into the bedroom, where she carefully laid Adam in his crib.

"It sure didn't sound like it to me."

"Look, I've been absolutely faithful to you since you moved in. I swear it. Come on honey, let's not fight."

"How about just **before** I moved in Jeff...about a month before to be exact. How about then?" her voice rising.

"Wha...what are you talking about...I," I stuttered as my memory flashed back to Hannah's visit.

"Did you fool around on me then...with Hannah?"

"No...of course not," I lied as I wondered to myself if she possessed some kind of psychic ability.

"Well let's just see you explain these then," she said as she reached into her purse and pulled out some pictures of Hannah taken during her last visit, which she flung in my face.

"Damn it Jami, those pictures are from a long time before that," I lied.

"Oh no they aren't. You bought that couch she's sitting on less than a month before I moved in. I know because I went with you and helped you pick it out, you lying bastard!" she screamed.

Our argument caused Adam to begin crying in his crib. I walked towards Jami with the intention of embracing and calming her, but she was too angry.

"STAY AWAY FROM ME, YOU FUCKING LIAR!" she screamed as she picked up a heavy wooden coat hanger and swung it viciously at my head.

I ducked as the thing slipped out of her hand and sailed two feet directly over Adam, who by this time was really wailing.

"You almost hit him, you stupid bitch!" I said as my right hand took on a life of its own and slapped her violently high on her left cheek.

"OW! Oh my God, you hit me. I can't believe you hit me," she said as she began to sob.

"Jami...I...I'm so sorry," I said as I stepped closer and tried to hold her.

"Get the hell away from me," she hissed.

I turned and stomped out of the house and sped off in my car. I stopped at the nearest phone booth and called Carol.

"Is your old man there?"

"No, I just hung up from talking to him. He's in Atlanta. Why do you ask?" she asked in a knowing and teasing tone.

"I'll be there in a minute."

"I knew you couldn't stay away forever. Come on over," she laughed.

I stayed there for several hours as we snorted cocaine, smoked pot and naturally, intercourse ensued.

I applied my usual illogical rationalization of what transpired between Jami and I to battle feelings of guilt as I returned home and pulled into the carport.

"Man, this was not my fault...not this time," I convinced myself as I walked into the house.

I walked into the den. She was sitting on the couch holding Adam and I saw her eye. It was already red and swollen. Obviously it would be black by the end of the next day. My earlier assessment regarding my culpability collapsed instantly.

"Oh my God Jami…I am so sorry honey. Oh my God…"

She sat there in silence. I went over and gently took Adam from her arms and pressed his little warm body as close to my heart as I could. Then I began to pace. I said how sorry I was and how much I loved her, both of them. Tears flowed down my face as I clung to the tiny life in my arms. I couldn't believe that I had hit the mother of my child. Not another woman, not again. I paced the house with Adam sound asleep on my chest. I continued to pace and whisper that I was sorry, very sorry, for nearly an hour. I was truly remorseful, to the point of nausea and right after I put Adam in his crib, I literally vomited.

Jami's eye turned black, very black, by the following morning. It was so bad that she wore sunglasses whenever she went out for the next two weeks and every time I looked at her, I cringed in shame and regret.

I told myself that, God or no God, I was going to really straighten up. However, the die had recast. I had once again tasted the fruit of another woman and I knew that I was too weak to resist the lure of other females. I realized that infidelity was a part of me and it was extremely likely that I would be sampling various sexual entrees in the near future.

The future happened two days later. I saw Brittany at Friday's at lunchtime and we ended up rolling around in her bed that night. I went home with a big lie about having to go out of town for Mr. Reeves, but Jami was a lot sharper than Mary Anne. She didn't buy the story, so she surreptitiously called my office and found out that I had no business out of town for over a week. She didn't mention a thing to me at that time.

Tanya was coming to town the next week, and I called her and arranged to meet her at the Hyatt the following Friday night. I spent the entire night getting very intimately reacquainted with the seductress. By the time I stumbled out of the hotel the next morning, I was exhausted.

When I pulled into my driveway at a little past seven AM I noticed that Jami's car was gone, and when I entered the house, I found out why. The house was empty. She left me a note telling me that it was over. She had had enough. She would make arrangements to pick up her things as soon as possible. Jami, Johnny and Adam were gone, along with another one of my opportunities for a happy, fulfilling life.

CHAPTER 18
ANOTHER WAKEUP CALL IGNORED

"We have dealt the devil no serious blow by calling him neurosis,"
(Carl Jung)

I discovered that they had left on a cold and windy November morning. I walked slowly through the house, which was empty and devoid of life. I wandered into the bedroom and stared into Adam's empty crib. I was now certain that the God I had been praying to, either didn't give a damn about me, or didn't even exist. After all, I had sincerely asked for the guidance necessary to straighten out my life and things were worse than ever.

I went downstairs, took the phone off the hook, closed the curtains, grabbed a bottle of Crown Royal from the bar and collapsed on the couch. I pulled out a mirror and dumped out a couple of grams of blow. After snorting several lines and taking a couple of strong pulls off the bottle, I started rolling joints. And after I was good and fried, I repeated the entire process again and again until passing out.

I had the wildest and most vivid dream of my life. Adam was a two-year old toddler and there was a beautiful little blonde-headed girl about the same age with him. They were standing in front of me smiling and holding hands. When I asked Adam who she was, he said that she was his sister Wendy and that they wanted for me to play with them. I bent down towards them in order to take their little hands. Julie and Jami suddenly stepped into the way.

"Uh uh, you can't play with them until you get rid of all that poison," they chimed in unison and pointed behind me.

I turned around to see a gigantic mound of cocaine. There were half naked women laying all over it. I saw Carol, Tanya and Brittany among countless others I didn't know, or at least didn't recognize. They were all spreading their legs and calling for me to come to them. Then I felt a tug on each hand. It was Adam and Wendy pulling on me as they looked up at me with their angelic faces. I looked back at all the sirens and then back down at the two children. The cocaine and women were powerful and incredibly enticing and each time I looked at them, it became harder and harder to resist.

The children began crying. They pulled away and moved between me and my weaknesses, and although they were now directly in my field of vision, I remained focused on the coke and the women. The longer I stared at this incredible scene, the louder Adam cried and the fainter Wendy became. Jami and Julie approached and both gave me a look of disgust. Jami picked up Adam and walked away. Julie screamed and when I finally tore my gaze away from my two vices, I saw that Wendy had completely disappeared. Julie started screaming Wendy's name over and over. I then noticed another female figure stepping out of the shadows. It was Mary Anne laughing and pointing at me, as Julie kept crying and screaming hysterically for Wendy.

"Wendy...Wendy...WENDY!"

"WENDY!" I woke up to hear myself yelling.

I was laying on the couch and absolutely drenched in sweat.

Jami went back to work and moved into an apartment complex, but she wouldn't tell me where. I gave her money for Adam each week from the drive thru lanes at the bank, which she grudgingly accepted. When I called, she wouldn't talk, except to tell me that I couldn't see my son, at least not until we had gone to court in order to set up the formal processes of paying child support and visitation.

The next month was more or less a blur. I stayed so drunk and high, I could barely recall any of it. I pulled multiple all-nighters, even a couple of all-weekenders! I had a vague memory of flying to Atlantic City, but the details had been washed away by mass quantities of booze and drugs. I remembered that Carol had spent a few nights in my bed followed by several different trollops, whose names I could not recall. Heck, maybe I never knew their names!

I did remember calling Hannah. I dialed her number one night and she sounded as though she had just woken up.

"Hello."

"Hey beautiful, do you know who this is?"

"Of course I do...it's my honey Tommy," she answered sleepily.

I hung up the phone. Then I called Candy who was more than willing to come over to cheer me up. She was there within an hour and we immediately began snorting coke and screwing all over the house. About an hour later the phone rang.

"Hey, if that's for me, tell them I'm not here," she said.

"And why would someone be calling here for you Candy?" I laughed as I reached for the phone. "Hello."

"Let me talk to Candy," said an unknown voice on the other end.

"Ah...she's not here," I said as I gave her a quizzical look.

"Yeah, she's there. Now let me talk with her, you asshole."

"Dude, like I said, she's not here, and you need to find someone else to play with," I said as I hung up the phone.

"Why the hell did you give my number to that idiot?"

"I'm sorry, it's Bobby...this guy I've been dating. I only gave it to my mom and told her to only call if it's an emergency. I guess she must have given it to..." She was interrupted by the phone ringing again.

"Hello."

"Listen motherfucker, I..."

I slammed down the phone.

The guy called back more than a dozen times, until I had reached my boiling point.

Then it rang again.

"Hello, may I help you?" I answered mockingly.

"For the last time ass-wipe, let me talk to Candy."

"Well I would Bobby, but you see, you wouldn't be able to understand her right now...because she's got her mouth full of my dick," I said, slamming down the receiver.

Less than an hour later the loud sound of breaking glass echoed through my bedroom. The guy had thrown a damn rock through the window! Five minutes later the phone rang again.

"Hello!" I yelled irately.

"Hey *seenyor*, this *ees* your local Mexican window *feexers* and we were wondering if you needed any of your windows *feexed*," he said with a very bad and very fake Mexican accent.

"I hope you're enjoying yourself you jerk wad, because you won't be laughing long *seenyor*. I'll be seeing you," I said calmly and hung up the phone.

Then I made Candy tell me everything she knew about the guy. She described him in detail, including what kind of car he had, that his name was Bobby Huggins and that he was just a 22 year-old punk. She also gave me his address and told me about Woody's Place, the seedy neighborhood bar he frequented.

Several days later I got Howie to ride with me over to Bobby's house. Howie was a friend I could always count on when trouble reared its head, so I brought him along in case the guy had a buddy or two with him. I pulled in front of his house where some teenaged boy said we had just missed him and that Bobby and some other guy had just pulled out on their way to Woody's Place, the dive Candy had told me about. So we sped down to Woody's Place, and there was his black, beat up Grand Prix just pulling into

the parking lot. I stopped my car, got out and walked quickly over to Bobby, who had just shut his door.

"Hey Bobby, how ya doing old buddy?" I said, making sure he was indeed the reprobate who had smashed my window.

"Hey, what's up…uh"

That's as much as he got out of his mouth before my fists began colliding with his face. I had already hit him about a dozen times, before his pal came running around the car. But he quickly stopped in his tracks when he saw Howie turn to face him. By this time Bobby was blubbering and folded up on the ground. I started to give him a few well placed kicks, but when I looked down at the human accordion and saw that there was no fight left in him, I stepped back.

"Now I figure that what I just gave you is just about equal to the eight hundred dollars worth of window I had to replace…but if you disagree, just let me know. You obviously have my number, so give me a call if you want to discuss this further, and I'll get back with you, okay?"

The following Tuesday Jami called me wanting money to buy clothes for Adam. I offered to take them to the mall and buy him whatever he needed, but she refused, saying that she didn't want to be around me and that she wasn't about to let me take Adam anywhere by myself. I asked Jami if she would allow it if I got Bikina to go along with us, which resulted in her cussing me and slamming down the phone. I sincerely wanted to take care of my little boy, but I also wanted Jami to know that I was not going to be browbeaten into doing it her way. And since we were both extremely obstinate individuals, we constantly argued about anything connected to Adam's financial support. I kept sticking a hundred bucks into the tube at the bank once a week, but that was all she was getting until she started letting me see him.

Being a full time jerk is hard work. But even losers need a break from their routine now and then, so I decided to take one. I made the decision to give church a try. I picked out a small Baptist church close enough to my house to be convenient, but far enough away so that the probability of knowing anyone would be low.

I knew the Bible fairly well, but had not been to church since I was in military school where all the cadets were forced to go every Sunday. The first Sunday morning I attended church, I locked eyes with a well-endowed blonde cutie who was singing in the choir. After the service she changed out of her scarlet choir robe and approached me under the guise of welcoming me to their little congregation.

She was twenty-nine and her name was Lola Myerson. She had the face and demeanor of an angel. It's been said that looks are deceiving and Lola did nothing to refute the aphorism. She invited me to lunch and by nightfall we were doing the mattress mambo in her bed. My intentions concerning going to church were good, but resulted in little more than another notch in my bedpost. Lola went to church every Sunday and Wednesday, but she was engaged in her own struggles. She loved sex and as I quickly found out, she loved marijuana and cocaine as well.

Another coke whore, and in church of all places…whodathunkit? I thought to myself the first time I watched her bend over and suck up a couple of healthy lines of blow.

I continued to see her along with Candy, Brittany, Tanya, Carol and another half dozen or so women. The next time I went to Brittany's apartment, I walked in on her freebasing with two other girls, but now even I was too smart to begin doing that crap again. Brittany was pretty and fun and I really liked her, but I knew that I had to stay away if she was going to be messing around with that poison.

"Brittany, give me a call if you decide to give up doing that shit," I said as I turned around, shook my head and walked out.

She never even looked up from the pipe.

Bikina, Danny and Wes and I were sitting in my den on a late Thursday evening about a week later. We heard something that sounded like a gunshot and some other noise coming from upstairs. We hurried upstairs to investigate and found a bullet hole in the picture window in the living room. The bullet had gone all the way through the wall on the other side of the room and into a kitchen cabinet where it shattered a couple of glasses.

"That little son of a bitch, I'm gonna kill him."

"Who Jeff…who did this?" asked a frantic Bikina.

"That little punk who busted out the window back in my bedroom. The one I beat the shit out of. It had to be him."

"Jeff you need to get a gun. This guy is obviously nuts," said Wes.

"No he doesn't, Wes. What you *need* to do is call the police and let them handle this," said Bikina defiantly with her hands on her hips.

"I'm not calling the cops Bikina."

"Well you need to do something Jeff. At least let me bring you a pistol over here in case this nut comes back. Tina's father left her a bunch of them when he died and they're just lying in the upstairs closet gathering dust," said Wes.

"Yeah, okay…whatever."

"No Jeff, don't. The last thing in the world you need is a stupid gun," said Bikina.

"So what should I do Bikina? Let the little punk get away with this? I don't think so. Yeah Wes, go ahead and bring one. What kind anyway?"

"How about a Ruger .357 Magnum, but I don't have any bullets for it."

"Well what good will that do?"

"I have some that'll work in it. They're Teflon coated. I'll bring them over tomorrow," Danny offered.

"Teflon? Why Teflon…can I fry an egg on them? What does that mean?"

"It just means they're good bullets Jeff...trust me," said Danny as he shook his head at my naiveté when it came to firearms.

Danny returned the next afternoon and handed me eight cartridges.

"And hey, be sure to shoot him in the front, even if he's on your property...okay?" said Danny seriously.

"Danny, I don't plan on shooting anybody. In fact I don't even have the gun. Wes hasn't brought it over yet."

But Wes showed up early the next morning and handed me the pistol. As soon as the weapon touched my hand, I experienced a strange sensation. I hated guns. I always had, probably stemming from the time in my childhood when my mom fired that pistol in her bedroom. The only weapon I had was a set of nunchakus that I sometimes took with me in my car when I traveled.

I didn't like having the gun, but I took it just the same. I had stashed the bullets in my locked briefcase, so I opened it up and placed the unloaded revolver inside.

"Man, this is insane, I don't want to shoot anybody, much less kill 'em," I said aloud.

My life continued down the same predictably destructive path. I periodically went to church. I argued with Jami about Adam and about money over the telephone. I engaged in fornication with what must have been a significant percentage of the attractive twentysomething year old females in Nashville; at least the ones who did cocaine. I used and sold pot and coke and partied like the end of time was imminent. The critical and ominous difference was now I had possession of an extremely powerful and dangerous handgun.

I partied in the New Year in my normal fashion. I laid down wagers for every college football bowl game, including over and under bets, and even halftime bets on each game. In spite of being ahead in every single game at halftime, I lost nearly every bet.

My only wins were point-total bets and the halftime bet I made on the LSU-Nebraska game. I initially thought that I would win over ten thousand bucks, but ended up shelling out around forty-four hundred. So 1989 did not start out well for me, and if I had been paying close attention, I might have heard the heavy footfall of karma as it began to rumble toward me.

I hadn't seen Adam for months and it troubled me that I was probably going to miss some important milestones in his life. I thought about how I could miss his first word, his first step, and even the first time he would say "Dada." When my traits such as narcissism, violence and insane fearlessness were juxtaposed with my vulnerability and love for Adam (and Hannah), the complexity of my psyche was apparent. The ultimate battle for supremacy inside my chaotic and drugged mind would soon decide the fate of a lot of people.

I called the bank one day and asked Jami if she would go to church with me the following Sunday. I hoped that she would consent and bring Adam along, but she gave me an abrupt *NO* and hung up.

Lola called on Sunday morning and asked if I wanted to go to the morning service with her. I said yes. She parked her Mustang in the front of my house and came inside. We decided to take my car, but first Lola needed to get her purse from her car, so I pulled around in front, got out and opened the door for her.

Just as I shut her door, Jami pulled up in front, staring in disbelief at the young woman in my car. She was all dressed up for church and had little Adam all decked out in his car seat, apparently having changed her mind. I took a couple of quick steps towards them to get a better view of Adam, when Jami screamed an obscenity or three, flipped me the bird and sped off in a rage.

I knew that she was angry, but didn't have any idea how mad she was until I returned to my house after church. There were two big ruts in my manicured front lawn from what I surmised to be the rear wheels of someone's car. I went inside and walked through the house. All of the telephones and the answering machine were missing, along with a giant novelty plastic beer bottle that was in the den and which had been filled with nickels, dimes and quarters. The thing had to weigh a couple of hundred pounds. That caused me to temporarily doubt that Jami had been the culprit. Then I went upstairs and discovered that practically all the food from the cabinets and the refrigerator was gone, while all the places where I hid cash and drugs were undisturbed.

"No thief breaks in, takes the food and leaves money and dope. It had to be that little bitch," I said aloud.

Early Monday morning I walked over to my next-door neighbors' house to borrow their telephone. I phoned Jami at the bank and threatened to call the police unless she brought back the phones and answering machine.

"They're sitting next to your car under your carport," she said matter-of-factly and then hung up abruptly.

I walked to the back of the house and sure enough, there they sat along with the giant bottle of coins.

"How in the hell did she pick that thing up?" I asked aloud while scratching my head in disbelief.

Since two ex-girlfriends had now used their keys to my house to burglarize me, I decided it was time to change the locks.

"I should have changed them when that loony Mary Anne left," I grumbled aloud to myself.

Unfortunately, very unfortunately, I never got around to actually doing it.

As March rolled around I found myself hanging out in different haunts. I had been barred from the Gold Mine for punching out the bouncer and I rarely went to Chevy's or anyplace where I thought there was a chance of running into Mary Anne or Jami. Since Bikina started bartending at a country and western bar called Billy's, I began to spend most of my partying hours there.

Billy's was a rough place and since I almost always went there alone, I began to keep the loaded Ruger pistol in my glove compartment. I had been patronizing Billy's for about a month when one Saturday night while I was sitting at the bar talking with Bikina, her eyes focused intently on something behind me.

"Oh my God Jeff, don't turn around."

"Why, is some guy trying to rope a cow?" I laughed.

"No, it's Jami and she's staring a hole through you."

"Okay then, that's all for me. Here's about what I owe you. I'm out of here. See you later Bikina," I said as I turned up my drink, guzzled it down and hightailed it towards the door.

I made it quickly to my car and was getting inside when a very drunk, but still beautiful Jami came running towards me.

"Hey Jeff, lets call a truce. Smoke a joint with me...please."
"Sure I will...if you'll let me see Adam."

"Aw, he's at the babysitter's for the night, but you can see me, unless you're on your way to...whoever's house...or you don't want to."

"Okay, come on and get in."

She jumped into the passenger seat and as soon as she closed the door, she reached and opened the glove compartment.

"Where's the coke. I want a hit...I...oh my God Jeff. You have a damn gun in here."

"Sorry, I've had a little trouble lately," I said as I reached over to close the compartment and lock it.

She wanted to smoke a joint and go for a drive, so we did. When I stopped for a red light, we looked at each other briefly and then began kissing passionately. Long after the signal changed to green we remained lip locked at the intersection, making out like a couple of sixteen-year-olds.

"Wanna come to my apartment and spend the night with me? Then in the morning, we can go and pick up Adam...okay?" she asked when we finally came up for air.

"Jami, are you serious? There's nothing I'd rather do!"

We began dating again and I saw Adam nearly every day for the next three months. It was the best our relationship had ever been. We were together nearly every night and during that time I remained faithful to her. I loved going to Adam's one-year birthday party, and afterwards I took him to the toy store and bought him practically everything that turned his little head. Jami was so happy with the way things were going that she insisted that I take a key to her apartment. It was another chance for me to have a good life. Unsurprisingly, it was also another chance for me to screw it up.

One Tuesday about one o'clock in the afternoon my doorbell rang and I opened the door to see Carol's very seductive profile.

"Hey there lover. I am so horny. I haven't been fucked in months and I need some dick...and I know I came to the right place!" she said as she slid by me and walked eagerly back to the bedroom.

I followed her and in seconds we were naked. She was telling the truth. She was horny, so horny that she clawed my back up with her fingernails, not that I minded much. But I did have to get her out of the house soon. We had been in bed for hours and Jami would be getting off work and she would often drop by unannounced. So I ushered her on out the door, made the bed and tried to think of any obvious clues to my afternoon delight. There were none. Good. I was home free, or so I thought.

But that night while I was at Jami's, she spotted the claw marks on my back when I got out of her bed. And in spite of the pitiful attempts I made to explain them away, she screamed a cluster of profanities and tossed me out. Same program, different day!

So I returned to my collection of women and to patronizing escort services. On the 8th of August, Gloria Lovelace, the owner of one of the services I frequently used, called me and said that she needed some coke. I told her to come on over and she was there within thirty minutes. I had often spoken to her, but only over the phone. When she walked inside, I was pleasantly surprised. She was a hot-looking blonde, who almost immediately began flirting with me.

"So you're the stud that so many of my girls have been falling in love with," she said as she batted her eyes.

"Yeah, right...as if I believe that."

"No, seriously, most of them are always begging me to send them whenever you call and always talking about how you're one of the best lovers they've ever had...and just generally carrying on about you. I just wanted to see what all the fuss was about."

"So that's why you came...to find out for yourself?" I laughed.

"Sure, where's your bedroom? Back this way? Come on, we don't have a lot of time," she sang without hesitation as she laid down her purse on my living room sofa, and struck out for the bedroom as though she had a GPS reading on my bed.

"Skankorama!" I silently mouthed as I followed her bouncy little derriere down the corridor.

We went to the bedroom and did mattress exercises for around thirty minutes. Gloria had said that she was in a hurry, so she dressed quickly and we went back to the living room. I laid an eight ball of coke on the coffee table, while Gloria counted out two hundred and fifty bucks and handed it to me. Then she kissed me goodbye, said that she hoped to have some more *fun* with me soon, scooped up the eight ball and left.

The same thing happened two days later on the 10th of August but without the sex, because I had a real estate closing I was late for. Besides, the truth was that she wasn't that great a lay. She reminded me of a smaller version of Mary Anne, which was less than an arousing recollection.

This was the month of August, which had been less inauspicious throughout my life than, say those who lived in Pompeii on August 24, 79AD, but typically ill-fated for me nonetheless. This year would be no different. Gloria had indeed heard from several of her employees about me. But it wasn't about my sexual prowess so much as it was about
my generosity with cocaine. She had found out that some of her girls had been coming back to my house and offering their *services* to me for free or at least with no cash for her.

Therefore, being the cunning businesswoman that she was, Gloria talked to a cop she knew who was a member of the local vice squad. She had convinced him to put a wire in her purse while she made two buys from me.

The cosmic forces that had shielded me from so many crises failed me this time and with unexpected consequences. It would have been so much better if I had been arrested right then and right there.

It was nearly midnight on Thursday, the 11th of August. Bikina and I were playing backgammon in my den, when we heard a noise that seemed to come from the front area of the upstairs. I jumped up, ran to my car in the garage, got the Ruger, bolted past Bikina and ran out the door and around to the front of my house.

"Meow,"

It was just a cat that had knocked over a loose brick from the retaining wall near the corner foundation. I walked back in, laughing as I told Bikina what had happened.

"Put that damn thing away Jeff. You know how much I hate those awful things!" she yelled.

"Okay Bikina, relax...I'll lock it up," I said as I opened the briefcase, shoved the gun inside and quickly shut and locked it.

Karma was busy lining things up; a cumulative payback...

The next night was Friday and since I had grown tired of all the wannabe cowboys at Billy's, I headed back to Chevy's for a change of pace. Nearly the first familiar person I saw was...Jami of course. She had been drinking quite a bit. She came right up to me and gave me a big, wet kiss.

"I hate you and...I love you...do you know...oh...whatever. Look, can we just have some fun tonight?"

"That'd be okay with me Jami, but are you sure that's what you want?"

"Jeff, I just...want...I think that we should see other people, since you're going to anyway. Soooo, let's just date. We can see each other when we want to. You'll pay me child support and you'll get to see Adam. That way everybody's happy!"

We stayed for another hour and then went back to her apartment, where I paid the babysitter and went in to kiss little sleeping Adam goodnight. Johnny was spending the night with his grandmother, so we went into his bedroom and made love. I spent the night.

The next morning I spent some time with Adam. We watched cartoons and played with his toys together. Before I left, I talked with Jami to find out how serious she was about seeing other people. After mutually deciding that it was the best arrangement we could manage, at least for the time being, I kissed her goodbye. I told her that I'd be back around noon with some takeout food for lunch.

After going home and taking care of two dope deals, I stopped by a KFC and headed over to Jami's with a bucket of chicken, several side dishes, desserts and drinks. We went down to the complex's pool and had a great day in the sun. After a couple of hours, I got up to leave.

"So...do you want to do something with me tonight, or do you already have a date?" I asked as we walked to my car.

"Actually, I have plans to go to a party for the complex's softball team with Daphne tonight...wanna come?"

"I think I'll pass on that...but...ah, wanna meet me later?"

"Okay...what if I meet you at Chevy's around midnight. Would that be too late?"

"No, that'd be perfect. So I guess I'll see you then...and there."

Then I pulled out a wad from my pocket and handed her two hundred bucks. She thanked me and gave me a big kiss. Then I bent down, picked Adam up and gave him a big hug and a kiss goodbye.

"See you later little man. Bye beautiful," I said with a wink.

That night I went to a bar called Buzzard's to pass the time until the planned rendezvous with Jami. It was about nine o'clock when I ran into Carl Michaels, a close friend who had taken part in my drug intervention.

"Hey Carl old buddy...how you doing?"

"Hey Jeff...hey, let's go out to your car. I've got some killer weed I want you to try." So we went to my car and smoked two joints and snorted several lines of coke.

Then I pulled out a bottle of Crown Royal and we took turns swigging.

"So, what are you up to tonight?"

"I'm supposed to meet up with Jami at Chevy's in a couple of hours. But until then,

I'm just getting blasted."

"JAMI?"

"Yeah...Jami."

"Man, I heard you guys broke up for the fiftieth time."

"Nah, we're okay now. In fact we agreed to see other people so..."

"Jeff man, all you two ever do is argue and fight. You need to stay away from her before one of you kills the other one!"

We finished the bottle and went back inside, where we got drunker and wilder. By the time I left for Chevy's, I was about as inebriated as I could be while still standing.

I arrived at Chevy's twenty minutes past midnight and right after I paid the cover charge, I ran into Gloria and a guy she introduced as Barry, her husband. After Gloria made a few comments about how trashed I looked, I slipped away. I felt uncomfortable being around her husband, since I had just nailed her a few days before and besides, I didn't want Jami to see me talking to such a tramp.

Then I spotted Jami waiting at the door, so I went over and paid her cover charge and bought her a drink, a Long Island Iced Tea.

"You're late."

"And you're drunk," she replied curtly.

"Come on back to a booth and we'll do some coke," I said loud enough for everyone in the general vicinity to hear.

"NO! And be quiet. Everybody's staring at us."

"Fuck 'em...come on," I slurred as I grabbed her hand.

"No Jeff, stop it...you're embarrassing me," she said as she snatched her hand away.

"WELL FUCK YOU TOO THEN...PRINCESS!" I yelled.

She threw her drink in my face! Then a guy right behind me grabbed me by the shoulder. I spun around and knocked him down. It was someone I knew; in fact we had played Little League baseball together. I tried to help him up, but one of the bouncers came over and told me to leave. Once outside I immediately took off running to the rear of the place. There was a fenced in area in the back for people who liked to sit outside, and I hit the fence on a run and vaulted it cleanly. I then reentered and walked up to the other bar.

"Give me a Long Island Iced Tea, please."

I quickly spotted Jami talking with some girl. I walked right up to her and threw the other drink in her face.

"There's another drink for you...bitch!"

Two bouncers grabbed me and escorted me into the parking lot. Some tall guy was laughing and pointing at me, so being my usual self, I walked right up to him.

"You got a problem?" I asked, angry, aggressive and extremely intoxicated.

"No, but you're gonna have one if you don't get the hell out of my face."

I immediately threw a right hook and caught nothing but air, while my face did catch the guy's fists a few times. I was so drunk that all I could do was grab on to my opponent and try to tackle him. We were rolling all around in the parking lot, and I was definitely getting the worst of it when the cops arrived and pulled the guy off me.

One of the cops handcuffed me, threw me in the back of his cruiser and said I was under arrest for disturbing the peace, public intoxication and anything else he could think of. Then he took off out of the parking lot. As we rode toward the police station, the cop pulled over on the side of the road and looked back at me in the rearview mirror.

"Listen to me man."

"Yeah...I'm listening."

"Look, I'm supposed to be getting off in another twenty-five minutes...and if I take you downtown, it's gonna be at least a couple hours before I get through with all the paperwork...and I've got a new baby and a bitching wife at home. So look, if I cut you some slack, if I let you out at a payphone, will you promise me to call a cab and not go back to your car?"

"Sure...yes sir!"

So the cop pulled over at the next phone booth and let me out.

"Remember...call a cab...deal?"

"Deal. And thanks...thanks a lot."

If I had been locked up that night, it almost certainly would have saved so many people a great deal of sorrow. But a cosmic force was gathering strength, and joined with my insatiable lust for trouble, karma was about to collect some payments - past due ones.

As soon as the police car was out of sight, I started the trek back to Chevy's. I stopped and looked at myself in the tinted glass of a car window and other than a fat lip, I saw no visible marks, although my chin and nose were pretty sore. I made it back to my car, hesitated for a moment as I considered going back over the fence again, but I thought better of it and got into my car. I headed back to Buzzard's and drank shots of Crown until they closed the place sometime around three. Then some slut I had been talking to at the bar went with me to my car, where we snorted a bunch of coke and she performed oral sex on me.

I was thoroughly wasted, but I somehow made it home in one piece. As soon as I opened the sliding glass door and walked into the den, I noticed that my briefcase that I had placed on top of the bar was missing. And so was the loaded handgun that was inside. I put my keys and wallet on the bar and looked around to discover that a few other things were gone, including a stack of child support checks.

"Jami!" I said through clenched teeth.

Reeling from all the booze I had imbibed, I pulled out a bag of coke from under the bar and snorted several lines. I was attempting to fortify myself against the wave of sleepiness that came with such extreme drunkenness. Then something on the floor caught my eye. It was Jami's little brown address book! It was 4:21 AM, but I didn't care. I dialed her number.

"Hello,"

"Listen you little bitch, I know you broke in and..."

"Click."

She hung up. I dialed it again...busy. She had taken the phone off the hook.

I was livid! I stormed out of the house and got into my car...no keys. I had left them on the bar along with my wallet.

"Screw it," I said out loud.

I reached into the side pocket on the door where I kept the extra key. The engine roared to life and I shot out towards her apartment like a heat-seeking missile.

Barring another divine intercession, it was inevitable that the predictable was about to happen. My personal miracle market was closed for repairs. All the paths I had taken and all the choices I had made put me in this precarious position. I was primed to make yet another crucial decision, a decision that would culminate in a senseless, horrible, irrevocable tragedy.

PART IV NIGHTMARE TIME

*One definition of insanity is doing the same stupid thing over
and over and expecting a different (and better) result.
(Origin unknown)*

CHAPTER 19
AUGUST 13, 1989

We as human beings are capable of fulfilling either beautiful dreams or horrible nightmares.
(A. P. Brooks)

I sat in the warmth of the fading Florida sun and stared down at the bloody Ruger revolver in my hands. I let my body go completely limp and collapsed back onto the sandy beach.

"What the hell happened?" I said aloud.

There wasn't a soul in sight. It felt as though I was in an episode of some D-rated reality show that had gone unimaginably astray. Much earlier that day, I had screeched to a stop in the parking lot in front of Jami's building and ran up the stairs to her apartment. Even in my drunken stupor I had enough mental acuity to be conscious of the fact that there was a loaded gun somewhere in her apartment. Therefore, I considered the element of surprise to be especially important to my welfare.

Having left my keys, including the one to her apartment on the top of my bar, I weighed my options...either through the door or through a window. I chose the door. It was a substantial wooden door. I gave it a hard smash with my right shoulder. Nothing. I backed up as far as I could and with a running start and a vicious kick, I blasted the door free of its hinges. I shoved it open, forced it back into the doorjamb and turned around just in time to see Jami scrambling and grabbing her phone on the wall. I hurried over, yanked the phone out of the wall and tossed it on the floor. Little Johnny came stumbling out of his bedroom.

"Momma, I heard a noise," he said sleepily.

"Put him back to bed and give me my shit," I said with an eerie calm.

As Jami gently guided Johnny toward his bed, I spied my briefcase on the kitchen counter. I relaxed, thinking that the handgun factor was now out of the equation. Jami reentered the room.

"Where are the cancelled child support checks Jami?"

When she reached down towards the sofa and into her purse, I assumed it was to get a cigarette. The diffused lighting streaming through the partly open Venetian blinds from the outside security lamps rather dimly lighted the room, but even so I instantly spotted the gleaming metal of the Ruger as she withdrew it from her purse. I grabbed her hand and snapped it into the air. She struggled and twisted around in an attempt to break free as she tried to bite me on the arm or hand.

Keeping both hands tightly clasped around her hand and the gun, I moved my head back a bit and then threw it forward, bashing her directly in the face with a vicious head butt. It was so forceful that the impact nearly knocked me out. As we tumbled to the floor, the gun fired and I felt the bullet graze the side of my right hand ever so slightly. The roar of the weapon scared her so badly that I easily pulled the gun from her grasp. I stood up and felt the warm flow of blood coming out of my nose and noticed that there was blood all over her face as well. I walked over to my briefcase and laid the Ruger down on top of it. Then I turned and stepped toward her, making sure that I stayed between her and the gun.

"Jami, why the hell did you do that?"

She rose to her feet and embraced me as she began to cry.

"I'm sorry. It was all my fault...I love you..." she sobbed.

I relaxed and stepped back to survey the damage I had inflicted. Her nose was bleeding badly.

Suddenly, she bolted past me and snatched up the Ruger again! The same scenario ensued. This time she had both hands on it and both of my hands were clamped firmly on top of hers. I literally lifted her off the floor and as she came back down I attempted to head butt her again. But her entire body was thrashing about wildly. My first two attempts were glancing blows that injured me more than her. On my third attempt however, I caught her fully on her nose and forehead. It almost certainly knocked her out and she began falling back toward the couch. Her hands slipped off the revolver and as I jerked it away, it thundered again.

The soft light in the room, together with the brilliant muzzle flash, enabled me to witness the awful spasm that rippled through her entire body. The shot hit her right between the eyes, and left a permanently seared impression on my consciousness. It was a nightmare scene that would literally haunt me for the rest of my life.

For what seemed to be an eternity, I stood there, bleeding and motionless, scared and panicky. I staggered back to her bedroom where Adam was. He had slept through the entire catastrophic event. I took a notebook from the top of the dresser and wrote a note:

Dear Hannah, Adam, Wes and Mom,

Jami has messed with my life for the last time and I am going to kill her and then kill myself. Hannah, I'll always love you. Wes, our friendship deserved so much more. Mom, Adam and Julie, I'm sorry.

Jeff

I never did come to understand why I left such a crazy note, and the oddity of it still puzzles me today, but I did other things that morning that were equally beyond the realms of logic and reason. If I had stayed and called the police, the outcome would still have been very bad, but not nearly as bad as fleeing the horrible scene. I fled.

After writing the note I went to the front door, but I couldn't get it to budge. I went over to the sliding glass door and opened it. And just as I was walking through it, I heard a tiny voice behind me.

"Jeff, take me with you," said Johnny as he grabbed my hand.

"No honey, you have to stay here," I said softly as I slid the door closed.

I had forced a six year old child back inside with his bloody, dying or dead mother, not to mention the fact that I had left my sixteen month old baby boy in there as well!

As I walked to my car, I realized that I had the pistol in one hand and my briefcase in the other although I had no memory of picking up the latter. I also noticed that the entire front of my pants and shirt were saturated with a mixture of our blood, hers and mine. Even the gun was bloody. I reflected for an instant on how sticky it felt. In a near state of shock I got into my car, shoved the gun into the console and drove away. I had no wallet or ID, but with three hundred and forty-four dollars I found stuffed in the glove box, along with an ounce of cocaine and three ounces of pot in the compartment behind the seat, I drove onto the entrance ramp of the interstate and headed…south.

I drove and drove and drove…and then kept driving, oblivious to the fact that the blood all over me, my face, hands and clothing, had dried. When I partially emerged from my mental fog, I pulled into a self-service carwash bay somewhere in Georgia. I got out of the car and used the carwash wand to clean myself, five minutes of soap, followed by five minutes of rinse, clothes, shoes, everything. I didn't give a damn.

My perspective at that time was that everything that had just happened was her fault and that now my life was over. I took off the t-tops, got back into the car, still soaking wet and lowered both windows. When I looked in the rearview mirror to examine my injuries, I was surprised to discover that I had one hell of a black, swollen left eye. I pulled a pair of very dark sunglasses out of the console and put them on to conceal it.

I got back on the interstate, sped up just a little and allowed the inrushing wind to dry my clothes and me. A little later I stopped for some gas, and then drove all the way to Orlando. Once there, I got another full tank of gas and considered getting something to eat. Instead I used a drinking straw to snort some cocaine from a loose pile at the bottom of the console. Then I drove on, and didn't stop until I was somewhere north of Miami. I had been on the road for the better part of a day. I was going to get a motel room, but thought that I should conserve as much money as possible for gas and food. Right then I just wanted to think.

I parked my car, pulled off my shirt, shoes and socks and got out and began walking up and down the beach in a daze. After wandering around for a short while, I returned to my car, wrapped my shirt around the gun and walked back to the beach with it at my side. The sun was gradually disappearing over the horizon and there was no one in the general vicinity, so I just sat down right in the sand. I took the gun and shoved it under my leg. Then I put on my shirt and lay back in the sand.

Time slipped by but my internal clock was no longer functioning. I sat up again and realized that I had been lying there for quite a while. I was experiencing a revolving array of emotions and sensations. There was fear, confusion, exhaustion and hunger, then anger, regret, pain and shame...and then it would start over again. My mind was racing as I glanced down at the metal object once again in my hands. I thought about pointing the barrel to my temple and pulling the trigger, but what if I missed? It seemed more likely that the intended purpose would be served if I put it in my mouth and shot upwards into my brain. I considered my options as I turned the gun over and over in my hands, as the image of my mother sitting on her bed with a gun in her hand flashed through my mind. I really intended to die, but for some reason, I never managed to raise the Ruger to my head. If I had overcome that hurdle, the odds were good that I would have pulled the trigger.

I returned to my car and fell asleep until the heat from the Florida sun woke me. Overcoming the struggle against fatigue by snorting some cocaine, I continued my southbound Odyssey. But after going through Miami, I was oblivious to the fact that I had somehow turned westward onto what is known as Alligator Alley. I had driven all the way across the entire width of the state before realizing that I was then heading north along the western or gulf side of the state.

When I reached Tampa, I decided that I really needed to get something to eat. I'd gone nearly two days without food and although hunger pangs were present, I didn't feel much like eating. I grabbed some fast food and forced it down while sitting in the car in a hotel parking lot facing the Gulf of Mexico. Then I slept in the car again that night.

The next morning I ate breakfast and drove around Tampa. I saw an international newsstand, and pulled over to see if they had a copy of Nashville's Sunday paper. They did so I bought a copy and saw that the horrendous nightmare had made the headlines. There was a large picture of Jami and a smaller one of me alongside the disturbing article. After tearing off the front page and the continuing article on the reverse, I tossed the rest of the paper into a trashcan and headed back to my car.

I read the story, folded it and laid it on top of the gun in the console. I drove down the beach, still considering the best method of suicide, when the sight of a pretty bikiniclad brunette caught my eye. She was carrying a big purse on her shoulder and was apparently hitchhiking. And even though a sexual encounter was one of the last things on my mind, I pulled over, perhaps out of instinct.

"Thanks for stopping. My name's Kellie. Where were you headed? Hey what the hell happened to your eye, honey?" she asked as she slithered into the passenger seat.

"I ran into a doorknob…on a very tall door," I answered.

"You're funny…and cute, except for your eye. Hey, let's stop and get some beer," she said.

"I'm kinda broke except for some blow and weed," I lied. "Do you know anybody that might be interested in buying some?"

"Yeah, sure…well maybe. Look, pull into this market and go in and get us a six-pack of beer. It's hot and I'm thirsty. And if you really have some dope, we can go somewhere to cop a buzz and even *party* a little…that is if you want to. Here, here's ten dollars," she said with her eyes perked up by the mere mention of cocaine.

I took the bill from her hand and went into the convenience store. While waiting in line it occurred to me that she might be rifling through the rear compartment and stealing my dope. I put down the beer and ran out of the store. I looked towards the car and saw her door swing open. She took off running down the beach.

I hurried to the car and saw that the console was open. Then I looked behind the seat and checked on the dope. It was still there. Then it became obvious to me what had happened. She must have opened the console and seen the bloody gun, the article about Jami and the picture of me and bolted from the car in terror. She must have been scared witless, because she had forgotten her big purse! I immediately drove off quickly, thinking that she would run straight to a payphone to call the police.

Man, I have got to change cars…and fast.

After driving two or three miles up the beach, I pulled into the crowded parking lot of a big motel. I backed up in a parking space in front of a large retaining wall so that my license plate couldn't be seen, just in case the girl had gotten the number. I went through her purse, and other than three one-dollar bills and her driver's license, which I considered altering to use for a fake ID, there was nothing of interest for me.

After rolling a couple of joints, I walked down toward the beach and threw the purse into a dumpster. I stayed on the beach until way after dark, just walking around and thinking about what to do. For the time being I decided to go back and sleep in the car for one more night and then try to swap cars and find a place to crash the next day.

It was about three in the morning and I was twisting and turning uncomfortably in the cramped seat. I kept thinking about the little phrase Jami used to say to Adam.

"Just a minute...just a minute...Momma's coming...just a minute."

My misery was interrupted by the sight of two guys who were apparently sneaking out of a room on the second floor of the motel. They had what appeared to be two pocketbooks and when they finished ransacking them, they dropped them and took off down the stairs. As soon as they were out of sight I crept up the stairs, scooped up the purses and took them back to the car. I hoped that they had left some credit cards or some money in a hidden compartment, but after an initial assessment, I determined that the thieves had left nothing valuable. After further examination however, I found out the purses did contain a couple of sets of car keys, one to a Nissan and the other to a Lincoln.

"Yes...thank you!" I whispered.

Both purses contained various Canadian papers including passports, so it was simple to locate the two vehicles and choose which one I wanted to trade for my car. I simply walked through the parking lot until finding a black Lincoln with Canada plates. Bingo! I drove it to another crowded motel parking lot about a mile down the road and walked back. After quickly finding the other victim's silver Maxima, I repeated the process. Then I drove my car to the same motel, where I took out everything I thought that I might need or could possibly sell from my car, including the license plates, t-tops and of course the stash of drugs. Opting for the car with better gas mileage, I moved all of my stuff along with the gun to the trunk of the Maxima. Then I took everything of value out of the Lincoln, including a big box of liquor, threw it into the back seat of my chosen ride and after replacing the Canadian license plate with my own, I drove away.

I was beginning to feel a little better about the circumstances, so I checked into a moderately priced motel about five miles away, looking forward to my first good nights sleep in days. But as soon as I drifted off to sleep I began dreaming of the sweet little, reassuring refrain:

"Just a minute...just a minute...Momma's coming...just a minute."

Then I dreamed about her lying in her casket with hundreds and hundreds of flowers surrounding her lifeless body. There were countless family members and friends around her, crying and saying how beautiful she looked. Then I was suddenly at my dad's funeral and my mother was standing by the casket which contained the fake head on my father's body. She was telling everyone that Jack wasn't really my father. Then I was in yet another funeral home. This time my grandfather and Jerry McCord were in two shiny black coffins, side by side. I walked and stood between the coffins. I looked down at my grandfather, but when I turned to look at Jerry, I saw Jami talking with the little girl named Wendy I had dreamed once about.

"Oh Jeff, isn't she just the most precious thing you've ever seen. Adam needs a little sister. Let's have a little girl...okay?"

I woke up gasping and drenched in sweat.

I couldn't go back to sleep, so I got up and turned on the television without any sound. As I sat there in the glow of the TV, I began thinking about how much grief I had caused for so many people. I thought about what Hannah would say when she heard the news and wondered if she would even care. I thought about Little Adam, Johnny and Jami's family.

Oh my God...what have I done...oh my God, how in the world did I let this happen? How? How? Oh my God. I killed her. Oh my God...oh my God...oh my God...oh my God!

There are no words to express how sick I felt as the terrible deed I had committed began to sink in. All the sadness and horror that her family was going to have to endure seemed to pass directly through my soul as I fell back into a fetal position on the motel bed.

While the scope of a single person's death may be dwarfed by mass casualty events such as the attack on the World Trade Center, the attempted genocides in Serbia and Africa and the Nazi Holocaust, nothing would ever supplant Jami's death as the worst thing that ever happened in my mind. Why? Because I caused it, all of it.

After remaining in the same position for nearly an hour, I got up and took a long, hot shower. I stopped by the motel office and paid for three more days, which came to over a hundred and seventy-five bucks. Then I went to the Maxima to get the rest of the dope. I also grabbed the box full of plastic liter-sized bottles full of various types of liquor.

"Maybe I can overdose on booze...or at least drink myself into a coma," I said aloud as I walked back up to the room.

I hung the "Do Not Disturb" sign on the outside of the door and proceeded to take a journey on a serious two day drunk. But this time it wasn't the partying kind of drunk. This was my attempt to slide through one of the cracks in the cosmos to the hell C.S. Lewis was writing about in his book <u>The Great Divorce</u>.

When I awoke two mornings later, the spinning room was completely trashed. I hadn't shaved or showered during that time, but I had puked in a couple of different places in the room. I walked to the mirror and confirmed my suspicion that I looked as bad as I felt. After taking a shower I went outside and stumbled down the walkway to see if my stolen car was still there…it was. As I walked back to the room I looked inside the open door of an adjacent room. There on the table right next to the door sat a tan leather purse. The thought of credit cards and cash was on my mind and my heart began beating wildly as I stuck my head in the doorway and looked around. I saw a shadow moving around in the bathroom as I quietly picked up the purse and snuck back to my room. I dumped everything out in order to carefully examine the contents.

"Damn!"

The only useful things I found were eleven bucks and a credit card for a regional department store chain that was issued to a Teri Smith. Shoving the money in my pocket, I began wondering if I could get away with using a woman's credit card. If I could pull it off, I could take whatever I bought to a different store in the same chain and try to get a cash refund. It was a master plan hatched by a now *accomplished* purse-snatcher.

Two days later, on a Friday afternoon, after buying a couple of changes of clothes and various toiletry items from a local K-mart, I realized that I was running low on cash. I decided to visit the department store, where I could try Miss Terri Smith's credit card. I went inside and tried to purchase a couple of hundred dollars worth of merchandise, but within minutes of handing the card to the clerk, I knew that the jig was up. The cashier must have surreptitiously pressed a button under the counter, because two burly looking security guards came up from behind me and grabbed me by each arm. They took me to the security office and called the police.

After truthfully telling them that I had no ID on me, the police assured me that they would have my name, address and any priors very soon after I was fingerprinted at the police station. As they led me through the aisles in handcuffs, I thought about the gun stashed in the Maxima's trunk in the store's parking lot and wondered how long it would take them to link it to me. It was five o'clock in the afternoon and by the time the clock struck six, they would have learned quite a bit about Jeffery Holden Collins.

My world was about to come crashing down. Not only would they find the Maxima, the gun and several pieces of blood-stained clothing. The Tampa police were about to suspect that on top of being a purse-snatching car thief, I was also a serial killer.

With my stupid, violent, selfish, destructive, drug abusing, whore-mongering lifestyle, I had single-handedly unraveled the very fabric of the lives of two innocent children and opened a veritable floodgate of sorrow onto multiple family members and friends.

CHAPTER 20
IN THE NEWS

"Life is a tale told by an idiot, full of sound and fury, signifying nothing."
(William Shakespeare - Macbeth)

The news media aims to titillate the public. More viewers mean more ad revenues and more profits for the station. The media understand that viewers love dirty laundry, so long as it's not their own. My sad saga had plenty to serve up: sex, drugs, murder and a violent killer on the lam from another state with possible links to multiple murders in Tampa!

As soon as I was brought into the Florida courtroom bright and early on Monday morning, I heard the humming and clicking from over a dozen cameras. There was a litany of charges against me: grand theft auto, possession of narcotics, unlawful possession of a firearm, fraudulent use of a credit card and illegal use of license plates. Then after the Assistant DA said that I had warrants for burglary and first degree murder in Tennessee, he added that the Tampa police were also investigating some possible links I might have to two local homicides.

"What the hell is he talking about?" I whispered to the representative from the public defender's office.

I found out that very afternoon. Detectives took me to an interrogation room and told me that a twenty-six year old woman had been shot in the head in the same motel where I had left my car. Not only was she from Nashville, she had also been involved in a bank robbery that occurred at the same branch where Jami worked. Furthermore, her birthday was the exact same day, month and year as Jami's, and she had worked for one of the escort services I had called on numerous occasions! Chills ran up my spine...but that wasn't all. They had found the ID belonging to the bikini-clad hitchhiker I had picked up, and she was now missing.

"Look Jeff, it's obvious to us that you had something to do with the death and/or disappearances of these women...and if you talk with us now at this stage in our investigation...well, we *might* be able to save you from a lethal injection after you rot away on death row for ten years or so."

"I have no idea what you're talking about. And hey, I saw the news this morning, and they said that that girl was killed in her room on *Saturday* morning."

"Yeah...so?"

"I was arrested on *Friday* night!"

"Well...ah...then...ah...what's your alibi for the disappearance of Kellie Elliott?"

"Who?"

"The twenty-year-old whose ID was found in the car you stole. She's been missing for several days now and probably lying in some ditch where you left her with a bullet in the head."

"You guys are nuts. That girl got scared when she saw the gun in my car while I was in a convenience store. She took off running down the beach and that's the first and last time I ever saw her."

"Well Mr. Collins, you're gonna be charged with two homicides irregardless…and then we'll just see who is nuts."

"Actually, irregardless is not a word. What you meant to say was…"

"Get him the hell out of here!"

I knew that they were barking up the wrong tree with the talk of that serial killer crap. Hell, I wasn't even concerned about any of the charges in Florida. I knew my real trouble was waiting back in Nashville. I also knew that representatives from the police force there would soon be paying me a visit in Tampa and that I would be extradited back home to stand trial for killing Jami.

Sure enough, two detectives from the Nashville Metropolitan Police Department came to see me at the end of the week. After I was properly read my Miranda rights, I refused to answer any of their questions.

"There is one thing I feel like I need to say. You guys need to know that there were *two* gunshots in her apartment that morning…and I think that being able to prove that two shots were fired would go a long way toward lessening my culpability in this situation."

"What are you…an attorney?"

"No just someone who knows a little bit about criminal law. So if you could…I realize that it's your job to convict me, but would you go to her apartment and see if you can find the other bullet?"

"Jeff, our job is to get to the truth no matter how it turns out. So yeah, I'll go there and have a look around personally," said the chubbier detective.

I was rather surprised to discover that Florida was willing to drop all the charges that they had against me, if I would not resist extradition to Tennessee. And after quickly agreeing to forgo any appeal of my extradition, the Metro cops told me that they would be back the following Monday, a day after my 37th birthday.

They picked me up around five o'clock on Monday morning and brought me a bright orange jumpsuit to wear. The drive back to Nashville was daunting. The two detectives took turns driving and both seemed to be auditioning for NASCAR. Another guy that was being extradited and I bounced and flopped around in handcuffs and leg shackles in the back seat as we seldom went slower than eighty up the interstate.

"Hey, how did you guys get them to let me go? They thought that I had killed two women in Tampa," I said in between bounces.

"Well, the one that was missing showed up at her sister's house last week...and they found out that the hooker from Nashville was shot by her ex-husband. You're a lucky bastard. They love to give people the juice down here," said the chubby cop from the passenger seat.

"Lucky? Are you kidding me? Both of those accusations were blatantly absurd. One girl was just missing and they already had me convicted of decapitating her or something. And the other one...the hooker...she was killed over twelve hours AFTER I was arrested. And you call me lucky? Come on man."

We drove in total silence for hours until we pulled into a fast food joint for lunch. After they had let us relieve ourselves and we had all scarfed down our *unhappy meals*, it was back to the races. On the second stage of the journey, I decided to find out if these cops really wanted the truth or were merely preparing to put my neck in a sling.

"So detective, did you ever get a chance to go back to her apartment and look for the second bullet?"

"Uh...yeah...we went back over there alright...spent a long time looking too. And we even took a metal detector...used it all over the living room, the kitchen and the kitchenette areas. But it...uh...never beeped, not one time," said the one driving as he looked at me in the rear view mirror.

"It never beeped at all the whole time...not even once? Are you sure that there was a battery in that thing?" I asked looking back at him.

"Oh sure...positive...I checked it myself. That's a fact...yes siree."

"And it never beeped a single time?"

"Nope...never...not even once."

"So you're telling me that it never went off a single time, even around the metal fireplace, the metal refrigerator, the metal dishwasher, the metal stove or all the countless metal nails and studs in the wall of that building. Man that must have been one lousy metal detector you had there, huh?"

Thus my suspicions were confirmed that the police were not interested in the truth. Their motivation was sadly similar to that of the news media, titillation and profit, even if the profits were non-pecuniary. This was going to be an extremely rough road and I expected no search for the whole truth from the police. Therefore I kept my mouth shut for the remainder of the trip.

Once we arrived at the courthouse in Nashville, the media descended on me like hyenas on a crippled gazelle. Dozens of flashbulbs punctuated the gloomy afternoon, while the cameras clicked endlessly. I was peppered with seemingly endless questions about how and why I did such a terrible thing. I put my head down and walked through the throng of blood-sucking reporters as fast as my shackled feet would allow. I was processed into the jail with the customary fingerprinting, mug shots and the accompanying paperwork. For the next twenty-four hours I was kept in a "suicide watch" cell and then rather abruptly released into the general population.

"Gen-pop" was quite a culture shock for me. The place was absolutely filthy and the food was virtually inedible. For someone who thought that I had seen it all, I realized that I had not seen a great deal of things, and that some of them were such that I would have preferred to have never seen at all. There were rampant displays of homosexuality, unbridled gang activities and fights every day. Not surprisingly, by the end of my first month in jail, I had been in two violent altercations myself.

One occurred during a basketball game and another when an inmate attempted to take my shoes. And since I had been victorious in both skirmishes, the other inmates learned early on that I was willing and capable of defending myself. I was taken aback when guards and inmates would say things like, "Hey there TV star." I suffered the twisted insults, somehow managing to keep my mouth shut.

Inmates with money could easily procure a cup of julep. Julep might evoke images of a sparkling cocktail for the Kentucky Derby, but in this instance, the meaning is much different. Julep is the jailhouse wine which is "cooked" in plastic garbage bags through the fermentation of old fruit. I found the un-potable swill dreadfully rank. It tasted even worse, but you could actually get drunk from drinking it. The problem was that you were more likely to get sick as well. If one preferred reefer, jailhouse joints sold for two or three bucks. The joints were about half the size of a toothpick, and to get high you'd have to smoke about five of them.

A great deal happened in the ensuing weeks. Several lawyers, who said that they were "sent by one of my friends" to talk to me, stopped by to offer their services in the impending trial. After taking their cards, I promised to make a decision soon. My bail was set at one million dollars and I was told that it would surely be raised higher if I somehow managed to come up with the money.

I received more than twenty letters of support during the first week, along with one hate letter that I suspected to have originated with Mary Anne, especially after I saw her on the local evening news the next day. She was talking about me, and although her face had been blurred out, there was no mistaking her identity.

"Oh he's the devil...let me tell you. He once told me that he would mess me up so bad that a team of plastic surgeons from Los Angeles wouldn't be able to put me back together. And he'd do it, too. He beat me all the time. And when I think of Jami and those poor women down in Florida...why that could have been me!" she said sobbing into the camera for the titillation of the viewers of greater metropolitan Nashville.

"Man what an evil lying bitch. That's great...just great," I said as I shook my head in disgust and walked away from the television.

The following day they interviewed Jami's sister, Pepper.

"My sister couldn't have defended herself against a kicking rabbit and I hope that he takes his dying breath in prison," she said to the reporter.

Without exception, every report about Jami's death raked me over the coals, which was to be expected. For all practical purposes, the media had me tried and convicted long before the actual trial was even scheduled to begin.

A great number of my friends came by to see me. They brought money, clothes, and toiletries and told me that they would support me throughout my ordeal. Bikina, Wes, Tina, Howie, Bo, Brittany, Danny, Candy, Gary, David and Jean Bell, my sister Joan, Carl Michaels and many others visited me during the first week. Carl's parents, who I had never actually met, came to visit and put two hundred dollars on my inmate account. Even Carol snuck in to see me several times. But each time that I was called for a visit, I hoped to see the one face that I truly longed to see, the one face that never showed...Hannah's face.

My Mom and Mel wrote to me from Arizona with their pledge of love and support. They offered to hire an attorney or help in any way I needed it and sent along five hundred bucks. When my younger sister Jeanne sent me a card telling me how much she missed me and loved me, I just about lost it.

There was plenty of bad news, too. When investigators questioned the people that I worked with, Mr. Reeves denied even knowing me. My real estate broker reluctantly admitted that I had made a "couple of sales" over the years, but added that he barely knew me.

All of the big name attorneys wanted in excess of a hundred thousand dollars to represent me and that was just their fee. The necessary extras included a psychiatric workup, a polygraph expert, private investigation work and other miscellaneous expenses. I eventually chose a woman attorney named Kathryn Stern, who initially seemed very confident that she could obtain an acquittal for me, or in the alternative, a conviction for one of the lesser-included charges such as involuntary manslaughter.

Several weeks later the results of Gloria Lovelace's undercover work and the sealed indictment against me yielded fruit. One night, two vice squad officers entered the cellblock, handcuffed me and took me down to central booking, where they put me through the processes of fingerprinting and taking my mug shots all over again. I was subsequently informed that I was under arrest for two counts of selling cocaine to a police informant. (If only they had arrested me the minute I sold Gloria the dope!)

At Kathryn Stern's suggestion, I hired another lawyer named Steve Downs who specialized in drug cases. This attorney quickly filed a motion of discovery in order to find out who the informant was. The following week Downs came to see me and played the taped recording of the drug buys. I was astonished to recognize Gloria's voice.

"Okay Jeff...now I've already talked with the District Attorney and they offered to cut you a deal...four years for both counts, on the condition that you accept a guilty plea. And I think that you should take it, because if you take it to trial you'd more than likely get twice that much."

"So in other words, I paid you ten grand for a plea agreement?"

"Oh believe me, I've been paid ten times that much for a similar deal."

"Okay, whatever...tell them I'll take it."

The *good news* was that I would now be sent to a state prison and away from the horrid conditions of the county jail. I had been told by several veteran convicts that the food was better, the place was cleaner and there were many more activities.

I had arranged earlier in the week for Howie, Bo and Gary to go to my house in order to remove and store some of the more valuable items, such as my pool table, the washer and dryer, most of the furniture, television sets, stereo components and jet skis among other things. But when the three of them showed up during visitation hours that evening, they delivered more bad news. Someone had beaten them to the punch and had stolen practically everything that wasn't nailed down.

When Gary asked my neighbors, he was told the same story by each one. Mary Anne, along with two or three men, had pulled a moving van into my front yard the day before and had emptied out the house. One neighbor added that Mary Anne had spoken to him and said she was, "...doing it for Jeff."

Kathryn Stern came to see me the following week.

"Jeff, they're offering us twenty-five years in return for a guilty plea to Second Degree Murder. This would allow you the possibility of parole in approximately five and a half years. And it's my duty as your attorney to advise you to at least consider it."

"But the newspapers...the District Attorney...all the news shows...they've all tried and convicted me already. They've twisted everything around and made it sound like I planned all of it, that I went over there, beat the hell out of her and then deliberately shot her in the head. And that is absolutely not the way it happened Kathryn...no way, not even close."

"I hear you Jeff and I believe you, but they've charged you with Felony Murder, First Degree Murder and Burglary. And you know that if you're convicted, you're looking at a possible death sentence."

"Kathryn, I want to go to trial. No, I *have* to go to trial. It's important for people to hear my side, for my family and for Adam and all of my friends that have stepped up and all the people that care about me. I have to do it, Kathryn, even if they don't believe me...even if we lose. I just have to."

"Okay then, I'll let the District Attorney know that you've made your decision, and we'll go ahead and get a trial date set."

"Kathryn, have you thought about what we discussed earlier last week? About me writing to Jami's family and telling them how sorry I am about what happened?"

"Jeff, let's hold off on that for now. It's been less than...let's see...less than a year and their wounds are still so fresh. And...they're all still so full of hate right now."

"But this is important to me Kathryn. I need to do it now or as soon as possible...please."

"Once again Jeff, I'm advising you against it. Those people are out for blood, your blood. And even if you did write to them, I doubt very seriously that they would even read it and if they did, it certainly wouldn't be read objectively. And besides, the state could try and twist anything you might say and use it against you in court. So please listen to
me at least for now. After all, you're paying me to look after your best interests. Therefore you should heed my recommendations, especially in this case...okay?"

"Okay then. I'll wait for a while, but I want to explain it to them one day...or at least try to."

"Alright...maybe after the trial."

"Oh yeah, one more thing. Can you see about getting them to transfer me to a state prison somewhere since I now have a conviction for the coke? I heard that I can go and everybody that's been in both places tells me how much better it is than this dump. So would you look into it?"

"Sure, if that's what you want...are you sure?"

"Positive, this place sucks."

"Okay, I'll see what I can do."

There was an older convict named Frank that I had talked to earlier on more than one occasion about my case. When I told him what the state had offered, Frank told me that I should take the plea.

"Man you better take that deal and run with it Jeff. Always 'take low and go'...like the saying goes."

"No way Frank. I'm not gonna stand up in open court and say that I deliberately shot her. No sir!"

"Listen to me son, when you go to trial, there's a number that all of us convicts get real familiar with."

"And what number is that Frank?"

"Thirteen and a half Jeff...thirteen and a half."

"I don't get it Frank."

"Thirteen and a half buddy...one judge, twelve jurors and a half-assed chance at justice...thirteen and a half."

CHAPTER 21
THIRTEEN AND A HALF

"Abandon all hope ye who enter here"
(Dante Alighieri – The Inferno)

Prison was no day at the beach, but it was Club Med compared to the Davidson County jail, and I was grateful to Kathryn for greasing the wheels and expediting my transfer. The place was much cleaner and the food was a great deal better and more plentiful. The first time I got my clothes back from the laundry, I was surprised when they came back actually clean and dry. And like I was told, there was a lot more to do. There were various athletic tournaments, drug and alcohol classes and a moderately outfitted law library, where I spent as many hours as I could each week preparing for my upcoming murder trial.

I received yet another major blow that August which came in the form of another death, the death of my closest friend Howie. Howie was killed in a head on collision while driving to work one Tuesday morning. His death left behind a one year old son and devastated Sarah, his young pregnant widow. Beyond the tragedy of losing a close friend, this also meant the loss of an important material witness. Howie could have testified as to the victim's propensity for anger, something he had observed from being present during more than a few of our many quarrels.

More than a few writers have likened the legal maze we call our justice system to a guillotine, a sword or an axe falling. It cuts whatever it hits, but it also causes a great deal of collateral damage to the family and friends of those who stand accused, the kind of damage to which those who are not afflicted by such a situation remain blissfully ignorant. Adam's plight notwithstanding, my mother and Mel, along with my sisters suffered a great deal in my journey through the gamut of motions, trials and appeals. I was surprised at their enduring displays of love for me after all the years of estrangement, especially between Mel and me. But I shouldn't have been surprised. Mel was merely doing what decent people do - rally to a loved one in times of trouble, and I was definitely in trouble, big-time trouble.

The trial began in the spring of 1991. I had been incarcerated for a year and a half, and although I had become somewhat acclimated to the prison environment, I naturally hated being there. I looked forward to telling my story in public. I knew that the danger of spending my life in prison was very real, so I did my best to prepare for the worst possible scenario. When I refused the state's offer of a twenty-five year sentence in exchange for my guilty plea to Second Degree Murder, Ms Jane Crowell, the District Attorney threatened to seek the Death Penalty.

It seemed to me that the DA did not want to go through the work involved in conducting a trial and they were trying to intimidate me. Their case fell far short of what the vast majority of the death penalty decisions require in Tennessee. The worst possible outcome would be a conviction for First Degree Murder which carries an automatic sentence of life in prison, not the death penalty but still a daunting prospect.

I knew how to psych myself up before games in the various sports I had played. Now I had a need for something similar, yet radically different. I knew that I needed to steel myself against the possibility of a defeat, because if I didn't prepare for the worst outcome, the effect could be much worse.

My dilemma was that feathery thing called hope. A resilient feeling of hope kept popping into my head, and I kept beating it back into the recesses from whence it sprang.

The trial typically began as all murder trials do, with the Assistant District Attorney giving the opening statement to the jurors, telling them what an evil degenerate the defendant was, and how I had absolutely no redeeming social value. Then the counsel for the defense shared her opinion of me with the same jury, which differed greatly from the ADA's description and opinion.

"Ladies and gentleman, Jeffery Holden Collins is a Viet Nam Era veteran. He is a college graduate who worked his way through school. He is a successful real estate agent and businessman. He is a doting father who loves his son. He has ties to the community. Is he perfect? Of course not. But who here amongst us is without a few of the human foibles that separate us from the angels? Along with the state, we will tell you about many of Jeff Collin's faults. However, our revelations of his weaknesses will be done out of honesty. Theirs, on the other hand, will be used to distort what type of person he is and to lower your opinion of him. But in the end, the evidence in this case will speak for itself, and you will come to the logical and just conclusion that this was a horrible, tragic accident, a tragedy that could have and should have been avoided, but was not. And in the end, you will agree that a conviction for First Degree Murder can in no way be supported by the evidence offered by the state."

The state began with the usual array of crime scene investigators, such as blood spatter experts, photographers and other forensic experts such as ballistic specialists. The blood trail on the wall that ran the length of the hallway was classified simply as type A, without the normal plus or minus that signifies the Rh factor and which further identifies the source of the blood. All blood typing in this country automatically includes the Rh factor. The elimination of the Rh factor in the prosecution's evidence was clear prosecutorial gamesmanship. Jami's blood was A+ and mine was determined to be A-. Logic dictated that proving who left such a trail would be extremely important in the case. And since I was almost certain that I had used the wall to steady myself as I staggered back to the bedroom, I knew that such withheld information was going to hurt my case.

Little Johnny was allowed to testify in spite of Kathryn's objections that the child had not been in the room when the fatal shot was fired. And when he testified that he saw me "shock" his mom, I knew that the little boy had been manipulated and coached. I'm nearly certain that after Jami had put him back to bed, he hadn't come out of his room again until I was leaving, and such a testimony could only have come from prompting by someone else. When Kathryn cross-examined the child, he said that his mother had given him some cold medicine for the sniffles that night and that it had made him very sleepy. He also said that he didn't know what the word "shock" meant and that he had indeed been instructed on what to say by some ADA in the District Attorney's office!

Then Gloria Lovelace testified. After expounding about how I frequently called her business to use escorts, she described how she had decided to help the police arrest me for selling cocaine, thus ridding Nashville of a dastardly dope dealer. When she was asked about the melee at Chevy's on that notorious Saturday night, she testified under oath that in her opinion, I seemed quite sober!

Next it was Mary Anne's turn to hammer in a few nails and she had plenty to say. Most of her testimony was based on outrageous lies, such as how I had beaten the hell out of her on numerous occasions, and how I had even once broken her arm and nose. She added that for as long as she had known me, I had carried a gun wherever I went, the same gun that I used to kill Jami.

Licking her lips in anticipation, Kathryn tore into Mary Anne's testimony during a merciless cross-examination. The witty attorney did a masterful job of destroying each claim of this pitiful and troubled woman. Although she continued to rant about how bad a boyfriend I had been, everyone present in the courtroom understood that Mary Anne was just a bitter ex-lover who was the epitome of the adage about a woman scorned.

The trial appeared to be tipping in the direction of the defense when the pictures were admitted into evidence. They were terrible, ghastly pictures that would horrify the most callused heart. As soon as I saw them, I grew nauseated. Jami's lifeless body was shown lying on her sofa and there was so much blood, endless volumes of blood.
Where had it all come from? Was it possible that one human body could contain all that fluid? And she looked so dead...so horribly dead.

Those images were etched in my memory forever, perhaps as partial retribution for my stupid, reckless actions. The photographs of the crime scene were disturbing and inflammatory, and I immediately understood that the jurors were going to have a difficult time remaining impartial once they had seen them.

I stayed on the witness stand for three days, with one full day spent answering Kathryn's questions and explaining the circumstances leading up to Jami's death, and the rest of the time being grilled by the ADA Crowell. The state's attorney failed time and again in her attempts to trip me up or to expose some undisclosed canard. I had told the unvarnished truth concerning every detail about what happened that morning, so I couldn't be trapped in a lie. This was quite ironic given my predilection for bending, stretching and snapping the truth so often during my lifetime.

At the end of the second week both sides concluded their cases. The judge gave her instructions to the jurors. Among the lengthy list of instructions, the jurors were told that in Tennessee, flight can imply guilt, and since I did in fact flee, they were advised to use that information while pondering my fate. Subsequently the jurors were moved into their designated area for deliberation. And after doing so for the better part of the day, it was announced that they had reached a decision, and everyone was ushered back into the courtroom.

I had been in a holding area throughout the deliberation and several attorneys visited while I was waiting. They told me that the courthouse scuttlebutt was that the verdict in my case was going to be a conviction for manslaughter. That would carry around a five-year sentence. The prediction caused me to feel only a temporary sense of relief, because as soon as I felt my hopes rise, I began focusing on the chances of the worst possible judgment. I made a deal with myself, whereby I would return to the courtroom expecting a conviction of Second Degree Murder. That way a manslaughter verdict would be a comparatively welcome and fair conclusion.

The judge instructed me to rise for the jury's decision. I immediately complied along with Kathryn and her co counsel.

"Mister Foreman, have you reached a verdict in the above styled case?"

"Yes we have your Honor."

"And what are your findings as to each count?"

"As to the count of Burglary…we find the defendant…Jeffry Holden Collins…Not Guilty."

"As to the count of Felony Murder…we find the defendant…Jeffry Holden Collins…Not Guilty."

Kathryn placed her arm on my shoulders and my heart skipped a beat as the Jury Foreman paused for a moment.

"As to the count of First Degree Murder, we find the defendant...Jeffry Holden Collins...**Guilty**."

It was a sledgehammer blow. I felt as though every molecule of air was suddenly sucked from my lungs. Kathryn and her assistant put their arms around me, but I could barely feel them.

"Don't give up Jeff. We're going to appeal this and there are quite a number of issues that we can use. It's going to be rough and you're just going to have to be patient, but I promise you that I'll go right to work on this...okay?"

I could only nod my head as the two Correctional Officers, who had brought me to the courthouse each day for the past two weeks, led me out of the courtroom in handcuffs while the cameras whirled away. I felt as though I was having an out of body experience.

There was an odd passivity and stillness that accompanied the decisiveness of the jury's verdict. I felt as though I was floating along in some warm, deep river, with the currents pushing and turning me in random directions. Any willful effort on my part was irrelevant. I stared into space as I was guided away from the courtroom and to confront my destiny.

During the next week, I didn't talk with anyone except when it was an absolute necessity. I didn't call anyone and I refused all visits. Whenever I could, I stayed in my cell reviewing the details of the trial. And of course, I had many people to blame.

I mentally ran through the list of culprits. A significant portion of the fiasco of my life was my mother's fault for abandoning me so many years ago and my father's fault for dying and leaving me fatherless. It was Julie's fault for denying my request for another chance and it was even Hannah's fault for moving away and leaving me, in spite of how much I loved her. Candy deserved a great deal of the blame for giving my phone number to her little punk of a boyfriend. That moronic miscalculation initiated a cascade of events leading down the path that ended with that accursed gun in my possession. Then there was Wes who gave me the Ruger revolver and Danny who provided the bullets.

Gloria and Mary Anne shared responsibility too, especially in light of the fact that they lied disgracefully under oath. I was confident that nobody believed Mary Anne's claims that I always carried a gun, but who knew for sure? In any case, her attacks on my character certainly didn't help. And the despicable ADA who illegally coached little Johnny and put words in his mouth, the judge who practically told the jury that it would be okay to convict me since I ran from the scene...and the newspaper and the TV reporters...it was all their faults, both individually and collectively. In my mind, there were plenty of people and situations ripe for blame. Unfortunately, I failed to place the lion's share of the responsibility for everything that happened where it belonged, squarely on the shoulders of the convicted murderer who stared back at me in the mirror.

The verdict had been rendered on a Friday afternoon and the Saturday morning headlines read, "Collins Guilty of Murder 1." What made this intensified coverage astonishing was the fact that the Gulf War was relegated to the bottom of the front page. I couldn't comprehend how the outcome of my trial was deemed more important than the United States of America invading a sovereign nation. That very afternoon Jami's sister, Pepper, appeared again on my TV screen to reiterate her wish for me to take my dying breath in prison.

I went straight to work helping Kathryn to file my appeal. I spent literally hundreds of hours in the law library, studying case law pertaining to homicides, as well as statutes that might apply to my case. My appeal contained thirteen separate issues and it was duly submitted seven months after the trial.

About a year later, the Tennessee Supreme Court overturned my verdict. Their decision was based on "faulty jury instructions." The ruling was reversed and the case remanded. I was to receive another trial!

As the saying goes, the wheels of justice move slowly and sometimes they creak and moan in a sluggish crawl. It was another year and a half before the second trial was set to begin, but a lot of important changes had taken place during that time. The judge of my first trial recused herself for the next proceeding. Mel insisted on paying for a higher-priced attorney and contacted a well-known barrister who had already won acquittals in several high profile murder cases to represent me. The lawyer's name was Jonathon Davidson, and he assured me that this time, things would be different. Kenneth Walters, the judge in my second trial was rumored to be a man who was much more liberal than the woman judge who presided over the first trial. This meant that those horrible pictures might be ruled inadmissible. That was my hope and it was also the first main objective of my new attorney.

After I refused the state's offer again (this time it was forty years), the second trial began with an eerie similarity to the first. The crime scene investigators and forensics experts testified on behalf of the state, and further prevarications ensued. Gloria and Mary Anne re-presented their perjuries and once again Mary Anne was exposed as a liar, this time by Jonathon Davidson. Mary Anne was shown to be quite the fool when Mr. Davidson instructed her to give him the piece of paper she kept glancing down at during his cross examination. She initially refused but the judge ordered her to hand it over. It revealed a detailed list of things that I had allegedly done to her during our relationship, including a time I supposedly tied her up and hung her upside down in the closet! Of course, this event existed only in Mary Anne's head and it showed the depth of her delusions when it came to our disastrous relationship.

The admission of the crime scene photographs was discussed a great deal before the trial began and continued to be considered by the judge even after the trial started. The state claimed the photos were crucial to their case and the defense opined that they were too inflammatory and prejudicial. Judge Walters was in a quandary. In the end he decided to rule for the state, and again the gruesome shots of Jami were admitted into evidence and shown to the jury.

After losing the fight to exclude the photographs, Mr. Davidson fully understood the importance of my testimony. And because my testimony had become so crucial, I remained on the stand even longer than in the first trial.

The same ADA used the same tactics in her Herculean effort to impeach my testimony, but she failed once again. My attorney thought that my testimony had gone exceptionally well; so well in fact that he made a critical decision, and during the next recess we discussed his plan.

"Jeff, you were outstanding up there. I was watching the faces of the jurors during her cross-examination and I feel as though the vast majority of them are on board with us. Now what I'm thinking about doing is concluding our case when we go back in session."

"But, what about our other witnesses?"

"Son, I've been doing this for a long time. I've got a pretty good gut instinct as to which direction a jury panel is leaning, and my gut is telling me to quit while I'm ahead. Now ultimately it's your call of course, but I'm advising you that we're in the lead. Besides, it'll throw a good hard curveball at the head of the prosecution. They won't be expecting for us to rest our case at this point. So...what do you say?"

"Mr. Davidson, Mel's paying you a lot of money for your advice, so I suppose the intelligent thing for me to do is take it."

The jury was given their instructions and they retired to their chamber to deliberate. They had only been out for a little over eight hours, when everyone was suddenly called back to the courtroom. As they filed in, my attorney and I observed that each one of them made eye contact with me, which we assumed was a good omen. Then the jury foreman asked the judge for permission to view the crime scene photographs once more. So they were given the photographs and once again filed out of the courtroom for further deliberation.

I had been in the holding area for less than an hour when the announcement came that the jury had reached a verdict, and I was taken back to the courtroom to await my fate. This time none of the jurors so much as glanced in my direction.

"Uh oh, this is not gonna be good," I whispered to Mr. Davidson.

"Mister Foreman, have you reached a verdict in the above styled case?"

"Yes we have your Honor."

"And what are your findings as to the charge of First Degree Murder and/or the lesser included charges?"

"As to the count of First Degree Murder...we find the defendant...Jeffrey Holden Collins...Guilty."

Thirteen and a half, indeed!

CHAPTER 22
GOOD MORNING DESPAIR

"There is but one truly serious philosophical problem and that is suicide."
(Camus)

I could have had a rich life. I might have experienced joy while celebrating births, birthdays and other happy occasions. I might have experienced sadness too as I attempted to console a cherished friend in times of trouble or mourned at the funerals of family members. Instead, I was insulated from all the good things and the bad stuff that most people face every day of their lives.

I often spoke on the telephone with my family and the next time I called, I learned that Mel and my mother were determined to fly to Nashville in order to visit. She was in extremely poor health and wanted to see me and my sister Joan one last time before she died. I did my best to dissuade her, but she wouldn't be deterred, and two weeks later Mel guided her wheelchair into the visitation gallery along with Jeanne and Joan. Mom was at death's door. She weighed about eighty pounds and several types of incurable cancer had ravaged her body. She and I had about five minutes alone together, when the others went to buy snacks and drinks from the vending machines.

"Jeff honey, I want you to know something...that I love you very much and for what it's worth, I want to say I'm sorry for not being a better mother to you," she said as tears began to well up in her eyes.

"Hush Mom, you've been great, especially through all this crap. It was me who was such a terrible son," I said softly as I gave her a gentle hug.

"Mom, there is one thing I want to ask you..."

"Go ahead darling, anything."

"Well...what I have to ask...is...uh...what I need to know Mom, was Jack Collins really my father?"

"Yes honey, he absolutely and positively was."

"Okay then Mom, that's good enough for me. Thanks. I love you very much."

By the time our discussion ended, Mel, Joan and Jeanne had returned with the food and drinks. We all sat around the table and had a great visit, reminiscing only about the good times we shared together. It was very enjoyable to each and every member of my small and rather dysfunctional family. And as our time together came to a close, we said our goodbyes amid countless tears, kisses, hugs and promises of prayer.

Happiness in prison is rare. During those infrequent times, the sensation of joy is fleeting and fragile. My occasional moments of happiness invariably sprang from distant memories, and when I dwelled on them, my mood turned to melancholy, regret and despair. I realized how much I missed the mundane things in life, the morsels that we all take for granted. I missed simple things like driving a car, riding a bike, taking a walk in a park, holding a baby, looking in a store window, walking down a beach...even taking a bath! All the things that I never noticed became things I'd possibly never do again, and there was no one left to blame except myself.

As I reflected on my life, my thoughts would on occasion turn to suicide. I recalled how close I came to checking out during my time in Florida when I was particularly desperate. I made a list of pros and cons to help me decide if taking my own life was a viable, rational option to consider:

PROS

1. I was curious to see what was waiting for me on the other side (if anything)
2. I was tired of this life and very ashamed of my actions and depravity
3. There had been no answers forthcoming from God in spite of all my prayers
4. It would probably give Jami's sister, Pepper and the rest of her family some degree of happiness
5. My suffering would be over

CONS

1. It would hurt the people who loved me too much
2. I had not given up on my search for God
3. It would take away some of the punishment, which I viewed as a partial payment for what I had done
4. All my suffering might not be over and it might actually increase as a result of taking my own life

In the end I chose to live, although there were many times when my prayers included a "Richard Nixonesque" request for God to simply allow me to die in my sleep.

I continued to be haunted by memories of Hannah and my dreams were often about her. One particular dream was of the two of us sitting in the audience of Julie's high school talent contest. Julie won with a moving rendition of "Where Have All the Flowers Gone?" When I awoke, I realized that practically every song I heard reminded me of Hannah, so I did my best to quit listening to music from 1995 until 2007, more than an entire decade! Practically the only time music reached my ears was if someone else's radio was playing while I was in the vicinity. If my radio was on, it was almost always tuned to some type of talk format.

My rambling thoughts caused me to question my sanity. From the smattering of psychological courses I took in college, I recognized that I could possibly be diagnosed as a pathological misfit with delusions of grandeur, or more likely someone with a borderline personality disorder with a chronic substance abuse pattern.

I knew I was not a psychopath however. I was openly and sincerely remorseful about my actions, although I was also aware that Pepper and the District Attorney would say something along the lines of, "Yeah, he's sorry alright...sorry he got caught!" I decided that while many of my actions had undeniably been crazy, I really did not have the personal luxury of possessing the excuse of insanity.

I thought about my shortcomings in each of my significant relationships with women. Love had always meant the woman totally giving herself to me, with virtually no commitment on my part. It began to dawn on me how unfairly I had treated Julie and Jami. It wasn't as though I had never recognized my narcissism before, but now I saw how terribly wrong I had been.

It was June of 1995 and I was into my sixth year behind bars. My appeal of the second trial was submitted, and I resigned myself to the dismal reality that the answer to this appeal would be slow in coming. I also realized that the decision might not be the one I wanted to hear.

I grew weary of the battles, both external and internal. I was sick of the same clothes, the same food, the same concrete area called the "yard" with the same globs of spit that glistened profanely in the sunlight. I was tired of the razor wire, which crowned the fences that protected society from the likes of me. I was tired of books...favorites that I had previously read and those I had yet to read. I was sick of watching all the inane shows on my tiny thirteen-inch television screen. I was sick of the worn-out songs on the radio, especially since so many of them reminded me of Hannah. I was tired of the same old and new faces of the convicts. I was sick of the dunghill of a place that was now my home. I was disgusted and dismayed by all the snitching, sniping, and complaining. I could not bear the resentful, lazy bags of dirt that populated the prison with their backbiting, loudmouthed, argumentative, ignorance. These ignorant dregs posed in a manner to suggest that they had vast quantities of experience and knowledge. The scene was so transparently phony, it might have been comical if it wasn't so damn pathetic.

Prison could bring out the worst in anyone. The most tolerant and compassionate individuals might devolve into racism even if they weren't racist before arriving. In prison, you are compelled to interact with the absolute worst people of any given ethnicity; white, black, brown, yellow...oriental, occidental...whatever. It is too easy to let lethargy replace reason and then engage in the stereotyping that is the norm of institutional living.

I was also fed up with the religious hypocrites that seemed ubiquitous on the compound. Seventy-five percent of inmates that went to the church services did so only to buy or sell dope or to engage in other reprehensible prison business. Many of these frauds walked around with their hands stuffed inside the front of their pants, all tattooed, rapping about killing cops, raping women, cliqued up in some gutless gang of cowards. They shuffled along with a permanent scowl, trying to look threatening and militant, while their palms remained upturned, expecting you to feed their delusional sense of entitlement. All day long, it was "motherfucker this…Goddamn that…suck this…fuck that." The crude facades and endless vulgarities created a wall of defense for these men who never matured mentally. These were men who could barely read and write, men who had given up on hope long before they had reached adulthood, men who had irresponsibly fathered and then abandoned the next generation of prison inmates.

The general sense of hostility between the guards and inmates was often palpable. The clear exception was the bizarre perception that many inmates had of female officers. I was astounded by the notion that an inmate could think of himself as a good catch, even while incarcerated. With no money, no car and no future prospects, these inmates still considered themselves undeniably attractive to the women guards.

Even more shocking was how often the ploy worked! Some women guards would actually risk their careers, their health, their freedom and their self-respect by becoming romantically involved with inmates. In time I grew to understand and honor the heroic efforts that married couples made in order to remain together through such a horrible time, but I could never reconcile the notion that any woman would debase herself by actually beginning a sexual affair with an incarcerated man. Maybe it was the cold comfort that the woman would always know exactly where her man was at night. Maybe it was the excitement borne of breaking taboos or maybe it was simply a result of two lonely people with no other options. It was sad, regardless of the cause.

I was tired of shouldering the mountain of guilt I carried because of the tragedy I had caused. I was tired of a vague, nagging sensation that was seeping out of the deep recesses of my psyche. This shapeless thought had been troubling me for a long time and although I didn't consciously know what it meant at that time, I was weary from it as well.

I looked forward to the end of each summer when the vine ripened tomatoes from the prison farm were served to the inmates. This only happened for a handful of meals and since I loved tomatoes, I would ask my friends who didn't eat them, for their portions. During one such noonday meal, I had been fortunate to gather six servings of the delicious red fruit. I cheerfully carried my overflowing tray to a table, and I was just about to shovel in the first mouthful when I noticed a white substance floating around in the juice of the precious fruit. The tray hadn't been cleaned very well, and the remains from some breakfast grits had contaminated my feast! I walked to the trash and dropped the entire tray into the receptacle and walked away muttering obscenities about the kitchen dishwashers. Yeah, I was sick and tired of being sick and tired.

That August brought yet another dose of bad news. My sick mother died. The ceremony was in Arizona so I wasn't allowed to attend her funeral. I grieved and suffered through the next few weeks as I recalled all the years I had neglected to talk with her. For many years I didn't even send her a Christmas card, a birthday card or even a lousy Mother's Day card for Christ Sakes! And this unconscionable inaction on my part happened in spite of my getting cards and letters from her every year. Her death inflicted a great deal of heartache on me, but it also caused something inside of me to stir, something that had remained dormant for so long that its very existence had nearly faded into oblivion. Change was coming and this time change would not be a bad thing. If allowed, the many constraints of prison will stunt the intellectual growth of any normal human being, but my thirst and quest for knowledge would not permit my mental development to be inhibited. Although badly neglected in recent years, my desire to learn eventually resurfaced. I began by immersing myself in studies of the major world religions. I also read extensively on the thoughts and insights of various giants in the fields of philosophy and psychology.

I made a formal decision to seek out all I could learn about God, the cosmos and whatever else fate enabled me to discover. The reinvigoration of my intellectual curiosity brought other unexpected changes. I became more considerate and tolerant of others and I became progressively introspective. Ultimately, I began contemplating about how and why so many terrible things occurred in my life.

I had been obtaining marijuana for several years through several different avenues. One method simply entailed having a visitor smuggle it in to me, and although two of my former girlfriends had done so from time to time, Bikina was by far the steadiest and most reliable source of my pot supply. She came to see me every weekend and had even passed up modeling jobs in other cities just to come here on visitation days. I knew that it was because she loved me and out of a love for her, albeit a platonic love, I put an end to her misery the next time I saw her.

"Listen Bikina, I've been thinking and I...we need to talk," I said to her as we sat at one of the picnic tables in the outside visitation area.

"Oh yeah? Me too! I've been thinking a lot about us. You know what would be a good idea? I think that we should get married. Then, after your case is overturned and you go up for parole, it'll help your chances. I've learned that a higher percentage of married people make parole than single ones and..."

"Bikina, listen to me please. Are you crazy? My appeal may not be successful. I could be locked up...forever. And look at you. You're drop dead gorgeous girl. Just watch how all these animals stare at you every time you walk through those gates. You deserve a life...with someone outside."

"Jeff you're a fool. Don't you know that I love you? I always have and I always will in spite of the way you probably still feel...about...Hannah. I love you and I don't want anyone else. I'll wait for you and if you never get out, I'll still be here every time they'll let me," she said softly as tears began to fall.

"Bikina, you know how I feel about you. I love you too, but you know...it's not the same type of love that you have for me. I wish I did. And these days I find myself being much more honest than ever before...with myself and with other people. I'm sorry honey, but you and I both know that it's not the type of love that it should be. And most of all the type of love you deserve. So beautiful..."

"Oh Jeff, please don't say what I think you're about to say...please..."

"You've been such a great friend and you're such a beautiful and wonderful person, and since I really *do* love you, I'm gonna do something so totally not about me for once in my miserable life."

"Jeff...oh...no...please...I..."

"Bikina, I want you to go live your life. Please don't try to come back here anymore, because...I'm gonna have to take you off my list. You deserve to be happy. I want you to be happy."

I knew that in time Bikina would be fine and that she would discover a new, more genuine happiness. After the avalanche of sadness that I had caused for many people, it felt good to do something selfless...so..."anti-Jeff."

Bikina knew that it was useless to protest further, so she stood and embraced me. The tears on her face felt like warm rain against my skin as we held our embrace until the guard told us to refrain from touching each other.

"Goodbye Jeff. I...I'll always love you. You'll always be in my prayers and if you ever need me, please get in contact with me and let me know" she sobbed, turning to leave.

"Bye beautiful. Take care of yourself and have a great life," I whispered as I wiped my eyes and watched her walk away.

I knew that she would probably try to come back, so I quickly followed through on my promise and removed her from my list of approved visitors. I decided to take the rest of my ex-girlfriends off the list as well. I had been exploiting them in order to get weed smuggled in, and after an honest assessment any fool would know that that was wrong. I certainly didn't love any of them, at least not romantically, and since I thought that at least one of them might at least try to wait for my release, I knew that ending the pretense was the right thing to do. Besides, I had witnessed so many inmates drive themselves nuts worrying over some woman on the outside, and I wanted no part of that obsession. My new prison philosophy was to do my time by myself and without any semblance of romantic entanglements.

Within the next few months, I stopped accepting any visitors unless it was an absolute emergency. I tried explaining to my sisters and friends that it was just too painful when they left and how I didn't want them around all the cretins that lived with me in my cesspool of a home. Joan and some of my friends argued with me that the visits weren't so bad and that seeing me, even in that awful place, was therapeutic and comforting for them. It helped them to know that I was okay. They said that the visits were more for the visitors' benefit than for the inmate, but I wouldn't budge. No visits. Some of them understood and others seemed to have their feelings hurt, but as time went on they all grew to accept and respect my wishes.

I promised to keep in touch with everyone by telephone and through the mail, which I did faithfully. It was the next logical step in my journey to becoming a better man. I refused to inflict the gloom and misery that permeated the prison on the people I loved.

Shortly thereafter, I had a very disconcerting dream. I was in a vast desert and dying of thirst. My body was just about to succumb to the heat and dehydration when I spotted two figures walking towards me. It was Jami and Wendy, the little girl I had dreamed of years before, the child Julie and I had aborted. They were singing a little song as they grew closer.

"Just a minute...just a minute...we're coming...just a minute," they sang together, sweetly and softly.

I woke up immediately. It was the middle of the night and if not for my cellmate, I would have yelled out as loud as I could. Instead, I got down on my knees and began a silent prayer.

"Oh my God, I don't know if that was a message from you or not, but it's the closest thing that I've ever had, felt to...I don't know if it could be called an epiphany or not, but that's as close as I've ever come to one. It sure kind of felt like one or like one might feel. Oh God, I killed Jami and I helped Julie not to have

our baby. I can't ever make up for their lives, but I'm asking for your forgiveness. I don't know exactly how it works, but I'm asking both of them to forgive me as well. God, please, please let them be in existence so that one day I can tell them face-to-face how sorry I am. I'll do anything you tell me to...please. And God, right here, right now, I'm forgiving everybody for everything that they ever did to me. And I mean everything and everybody...Mary Anne, Bobby Huggins, Mom and Hannah for leaving me...everybody and everything. I forgive them all, and...I'm gonna change. I'm sorry for so many, many things. I'm sorry for doubting your existence, but if I'm ever gonna have a chance to see them one day in the future, then you'll probably have to...well, exist! Because if you aren't real, then I hope that I die in my sleep tonight, just like Richard Nixon prayed for. Now I know that I can never do anywhere near enough to make up for all the horrible things I've done in my life, but I'm gonna try. I don't even know if I'm...fixable, but I'm gonna try. I swear to...well...I guess...to you."

I got back in my bunk and fell asleep. When I woke up the next morning, I experienced an inner peace I had never felt before. And that very afternoon while channel surfing, I was floored by what I saw on Oprah Winfrey's talk show. It was one of her high school reunion shows, and there on the stage with the talk show queen herself, were several people I knew who had gone to school with her, including my cousin and Julie! She looked amazing. She was pretty, poised and articulate. She was married with children and seemed very content with her life. And then I realized that a strange thing occurred. Instead of feeling sad, envious or regretful, I felt a great sense of joy and a sense of relief from knowing how well her life had turned out. I was sincerely happy for her. It was an important milestone in my quest to become a good person.

CHAPTER 23
BEING THE CAUSE OF GRIEF

"Decay is inherent in all component things.
Work out your own salvation with diligence."
(Siddhartha Gautama's [Buddha's] last words to his disciples)

IF...it's such a little word that we say so often that it usually slips right off the end of our tongues unnoticed and when used in conjunction with the word ONLY, it can make a neat little phrase indicating regret. How many areas of my life could the words "if only" be applied to? Ten? A hundred? A thousand?

Plenty of people agree that it's inaccurate and unfair to define a person by their best moment or their worst moment. I hoped that the sentiment was true, but inside I believed that I would forever be known as "Jami's killer," the man who had orphaned my own little boy. I was a murderer who had been convicted in a court of law for brutally killing the mother of my child.

Within a year of my first conviction, I refused to wait any longer. I wrote out a letter of apology and addressed it to Pepper and the rest of Jami's family. And after allowing Kathryn Stern to read it and insisting on her reluctant approval, the letter was mailed. I spent a great deal of time hoping for some kind of reply, but one never came so I assumed that they probably burned it or threw it into the trash unopened.

I also knew that one day in the not too distant future, I would have to write another letter, one that would be much harder to write, but a letter that I needed to write no matter how difficult. I wanted Adam to hear my side one day, or at least I wanted to try and tell him my version of the events of the terrible morning of his mother's death. I promised myself that as soon as I considered Adam old enough to understand, I would write to him. That time came immediately after the tragic horrors of World Trade Center. But I continued to refine and expand the critical letter over the next two years. I finally mailed it right before he turned sixteen.

March 15, 2004

Dear Adam,

This letter is by far the hardest one I have ever written, and it has taken me over fourteen years to complete. I promised myself I would attempt to contact you around the time you turned sixteen. I thought about attempting to contact you countless times in the past, but I did not think your guardians would allow any communication with me, so I decided to wait until I could assume you were mature enough to make your own decision. I hope you take the time to carefully read it, but if you chose not to do so, I completely understand.

First and foremost, I want to tell you how sorry I am for taking away your mother and father by my stupid, careless, tragic, horrible acts. Unfortunately, my ability to express the depth of my shame and remorse is woefully inadequate. I have prayed for well over a decade for your life to be as good, and as normal as possible under the circumstances. It is my deepest hope that you are a happy, healthy, normal young man. If not, the vast majority of the blame lies at my feet. It could have been so much better if a man, who conformed to the laws of society, and one who possessed more of a capacity to love and a greater ability to be loved had biologically fathered you.

In this letter, I plan to address only a few of the details about what happened on the Sunday morning of August 13, 1989. I will also provide you with access to the specific and factual minutiae available in the two volumes of transcripts of the two criminal trials. (My first conviction was overturned.) My sister Joan in Nashville has the first one and the second trial's transcript is currently in my possession. You may have either or both of them to read if you want. Then you may have some questions you would like for me to answer about what happened. Whatever you may ask, I promise to answer it truthfully, no matter how painful it might be.

In our youth, it is easy to believe that whatever we desire is no less than what we deserve, to assume that if something is wanted badly enough, it is our God-given right to have it. That is how it was for me. Things always seemed to come easy for me, money, material possessions, good grades in school, sports, etc. At the time, I considered this "talent" a blessing, but in hindsight, I suppose I now view it as a curse.

I blame only myself for all the bad choices I have made in life. At the age of nineteen, I began experimenting with marijuana, which led to using cocaine about a decade later. Along with my use of these two poisons also came quite a bit of alcohol consumption. I am ashamed to tell you that I also sold marijuana and cocaine for several years to supplement my "supplies." But, all of the grief I caused so many good people (and myself) cannot be blamed on my drug use. Although my choices to drink and get high account for a large portion of what has happened, my flaws as a human being were not limited to these terrible choices. The truth is that I was not a good person, and for the past fourteen years, I have attempted to discover why. I have met with only limited success.

I was born in the same hospital in Nashville, Tennessee as you were, 36 ½ years earlier in 1951. My dad was Jack Bernard Collins, and my mom's name was Maddie, although she later changed it to Lana. He was from Dallas, Texas, and she was born in Oklahoma. My father died after being run over by a large truck when I was nearly nine years old, and my mother passed away in 1995. She had been married to my stepfather, Melton (Mel) Snow, for about thirty-five years, and they lived in Tucson, Arizona. Mel passed away about three and a half years ago. When you were about five or six, they managed to spend some time with you. I hope you remember them. They were good, hard-working, decent people, who loved me very much, and did their best to raise me. I have two sisters, your Aunt Joan in Nashville, and your Aunt Jeanne, who lives in Phoenix, Arizona. Because of me, they have been unfairly shut out of your life. They had nothing to do with any of my mistakes, but continue to suffer because of them. They both love you and have kept you in their thoughts and prayers.

I grew up in Nashville, but graduated with high honors from a private college preparatory school. After dropping out of college after one year, I was drafted into the United States Army during the last of the Viet Nam War. I served from the summer of 1970 until the spring of 1972. I then went back to school for two years. I spent way too much time "partying" during my two years there, and left college to get married to a very beautiful and intelligent young lady named Julie. We had been "going together" for around five years before we were married. During our marriage, she worked as I finally graduated with honors with a Bachelor of Arts degree. I then tried law school for a couple of years. Many of my family and friends regarded my potential at that time to be practically unlimited. For the entire duration of our relationship, she was the perfect girlfriend and wife, while I was the perfect jerk! After putting up with all my many shortcomings for the better part of ten years, she finally left me in 1979. At the time of our divorce, I had pretty much lost control of my life. I dated many different women, used a lot of marijuana, went to countless bars, and inevitably, dropped out of law school. I was still lucky enough to land several jobs in management at various corporations, and I was very successful for a while as a real estate agent. It was about this time, when I began dating Jami.

I recall reading a book in which the author wrote about life's beauty and how death sticks so close to life, not only from a biological necessity, but because of envy. His theory was that life is so beautiful, that perhaps death fell in love with it. A life is a very precious gift from God, and now whether or not I am ever released, I will be directly responsible for two of them until the final beat of my heart. I am sure that you have been told how wonderful and beautiful your mother was, but no matter how great you have heard that she was, it had to be an understatement. She was one of the most beautiful women I have ever seen, and had an awesome personality. Jami was truly an exceptionally nice person and she possessed many other wonderful qualities. She loved you and your brother Johnny more than anything in the world. Except for your conception, however, I wish that she had never become involved with me. I never could see what she saw in me, or why she loved me. I certainly did not deserve it. When we met, she was working as a teller at my bank. We began dating in the summer of 1986, and you were conceived in the following summer of 1987. She was eleven years younger than I was, but much more mature and responsible. Your brother Johnny was around four years of age at the time we met, and she was a very good mother to him. Although she was a very sweet young woman, she also possessed quite a temper, which I could easily arouse to say the least. She was justifiably very angry with me on many occasions. And yes, she too used drugs, although not nearly to the extent that I did. I am hesitant to mention anything negative to you about your mom. It is not my intention to cast dispersions on her character, but simply to tell you the truth. Everyone has a temper, and drug use was a cancer and a sign of our culture and times, as it continues to be today. No one is perfect, and Jami had a few faults, but she was truly a genuinely good person.

As I said earlier, I was not a nice person. I was constantly unfaithful or mean to her, and she would do little things to retaliate. I think that I behaved like I did due to a fear of commitment, but I really do not have an answer, or at least a very good one. Because of my actions and her temper, we had a very volatile relationship. She would break up with me over some insensitive thing I had said or done, and I would talk her into giving me another chance repeatedly...and again. When she became pregnant with you, she and Johnny moved into my house and lived with me for most of her pregnancy, and on up until you were six months old. It was during this time when I appeared to straighten my life out a little. It was only an illusion. My drug use and infidelity continued, just on a smaller scale. When you were born, you were a perfect and beautiful baby boy, named Adam Holden Collins. Other than the doctors and nurses, I was the first to hold you. I was so proud.   Things were okay for about six months, when Jami caught me in a lie or something...I really cannot remember what it was, because I did so many wrong things. She left with you and Johnny and she would not let me see you again for six months. Then we ran into each other at a local nightclub and began seeing each other from around March through July of 1989. We got along well that summer, better than ever before actually, but my drug use and other faults and vices continued.

Then on that nightmare of a morning, as we were fighting over a gun, she was shot in the head. I then left in a panic and total state of shock. I later learned that she died in a matter of minutes. It was entirely my fault, my fault for coming to your apartment, for kicking in the door and for having a stupid gun in the first place. I was high, drunk, angry and stupid, a condition that proved to be fatal and tragic on so very many levels. I alone am totally and completely to blame. There were different theories and assumptions as to what exactly transpired that morning, but I am the only one who knows for sure. Johnny testified that he saw me "shocking" his mom in the first trial, when he was about six or seven years old, but he also said on the witness stand he really did not remember what actually occurred and that one of the assistant district attorneys had

told him how it happened. (You can read this in the transcript of the first trial.)

I have decided not to go into any further details, because I am afraid that it might seem as though I am making excuses, and that is not the case. Besides, there is no excuse for what I did. However, I will say this: It was horrible enough exactly the way it happened. The portrayal by the media and the prosecution made it sound even worse.

"Rehabilitation" is just a word. When used in connection with prison, it is a joke. The only real way people change is if they truly want to change, and believe me, it is not easy. There are no secrets, but one of the main keys is "remembering" your past mistakes. At the time of my relationship with your mother, I was a narcissistic, selfish, violent, immature jerk, who was *spiritually weak and morally bankrupt. I have caused unimaginable grief to my family and friends, not to mention what I have done to yours. I would love to have a "time machine" to use. I would travel back in time and have a very long talk with that "eighteen year old me." It could make a huge difference in how I lived my life, but unfortunately, such an option does not exist. Nevertheless, I have worked very hard over the past decade and a half to become a much better person than I once was. I have come quite a ways, but have light years to go, and there are many areas in which improvement could and should be made. I still remain a "work in progress." I can never ever atone for taking your mother's life. I believe that God has forgiven me, but I have still not completely forgiven myself. I may never be able to do so, at least not in this lifetime. Jami's family and friends hated me for what I did and they are indeed justified for feeling that way. I have prayed to God for their hatred to turn to forgiveness and compassion, for their sake as well as my own. Hate is such an exhausting and worthless emotion, but I certainly understand if you or any of them will never be able to forgive me.*

Look, I do not want to upset your life anymore than I already have. I just felt that this is something I had to do. If you never want anything to do with me, that is completely understandable. If you decide to come to my parole hearing sometime in the summer of 2010 and protest my release, I will not blame you in the least. Whether or not I am ever released, I can never pay for what I did. All I can do is try to become a better human being every day until I die, and always try to do the right thing. I believe that it was Mark Twain who once said, "Always do right. You will gratify some people and astonish the rest."

I am going to provide you with some addresses just in case you ever decide to get in touch with your two aunts, your cousins and a few of my closest friends. They are on a separate sheet of paper along with a few short notes on why you may want to contact them.

In closing, I must say I wish I had been the father to you that I should have been, and that I am extremely sorry for all the grief I have caused for you, Johnny and all of Jami's family and friends. We as human beings are capable of such beautiful dreams, but also such horrible nightmares. Many times over the years I have asked myself why things happened the way they did, why I made the choices I made, why she was the one who died instead of me when we were wrestling over that gun, etc. I just do not have the answers yet. Determining the exact value of Π (pi) may prove to be easier.

If you decide that you would like to contact me, I would love to hear from you. If not, I wish the very best life possible for you and all those people close to you. Whatever you do and wherever you go, you will remain in my thoughts and prayers until I take my final breath. I wish that I could sign this letter with something like, "All My Love, Dad," but I certainly have not earned such a privilege. May God bless you and keep you safe.

Earnestly,
Jeff

The letter was extremely difficult to write. I didn't know if I said the right things, whether I said too little or too much. Should I have left out the part about Jami using drugs? Should I have left out the part about her having a temper? Did I convey how much she loved Adam and how good a mother she was? Had I adequately expressed how repentant and remorseful I felt? I wanted to shout it from the rooftops to Adam, Johnny, Pepper and everyone I had hurt so badly by being the cause of the death of their loved one. I wanted them to know how much I was suffering. Maybe knowing that I was in tremendous anguish would somehow ease their suffering. Perhaps their desire for vengeance would be partially satisfied.

When I managed to find some degree of privacy, I once again prayed in my rambling manner.

"God please help me. I really don't believe that I can do this by myself. I'm begging for you to forgive me and I'm begging you to help everyone I've hurt to forgive me. I'm so thankful for the friends who still support me and I'm very grateful for Mel, Joan and Jeanne. So please bless them all in some very special ways. They've made all this so much easier. I still hate this place, but without them, well...I don't know how I would have made it. Thanks so much for letting me see Julie on TV a while back. It was great to find out that she's doing so well and I'm asking you to bless her as well. And as for Hannah, I have no idea where she is or how she's doing, but I hope that she's healthy and happy ...so please look after her too. Look, I'm gonna read the entire Bible, the Book of Mormon, the Qur'an and...well...any other so-called holy book you might want to send my way. I'll search for you until I feel like I've hit pay dirt, so to speak. Until then I promise to do my best regardless if my appeal is successful again or even if they tell me to lie down, be quiet and do this life sentence. As for Pepper and all the people who loved Jami, for all of them that I've hurt so badly...I'm very sorry. But, I know that no matter what I do or say, it won't mean spit to them. But I'm praying to you that one day in the future they will find the inner strength necessary to forgive me for what I've done, and if they can't ever do so, I'll truly understand. I'm also praying that you somehow make sure that Adam will at least read my letter. You know that every word of it is true and unfortunately it's...well, it's the best and the most I can do, at least for right now. Maybe one day I can...ah, I'll save that for another time. Okay then Father, God, Creator...or whatever title you want, that's about all for

now from one of your most wayward children. Thanks for listening to all of my grumbling and rambling. I sincerely want to do my best for the rest of the time I have in this lifetime, and...I want to become like the guy that Nietzsche talked about...the man that made virtue his addiction and if need be, his catastrophe."

PART V INTROSPECTIVELY

"To every thing there is a season, and a time to every purpose under heaven."

(Ecclesiastes 3:1)

CHAPTER 24
RELIGION...A SWING AND A MISS

"So many Gods, so many creeds, so many paths that wind and wind. While just the art of being kind is all this old world needs."
(Ella Wheeler Wilcox)

In July of 1998 I had been incarcerated for nearly nine years and my appeal of the verdict in the second trial had been pending for over three years. My attorney assured me that it was *almost always* a good sign whenever it took a long time for the Tennessee Supreme Court to decide a case. And since three years was the longest time my attorney had ever heard of, he felt nearly certain that I was going to receive some good news very soon. The answer came the next month...August. The month that had so often brought terrible news throughout my lifetime did so yet again as I read the ruling, which was a unanimous affirmation of the lower court's findings.

"What the heck is the deal with me and this lousy month?" I asked aloud as I refolded the letter, put it back in the envelope and tossed it onto the bunk.

The only legal remedies left open to me were either filing a Post-conviction Appeal based on ineffective assistance of counsel and/or going all the way to the United States Supreme Court. I had a better chance of winning the lottery...in Japan!

The court's rebuke was quite a blow, but it didn't knock me down. Genuine change had been manifesting itself in my character since my 44th birthday, about a month after the death of my mother. Shedding the final layers of the onion of self-pity, I refused to waste another second feeling sorry for myself. I was too involved and focused on several projects. My appeal to even higher courts and religious studies consumed a great deal of my time.

I had long questioned the existence of a God who was said to be involved in the smallest details of every human being's life, a God that knew the exact number of hairs on my head. Since coming to prison, I began an earnest and objective search for something that would convince me one way or the other. I read volumes of so-called holy books, books of apologetics on holy books, and even books detailing the minutia of holy books. I started by reading various editions of the Bible and moved on to the Qur'an, the Book of Mormon and a tome called *The Urantia Book*. I read all of them from cover to cover and without prejudging any of them. Every single one was read openly and eagerly. I read a great deal about Buddhism, the Upanishads and Vedas of Hinduism and about some of the most obscure religions such as Rastafarianism and Zoroastrianism among a myriad of others. I ventured into the troubling waters of the

Scientologists and the Jehovah's Witnesses, but I didn't stay there very long. I investigated the Asian religions of Taoism, Confucianism, Shinto and Sikhism, a blend of Hinduism and Islam. I even looked into the rather obscure worship of such things as the sun, the moon, various animals and Mother Nature.

I found it remarkable how often the God of an old religion would somehow resurface as a demon of a new religion. I examined the insights of the more prominent atheists, such as Richard Dawkins, Bertrand Russell and Lucretius. While I agreed with Russell and Lucretius's thinking that "...religion is a disease born out of fear and the source of untold misery for the human race," I knew that I could never be an atheist myself. I wanted to believe in something beyond this world too badly, even though I vacillated relentlessly between faith and doubt. My belief could not resist doubt because my faith was too weak to transcend it. And during the extended periods when my thinking was ruled by disbelief, doubts would rise about my disbelief as well. I continued to hope that a merciful, caring Supreme Being existed and I sincerely wished for an afterlife, all the while doubting and wondering if there even was a God at all. I wondered how important a single individual could be considering the untold billions of people (or souls) who have lived and died. I faced a plethora of unsolvable problems and unanswerable questions concerning every religion and every one of their holy books that I studied, especially the ones that claimed to offer an exclusive path to God.

I was raised as a Christian and fairly familiar with the Bible, but nevertheless I decided to reread the entire book from cover to cover. But again, the experience left me thoroughly confused. After deep consideration, I decided that the Bible appeared to be a book written by a group of nomadic, idealistic Jews who had perhaps lived in the desert heat a little too long, some three thousand years ago. The New Testament was added, and the book suffered through another two thousand years of countless translations and broad editorial license, many times by editors who harbored hidden agendas. To me, the bible was irreparably riddled with countless contradictions and inconsistencies.

My curiosity moved me to focus on the purported virgin birth of Jesus. I discovered that it was common knowledge among scholars that this miracle story is at least suspected to be the result of the mistranslation of the word *almah* in *Isaiah 7:14* which when correctly translated simply means young maiden, not virgin.

I wondered if Jesus was speaking about extraterrestrials when he said, "...other sheep I have which are not of this fold" in *John 10:16*. And was the first chapter of Ezekiel describing a spaceship? I was perplexed about the "144,000" souls that will make it to paradise in *Revelation 14:3-5*. Not only were they all virgin males, not one of them had ever told a lie and all of them were "perfect before God." Perfect! This despite Jesus' own admonition "Why do you call me good? No man is good."

"Does that mean that all the rest of us are doomed?" I asked aloud.

I was troubled by God's decision to kill everyone on earth except for eight people. It seemed to me that the "sons of God" mentioned early in Genesis were the true troublemakers. They took the daughters of man as wives. Why then did we mortals receive the bulk of his wrath? Furthermore, it appeared to be blatantly unfair that God allowed the hooligan renegade of an angel called Lucifer to come to earth just to bring down plague after plague, especially after being proven unfit for heaven.

I had a problem with Samson losing a bet because of his wife, and then expressing his anger by killing thirty Philistines who weren't even involved in the wager. I questioned the misogynistic philosophy of Paul, who in *First Timothy 2:15* wrote that women "…will be saved by childbearing, providing that she lives a modest life and is constant in faith and love and holiness." I wondered what happened to salvation through Christ!

To me, the Christian God often seemed extremely wrathful, arbitrary and capricious. Although God let David literally get away with murder, among many other serious sins, he struck down one guy for masturbating his "seed" onto the ground and another man for merely reaching out to steady the Jewish Ark of the Covenant. And although the Bible claims in *Acts 10:34*, that God is "no respecter of persons," he does seem to pick and chose quite a bit, the entire Jewish race for example, who the Bible says is his chosen people. And then there was the story about Esau and Jacob. God decides that he loves one and the other he chooses to hate, and right out of the womb to boot!

Heck, maybe I'm like Esau. That may be the reason why I never seem to get a straight answer to my prayers. But if I was God, I probably wouldn't answer a guy like me either.

I was taken aback when I read the fifth chapter of Numbers, which tells how the ancient Jews performed a ritual to determine whether or not someone's wife had been unfaithful. After the priest swept up the dirt from the floor of the temple and mixed it with water in a cup, the woman in question was required to drink the filthy quaff. If she didn't become sick, she passed the test. I wondered why those women put up with such nonsense, and if they ever tried to use the same procedure on a philandering husband.

I really wanted and needed someone to adequately explain Melchisedec to me. This enigmatic King of Salem and Most High Priest was mentioned in Genesis, Psalms and in greater detail in Hebrews. Here was a man without a mother, without a father, without a beginning or an end! In my opinion, his origin was more miraculous than that of Jesus. And if Jesus, who was supposed to be a direct descendant of King David, was truly born to a virgin and had no biological father on earth, why does the Bible bother to name Joseph in either of the varying lists of descendants found in Matthew and Luke?

Next I read the entire Qur'an as I examined the faith of Islam. I quickly discovered that in spite of the claims of Muslims that the Qur'an has remained the unchanged word of Allah since its inception, there was much evidence to the contrary. It is an accepted historical fact that Caliph Uthman, the third successor to the prophet Mohammad, ordered every copy to be burned that differed even slightly from the one he favored. It was one of the greatest purging of religious texts known to the ancient world.

When I read *Surah 21* and learned that Muslims were first told to bow toward Jerusalem when they prayed, and then the direction was changed toward Mecca, I wondered why. And when I studied *Surah 53* and the so called "Satanic verses," which were concerned with the three goddesses, Al-Lat, Al-Uzza and Manet, I understood why there was a contract taken out on Salmud Rushdie's life. The exposure of this major faith as one that once nearly made bizarre compromises with minor deities would certainly be unpalatable to most believers.

I was curious about the promise of seventy-two virgins for every Muslim martyr who gave his life in the name of jihad. Where would all these virgins come from? What did the virgins do wrong to deserve being reduced to little more than a bartering chip? Did the girls supernaturally remain virgins after having sex? Because with only seventy-two of them, I figured that most men would run through them within a few years, and with all eternity looming…what's a fellow to do? And what was a female martyr's reward?

Additionally, there's another question of mistranslation of the word virgin. I had to laugh when I read what Richard Dawkins said about it in his book, The God Delusion. Dawkins wrote that Ibn Warraq claimed that instead of virgins, the correct translation should be that every martyr will receive seventy-two "white **raisins** of crystal clarity." These are his words, not mine!

Did Mohammad really marry the six-year-old child named Ayesha and consummate the marriage when she was nine? In spite of all the explanations given by Muslims I knew, there was no way to clean up that story. Not that the incident could be much worse than the apparent insemination of the 13 or 14-year-old Virgin Mary by the Holy Spirit. Did this child consent to being impregnated? Can a young teenager even offer an informed consent for such a violation? Even if the conception was immaculate, certainly the trauma of childbirth on a little girl was a dangerous and horrifying burden. "The world was different back then," was a common excuse I heard, by people trying to justify what any reasonable secular person could logically construe to be religiously countenanced child rape. It is commonly accepted as fact that thousands of years ago, children were much *less* mature physically and mentally than they are today, so any attempt to mitigate the horror of these vicious assaults did nothing to endear me to these major religious characters or their advocates. The hypocrisy of venerating individuals and divinities whose actions today would put them *under* the prison, rendered traditional religions untenable in my opinion. If the God of Abraham represents the absolute truth, but simultaneously supports or justifies horrible crimes against children and then advocates wholesale genocide, then why do we call him God? I suspected and hoped that it was God who had been debased and misrepresented by ardent "followers" bent on their own deification, not the other way around.

Many believers of Islam claim that Alexander the Great, who was born 350 years before Christ, and Abraham, who lived eons before that, were Muslims. Simple math exposed this absurdity since Mohamed didn't roam the desert until the seventh century AD. And when I read in *Surah 18* that Alexander discovered that the sun set in a pool of black mud, I suspected that the transcribers of the prophet (Mohamed was apparently illiterate) may have been drinking absinthe. Or maybe it was another case of ignorance that prevailed.

My conclusion was that neither Christianity nor Islam was for me, but if I had been forced to choose, I would have to lean toward Christianity. A religion in which the Son of God came to earth in order to die for the sins of man, was much more appealing and merciful than a religion that required the sons of man to die for God in exchange for 72 virgins.

I liked and enjoyed Buddhism. I was initially shocked by the claim that Siddhartha Gautama, who would become the fourth Buddha of this kalpa, was born to Queen MahaMaya after she was impregnated by a "superb white elephant" during a dream. This bizarre conception notwithstanding, I considered the teachings of Buddha to be elegant and beautiful. They were based on Buddha's Four Noble Truths which are:

1. All existence is suffering
2. Suffering arises from craving and desire
3. Cessation of desire means the end of all suffering

    4. Cessation of desire is accomplished by following Buddha's eightfold path, controlling one's conduct, thinking and beliefs

Buddha encouraged his disciples to find their way to enlightenment themselves by his last words, "Decay is inherent in all component things. Work out your own salvation with diligence." The wording is very similar to Paul's counsel to the Philippians when he instructed them to "work out your own salvation with fear and trembling." Buddha said it centuries of years before Paul, and its message remains poignant today.

I was fascinated after reading the teachings of Buddhism and Hinduism, especially the ideas of Karma and reincarnation. I wanted to be able to recall this life when I arrived in the next one, but I certainly didn't want a rerun of all of my horrible choices from this life! Where was the point in that? But my main problem with Buddhism was that Buddha never concerned himself with the existence of God. In fact, according to Buddhist teachings, Buddha said that if God actually exists, it was inconceivable that such a God would be concerned about the day-to-day affairs of mortals.

Then I stumbled upon *The Urantia Book* with its 196 chapters and 2,097 pages of tiny print. Reading that book was a major undertaking, both physically and emotionally, but after completing the tome, I decided that *The Urantia Book* made more sense than any other holy book. It contained a logical explanation for the creation of the cosmos and for the existence of life on earth. It detailed how and why we developed down through the ages, describing a method similar to the one explained by Charles Darwin. I despised the endless debates between creationists and evolutionists. In my opinion the stance of strict creationists had become silly, as I witnessed their "theories" evolve, constantly contorting their arguments in new ways to account for each successive scientific breakthrough. Even the Vatican acknowledged Darwinian evolution, and besides, how could any rational thinker of the 21st century deny the genetic variability among people? *The Urantia Book* shed light on other mysteries of the galaxy. I did question the book's claims of authorship however, ostensibly because among other writers, it listed the mysterious Melchisedec.

After so many forays into diverse creeds, I found none suited to my personal beliefs, and none that really explained God. After years of searching in so many different places and praying daily for guidance, I found myself in essentially the same place spiritually as where I began so many years earlier.

*   Maybe this is all there is, but if that's true, then I'll never be able to tell Jami and Wendy how sorry I am...face to face...to tell them both how many thousands of times I've asked forgiveness and begged God to let me trade places with them.*

I attempted to keep my religious views to myself, but I was often provoked into defending my views, or overwhelmed by the ceaseless inanities spouted by some new, impassioned convert to Christianity or Islam. And after reading so many texts on the subject, I took exception to anyone, Christian, Jew, Muslim or Buddhist, who tried to convert me to a religion to which they themselves remained at least partially ignorant. Although I usually relied on reason and logic while discussing an issue, when the topic was religion I would often score with cheap debating points.

I often resorted to sophomoric, pedantic arguments, especially if I was talking to some unread yahoo trying to prove a point by referring to a book the guy obviously hadn't even read. "Tell me about who you think Melchisedec was" or "Can God make a rock so big that he himself can't pick it up?" were two of my standards. These discussions frequently concluded with me saying something like, "You really shouldn't say that something is the word of God, when you don't even know what it says!"

I had improved my demeanor, but I retained my sardonic wit and I wasn't always successful at suppressing it. Once I wrote a poem that described my feelings about religion, especially targeting Christianity. The editor of the prison newspaper at that time was a Christian and found the poem offensive, so it was never published.

Another Credo

Is it good to be a Christian…
Because of the free pass on the iniquitous road to heaven
Okay to fuss, cuss and lust
To be unkind, to disregard, to disrespect
To view another as inferior
As they judge and spew their sundry racist venom
Okay to lie, steal and rob
To deal and abuse dope, to maim and kill
As long as the Magic Words are invoked
"I repent Father, please forgive me"
Would it not be better to avoid wickedness
And consider all sin unforgivable without amends
Gandhi said that he would consider becoming a
Christian the instant they became more like Christ Is
it good to be a Christian…**?**

I thought about prayer and wondered about the meaning of *First Thessalonians 5:17*, "Pray without ceasing." I learned of a prayer that many people use from reading J.D. Salinger's *Franny and Zooey*. The character named Zooey relates a prayer that Catholics are instructed to say thousands of times each day. It goes something like, "Lord Jesus Christ, have mercy on me, a miserable sinner." The idea is that when you recite the prayer with sufficient frequency, it becomes second nature. Soon your heart supposedly takes over and the prayer is automatically said simultaneously with every heartbeat. I tried this for weeks before giving up when the concept began to feel pointless.

I prayed every night, but I restricted myself to asking forgiveness, giving thanks, asking for the strength and guidance needed to continue my spiritual quest, and to keep my loved ones safe. (And during especially stressful times while battling a bout of depression, I would sometimes pray the Richard Nixon prayer to die in my sleep.) I concluded that if God existed, his will would be done, regardless of my input, so why ask for anything?

In the end I rejected all religions. Christianity and Islam were dismissed for the reasons given, Mormonism for the absurdity of its origins (outrageous even when compared to other religious origination doctrines) and sects such as Jehovah's Witness because…well, such sects betrayed themselves by preying on the hopelessly ignorant. I likened most purveyors of static religion to dope dealers, because they required the faith (or addiction) of others to sustain what little, if any, beliefs they held.

After all the metaphysical barhopping, the thousands of prayers, and taking into account the logic of Pascal's Wager, I sidestepped the wisdom of Ockham's Razor, and arrived at a unique philosophy that was esoteric, eclectic and difficult to describe.

I was moved spiritually while reading Yann Martel's book, <u>The Life of Pi</u>. In this novel the lead character is torn between Hinduism, Islam and Christianity, and when his parents demand that he choose one of them, he exclaims, "I just want to love God!"

My heart screamed out a resounding, "YES!"

While the ordinary believer has had his beliefs made for him by others (usually by the happenstance of birth which dictates both geographic and parental influence), communicated to him by habit, and retained by threats of hell, my beliefs came from within. I had come to believe in virtue, kindness and doing the right thing for the right reason. My spirituality had been razed and built anew from the ground up. I maintained a personal relationship with God, and most importantly it was sincere. Although I continued to carry the burden of doubt, I believed in a caring God who was in charge of dispensing karmic justice. I refused to believe in any man's ability to tell me how to find

God, and rejected any attempt by mortals to act as the sole intermediary between God and me.

Many times people develop faith in order to provide a psychological safety net for their fears of whatever the supernatural may hold for them. That wasn't true in my case. My chief fear was not punishment, but the possibility that there might be nothing more than what there is in this lifetime, and I desperately wanted to survive into an afterlife. I wanted to stand before all the people I had hurt and ask for their forgiveness. I wanted the chance to atone for not being a better son, father, brother, husband, grandson, boyfriend, friend...and human being. Just a chance...that was my only hope, my prayer for a chance...a chance for redemption.

CHAPTER 25
UNDESERVED LOVE

"The quality of mercy is not strain'd. It droppeth as the gentle rain from heaven upon this place beneath. It is twice blest. It blesseth him that gives and him that takes... And earthly powers doth show like God's when mercy seasons justice."
(William Shakespeare – The Merchant of Venice)

It had been four years since the death of my mother, and during that time, Mel continued to send money and stamps in addition to picking up the bills for my legal fees.

During the summer of 1999 we were talking on the phone one Saturday morning.

"Listen son, I need to talk with you about something serious."

"Sure Mel, go ahead."

"I just found out that I have cancer. They told me it's incurable and I don't know how long I have left. So…I know that you don't like visits, but I'm flying to Nashville in two weeks to hopefully see Joan, Adam and the rest of my grandbabies. And I'd like to stop by and see you too, if you don't mind."

"Mel that'd be great. I'd love to see you. I'll get a special visit approved for any day you want."

"Well, how about a week from this coming Friday?"

"Consider it done."

Mel arrived early Friday morning and we had been talking and laughing about old times for a while when I turned to a serious topic.

"Mel, I want to ask you a question that I really need answered," I said solemnly.

"Sure son, shoot."

"Do you know if Jack was really my father or not…for sure?"

There was nearly a full minute of awkward silence as the two of us looked at one another.

"Jeff, I'm not gonna lie to you. I don't think that he was."

After another period of uncomfortable quiet, I looked down and asked, "Do you know who was?"

"No I don't son. I asked Lana more than once, but she never would tell me, and whenever I pressed her for an answer, she'd get mad, so I usually just dropped the subject. I'm sorry. I wish that I could tell you. I really do."

We finally got on the subject of his grandbabies and Mel was telling me how much Adam looked like me. Mel said that he was growing like a weed and seemed normal, happy and healthy when he visited with him for several hours the day before. I realized that I knew next to nothing about the son I claimed to love so much, the baby that I had held in my arms and promised to be a great dad to on the day he was born. We talked about Joan's children, and I suddenly faltered as if there was something I couldn't figure out how to say or even whether to say it. Instinctively, Mel simply placed his hand on top of the back of my hand and nodded.

"It's okay son. It's okay."

I just allowed the tears streaming down my face to drop onto the table like a summer's rain. I didn't care if a bunch of guards and hardened criminals saw me crying or what they thought about it. The man sitting across from me...he had been a father to me all along. I had been too stubborn to see it, to realize that Mel's love for me truly was the love of a father for a son. And despite the horrible things I had said to him and about him, despite our fight years ago, despite the imaginary rift that I constructed between us, Mel...my dad, had been there for me all along. And now before it was too late, I was blessed once again, this time with the opportunity to tell him just how I felt.

"Mel...Dad...I want to thank you for being a father to me and for loving me all these years, in spite of the horrible way I've treated you and in spite of all the terrible things I've done. I wish that I had told you all this before Mom passed away, but I'm telling you now.
And Mel, I love you very much."

That was the last time I saw him and as I walked back to my cell, my heart was so full of gratitude for such a chance to tell him and love for Mel that my feet seemed to barely touch the ground.

There were many friends and family members who had come to offer love and support at the beginning of my legal ordeal. An old convict once told me that my roster of free-world visitors would "thin out" over the years. He was right. A lot of them fell by the wayside and a few others completely turned their backs on me, one or two of whom I thought would never leave my side. But the ones that remained in my corner, how enduring they were...what unbelievable family members and friends! Perhaps it was the positive karma I had built over the years as I exchanged bad habits for good ones. But even that could not possibly account for the outpouring of love and kindness.

Brittany kept in touch through countless cards and letters and she even offered to marry me, thinking that it might improve my chances when I met the parole board. Kenny Collins and his family sent a Christmas package every year and Kenny and I talked on the phone at least once a month. My little sister Jeanne sent cards, letters, money and stamps practically every month, and she always told me how much she loved me and how proud she was to have me as her brother.

Barry Michaels, a close friend who I had met in prison, continued to stay in touch for years when he was released (after serving several years for a crime he did not commit.) Barry had become quite successful as the owner of a computer consulting business, and he offered me a car, a place to stay and a job whenever I made parole. David Beal, the beer bottle-hurling champion, had married a beautiful girl named Jean who he was dating before I was arrested, and it seemed as though the two of them had practically adopted me when I went to prison. Every year at Christmas, David sent several hundred dollars to use to buy gifts for indigent inmates. There were plenty of these men who had no money, men no one outside the fence gave a damn about. I had a great time playing Santa Claus and when I asked David for permission to give his address so that the grateful men could send thank you cards, David said, "No, just let them think it's coming from you."

Jean sent hundreds of books, countless food packages, sweatshirts, sweatpants and running shoes. I talked with her about as often as I talked with David. I remember one poignant conversation with Jean on the phone. I was trying to convince her to read the copy of *The Urantia Book* that I sent to her.

"Jean, I really do hope that you read it. It answered so many questions for me."

"Jeff, I've read some of it, but...well...you have more time on your hands than I do." "OUCH!" I laughed.

"Do you know something, when I first met you years ago, I really didn't like you very much."

"I understand. I didn't care much for that guy myself."

"But I love you now," she said.

"And I love you guys too."

What family and friends! And as the years rolled by, I continued to receive letters of support from other friends who kept me in their prayers all the time I had been incarcerated. I realized that I was one fortunate man!

I became entrenched in the banal routines of prison life, always cognizant of the indolent forces aligned to reduce me to just another institutionalized automaton. My athleticism, or what was left of it in my mid-forties, combined with my education and intellect, continued to set me apart from most other miscreants. I was assigned to work in the recreational department where I made the maximum wage allowed; a whopping fifty cents an hour. In the recreation department, I served as the officiating clinic instructor and trained inmates to be officials for basketball and softball tournaments. I also served on the Grievance Committee, the Inmate Council, wrote numerous articles for the institutional newspaper and participated in a handful of other extracurricular activities. I stayed very busy and preferred it that way.

Several years earlier I was called into an office near the front of the prison. I immediately recognized the warden and a counselor with whom I was very familiar. I felt a sense of panic rising inside, certain that someone in my family was seriously ill or had died, but this time it turned out to be positive news.

"Good morning Mr. Collins, please come in and have a seat," said Warden Hornbuckle with a smile.

"Good morning Warden and Mr. Bell."

"Jeff, we need a favor from you. We're going to be starting up a program for groups of high school and college students to visit this institution and listen to a few inmates talk about prison and how they came to be here. And your name has been recommended to me by more than a few people, officers and others who have told me that you'd be perfect for such a program," she said.

"What exactly would it entail?" I asked.

"Oh just walking around the compound with them and Counselor Bell when the groups visit, standing up in front of them and telling them what it's like in here, you know, your story...as much of it as you'd like to share...that sort of thing."

"Warden, I'm not much of a public speaker. I don't know," I said.

"Oh Jeff, you'd do great. I've talked with you enough times to know that you're more than capable of doing this. But it's your choice. It's completely voluntary. There are no privileges attached, no extra good days or anything other than my appreciation. But like I said, it's your decision."

"Okay Warden, I'll do my best."

And I did, too. The first time I was a little shaky. Speaking before a group of people was new to me and it showed. But by the third tour I began to feel more comfortable. And although I didn't foresee a future as a professional speaker, I began to reap some benefits. I was up front and honest from the outset. I felt I owed it to the students and to the people in my own life, so I was always candid about what I had done to be in prison. I had long ago ceased to blame others for anything that occurred in my past. And by doing so and sharing the intimate details of that awful morning with one group of strangers after another, the process began to serve as a form of catharsis.

I continued to feel nervous even after speaking to more than 100 groups, but I also continued to feel better about myself each time the students exited through the prison gates. I considered the opportunity to meet with them a great blessing.

I began the tours by telling the students my name, age and my sentence. I downplayed my college education and the material successes I had experienced earlier in life. Although I had no actual script, I usually said something like the following:

"I'm going to ask you to suspend any preconceived notions you may have about convicts, prison and our judicial system. What you're about to experience is reality, not television. Your pity is unnecessary, but compassion is appreciated. Avoid being gullible, but please show understanding. For you, this will hopefully serve as a lesson. It'll be therapy for me.

"I've been locked up for more than twenty-one years. By the end of this tour, I'll have told you what I did to get here and at that time, you'll have a chance to ask me questions. I promise to answer any question you have as truthfully as I can. Fair enough? Let me start off by saying I'm scheduled to meet the parole board sometime in 2010. By then I will have served 21 years or somewhere in the neighborhood of 7,665 days.

"Success always seemed to come easy for me. Things went so smoothly when I was young that I considered myself blessed. Now I suppose I consider it a curse, or at best a badly mishandled benefit. I believe that character is formed in times of adversity and perhaps I had it too easy. By my own amateurish self-analysis, I have deduced that my gifts may have hurt my moral growth and stunted my need to expand or further develop my character. I didn't stand for something positive and like Martin Luther King said, '...the man who doesn't stand for something will fall for anything.'

"Let me bore you with a few statistics for a minute or so. There are approximately 300 million people in the U.S. and today we have around 2.5 million people incarcerated, more than any other nation in the world. There are more than 5 million people on parole or probation. Therefore, there are more than 7.5 million people in the national system or one out of every 31 adults! This country incarcerates people at a rate more than five times that of most European countries. Per capita, America has the largest number of people incarcerated of any country on earth, and more than any time throughout history, even higher than during the peak of the gulag era when Joseph Stalin ruled the Soviet Union. When I was a teenager, I believe that there were four prisons in Tennessee. Now there are over twenty different sites. How many will there be when you reach my age? There are many areas in which the U.S.A. appears to have made mistakes, but we know how to build prisons.

"Life holds many things in store for us. There's happiness, adventure, love, success, joy, etc. on one hand; then there is misery, hate, gloom, desperation, despair, failure, pain and death on the other. Every one of these situations will almost certainly find each one of you. It's kind of stupid to volunteer for the negative ones or to search for them by making bad choices, choices like the ones I've made so often in my life.

"We as human beings are capable of fulfilling beautiful dreams or creating horrible nightmares. My life is the perfect example. Sadly, the majority of you will never have the opportunities that I wasted. I was the kid the other kids' parents liked. My potential was considered by many to be unlimited. Somewhere along the way, the train got derailed. My good guy façade continued, but in reality I was just a liar, a fake and a drug addict and dealer. One definition of insanity used in psychology is doing the same stupid thing over and over, all the while expecting a better or different result. My choice to use drugs is a very good example. Drugs, man don't buy into the lie. There's a good reason why it's called dope!

"What I caused was not fair to so many people, but fairness doesn't govern life or death. I can never escape my past, nor should I be able to, but I battle each day to make my peace with it, as I deal with a primal sense of shame and humiliation.

"Prison certainly is no guarantee for rehabilitation. Each individual must decide for himself as I decided years ago. The positive changes in me have been slow to develop and sometimes painful to accept. During my evolution into a better person, I went from being very self-involved to hating myself. Hating yourself takes a lot of energy, and I had to overcome my self-hatred before I began to grow. I'm still working on me. I'm just another flawed human being. There are no secrets, but I believe that one of the keys to rehabilitation is remembering. I have to battle daily against allowing prison to dictate my mentality, which is extremely difficult at times. Everyone here (with very few exceptions) has failed the test we call life. Upon our arrival into prison life, not much in the way of self-improvement is expected. Most of the men here are content to live down to these low expectations.

"Guys in here are routinely granted parole, provided they have a job and a place to stay the moment they leave. This is next to impossible for many of the men. Many have no family or friends to help. Therefore, unless they are fortunate enough to find a halfway house willing to accept them, they remain in prison until their sentence is completely done, all the while becoming more and more bitter. Then society is amazed when they engage in more activity that is criminal. And remember, over 95% of us will be back on the streets with you sometime in the future.

"Recidivism is an insidious "revolving door" process. I can't tell you how many guys I've known who violated parole and came back through these gates. Some of them never had much of a chance on the streets. Others seemed to want to come back. It's hard to succeed in life for a normal person without a record. For some parolees and ex-cons it's darn near impossible. What's the answer? In my opinion, it's more and better programs to educate and train those who don't want to return to their old ways. Again, most of us will be released at some time in the future. Wouldn't you prefer to see people released with training and education to help them avoid gravitating toward criminal activity, like breaking in your homes or robbing you? And that's not blackmail, it's straight statistics.

"I can't undo the tragedy for which I alone am responsible. I can't make a new beginning. However, I can make a new and improved ending. That is my intention each day in this place, and some days are much better than others in that regard.

"It would be wrong for me not to reiterate about the one common denominator for over 95% of the men in here...our decisions to get involved with illegal drugs. Like I said earlier, we call drugs dope for a very good reason...because they're stupid! We should call them brain remover! Inevitably, it begins with someone being curious or feeling peer pressure, so they try it thinking, 'I'll just take this one pill or smoke this one joint just to see what it's like. I know that I'm too strong mentally to ever become addicted.' Then a few *experiments* later...WHAM! They're hooked. If you think you can quit using dope anytime you want to, you're just kidding yourself. Consider the millions and millions of Americans who fail to quit, even after going to rehab and/or jail repeatedly. For a huge percentage of the people who are addicted to drugs, the only certain cure is death."

At that point I told them all about the morning of August 13, 1989. I gave them a brief account of what happened and then opened the floor for their questions. There were always a few tough questions, but I never hesitated to respond to them frankly and honestly. Then as the group got ready to depart from the facility, I would usually say a few final words.

"Look, I want you to know that every word that I've said to you today is the truth. I began talking to groups like this one because a former warden asked me to. At first, it was a little scary for me since I wasn't used to public speaking, and I'm still not totally comfortable, but I do my best. Over the years, it has taken on more importance for me. It's important that I tell the truth and then there are the benefits. No, I don't get any extra privileges, time off my sentence or anything like that. But this, what we just went through together is therapy for me, which helps to continually remind me of what I must strive to atone for, even though total atonement is impossible. And I want you guys to know that I'm very grateful for the opportunity to tell you about prison and about my life story in a nutshell. So thank you for coming and thank you very much for listening."

In August of 2000 another blow came in the news of Mel's death. It was a hot summer's day and I was on the ball field playing softball, when I was told that my sister Joan was waiting for me in the visiting gallery. And since I knew that she wouldn't be there unless it was an absolute emergency, I rushed back to my cell, changed clothes and took off for the visitation area. They had asked Joan to wait for me in a separate room so I knew that it was bad. As soon as I opened the door, she started to cry.

"Jeff, I know that you don't want us to visit…but…Mel died last night. I tried calling out here but I couldn't get hold of you and I'm sorry I had to come …" she cried.

"Don't be silly Joanie, it's okay," I said as I put my arms around my sobbing sister.

"Do you realize that this is the second time I've had to tell you that our daddy has died?" she said softly as she hugged me tightly.

"And both of them in August, too," I replied.

I was so glad that Mel and I had made amends and that we had become friends as well as father and son. It was a great blessing to me that would forever be a reminder of how fortunate I was to have had a parent who loved me unconditionally, especially in the face of my lifetime of screw-up's.

The next month, September, the month that often took away some of the pain that August brought, held a blessing once again. I was out on the yard playing Scrabble with my friend Raymond and I noticed that some new arrival had been running in the heat of the day for over an hour.

"What the…oxo…that's not a word. That's a prefix," said the new guy as he walked up to the table dripping wet with sweat.

"Oh really…are you a Scrabble expert?" I asked as I looked up at the long distance runner.

"No, but I know enough about chemistry to know that that's a prefix."

"Were you a chemist on the street?"

"Yeah, something like that."

Something like that indeed! He was a very accomplished trauma surgeon who had gained national recognition for his skills. He had also taught future surgeons, and written various textbook chapters and research papers, which appeared in prestigious medical journals. On top of being a brilliant human being, he was athletic and talented in many other areas. His name was Doctor Greg Priest and at first I resented him because I detected a bit of a smart aleck. However, when I discovered that the doctor was indeed quite a smart aleck and that he was much smarter than I was, I immediately made a reassessment. It was an exceptionally good move. Although he was ten years younger than me, the doctor became the friend of a lifetime. I learned so much from him in many areas. The guy knew so much about so many different things. He taught me skills ranging from origami to mending softball gloves, although I never came close to doing it as well as the doc. And the more I hung around him, the greater my admiration became.

When one of the editors of our institutional paper went home, Greg took his place. That was fine with me, since the newspaper office was in the back of the gym where I worked. In a relatively short time, he became someone who I felt I could trust with literally anything. We talked about everything under the sun and eventually the topic of religion arose. I learned that Greg was an agnostic leaning far toward atheism, which troubled me a little. I still prayed every day and would not give up my belief and hope that God existed. I enjoyed the countless stimulating conversations we had on the subject and admitted that Greg made some excellent points, but decided that it was an area in which we would have to agree to disagree.

I always hated running in spite of being involved with athletics practically all my life. I associated running with punishment like when a coach made me run laps due to something like a missed lay-up. But since Greg seemed so committed to it, I wanted to give it a try. I was pushing fifty and since I was having a harder time keeping up with the younger guys, I knew that I was going to need a form of exercise other than basketball and softball pretty soon if I planned to stay fit. So I tried jogging and I hated it, but I stayed with it until I built up my endurance enough to run over three miles a day and then over six miles. And finally after years of training I ran a half marathon. Of course all the while, I saw my best friend whizzing by me effortlessly and usually running twice as far. I had always been the one who excelled at practically any sport, but here was something new. But due to the admiration and respect I had for Greg, I actually felt proud rather than envious.

"I hate you," I would laugh as Greg lapped me time and again.

Later on when the other editor left, I jumped at the chance to work with him on the newspaper. We had such a good time and enjoyed each other's company so much that it didn't even seem like a job. We had a blast writing articles that poked fun at everything from President Bush's wackiness to making fun of our own individual foibles. I became a better writer because of the doctor but nowhere near as gifted as my younger mentor, and I became a better person as well. Greg was tolerant, honest, kindhearted and abhorred violence. I found myself emulating him more and more as I continued shedding bad habits.

One day we were talking about another inmate who worked in the gym with us who had been sending letters to the warden's office. These "notes" were full of fabricated lies about the two of us and included our close friend Raymond, too. The note-writer was a lazy, obese, gender-confused neurotic who seemed to think he was the second calling of Billy Graham, but acted more like Caligula on crystal meth whenever he was around young inmates. He was a miserable and pathetic creature who had more issues than it's fitting to number here. I decided to try my hand at poetry and composed a poem about the prison snitch:

> He revels in backstabbing, backbiting and nasty fabrication
> Darkness is his lord behind his facade of farcical veneration
> Anonymity is the cloak he dons as he metaphysically barhops
> When there is work to be done, into the darkness he always flops
> Neither loyalty nor gratitude ever pierces his delusional murky essence
> His joy is derived by deceiving others and disguising his spinelessness
> Oh how he revels as he steals and cheats underneath his illusionary mist
> But believe this thou vile and pathetic wretch, Karma does indeed exist!

I then read it out loud to Greg and then we both began laughing uncontrollably.

"That's great Jeff, but it needs a name."

"How about Karmic Suicide?"

"Not bad...not bad," said Greg as he scratched his head.

"I've got it...Kamikaze!" I bellowed.

"No...wait...Karmakaze!" shouted the doctor.

"Perfect! Perfect! Karmakaze, that's it for sure!" I yelled back at him.

In August of 2006 I received a ruling from the Tennessee Supreme Court denying my petition for relief due to ineffective assistance of counsel. Then in September I received great news in the form of a letter from Adam's legal guardian. Her name was Pamela Messenger and she wanted to help me establish contact with Adam. To me, she was an angel sent from heaven! She said Adam had read my letter of March, 2004 and was thinking about sending me a reply. I promptly wrote a letter back to her and included one to Adam as well.

Within a week I received a letter from Adam. My son! Adam wrote that he had forgiven me for the death of his mother and he hoped we could get to know one another. I was beside myself with joy. I prayed earnestly in thanks to God at that very moment, for Pamela and for the forgiveness of my son. Over the next few months, we wrote back and forth. I discovered that Adam had not had an easy time of it. He had problems, which was in large part due to the tragedy that I, his biological father had caused, but this was a chance for us to have some type of relationship.

Then like clockwork a year later at the end of August of 2007, my Petition for Certiorari was denied by the United States Supreme Court, yet another one of the many blows that August delivered. I knew that my final chance for an early release was gone, and that my first slim chance at daylight wouldn't be for another three years in the summer of 2010. I allowed myself to feel a little disappointed, even a little depressed, but it was only to last for a few days, because September arrived. September, the month that had so often served as a cleansing summer rain for the inundation of the woes of August. September held good news once again.

I received a letter postmarked from South Carolina with my name and address handwritten on an envelope with the name of some company as the return address. How I knew was anyone's guess but I was somehow certain that it was from Hannah, Hannah Jane Preston, the love of my life. I ripped open the envelope and devoured her words with my heart as well as my eyes. She wanted to know if I remembered her.

"DO I REMEMBER YOU!?!" I shouted.

There were very few days that I had managed to get through without thinking of her. I wrote her back immediately and we began to communicate through the mail. She told me that she had survived breast cancer and was divorced after having been married for a long time, and that she had graduated from college with a Masters degree in psychology. She sent some current pictures and I lost myself in the blue of her eyes. She was my dream girl, my soul mate. I wanted to see her, to hold her, to tell her I loved her, to walk with her, to sleep with her, to make passionate love to her, to do laundry with her...to do everything with her. And although I was painfully aware that none of that could happen unless I was released, I couldn't help how I felt about her, this woman who had always been so special to me.

As soon as possible, I got her number put on my list of approved numbers and called her. She sounded wonderful and happy. I knew that the direction I was heading in probably wasn't a good idea, but I didn't care. In spite of having established my unbending policy of no romantic entanglements many years before, this was different. There was no way I was going to be able to resist her. I was certain that she still had men chasing after her and that she would be going out on dates, but I didn't care. I was just as wild and crazy about her as I had been two decades earlier. Only now I was neither wild nor crazy, and the days of drugs and alcohol were long gone, gone the way of several of my worst vices, including my pathological jealousy and my predilection for violent behavior. And she had changed for the better also, having shed the vice of drug use years before. And when she decided that she wanted to drive here to see me all the way from South Carolina, I immediately repealed my no visitation policy for her. After two visits we began talking seriously about getting married. She came several times and her visits were by far the best days I have ever had in prison. I was so grateful to reconnect with this wonderful woman.

I received a letter from Adam in autumn of 2008 from which I learned that I was now a grandfather! Adam had enclosed a small picture of my granddaughter, and she was beautiful. I stared at the picture and saw the pretty little red haired baby girl named Katy. She looked so much like Jami that I was taken aback. I knew that it was a long shot, but I hoped to meet her and maybe be a part of her life one day.

Then came March 30, 2009, the day Greg was finally released. I was extremely happy to see one of the greatest friends anyone ever had go home to his beautiful and loving wife and their two incredibly gifted and pretty daughters. But at the same time, I was filled with anguish and despair over the reality that the doctor was gone. He had been my lifeboat in a sea of insanity, and now the ship had sailed away to the sweet paradise of freedom and far away from the miserable, polluted shores of my island of hopelessness. After seeing Greg off amid promises to stay in touch, I returned to my cell where I found a card from Greg on my bunk. It said that I had saved his life with our friendship and that he loved me like a brother and promised to always be there for me if I ever needed anything. Tears of happiness for my friend began streaming down my face, as I sat there on my bunk in my vermin infested cell and prayed a prayer of thanks.

"God, you have to exist. There is no other answer that could possibly account for all of the blessings and all of the love that I feel from so many people. There's just no other way other than some kind of heavenly mercy, some type of celestial love. I have so much that I want to thank you for...for the kids that come here for the tours, for Mel, Jeanne, Joan...for letting me say goodbye to Mom...for letting me thank Mel and tell him that I love him and call him Dad before he died...for Kenny...for David and Jean and all they've done for me...for my friendship with Greg...for my health...and especially for Hannah getting back in touch with me. Oh my God, I'm so unworthy of all those unbelievable people and wonderful things that I've been blessed with over the years. Thank you. And thank you for Pamela getting me in touch with Adam and letting me see a picture of Katy! God I am so sorry I have doubted you. I believe in you. I don't deserve any of these blessings. I know that. I've come a long way, but I haven't undone any of the harm and the

hurt I caused. God, please comfort all the people who hate me for what I did and bless them all as well as all of my wonderful family and friends. All the money I had, all the dope, all the cars, the house...all the toys and all the women...I don't miss any of that stuff. Well, I guess I do miss one woman in particular, but you probably know that. God, if I could only undo the crap I've done. But I can't, so all I can do is ask forgiveness, which is another thing I don't deserve. But today...right at this moment in time, I believe that you have forgiven me, although I can't imagine why. And while I can't promise that doubt won't creep back into my thick skull ever again, I promise to keep trying to find the right path to you and to keep trying to become a better man. That's about it. Please bless my buddy and his family in some very special ways. I'm sure gonna miss him."

CHAPTER 26
THAT ABORTED CHILD

"...If a body catch a body coming through the rye..."
(J. D. Salinger – Catcher in the Rye)

That baby of the seventies, the other life I felt responsible for taking, kept slipping into my thoughts, a little angel who continued to frequent my dreams. How old would she be now? Was it a boy or a girl? It? She must have been a little girl. I hated calling her "it," even in my thoughts. I believed it was a little girl, a little girl that looked like Julie, the blonde headed angel named Wendy who appeared in my dreams.

I was sure that she would have been pretty and smart, just like her mother. I was equally certain that Julie would have loved her more than anything in this world. I wondered if she ever thought about our baby the way I did. She probably did, she was simply too insightful and caring not to. I hoped that the profound regret I felt wasn't troubling Julie as much as it troubled me. She was so young then...yeah, so was I, but Julie was different, she was a better person than I was. She was intelligent, nice, pretty...there just wasn't anything negative I ever could say about her.

Julie was so scared when she told me about the pregnancy. I remembered her trembling voice and the panicked look on her face. But why after all this time had passed had I suddenly begun dwelling on this baby, my daughter...my Wendy...on this lost angelic essence of an almost life?

If I could go travel back in time to change things, maybe I could have learned to be in love with Julie. Who knows? And as for the baby, well naturally I would try to be a good father, especially if I realized how horribly my life would turn out from making all the wrong choices. I was haunted by thoughts of what might have been. Every time I heard one song by...I think that it was by the band Toto, a couple of the lines made me realize how I should have felt about my daughter...my baby girl...Wendy.

"It's gonna take a lot to drag me away from you.
There's nothing that a hundred men or more could ever do.
I bless the rains down in Africa
Gonna take some time to do the things we never had."

Perhaps it was just a natural culmination of self-inventory and analysis, a totaling of a life's worth of mistakes and the demoralizing consequences. Of all the things I regretted, I felt that the abortion, the discarding of this precious life, was possibly the second worst thing I ever did or let happen. It was a deliberate, selfish and cowardly step toward extinguishing a human life. The results of my action or inaction would surely be viewed with the same gravity and resolve by the twenty-four jurors in my two trials who unanimously judged me guilty. Furthermore, didn't the fact that the loss of her little life stemmed from my desire to avoid an inconvenience make it much worse?

I have reflected deeply on the whole "when does life really begin" debate for several years. Many logical people argue that it begins at birth, while others who are just as logical maintain that conception marks the spot. A misconception regarding a conception, that's what it had to be by either the pro-life people or the pro-choice group. But which one?

Being painfully aware that I was one of the last people on earth with the right to dictate morality, I once reasoned that a woman should have the choice. After all, wasn't it her body? I realized that all innocent children do not become blameless adults. What if my mother had aborted me? Might that have spared another life? Was it possible that there was a balance, a compromise? The whole issue was dreadfully convoluted and confusing. But all that confusion ended with the appearance of the little angel named Wendy, the unborn daughter who visited me in my dreams.

Any uncertainty further receded as I researched abortion and the case of *Roe v. Wade*, the landmark decision by the United States Supreme Court, which legalized abortion in the United States. The plaintiff in this case was designated "Jane Roe" but her real name was Norma McCorvey, and after I read what she had to say in an affidavit twenty-seven years after the ruling, I subscribed to a very different view of abortion:

"My name is Norma McCorvey...I was the woman designated as 'Jane Roe' as plaintiff in Roe v. Wade, the United States Supreme Court decision that legalized abortion in the United States...the courts...I feel used me to justify legalization of terminating the lives of over thirty-five million babies. Although on an intellectual level I know that I was exploited, the responsibility I feel for this tragedy is overwhelming."

I knew the pain felt from the responsibility of a single child being aborted. I could not imagine how much hurt and guilt this woman must have endured.

When her case was before the United States Supreme Court, Norma McCorvey's attorneys assured her that the fetus growing inside of her at the early stage of gestation was merely tissue. Years later when her naiveté had faded, she realized that it was more than tissue. In her opinion, and one that I now share, that tissue was a life and carried the potential to become her child. After the abortion, McCorvey worked in several abortion clinics and to her horror, she discovered first-hand how ghastly such places could be:

"One place where I worked in 1995 was typical: Light fixtures and plaster falling from the ceiling; rat droppings over the sinks; blood splattered on the walls. But the most distressing room in the facility was the 'parts room.' Aborted babies were stored here. There were dead babies and baby parts stacked like cordwood. Some of the babies made it into buckets and others did not, and because of its disgusting features, no one ever cleaned the room. The stench was horrible. Plastic bags full of baby parts that were swimming in blood were tied up, stored in the room and picked up once a week. At another clinic, the dead babies were kept in a big white freezer full of dozens of jars, all full of baby parts, little tiny hands and feet visible through the jars, frozen in blood. The abortion clinic's personnel always referred to these dismembered babies as 'tissue.' Veterinary clinics I have seen are cleaner and more regulated than the abortion clinics I have worked in."

I hoped and assumed that the clinic descriptions were somewhat hyperbolic and inflammatory. I knew that most pro-choice practitioners also wanted to eliminate the need for abortions and that these doctors and nurses really cared about the welfare of the women involved. Both sides wanted to eliminate the need for any abortion. But pro-life advocates desire to spare the lives in the balance of the unwanted pregnancies. I knew that these lives represented a staggeringly large number. I wondered if McCorvey's description of the clinic conditions were the same as when Julie and I decided to end her pregnancy. And although I had gone to the clinic with her, I merely sat passively in the waiting room while she disappeared through the door to the horrible room where it took place. Had Julie seen appalling things like the filth and tiny body parts described by McCorvey in her affidavit?

I theorized that our culture has become anesthetized to the word abortion and the practice of abortion through sheer repetition, a protective reaction to sensory overload. I understood that there were exceptional cases, such as rape or when the mother's life is in jeopardy, but were those babies any less human, any more guilty and deserving of death? It was a conundrum, but I now knew where I stood on this contentious issue.

McCorvey felt responsible for over thirty-five million abortions, and that was from 1973 to 2000 in this country alone. Extrapolating on her number, I decided that the all time worldwide total would surpass one billion. One billion...a thousand million! It became my opinion that no matter what side of the debate someone fell on, and no matter how many Supreme Court decisions were handed down, if a logical and sane person looked objectively, they would have to agree that the potential life of a human being is terminated every time an abortion was performed. What could have been a baby boy or girl became a lifeless carcass.

There were other troublesome areas, such as the fertilized, frozen, un-inseminated embryos left over from *in-vitro* fertilizations. These embryos have the same potential to become people as aborted fetuses, and yet they are destined for disposal. Is the difference legitimate? Should infertile couples be denied a chance at parenthood because a single cell holds the full potential of a complete human? And what about the benefits related to stem cell research? Should millions of people suffer and die from curable illnesses because unused frozen embryos once held the potential for human life? Was it morally preferable to keep the embryos perpetually frozen or to throw them away, than to use them to cure a disease afflicting millions of good people?

I decided that there could be no compromise when it came to human life, and perhaps my stance was especially firm because of my own life experiences and the deaths that weighed heavily on my conscience. Could it be that I saw the abortion issue as a chance to dilute my own guilt over Jami's death? I knew enough statistics to realize that many of my close friends and a huge percentage of people in this country have been directly involved in aborting a fetus. Maybe some of the ADAs, the jurors and even the judges were silently burdened with the abortion of a pregnancy. If all those millions of people could also be labeled murderers, would that somehow lessen the sting of my self-assessment, or of my stigmatization? Not likely. My decision regarding abortion evolved from my own self-loathing and regret, not the other way around. It added the burden of another death to my already strained conscience.

The knowledge that millions of people are implicated in the deaths of babies did little to console me about my own shortcomings. Rather, it strengthened my desire to take full responsibility for the deaths I was implicated in. I had no intention of impugning other people and their choices, but for myself, I decided that the taking of a human life was wrong. I thought about how unfair it was that people generally consider the woman as the only person making the weighty decision of whether or not to abort a baby. What about the man who knows and agrees with the decision, like I did in Julie's pregnancy? Wasn't I equally culpable, maybe even more responsible than Julie since I wasn't stressed from all the hormonal changes and since I was older and should have been the more mature person? I realized that I was just as much to blame, if not more.

I felt disgrace, so much so that I never mentioned the abortion to another soul until I was nearly fifty-five years old.

I often considered what my life would have been like if Wendy had been born. Would being a father to a baby girl have caused me to straighten up my act? Julie surely would have been one terrific mother. Would she have said something sweet and precious to our baby girl in the middle of the night like Jami used to sing to Adam? Something enchanting that would reverberate forever in my memory?

"Just a minute... just a minute Wendy... just a minute...Momma's coming... just a minute."

Naturally, there were countless people who had grieved and mourned over Jami's death. But, who mourned over Wendy? No one...well, perhaps Julie. Maybe she held the ache inside and never said a word to me or to anyone else. Maybe she still had regrets. But we had a good reason, didn't we? We were so young with our whole lives ahead of us, and a baby would have been so difficult and inconvenient. INCONVENIENT! So, for the tidy sum of three hundred dollars, our inconvenience disappeared and the little mass of tissue that would have become Wendy was thrown out with the clinic's garbage. No need for tears. No need to select a casket. No need for family members and friends to console one another at the funeral home. No need to purchase a grave plot. No need to watch with anguish as the lifeless flesh of our baby was lowered into a hole and covered with dirt. One of the wonders of our existence is the miracle of birth and nobody should have the right to destroy the marvel of human life for the trivial expediency of convenience.

I recalled reading about a conversation McCorvey had talked about in her affidavit. She overheard a young woman crying as she talked on the phone with her mother, right after she had an abortion:

"I just killed my baby. I'm so glad you never killed me!"

And now every time I think of Wendy, and I think of her often, the hurt, heartache and regret overwhelm me. My daughter...my baby girl...the angel I'd gladly give my life for today.

I recall a prayer I once prayed.

"God please hear this prayer. This may sound a little crazy but I'm asking you to somehow let Wendy hear what I want to say. If there's a way, I'd really appreciate it. Anyway, here goes. Hello angel, it's your dad...or at least the guy who should have been your father. I'm gonna call you Wendy. Now if you're a little boy, it's gonna sound silly, but since you've been a beautiful little blonde headed girl

every time you've popped up in my dreams, I'm gonna stick with Wendy. Honey, I was such a bad guy...a horrible...a miserable excuse for a man when you were growing inside your mom. Please don't blame her. It was my fault. I should have been a man instead of the coward that let it happen. I am so sorry and I know that sorry means so little. I know that it changes absolutely nothing. I wish that it did. I wish that there was so much more that I could do, but there's not. I've tried so very hard to change and I have to a large extent. The person I was...the guy that I hated is gone and I know that I'm a better man today. But it doesn't change the fact that you never had a chance to take a single breath, and it doesn't change the fact that Jami's body lies rotting away in a grave because of me. Angel, I am so sorry, so very sorry. I hope that you can hear this. I hope that you can somehow forgive me. I hope that you're in a good place. Maybe you've met Jami. She would have loved to have a little girl just like you. Oh my God...oh my God...please, please forgive me. So little darling, I suppose that all I can do is to keep on trying to improve myself and I promise to do just that in every way I can. Goodbye Wendy...and if you want to, please come back and visit me in my dreams anytime you want to. I sure hope that you heard me. Okay God, that's about all I've got for now. I'd really appreciate it if you can please let Jami and her know how sorry I am and ask them to forgive me and please take good care of them. What the heck am I saying, if they're with you, of course I know that they're in good hands. Please give me the strength, wisdom and guidance to stay on the path I'm on. You know how much I want to see them both one day, and you know that I can never deserve to see them, but I'm gonna do my best from here on out. I'm still searching for the right path to you, so any tips you want to send my way would sure be appreciated. Thanks again Lord...amen."

CHAPTER 27
THE UNKNOWN

"All the truly important conflicts are fought within ourselves."
(Buddhist maxim)

Leo Tolstoy wrote that he fell woefully short in the light of God's ideal, so much so that it drove him to the brink of insanity in spite of his belief in Christ. I understood that in Christian thought, the ransom of Christ stands in lieu of man's ability to attain perfection and since I wasn't a Christian, I had no such luxury. And upon learning of Tolstoy's descent into madness, I figured that such a powerful conviction probably wouldn't help me even if I did believe in salvation through Christ.

Why had I lived instead of Jami? Why wasn't I dead from suicide or stricken with some painful, terminal disease? Why had I survived innumerable close calls with death? My guilt from Jami's death was immense. I left one child motherless and orphaned my own son, for God's sake! And I had taken away the chance at life from my aborted child. Why hadn't one of my brushes with death concluded the disturbed portrait splattered on the canvas of my life? Was Jack Collins my father or not...and if he wasn't, who was...and what was he like?

I had so many unanswered and unanswerable questions. Did the caring and merciful God that I choose to believe in really exist? Had any of the thousands of prayers I had said been heard? Would I ever have an opportunity to truly atone for my mistakes - if there was an afterlife? What price would I be required to pay after this life...after man's law had exacted its cost? What would cosmic law demand? And if there was an afterlife, would all the people I wanted to apologize to be there? What about Adam? Had my son really forgiven me for taking the life of his mother? Could I maintain hope that Johnny would someday forgive me as well? My responsibility for leaving both children motherless, along with residual feelings of guilt over Julie's abortion, had greatly influenced my personal philosophy. This monstrous regret and endless yearning for atonement was the essence of the force behind my search for God, just as it was the forceful inspiration fueling my desire to be a better man.

The punishment for homicide resulting from man's law is often harsh for those who are found guilty. That's as it should be. Life is precious. The time required for retribution and/or punishment in the various states of this country ranges anywhere from a few years to the death sentence. The penalty depends on the state, the level of the conviction, the mood of the jury and sadly, the ability of the defendant to retain competent counsel. Those forces and their ensuing consequences are all part of the tangible world.

The cosmic or karmic requirement may be substantially more than the mortal one - if I am ever able to finally settle my debt. I bear the responsibility for the loss of two miracles of life, one who loved me and another who would have. I thought of karma as an independent entity and perhaps that's what it is. Karma may allow Pepper's wish to come true - that I take my dying breath in prison. That scenario may be the metaphysical price for my part in the death of Jami, and my compliance with Julie's decision resulting in the nonexistence of that innocent little angel who never saw the light of day or took her first breath of sweet life.

Forgiveness is a complicated word. It's easier to say than it is to sincerely offer. Oprah Winfrey once said that forgiveness can be granted without regard for the person being forgiven, and that it does not alter the way you have to feel about the perpetrator of a crime. But forgiveness is at its essence a concept that requires a relationship, and forgiveness implies that the relationship will change in a fundamental way. That change requires the involvement of two people. Can you really forgive a person after they are dead? Maybe, but it certainly holds different import. And unless it occurred in some supernatural manner I don't believe that a dead person could forgive. A rape victim may forgive her assailant, but a murder victim is denied the chance to even consider that option. One of my greatest problems was that Jami could never forgive me, at least not in this life.

I recalled an old Spanish proverb that said something like, "Revenge is the sweetest taste on the lips of those who are in hell." I had once blamed others for my plight, but after all the effort I had put into attempting to understand myself, I came to the realization that there was no one else to blame. When I had sincerely forgiven everyone for everything, both real and imagined, and let go of all of the hate and contempt I held for so many people, I experienced a wonderful and amazing feeling, like setting down a heavy load I had been carrying around for years. I wished that those who still hated me could let go of their hatred and their desire for revenge, so that they too could experience such an uplifting sensation.

I had come a long way towards becoming a better person. It had been an epic battle between the good and evil within. For a long time I allowed evil to dominate, but over the past fifteen years, good had made an unlikely and miraculous comeback. I had worked diligently on myself and had overcome many vices. I still had issues to confront, but I had made tremendous strides in several areas, including one of the most important, my temper. And though it may sound trivial when compared with discovering how to deal with my anger issue, I was nonetheless very proud of the fact that I had long ago quit smoking marijuana and had stopped using profanity, vices of mine that would never be seen *or heard* from again.

For over twenty years I observed the dregs of society all around me, guys who were often better off inside than they were on the streets. They had nothing, they knew very little, no one gave a damn about them and nobody expected anything of them. Many were toothless, crippled, diseased and dying, mentally ill, forgotten and renounced by their families. I saw these people every day, their eyes glazed over revealing dull, blank and hopeless stares. I felt so fortunate when I saw these pathetic men, and I knew that someone powerful must have been watching over me. If not, I certainly would have become one of the men with glazed over eyes.

"Dear God, there's probably not gonna be a happy ending for me. I haven't made up for crap. That light I think I see at the end of a tunnel, it's probably the proverbial headlight of an oncoming locomotive. There are so many things that I wish that I had done differently, so many things I wish I could change. But, I'm still so blessed for some reason. I'm so much better off than so many of these wretches in here. Why that is I just can't imagine. I'm thankful, but why do I deserve such friends, and sisters like Jeanne and Joan? And why have so many people continued to care about me, to love me?"

There wasn't a single day that passed that I didn't remind myself of how lucky I was. Sure, there were some bad days, even terrible ones, but by and large, I felt blessed. And although I had long since realized that I would probably never know my biological father's true identity, that detail didn't matter that much anymore. I accepted the likelihood that, along with Adam, Leonardo da Vinci, Alexander Hamilton and Erasmus of Rotterdam, I had been born out of wedlock. Hey, at least I was in excellent company! Sure, it would have been nice to know who my real dad was, but Jack Collins and Mel Snow treated me like a son and most of all they loved me like a son. And having both of those men as father figures were enormous blessings. Adam continued to write and said in one of his letters that he hoped to meet me in person some day. I hoped and prayed for the same thing, so that I might have a chance to be some kind of a father to him (and maybe even a grandfather to Katy.)

I often thought of Greg and his family and how grateful I was to have had such an amazing man as a close friend. It was true what I had read in *The Urantia Book*, "…the noblest of all memories are the treasured recollection of the great moments of a superb friendship." How often had just thinking back on my relationships with Greg,

Kenny, David, Jean and others lifted me out of the doldrums. And then there was Hannah. I was listening to music again and I was overjoyed to discover that so many songs still reminded me of her. I continued talking with her on the phone several times a week and she continued to tell me that she loved me. And when she said that she had never stopped loving me, my heart sang its own blissful song.

I loved Hannah as well, but I loved her beyond merely a physical love, it was a heartfelt soul-to-soul and mind-to-mind kind of love. It was such a powerful love that it brought a smile to my face several times each day. It transcended the fact that the odds were stacked against the possibility of us ever being together again. I felt as though my love for her was so pure that I wanted her to find true happiness with someone even if it wasn't me. I had come a long way from that jealous, self-centered maniac I once was.

I continued to devour books, to better understand everything I could, about life, joy, suffering, birth, death and the possibility of an omnipotent being who created us all and who continues to watch over and care for us. I believed and continued to struggle with doubt….but I believed.

In essence I had been transformed from an evil, narcissistic, lying, manipulative, whore mongering, thieving, drug addicted, dope dealing, violent, redneck, who had taken the life of the mother of my son and had overseen the forfeiture of my baby girl's chance at life, into a humble, kind, considerate, knowledge seeking, spiritual believer, who indefatigably persevered in a quest for love, virtue, God and redemption.

I held out unremitting hope for freedom, yet I refused to ask God to help free me from prison. Yes, of course I wanted to be free. I wanted freedom desperately, but I knew that I had no right to ask. Besides, I believed that God's will has to be done, so what was the point in asking? If my freedom was meant to be, it would happen and if not, it was in prison that I would remain.

I hoped for other things. I wanted to have an even more meaningful relationship with Hannah, beyond what we discovered through her occasional visits, cards and letters and over the telephone. I wanted a relationship with Adam and I wanted to spoil Katy rotten! But I knew any such chance of these things ever coming to fruition hinged on the decision of the Tennessee Board of Pardons and Paroles. The year 2009 came to an end and the arrival of 2010 came with a huge challenge. I had failed to adequately prepare for the crushing defeats of my seemingly endless trials and appeals. It was time to steel myself for more potential disappointment, this time from the parole board. I was scheduled to stand before them in approximately three months. I knew I must expect the worst, because another emotional setback would be devastating.

"Dear God, you know exactly what happened and exactly how it took place in her apartment that awful, crazy morning. You know how sorry I am and you know that I would gladly trade places with her the exact second that stupid gun fired. I know that I've asked you countless times before to forgive me and you know that I've asked Jami to forgive me too. And I believe that you have, but I'm not at all sure about even the possibility of her forgiveness. I hope she has, I hope she can. Now I'm asking you to give me the strength or whatever it is that I need to completely forgive myself, because I haven't really accomplished that yet. So please give me some help in that area. And God, I'm gonna need some more help from you soon when I meet the parole board. I don't know what's gonna happen. They'll probably deny me and that's okay. It's just that I don't want another inner struggle with depression like the ones I had after my trials and my last appeal. I want to be ready and strong enough for disappointment this time. Whatever happens I promise to do my best to face up to it. And I'm gonna keep on doing what I've been doing. Thanks for listening Lord. Amen."

Facing the unknown was a daunting task for me, but I was ready to accept the future. If providence saw fit for me to be granted parole, I planned to make the most of my time left on earth as a free man. If karma required me to take my dying breath behind these fences of razor wire and at least please Pepper a little, I would accept that destiny as well. No matter which scenario was to be played out, I understood that life was not going to get easier. I had come to view my life as a journey, a test that would continue until death and hopefully beyond. My struggle was a significant component of the motivation I had to go through each day, and I realized that there would always be another quest to begin, another mountain to climb.

My objectives of forgiveness and redemption were unattainable, at least during this lifetime, but that did not prevent me from trying. I repeatedly thought of Sisyphus, the cruel king of Corinth in Greek mythology, who was condemned to forever roll a huge stone up to a hilltop in Hades only to have it roll back down again and again. Sisyphus' struggle against eternity was all he had with which to fill his heart. The endless, individual journeys up and down the hill might have been all that sustained him. His journey could never end. His destination was unreachable, yet he pushed on determined to reach his goal. I imagined Sisyphus to be somewhat contented. I had an endless struggle, but I also had Hannah and many profound friendships that helped to sustain me. In this way I had a huge advantage over Sisyphus.

I knew that my life wouldn't, that it couldn't conclude with some happy fairytale ending. My success with self-improvement was a pyrrhic victory. It came too late and at far too great a price. And I knew that like Sisyphus, my redemption was unachievable, but however quixotic the quest may be, I was determined to strive for seemingly unobtainable objectives; to continue my search for God and to earn forgiveness from Jami and my baby girl…and to love and honor those who remained close to me.

EPILOGUE
ANOTHER TRIAL, ANOTHER JUDGMENT

*"There is nothing deep down inside us
except what we have put there ourselves."*
(Richard Rorty)

Although I was eligible for parole in May of 2010, my hearing was delayed for over nine months and finally held in late March of 2011. A parole hearing is like a mini trial, with a seven person panel of parole board members serving as judge and jury. There were advocates for my release and there were protestors who were totally against me ever getting out. Jami's father, who I had never met, said that he did not hate me but wanted me to spend the rest of my life in prison. Her son Johnny was there but did not speak. And then there was the prosecutor from my two trials, Ms Jane Crowell. She stated that I had never expressed any remorse beyond regrets over what my actions have done to my life, which of course was egregiously untrue. She went on to say that people like me do not change and that we are in fact incapable of being rehabilitated. Then for good measure she twisted the actual testimony from my two trials and added various bits of erroneous information for the parole board members to hear. To the credit of my advocates, they sang my praises loudly. Barry Michelson publicly offered me a job, a place to stay and even a car. Two high ranking prison officials who I have known for more than a decade stood before the board and proclaimed me rehabilitated and a good person. Several others spoke eloquently on my behalf as well. My sisters were both quite ill and could not attend the hearing. Joan had recently undergone surgery and Jeanne had an inoperable brain tumor. Hannah was not there either. She had grown extremely frustrated and depressed from the continuing delay in my hearing and we were not getting along over the telephone like we once did. According to her, every argument we had was 100% my fault, and because I was unable to look at it objectively, I could not state unequivocally that her claim was totally untrue. She admitted that she was harboring a great deal of animosity and resentment over things I had done over a quarter of a century before, as well as all my actions which led to my current situation. Additionally, she had been drinking quite a lot and at times she was rather cold to me. For whatever reason, she chose not to come.

At the end of the hearing the hearing officer said it was obvious that I had been a model inmate and I had done everything I could possibly do over the past 21 years to change for the better. He also stated for the record that he himself believed that I had indeed changed. He congratulated me for completing classes in anger management and substance abuse and went on to thank me for my military service. He concluded the hearing by saying that the final decision would be made within the next few weeks and I would be advised of the result in the near future.

I wish that I could wind things up like the happy ending in a fairytale, but unfortunately, this was real life. The board's final decision to deny my request for parole came a month after the hearing, and it was not what I had hoped to hear. I suppose that great cosmic commander in charge of dispensing karmic justice was not through collecting from me and I could almost hear karma screaming, "Here's some more payback Mr. Collins!" The wound is fresh, still open and bright red, but I feel a need to reveal the ramifications of my continued incarceration.

When she heard the news, Hannah's anger and disappointment seemed to be directed more at me than at the Parole Board. She quickly decided that she couldn't deal with the prospect of waiting for me until I met the parole board again. She went on with her life, and within a month of the final decision by the parole board she began dating. She found another guy. They went out on a date one Friday and by Sunday afternoon, it had evolved into a full-blown relationship; *at least from my vantage point*. But then I never could be very rational when it came to Hannah. Talk about speed dating! It was confusing to me, since we had come so close to getting married just months before. We had gone so far as turning in a marriage application to the institutional chaplain. If I had made parole, we planned to move to a sleepy little fishing village on the North Carolina coast, where I would work for Barry Michelson's company. In any case, I wish Hannah continued health and happiness, and I wish the same for anyone she chooses to be with. At the risk of sounding like I'm boasting, I experienced a sense of pride from having already forgiven her, even though I initially felt abandoned and betrayed. I believe that this was another good indication of how far I've come. I must admit that such a fine and noble concept ran much smoother in my head than in everyday applications, but I'll work on it.

Ultimately however Hannah had given me over three years of something to look forward to...talking with her on the phone, writing her and seeing her when she could make it here for a visit. I believe that the nine month delay coupled with the board's decision pushed her over the edge and caused such a response. In her defense she had gone above and beyond merely being a faithful girlfriend, and she will always be very special to me. Besides, her decision was what almost any normal person would have chosen and it was understandable to any logical mind. But now she is gone and I'll have to go through this alone. I have about 17 years of experience flying solo, so I'm confident that I can do it again. It may not sound all that manly to say, but I have to admit that she broke my heart when she gave up on us and found a new love so quickly. Of course it would have been much easier if I had never known how great it was to have her in my life again, but that's the way things go sometimes. I knew how dangerous it was to become romantically involved while incarcerated, and I could have stopped it before it ever began. It was my own fault.

I did manage to find a couple of blessings even in that difficult situation. I had to recover from losing her before, so I know that I can recover from losing her again. And I know it's a veritable certainty that I will never have to endure anything like that again. I've battled back and forth in my mind over whether or not I would prefer for her to have written to me back then; some 3½ years earlier. In the end, if I had it all to do over, I admit I would welcome her letter every time. If it appears that I dwelt too much on being with her, it was probably true, but I also desperately wanted freedom, almost as much as I wanted her. Like she once said to me, "You can't help who you love." And yeah, I do still love her and I always will.

In the aftermath of the board's decision, I agonized over my bleak future. I believe that any normal person who gets figuratively punched in the gut like I was considers ending it all. I honestly did reconsider Camus' one truly serious philosophical problem, but any thoughts of suicide were quickly dispelled. I felt as though there was simply too much left to do. There were days when I realized how much I still hated myself and there were nights when I once again asked to die in my sleep. Nevertheless my life continued on and I once again became determined to face my problems and go on with my journey. And of course I appealed the board's decision, but there is virtually no chance for a successful appeal since the appeal is heard by the same board members who declined my request for parole.

After feeling temporary disdain for all those against me, I looked at my state of affairs in the light of reason. Could I have been anything I wanted to be? No, not a nuclear physicist, brain surgeon, professional football, basketball or baseball player, but I could have been happy and made other people happy as well. It's often been said that karma is a bitch, but I disagree. From the judgment of my own actions, I am hers to reward and punish. In the end it'll be all right or it won't. And I'll be okay or I won't. Only time will give the full measure of such outcomes.

After considering once again how extremely blessed I still was, I made the decision that whether or not they ever release me, I'm going to continue to be the best father, friend, brother, writer, runner and human being that I can be. I will continue my quests for forgiveness, redemption and the true path to God right up until my last breath is exhaled.

As for Jami's father I understood his wish for me to spend the rest of my life in here. I was and always will be so very sorry and regretful for the tremendous pain and grief I caused him and every person close to her. I wish them all closure and peace.

I could have had it all. I could have been so good to so many people. I could have...

Technical Support

Editing
Craig Nunn, MD

Formatting
Craig Nunn, MD
JR Davis

Cover design
Ben Damron

Fact / Quote checking
Rebecca Brown

Proofreading
Steve Emery
Jean Bell
Bryan Haas
Austin Smith
Robert Harrison
Kevin Mingis
Charles Lord, esq.
Ben Damron
Steve Diffee

44

About the Author:

Allan Brooks is a graduate of the University of Tennessee. He is a Vietnam era veteran with an honorable discharge. After serving more than 28 years of a life sentence, he was released on parole and is living in Nashville, Tennessee. Allan is working for a non-profit that serves the homeless people of Nashville. His next book, *Ransomed beyond Karmakaze*, has just been released for publication and is now available.